She shrugg  **eve**
what it like

His changeable eyes alerted, their sparkle intensifying. Slowly he scanned her, lingering at her breasts before returning to focus on her lips. Heat scoured Valeria in the wake of that glance.

"Is it sure you are?" he murmured.

"Certainly," she lied. "You will conduct yourself as the perfect gentleman I have pronounced you to be."

He raised his teacup to her in salute. "A bargain it is, Lady Arnold."

With a calm Valeria was far from feeling, she held out her hand. "Until tomorrow, then, Mr. Fitzwilliams."

He came over and kissed it. "Until tomorrow."

Scarcely breathing, Valeria watched him walk out, her fingers burning where he had held them, her hand tingling where he had kissed it. Legs turning shaky, she collapsed back into her chair.

Oh, my, this was definitely not wise. And she was going to do it anyway…!

As a child, **Julia Justiss** found her Nancy Drew books inspired her to create stories of her own. She has been writing ever since. After university she served stints as a business journalist for an insurance company and as editor of the American Embassy newsletter in Tunisia. She now teaches French at a school in Texas, where she lives with her naval officer husband, three children and two dogs.

Recent titles by the same author:

THE WEDDING GAMBLE
THE PROPER WIFE
MY LADY'S TRUST

MY LADY'S PLEASURE

Julia Justiss

MILLS & BOON®

DID YOU PURCHASE THIS BOOK WITHOUT A COVER?

If you did, you should be aware it is **stolen property** as it was reported *unsold and destroyed* by a retailer. Neither the author nor the publisher has received any payment for this book.

All the characters in this book have no existence outside the imagination of the author, and have no relation whatsoever to anyone bearing the same name or names. They are not even distantly inspired by any individual known or unknown to the author, and all the incidents are pure invention.

All Rights Reserved including the right of reproduction in whole or in part in any form. This edition is published by arrangement with Harlequin Enterprises II B.V. The text of this publication or any part thereof may not be reproduced or transmitted in any form or by any means, electronic or mechanical, including photocopying, recording, storage in an information retrieval system, or otherwise, without the written permission of the publisher.

This book is sold subject to the condition that it shall not, by way of trade or otherwise, be lent, resold, hired out or otherwise circulated without the prior consent of the publisher in any form of binding or cover other than that in which it is published and without a similar condition including this condition being imposed on the subsequent purchaser.

MILLS & BOON and MILLS & BOON with the Rose Device are registered trademarks of the publisher.

First published in Great Britain 2004
Harlequin Mills & Boon Limited,
Eton House, 18-24 Paradise Road, Richmond, Surrey TW9 1SR

© Janet Justiss 2002

ISBN 0-263-83982-6

Set in Times Roman 10½ on 11½ pt.
04-1004-81260

Printed and bound in Spain
by Litografia Rosés S.A., Barcelona

To my editor, Margaret Marbury,
for her support and encouragement.
Working with her has been
this lady's pleasure.

Chapter One

If fornication were going to occur, it wouldn't be in her hayloft. That decided, Valeria Arnold frowned as she watched her maid, Sukey, loosen her bodice lacings to reveal more of her generous bosom, then turn the corner of the path leading to the barn, "assignation" written in every sway of her ample hips.

Now, how to enforce that resolution?

Valeria had been coming in for tea after her usual morning ride when she noticed Sukey, after a furtive backward glance, slip her sleeves off her shoulders and scurry out the kitchen door. Since the maid was now out of sight and well beyond hailing distance, if Valeria truly wished to stop her she'd have to follow the girl.

Well, if one must do something unpleasant, best to proceed quickly and be done with it.

Laying down her riding crop, Valeria lifted her chin and strode to the door. At the last moment she paused to pick up a stout walking stick from its stand beside the cupboard. In case her firmest governess's manner wasn't enough to dissuade the ardent youth awaiting Sukey, it wouldn't be amiss to come prepared.

Her courage nearly failed her when she reached the barn.

From within its stout walls emanated Sukey's high-pitched giggles, interspersed with soft shufflings and low-toned masculine murmurs. Valeria took a deep breath and wiped nervous palms against the woolen skirt of her habit.

She'd call out a warning. No sense barging in unannounced and surprising them at…whatever they were now doing, she decided, her cheeks warming at the thought. The idea of viewing a man whose unclothed body was not in the last throes of deadly illness fired that warmth to flame.

Nonsense, she told herself, raising chilled hands to cool her hot cheeks. A respectable widow shouldn't be having such thoughts. Especially—honesty compelled her to add—when in this remote corner of Yorkshire there was so little opportunity for her to act upon them.

She pulled the barn door slightly ajar. "Sukey Mae, are you in there? Cook needs you in the kitchen at once!"

At the sound of a gasp, followed by frantic rustlings, she entered.

Valeria saw Sukey first, hastily re-lacing her nearly bare bosom while her skirts, which must have snagged the edge of a nearby hay bale when she dropped them, were still hiked up to reveal a froth of white petticoat. Valeria's gaze moved to the man beside Sukey and stopped dead.

Tawny hair gleamed in the shaft of early morning sunlight, and the tall, well-muscled body that lazily rose to impressive full height was not that of the fumbling farm boy she'd expected. Golden cat eyes swept her with a glance from head to toe, their expression half annoyed, half amused, as finely chiseled lips curved into a smile.

"A ménage à trois? Who would have thought to find such delights in the wilds of Yorkshire?"

His voice whispered of Eton and Oxford, even as the fineness of the half-unbuttoned linen shirt, the width of the cravat tossed on the hay, and the expensive simplicity of the form-hugging buff breeches shouted Bond Street.

The stranger's smile broadened, and Valeria realized she must have been staring with mouth agape. Though in truth, such a man was as out of place in this remote section of England as if he'd dropped from the moon. Wherever had Sukey stumbled across this London dandy?

Valeria shut her mouth with a snap. Before she remembered her purpose, though, she had to admit a certain sympathy for the susceptible Sukey. With his smiling eyes and rakish grin, the gentleman before her could tempt a saint to dalliance.

"Sukey Mae Gibson," Valeria said, her first attempt at a stern tone coming out more like a croak. "You will return to the kitchen. We'll speak of this later."

Finishing the ties of her bodice with a jerk, Sukey gave her a sullen look. As she stepped past him, the unrepentant rogue had the audacity to wink at the girl. A foolish grin sprang to her lips before she turned back to Valeria. "But Mistress—" she whined.

"At once, Sukey," Valeria interrupted. "Before I forget that it is a Christian virtue to forgive."

What no other housewife in the county would, Valeria added mentally, with a rueful sigh at the compromises poverty compelled.

She kept her unflinching gaze locked on Sukey until the maid, with slow, reluctant steps, exited the barn. Then Valeria turned back to level the same stern look on her uninvited visitor.

"You, sirrah, will do me the favor of leaving my property by whatever means you came, and returning to wherever it is you came from."

Apparently possessing not a particle of embarrassment, the man merely inspected her once more from head to toe, his gaze curious. "Will I now?"

He spoke the words with a slight lilt, whose origin her precise mind was distracted into trying to ascertain until she realized the rogue was approaching. Before she could move, with a smooth panther's gait he had reached her and seized a curling wisp of hair, escaped from its pins during her ride, between two tanned fingers.

"You so unkindly interrupted my morning's plans. Why should I not take you instead?"

Seen up close, the golden eyes mesmerized. For an instant, she couldn't seem to move—or breathe. Then she caught the odor of brandy, the lingering scent of cigar smoke. He was more than half disguised, she realized. Rather than rising early, he'd probably not yet been to bed. Her first thought—to wonder again where in the world he had sprung from—was rapidly swamped in acute awareness of the heat and scent of him hovering over her.

"You shall not," she said sharply, dragging herself back from lassitude to slap his hand away.

"And why is that, pray? 'Tis ready for kissing you look."

Since her rapt gaze *had* focused on his lips, she'd best not debate that. "You have the appearance of a gentleman, sir, and therefore would never take an unwilling lady," she pronounced.

To her surprise, the man threw back his head and laughed. "Sure, and you're wrong on both counts! Shall I show you how much?" With the spurned hand, he reached out to tilt up her chin.

Valeria's gaze locked with his. She tightened her grip on her walking stick, though as the gentleman's height and reach far exceeded hers, should he really choose to attack her the wooden pole wouldn't prove much of a weapon. But despite his threat, she felt no fear.

"I'd prefer you didn't show me. I'd also prefer if you'd refrain from enticing my maid."

He released her chin, his glance sympathetic. "You waste your time there. The girl's as light-skirted as they

come. If not me, 'twill be another lad she raises her petti-
coats for, sure as dawn follows moonlight.''

Valeria stifled a sigh. "But not in my barn."

With a lithe movement the man caught up his discarded
jacket. "I wouldn't be too sure of that."

Nor was she, but she wasn't about to discuss with this
bosky stranger what necessity forced her to tolerate. "I trust
you can find your way out. Good day, sir."

She turned on her heel, but the man caught her shoulder.
Startled, she looked back at him.

"Is it sure you are that you're unwilling?"

A shudder of heat radiated from his hand throughout her
body. Something buried deep within her, a longing long
denied, stirred in response.

Don't be a fool. Jerking her shoulder free, she stepped
away. "Yes," she said crisply, and strode off.

His soft chuckle followed her. Just before the barn door
closed, she heard him murmur, "Liar."

Was she unwilling? Valeria wondered as she made herself walk purposefully to the house, resisting the temptation
to glance back and watch the man leave.

Of course she wouldn't consider lying with a chance-met
stranger—certainly not one so undiscriminating that he'd
been about to tumble her maid! But neither could Valeria
deny that the stranger's sheer virility had awakened a firmly
suppressed desire for the physical bond marriage promised.
A promise that, in her case, had never been fulfilled.

The inevitable wave of pain, muted now, swept through
her. She couldn't prevent herself thinking of Hugh—tall,
broad-shouldered, black hair curling over a gold-laced uniform collar, dark eyes gleaming with health and high spirits. The man who'd been her brother's best friend, hero of
her adolescent fantasies, and briefly, her husband.

He'd want her to remember him like that—not as he'd
been last summer, wasted with fever, his flesh hanging on

a too-large frame, eyes sunken in a face yellowing with the pallor of approaching death. Shuddering, she once again banished the image. Best to bury it deep, along with any memory of her disastrous wedding night.

Impatiently she shook off a vague sense of guilt. It was only natural, having known so little of the delights of love, that she'd be tempted by a cat-eyed stranger whose lips and hands promised expert skill in the arts of seduction.

Doubtless more skill than her erstwhile suitor possessed. The idea of comparing stodgy Arthur Hardesty to that tawny-haired personification of male carnality was so ludicrous, she had to laugh out loud.

Her attraction to the stranger was equally laughable. Should she ever meet him in his true setting—a London drawing room—she would hold as little appeal for such a man as her low-born maid.

Still, if she wished to relieve the tedium of her dull existence with visions of a torrid interlude, 'twas a harmless enough diversion. Wherever the stranger had sprung from, he wasn't local. Probably he was some traveler passing through whom Sukey had somehow encountered at the posting inn when she went to town for supplies.

Aye, no need to chastise herself for wistful fancies. After all, Valeria would never see the rogue again.

Laughing softly, Teagan Michael Shane Fitzwilliams let appreciative eyes linger on the retreating figure of the lady in black. With curves as delightful, if not quite as ample, as those of the maid she'd routed, Lady Mystery was much more intriguing.

Euphoric over winnings that would keep him in clean linen and adequate victuals for the next several months, Teagan had decided to take a dawn ride to blow away the smoke and liquor fumes of a hard night's play. Had he not still been three parts castaway, he'd never have followed—

it would be a misnomer to term responding to that walking advertisement for the world's oldest profession ''seduced''—the saucy maid whose bold glances and ample curves had attracted his attention at the posting inn.

Though his body still protested the abrupt termination of its favorite recreational activity, his head was more than willing to exchange a quick tumble for the possibility of a more challenging partner.

The maid had called her ''mistress,'' so his proper lady must be in charge of the small manor whose stone walls he glimpsed beyond a curtain of trees as he walked out of the barn. A widow, in her somber black garb? Or mayhap a woman who cared little for her husband, for no wife who enjoyed bed sport would risk employing a wanton like Sukey.

Either way, he'd read attraction in her eyes—and longing. Exactly the combination that offered the potential of a mutually profitable interlude.

Though serviceable, Lady Mystery's habit had never seen the inside of a London emporium, his discriminating eye said. But the hothouse flowers of the metropolis, with their endless need for flattery, gossip and manipulation, had been growing rather tiresome of late.

Let the other men pursue the tarts Rafe Crandall had brought to occupy those of his guests who tired of hunting or card play. Teagan would seek out his host and make some discreet inquiries about Lady Mystery.

A woman for whom he'd felt an immediate attraction. His half-aroused body hardened again. It had been a long time since he'd been able to combine business with pleasure.

His exacting eye for detail pulled up another memory, and his glow of anticipation faded. As he now recalled, her black habit had been not just unfashionable, but worn.

He tried to summon up a niggle of hope. Perhaps Lady

Mystery saved her newest garments for impressing the ton during her sojourns in London. If not, it appeared his comely widow was none too plump in the pocket.

Not even the sight of Ailainn, the glossy black stallion that was his one indulgence, erased his irritation at that conclusion. Society might deem Teagan totally irresponsible—an image carefully cultivated to provoke maximum irritation in his mother's sanctimonious English relatives—but he'd learned early the pain of a starving belly and an empty purse. A man living solely by his own wits could not afford to neglect his game and pursue a woman merely for the enjoyment of it.

He should put her out of mind, he concluded as he mounted Ailainn and caught up the reins.

As the stallion trotted down the path to Rafe's hunting box, Teagan urged his mount to a gallop. The sheer beauty of the animal's powerful stride, the siren song of the wind rushing by him—scouring away the smoky debris of yesterday, making him new—carried off his vexation and revived his spirits.

Pulling up the stallion at a rise overlooking his host's dwelling, Teagan threw back his head and laughed aloud, caught up in the sheer joy of being alive on such a glorious morning.

Perhaps it was the same quixotic stubbornness that had led his mama to defy her family and follow her heart and the sweet-talking rogue who'd left her to die alone in a Dublin hovel. A man, her censorious relatives never tired of reminding him, Teagan resembled to the life.

Or that all Irishmen were fools—had his English relations not drummed that fact into him as well?

Whatever prompted him, stubborn fool of an adventurer that he was, he decided on the spot to pursue his Lady Mystery anyway, be she wealthy or not.

Chapter Two

Surveying the ruins of what had been her favorite vase, Valeria stood in the parlor trying to curb her temper. It being of little use to chastise the already weeping Sukey, she'd sent the useless girl to her room.

Valeria bent to pick up the largest remaining piece, a whimsical array of birds and flowers in blue and white pottery that had been her brother's last gift before he was killed at Talavera. Like Elliot, the vase was now shattered beyond repair. She took a deep, shuddering breath, working hard to suppress her own tears.

Remembering brought only sorrow, and heaven knew she'd grieved enough. She forced herself to concentrate instead on the practical matter of gathering up the shards.

She had to grin wryly. Her dressing-down of the hapless Sukey had succeeded all too well. Finally appearing struck by the dire future that awaited her on the streets or in a brothel, should Valeria repent of her mercy and discharge the girl, Sukey had been tearfully eager to please. But since, as she'd sobbed to her mistress after this latest mishap, she was still "powerful agitated by that smooth-talkin' London gent," the girl's distracted efforts this morning had resulted first in burning today's bread, then in scorching Valeria's

best lace tablecloth and now in the destruction of one of
her last physical links to her brother.

To distract herself from the anguish of that thought, Valeria deliberately conjured up the handsome stranger who,
she had to admit, had left her a bit "agitated" as well. She
was still kneeling, a half smile on her face, her mind tracing
the image of his delicious physique and knowing eyes as
one's thumb would caress the smooth surface of a gem-
stone, when Mercy, her nurse-turned-lady's maid, peeked
in the parlor door.

"There ye be, Missy! Sorry I am to tell you, but Sir
Arthur and Lady Hardesty are here. I tried to fob 'em off,
but knowin' you was home, they insisted they must see
you."

Valeria groaned. With Cook muttering in the kitchen
over the bread, her elderly butler in high dudgeon about
the ruined tablecloth and the estate books still needing attention, she had neither time nor interest in these uninvited
guests courtesy now compelled her to entertain.

Uttering Portuguese profanities under her breath, she
raked the broken pottery into her handkerchief. "Did you
answer the door?" she asked over her shoulder.

Her old nurse bent to help. "Aye. Sorry, Miss Val, but
Masters were still in the pantry, sulkin'. I'll take these to
the kitchen for you."

"Blast. Then I shall doubtless have to endure Lady Hardesty commiserating on how my 'unfortunate circumstances' force us to retain a butler too old to perform his
duties." With a sigh, Valeria stood and handed her nurse
the handkerchief. "Please do take these. I'd prefer not to
have to explain what happened, and invite another homily
on why it was false charity to hire Sukey."

Valeria dusted off her hands and gave her hair a quick
pat. "Send them in, then, since you must."

Her impressive bosom jutting before her like the prow

of a warship, Lady Hardesty sailed into the room. "My dear Valeria! So kind of you to receive us unannounced. And I do hope poor Masters is not ill. Your maid Mercy had to admit us."

Valeria damped down her irritation. "He's quite well, thank you. Not expecting callers this time of the morning, he was busy with other duties."

"Yes. So unfortunate it is not within your means to employ an underbutler or a footman to assist him."

"Should you like tea?" Valeria asked, determinedly ignoring the comment.

"Oh, yes. 'Twill help settle my nerves, which, I declare, are quite shattered. Only the knowledge that it was my inescapable duty to poor Hugh gave me the strength to drive out today!"

"Here, sit, Mama, and make yourself comfortable. Lady Arnold, I trust I find you well." His forehead perspiring under the burden of escorting his suddenly drooping mama to the sofa, Sir Arthur managed to sketch her a bow.

"Quite well, and you, Sir Arthur?" Valeria did not bother to inquire what dire news had prompted Lady Hardesty to drag herself from her morning room, knowing the woman would soon inform her at length, whether Valeria wished to know or not.

With a pant, Sir Arthur settled his mother's bulk on the cushions, then turned to fix a smile on Valeria. "You are looking particularly lovely today."

Since she was garbed in one of her oldest gowns, with her hair still sprouting wisps blown free by her ride and her sleeves ornamented with flour, she could manage only a noncommittal murmur in reply.

Arthur did possess a sweet smile, Valeria reflected. If it weren't for the fact that his sweetness was cobbled with an intellect dim enough to consider such absurd compliments flattering, a body already tending to the corpulence so ev-

ident in his mother—and a mother who kept him firmly
under her thumb—Valeria might think more seriously about
letting Sir Arthur relieve her of the burden of managing
this barely profitable sheep farm.

"...awful danger!" Lady Hardesty tapped Valeria on the
arm, recalling her wandering attention. "A peril to every
decent woman in the neighborhood!"

"What Mama means," Sir Arthur inserted, "is that Rafe
Crandall—Viscount Crandall's youngest son—has brought
a party of rather...disreputable guests to his hunting box."

"A property, my dear, that borders your land!"

"For seven and one-half acres on the west," her son
clarified. "Although the greater length of it, one hundred
thirty-six acres, adjoins Hardesty's Castle."

Of course Sir Arthur would know to the acre where the
property lines went, Valeria thought. Her suitor, she often
suspected, valued her more for owning fields that marched
with his own than for any beauty or charm she might possess. A lowering reflection, that.

"And the...persons that wild boy brought with him!"
Lady Hardesty continued. "Why, 'tis perilous for any decent woman to walk the streets. After all your devotion to
him, I knew dear Hugh would want me to warn you to stay
behind locked doors until that revolting party departs."

While Sir Arthur looked at her and saw acreage, his
mother perceived a woman who'd nursed her son's boy-
hood friend for months. And who thus might be expected
to meekly do the bidding of a second husband—or mama-
in-law. Not in this life, Valeria silently vowed.

"Now, Mama, 'tis not as dire as all that," her son
soothed. "I daresay as long as Lady Arnold remains on her
property she will be quite safe. However, as some of the
guests will be shooting—and probably not in a condition
of absolute sobriety—it would be wisest for her not to
ride."

"There's a greater danger to riding out than bosky hunters. Arthur, did you not tell me you'd seen the man yourself yesterday at the Creel and Wicket, bold as brass?" Lady Hardesty shuddered. "Why, they say those golden cat's eyes can hypnotize an unwary woman."

Valeria's attention had wandered again, but at those words she snapped to attention. "C-cat eyes?"

"Nonsense," Sir Arthur reproved. "Ladies have always found Teagan attractive, but I've heard naught of hypnotizing."

"Who knows what Irish riffraff is capable of," Lady Hardesty sniffed.

"Only half-Irish, Mother. His mama was good English stock—the Earl of Montford's daughter, you will remember. How else could Teagan have gotten into Eton and Oxford?"

"One of the guests is a rake and the, ah, natural son of an earl's daughter?" Valeria asked, pulse leaping at the memory of golden eyes and smiling lips bent kissing close.

"No, she actually married the Irishman—her father's *groom!*" Lady Hardesty said. "To think Lady Gwyneth would show so little consideration of what is due her station!"

Irish, Valeria thought. So that explained the lilt.

"'Twas only what she deserved," Lady Hardesty continued, lips pursed in disapproval, "when the blackguard deserted her and the child, leaving her to die penniless. Why, 'tis said the boy lived on the streets until some clergyman was kind enough to restore him to her family. By which time he was already an accomplished thief."

"You exaggerate, Mama. Teagan must have been only six then, for when I met him at Eton he wasn't yet seven." Sir Arthur turned to Valeria. "We're speaking of Teagan Fitzwilliams, Lady Arnold. His reputation is very bad, I fear. But the young man I knew was not evil, merely wild."

"Wild enough to study vice early. Didn't you tell me they called him 'cheat' at school?"

"'Jester,' Mama. For the card tricks and sleights of hand he used to perform for us."

"Whatever he was as a boy, you can't deny he's turned into a gambler and a heartless rake."

"I cannot condemn him simply because he makes his living at the green baize table, Mama. What else was he to do, pray, when his mother's family virtually cut him off after Oxford? And, I must own, I think the stories of the many women he's supposedly seduced vastly exaggerated."

Lady Hardesty sniffed again. "Of course they cut him off. How could they not, after he was dismissed for seducing the wife of the dean!"

"'Twas his mentor's daughter-in-law, Mama."

"Well, the entire ton was in an uproar over the way he carried on with the wife of old Lord Uxtabridge. Now, you may say I exaggerate—" she turned to her son, who with half-open mouth did seem to be about to protest once more "—but Maria Edgeworth has sent me all the town news for years, so I believe I can speak with more authority about this matter than you!"

Having effectively squashed her son, she addressed Valeria again, clearly eager to spill yet more gossip. "After Uxtabridge, who should have known better than to buckle himself to a chit young enough to be his granddaughter, there was Lady Shelton, and—"

"Mama, you're putting Lady Arnold to the blush," Sir Arthur exclaimed, regarding Valeria with alarm, as if he expected her to swoon at any moment.

Glad her thick-headed suitor read embarrassment in the flush of excitement he must have perceived on her cheeks, Valeria was, for once, shamelessly eager to plumb every tidbit Lady Hardesty could be induced to offer. "My nerves are quite steady, though I thank you for your concern, Sir Arthur,'' she said placatingly. "But I believe Lady Hardesty is correct. I ought to know the whole."

"Indeed." Her ladyship flashed her son a superior look. "Gentlemen try to dismiss the villainy of their sex, but we ladies must acknowledge it if we are to protect ourselves adequately. And I would consider myself failing in my duty to dear Hugh were I not to insure that his sweet widow, whom I trust has no idea of the devilment of which men are capable, was sufficiently armed."

Valeria had the grace to feel a twinge of guilt, but not enough to stop the flow of information. "I appreciate your concern," she said demurely.

Lady Hardesty patted her hand. "You know I look on you almost as a daughter, dear Valeria. So, though it grieves me to speak ill of one whom Arthur once considered a friend, I must warn you Maria tells me this Fitzwilliams fellow never loses a hand, leaves a bottle, or spares an opportunity—excuse me for stating the matter so crudely—to debauch a complacent man's wife."

"Being a widow, I should be safe then."

Her ladyship ignored the remark, as she did any attempt to deflect the conversation from the direction in which she desired it to proceed. "I daresay no woman is safe. Indeed, I begin to feel it my duty to dear Hugh to insist you stay with us at Hardesty's Castle until Crandall's party and That Man have departed the neighborhood."

Valeria caught her breath in alarm. That would guarantee she'd never encounter the rogue again—and make her a prisoner to Sir Arthur's ponderous suit and Lady Hardesty's none-too-subtle maneuvering.

"Indeed, Lady Hardesty, you are much too kind!" Valeria said quickly. "But I could not put you to so much trouble, with your nerves in such a state. Besides, the shearing will soon be upon us. I simply couldn't leave such important preparations to mere underlings,'' she concluded, hoping to draw support from Lady Hardesty's well-known contempt for social inferiors.

"You have an admirable sense of duty, Lady Arnold,'' Sir Arthur said. "Perhaps I could step in to assist—''

"Oh, no, Sir Arthur! With the vast responsibilities of your extended acreage, I simply couldn't ask you to burden yourself with supervising mine as well.''

"Dear lady, no service I could do you would ever be a burden.''

Oh yes, he'd love to assume the management of each and every one of the six hundred-some acres Hugh had left her, she thought sardonically, and then caught Sir Arthur flashing his mother a significant look.

Lady Hardesty rose. "Valeria dear, I nearly forgot. I brought with me my receipt for whitening lace, which by the looks of the hangings in the entryway, your housemaid could certainly use. If you'll excuse me a moment, I shall take it to her.''

Valeria rose as well, determined to forestall this blatant attempt to leave Sir Arthur alone with her. "So kind of you, but another time, perhaps.'' After frantically scanning her mind, she hit upon an excuse that might prompt the Hardestys' speedy exit. "You see, Sukey Mae is laid down on her bed at present. Nothing to worry about—a putrid cough only. I was about to prepare her a tisane when you arrived. Indeed—'' she added a delicate cough ''—my own throat is so scratchy, I believe I shall prepare myself one as well.''

While Sir Arthur shot up from the sofa with the speed of a Congreve rocket, Lady Hardesty hastily deployed a handkerchief over her nose. "Lady Arnold, you should have warned us immediately that you were feeling unwell! Surely you recall the delicacy of my lungs. Come, Arthur, we mustn't linger.'' Her hawklike eyes looking aggrieved over the handkerchief, she headed out.

Valeria followed them. Despite her praise of careful nursing, Lady Hardesty had such a horror of illness she'd not come next or nigh her ''dear Hugh'' in all the months he lay dying, Valeria recalled bitterly.

Remembering that, she allowed herself to cough again, harder this time. Lady Hardesty speeded her steps.

''I'm sure I'll be right as rain in a day or so. Thank you so much for stopping by,'' she called after her departing guests. And then stood, immensely pleased with her ploy, listening to the echo of the front door's slam.

An Irish rogue, she thought, lips curling into a bemused smile as she wandered back into the parlor. An Irish rogue with a winning smile and an intimate gaze that could charm leprechauns out of the air, she suspected.

And foolish women out of their virtue.

A cheat and a liar, as Lady Hardesty claimed? Knowing how the worst sorts of rumors made the best gossip, she was more inclined to credit Sir Arthur's memories of an orphan barely tolerated by his mother's disapproving family.

Valeria recalled the keen intelligence of those golden eyes, the hard strength of that muscled body. But with very little effort, having been orphaned young herself, she could imagine what it must have been like for a boy of six, forced to scrabble for survival on the streets after losing his one remaining parent. A boy suddenly transported out of everything familiar, and given over to relations who, if she knew aught of aristocratic English families, never let the child forget that his father was a wastrel, his mother a fool and he an Irish beggar dependent on their charity.

Small wonder the lad had grown up a hellion.

But not, she was quite certain, a heartless womanizer.

Despite his disclaimer to the contrary, Mr. Fitzwilliams

had behaved as a gentleman. After all, she'd been alone with him, virtually defenseless, with little chance of retribution to follow should he have taken advantage of her. A true predator—with a shudder she recalled encountering several such individuals while in India with her father— would never have passed up such a golden opportunity.

No, he'd not acted the rake, and his teasing words had left her enticed rather than threatened.

Of course, having Lady Hardesty command it and Sir Arthur recommend it, she couldn't possibly remain at home. She would ride in the morning, as she always did.

And if she should encounter the fascinating Mr. Fitzwilliams?

Her heartbeat galloped and she felt shaky. Heat flushed her cheeks, then cold. In the pit of her stomach a curious spiral began, and the tips of her breasts tingled.

Yes, she lusted after the man—as apparently so many other women had before and probably would after. Still, she couldn't stop her fevered imagination from wondering what it would be like to have the rogue's lips upon her own, those long tanned fingers caressing her, that strong torso leaning over her, thrusting the most intimate part of his body into the most intimate part of hers. A powerful wave of desire and longing swept through her.

And as she struggled in rural remoteness, striving to accumulate the financial means of escape, it seemed the vague yearnings of girlhood only sharpened. She'd scarcely been married before being widowed, so the passion churning within her had never been allowed free rein. How she ached to fully experience that rapture of which bards through the centuries had sung, sensual delights which, unless Arthur Hardesty finally wore her down into accepting his suit, she might never taste.

With Arthur, a taste would likely be all she'd get.

She was back on her knees, brushing together a few bits

of the broken vase that had escaped her hasty earlier inspection—and by some mercy, Lady Hardesty's gimlet eye—when the idea struck her. Her hands froze on the shard.

Teagan Fitzwilliams, Lady Hardesty claimed, was a master of seduction. As Valeria knew from personal observation, that tall, golden, compelling gentleman appeared to be everything a woman could wish for in a lover, capable of making even an on-the-shelf widow like Valeria feel desired.

Teagan Fitzwilliams would be in the vicinity of Eastwoods for a few days only. And if, in that time, he happened to initiate her into the rituals of passion of which he was so obviously a master, no one need ever know. Should she encounter him, and he rebuff her, no one would ever learn of her humiliation. And should he take her, after a few days he would depart, sparing her the embarrassment of ever facing him again.

But in her heart, her body, the wonder of the passion with which he gifted her would burn forever.

She raised a shaking hand to her face. She must have taken leave of her senses. The idea was insane!

But once conceived, the notion refused to be dislodged. Her senses hummed with it, thrilled to it, beat with an urgent pulse that whispered, "Do it."

A sharp pain pierced her finger and she opened her fist. She'd clutched the pottery shards so tightly one had cut her.

Would that her feckless mind should receive so painful a check, she thought, inspecting her bleeding finger. If she did something so rash, so wanton, so…unladylike, she was apt to suffer much more than embarrassment. Men might indulge their passions with impunity, as her reckless body urged, but men did not bear children. Could she be irresponsible enough to risk that?

But her courses, always extremely regular, would be upon her in a day or so. Mercy had blessed that very fact three years ago, confiding on Valeria's wedding night that as no woman Mercy had ever known had conceived so near her time, Valeria would be spared the possibility of bearing a child who might never see its soldier father.

There wouldn't be a child. But there could be pleasure—pleasure such as she'd never known and likely would never have a chance to find again.

She wouldn't dare.

How could she not?

Trying to squelch the unaccustomed turmoil in her normally well-regulated mind, Valeria rose on shaky legs and went to dispose of the broken pottery bits. Noticing the blood pooling from the cut, she brought her finger to her mouth.

The suction of her lips against her throbbing digit set her body tingling again. How would it feel were it his lips against her hand…her belly, suckling her puckered, aching nipples?

Another wave of heat swept her, then a light-headedness that made her dizzy. She stumbled into the kitchen, startling Cook by leaning against the dry sink to splash water on her flaming cheeks.

She would think on this no longer. Let fate decide.

She would ride tomorrow as usual. If she happened to encounter Teagan Fitzwilliams…let happen what may.

In the late afternoon, after a thorough washing and pleasant dreams of a certain dark-haired lady in a black riding habit, Teagan went looking for his host. He ran him to ground in the back parlor, playing billiards for pound points with several other gentlemen. For a few moments Teagan simply watched, gauging the mood and degree of sobriety of the group so as to decide how best to discreetly obtain the information he sought.

Rafe, as usual, had a half-empty glass of brandy in hand. Markham and Westerley, dissipated younger sons of an earl and a marquess respectively, looked equally live to go. Only the last member of the group, a plainly dressed older gentleman, appeared completely sober.

In fact, as he was normally rather a straight-laced government man, Lord Riverton made an odd addition to Rafe's assemblage of hard-drinking, high-stakes rowdies. However, as the man had cheerfully lost a considerable sum to him last evening, Teagan was prepared to be affable.

"Gentlemen." Teagan greeted the group.

"Ah, Jester." His host turned spirit-brightened eyes toward him. "Good night you had, eh? Riverton went down by several thousand, and Markham here should have provided you enough to pay off your tailor."

Teagan gritted his teeth. Suppressing the automatic anger that still flared at his well-bred, well-heeled acquaintances' mockery, even after ten years of playing this role, he forced himself to make a light reply. "Aye, and it's a new pair of Hoby's best boots I intend on winning from him tonight."

"Here, here!" Westerley called as Rafe slapped Markham on the back.

"Before that, I've a mind to do some riding. I wondered—" Teagan began.

"Try the red-haired tart," Rafe interrupted.

As the other men hooted, Markham added, "The blond filly's got a nice tight saddle as well."

After waiting for the merriment to subside—and noticing Lord Riverton's curious glance focused on him, Teagan continued. "I appreciate your recommendations, gentlemen, but 'twas riding of a more equine nature I intended. My black needs exercise."

"Damme, why won't you sell that beauty to me?" Markham complained. "Don't know how you afford him."

"Why, by winning blunt from obliging gentlemen such as yourself," Teagan replied.

"For the black I'd pay you more than enough to keep you in booze and strumpets for a year!"

"A tempting prospect." Teagan assumed a thoughtful pose, as if considering Markham's offer. "But then, were I to turn Ailainn over to the likes of a rider like you, sure and the stallion would never forgive me."

While the other gentlemen laughed, Teagan addressed Rafe. "Can I ride in any direction, or have you left a jealous husband hereabouts who's like to shoot at me if I stray onto his land?"

Rafe grinned. "Jealous husbands are your forte—I stick to doxies. Might want to stay away from the north—Sir Arthur Hardesty's just the sort of sanctimonious prig to chastise a fellow for trespassing. Not much of a view to the west, but the woods to the east are pretty enough." His grin widened. "Especially if the widowed Lady Arnold happens to be riding."

"A widow, you say?" Westerley chimed in. "Sounds like just the thing for the Jester! Wealthy, is she?"

"Alas, no—sorry, Jester, she's nearly as indigent as you," Rafe answered. "When her soldier-husband cocked up his toes, the barony and its land went to a cousin. He grew up here at Eastwoods—his mama's property, so it wasn't entailed. If that little sheep farm brings his widow above five hundred a year, I'd be vastly surprised."

"Definitely not for the Jester, then," Westerley said. "He prefers 'em rich—and grateful."

Teagan merely raised a noncommittal eyebrow. Outwardly he followed the conversation, nodding or commenting as required, while his mind ticked off the tidbits of information. So she was "Lady Arnold." Well, until he learned her given name he'd continue to call her Lady Mystery. He didn't wish to think of her by the mark another man had left on her.

About all he'd left her, apparently. No wonder she looked so hungry. He felt an answering hunger sharpen within him.

"Pretty widow, you said, Rafe?" Markham was asking. "Maybe 'tis my duty as a gentleman to ease her loneliness."

That comment jolted him out of reverie. The idea of the corpulent Markham forcing his inebriated hands and whore-mongering body onto Teagan's slender Lady Mystery spiked the rage that always smoked beneath his surface.

"Really, Markham," he drawled, "if the lady's truly as comely as Rafe says, I fear she'd prefer the sheep."

Markham glared, but with the other men seconding Teagan, didn't hazard a reply. When he stopped laughing, Rafe added, "Even were Markham as handsome as Jester, I doubt the widow'd have him. Totally devoted to poor old Hugh, she was. He'd taken some sort of ghastly wound, and she nursed him for months. Died in her arms, the story goes." Rafe thumped his chest and sighed. "So romantic."

"Stop, you'll have me in tears." Westerley tittered. "I might have to make a condolence call—if she's worth the trip, Rafe?"

"Only if you like a heart-shaped face with big brown eyes, lots of wavy dark hair and a figure..." He traced an hourglass shape with his hands.

Enough, thought Teagan. Lady Mystery was *his*. "Doubtless you'll sober up sufficiently en route that you won't run your mount into a tree," he said. "Best hurry off, though, since you'll have to sit an interminable time sipping tea in a stuffy parlor while you figure how to charm her out of her skirts. But if you'd rather do that than avail yourself of the beauteous company our kind host has so thoughtfully provided…'' He let the sentence trail off and shrugged. ''The redhead's a hot one, you said?''

His irritation apparently forgotten, Markham brightened. ''Aye. Come to think of it, this game is cursed flat. Think I'll go find that little ladybird.''

''Give me your cue, then, Markham,'' Teagan said. ''Westerley, are you off, or can I count on lining my pockets with more of your gold?''

Teagan held his breath while the man stood frowning, knowing he could not push further without arousing suspicion. ''I'm in,'' Westerley said at last. ''No female's worth sobering up for, 'specially not one that needs persuading. Save me the blonde, eh?'' he told Markham, and leveled his cue.

Relieved, Teagan looked up to find Riverton studying him. His lordship had taken no part in the banter, continuing with his game as if oblivious. As he looked at Teagan now, though, the man's lips slowly formed a grin.

Teagan had the oddest feeling Lord Riverton realized exactly what he'd wished to accomplish in that conversation.

Nonsense, he thought, shaking off the notion. He raised his cue, took a careful breath and sighted the ball. If Lady Luck continued to smile, when next he went riding, his pockets would be plumper by several hundred pounds. Business accomplished, he'd have earned the leisure to pursue only pleasure—his, and that of one special dark-haired lady.

Chapter Three

As her mare crested the ridge, Valeria looked down across the pasture to the stone roof of Eastwoods and tried to quell a sharp disappointment. She had nearly completed her normal route—had dawdled, even—but had caught no glimpse of a cat-eyed rogue. Either he did not ride this morning, or he'd taken care to avoid censorious widows.

The depth of her disappointment irritated her nearly as much as the pitifully nervous, flustered state in which she'd begun her ride. Specter, her gray mare, had sidestepped as Valeria mounted, and shied at every turn during the first half hour, unsettled by her equally unsettled rider. At least now Valeria had herself well in hand.

Irritation drained away, and, as she gazed at the view that signaled the end of her ride, a deep sadness welled up. There'd be no knight on a white charger to steal her from the tedium of her day and lift her to a glorious, fleeting pinnacle of delight.

No, she thought as she let the mare pick her way down the steep hill to the mowed pasture, today would settle into the same rhythm as all her yesterdays since Hugh's death, offering nothing more exciting than bills to pay, the shearing to schedule, Cook's complaints to soothe and Sukey Mae's inattention to correct.

Reaching level ground, she tautened the reins. Enough lamenting. Valeria Winters Arnold, soldier's daughter, would simply make the best of whatever life offered, which at this moment meant urging her mare to one last gallop across the meadow into the orchard.

Sensing her mistress's mood, Specter whinnied, clearly eager for the run. After spurring the horse to a gallop, Valeria narrowed her eyes, the better to savor the tempest of wind through her hair, against her face. Almost, she could imagine herself back on the vast brown plains of India, racing with Papa and Elliot on her first pony. Sharp longing pierced her for that lazy long-ago when every day brought new vistas, new experiences, and life seemed brimming with possibility. Tears, not entirely from the bite of the wind, pricked at her eyes.

Not until she was pulling up under the canopy of apple branches did she hear the pounding of hooves behind her. Surprise and dread clenching her chest in nearly equal measure, she turned in the saddle.

Racing toward her on a magnificent black stallion, golden hair incandescent in the sunlight, came Teagan Fitzwilliams.

Her hands went to ice, her mind to a blank. When he reined in beside her, laughing, she could think of absolutely nothing to say.

"Sure, and a fine morning it is for riding, ma'am. 'Tis a lovely mount you've got there."

His unusual cat-eyes seemed to catch and refract every golden sunbeam, appearing ten times more luminous now than in the shadowed barn yesterday. "Y-your stallion is finer…" she began before, captivated by the twinkle in their kaleidoscope depths, her words trailed off.

Lady Hardesty was right, she thought wonderingly. His eyes did hypnotize.

She realized she was still staring, her lips half-open. Lud, she must look like a drooling dimwit.

So much for enticing him! She felt the heat of embarrassment all the way to her toes.

Before she wrenched her glance away, though, she got a good enough look to realize that full sunlight magnified not just the attraction of his eyes, but the perfection of every feature—straight nose, high cheekbones, sensual lips, thick hair of a shade that mingled corn silk and strawberry, and cried out for a woman's fingers to comb through it. Even his tanned skin was marvelous, dusted with an endearing sprinkle of freckles.

Merciful heavens, how could plain little Valeria Arnold think such a godlike creature would ever give her a second glance?

Her fingers trembling again, she fumbled to pull the slack reins taut, ready to kick Specter to a canter and ride away before she humiliated herself totally. But when Mr. Fitzwilliams spoke again, courtesy forced her to halt.

"What reward shall we offer for so capital a run?"

Kisses was the only idea that popped into her head. As she could scarcely say that, she said nothing.

"Have you brought no treats? Whist, and with the trees so bare. Mayhap your mare can wait, but the stallion must have his now."

Struck by all the double meanings, she jumped when he reached out—then pulled an apple from his jacket pocket.

He meant the horses. Of course he meant the horses. Another wave of heat scorched her cheeks.

She ducked her head, mortified. She couldn't do this. She simply wasn't cut out for it.

At last she dared to raise her face, compelled by a need so acute she could taste it, helpless to depart without stealing one last, longing look into the forbidden face of pleasure.

Motionless, he stared back while she simply watched him, enraptured once more by the dancing light in his eyes.

Before she could summon the will to tighten her reins

and kick her horse forward, Mr. Fitzwilliams jumped down
from the saddle and stepped over to trap her gloved hand.

Her gaze flew back to his.

"Don't go, sweet lady," he whispered.

Bittersweet anxiety paralyzed her chest, robbed her of
breath. She must turn away, she must, before his knowing
eyes read in hers the naked hunger blazing there.

Then he smiled again. "Dismount, if you would. I've
enough for us both."

It took an instant for her to realize he meant the apple.
Breaking it in two, he held up a piece and waited.

She eased herself to the ground. After she took the chunk
he offered, he turned to feed his half to the stallion. Specter
nipped her fingers when she held on too long to the mare's
portion, watching him, her heartbeat quick-stepping like in-
fantrymen on the attack.

"T-thank you," she managed finally.

"Did you not think I'd come back?" he asked, facing
her once more.

She moistened her dry lips enough to speak. "Nay."

"How could I not? There's unfinished business between
us, Lady Arnold."

"What busi—oh! You know my name!"

"I made sure to find out."

Panic swept through her and she rifled a glance toward
the house. "But I mustn't be seen—"

"Whoa, steady now. No one knows I came."

"Is a rogue discreet, then?"

His eyebrows lifted, the half smile fading. "Ah, I see
you've been warned. It's flattered I should be, I suppose,
if my very appearance in a neighborhood is enough for
good folk to spread the alarm."

To her surprise, she heard bitterness under the banter.

"I'm a desperate character, a thief and a rogue. Have I
the right of it?"

"'Tis what I was told," she admitted.

"And what does the lady think?"

Her next words seemed to form of their own accord, without thought or volition. "I want you to kiss me."

Aghast when she realized she'd actually spoken the thought aloud, she braced herself for his laughter.

Instead, the cynical twist left his lips and his smile turned brilliant. "Anything for my lady's pleasure."

After looping his reins around one gloved hand, he stepped to her and tilted her chin up with the other.

The bottom dropped out of her stomach and she couldn't feel her fingertips. Every nerve in her body switched off save those at her lips, which awaited in screaming impatience the slow descent of his mouth.

Her eyes fluttered shut as she felt the warmth of his breath, then the gentle brush of his lips, soft as butterfly wings, teasing. When he brushed her lips again, this time tracing them with the wet blade of his tongue, he had to grab at her waist to keep her from falling.

The stallion shifted, tugging at the reins, and Teagan backed away. "So sweet," she thought he murmured, his voice thick, his breathing rough. But she wasn't sure she was hearing properly over the roaring in her ears.

She simply couldn't let him ride off yet.

Desperate purpose stiffened her and she called out, her voice sounding odd and breathy. "Mr. Fitzwilliams! Your...your horse. There's hay. In—in the barn." With a jerky motion she indicated the trail toward the manor.

To her mingled horror and relief, he nodded. And after he assisted her to remount, when she kicked Specter to a trot, his black followed.

She'd waited for him. A grin of pure delight on his face, Teagan kept Ailainn in line behind Lady Arnold, the better to savor the sight of her trim posterior bouncing on the sidesaddle.

The black habit was more threadbare than he remembered, but that confirmation of her poverty he readily excused, for the thin material molded that much more closely over the full breasts, slender shoulders and long, graceful line of leg. Curves as enchanting, as enticing as he remembered, and more.

A day of fantasizing over what he would do with and to those curves had strengthened desire to a fine edge. Teagan wanted his Lady Mystery as he'd not wanted any woman in a very long time.

But desire was only partly responsible for the savage, purely male satisfaction that swelled his chest. In her every hesitant move, in the enormous dark eyes clouded with confusion and hunger, he read the incredible truth.

Lady Arnold had never done this before.

All the women with whom he'd trysted, back to the very first, had been in greater or lesser degree masters of the game of seduction, using with practiced skill all the feminine weapons of enticement.

Lady Arnold, though, like the half-gentled colts he'd trained in his youth, was attracted but wary, ready to bolt at the first alarm. Her indecision, her utter vulnerability spoke strongly to him on some deep level beyond reason or explanation.

It sharpened his need, honed every sense knife-blade keen—and filled him with an odd tenderness. Lady Arnold, he vowed, would never regret taking her first lover. He would give her everything for which that yearning, doe-eyed glance begged—everything and more.

He mimicked her movements, slowing their pace to let the horses cool, then dismounting to lead them into the stable yard, delay heightening anticipation.

She motioned for him to bring Ailainn to a stall in the barn where he'd first met her—was it just yesterday?—then went to swiftly unsaddle and corral her mare.

Once finished, she hesitated at the paddock rail, her back to him, as if marshaling her courage. With a sigh that shook her slender frame, she turned and walked toward him, high color in her heart-shaped face.

He kept motionless, barely breathing, for she looked as if even now she might change her mind and flee. As she neared with hesitant steps, he slowly reached out his hand, wanting to lure her closer, ease for her the moment of first contact.

Trust me, he silently urged.

Lips trembling too much for the smile she tried to form them into, she raised her hand to his. Pure energy crackled between them as their fingers touched.

She gasped, moved as if to back away. He tightened his grip, pulling her gently toward him, then raising her gloved hand to his lips and holding it there until her resistance faded. Once again, her eyelids fluttered shut.

Teagan battled a fierce desire to seize her in his arms, free right now from its chains of uncertainty the passion simmering in her body. With vivid clarity he could picture her writhing beside him, under him, and knew he could guide them both to release more intense than they'd ever before experienced.

"Shall we go into the house?" he asked.

With a flutter of lashes, her eyes opened, panic once again in their depths. "No, I cannot! My maid…the butler… No, it must be here." She pulled her hand free and pointed to the hayloft. "Th-there."

As if having suddenly reached an irrevocable decision, she strode quickly to the ladder leading up to the loft, shedding her bonnet as she walked.

He followed, grinning, ambushed once more by tenderness. His sweet Lady Mystery, hiding out not from a jealous husband but from her household staff.

He wanted better for their first loving than a rapid tumble in a haybarn—fine linen sheets, champagne, hours of the slow teasing build to ecstasy. But he sensed for right now, this was all she'd allow. More, longer, later, he silently promised as he followed her up.

When her booted foot slipped on the ladder, he caught her against him, her deliciously rounded derriere pressed against the aching fullness at his groin. For a moment neither could move. Teagan's hands were shaking almost as much as hers by the time they reached the hayloft.

She scooted across the loft to stand facing him, back against a fragrant stack of hay bales, hands fluttering nervously at her sides.

Lady Mystery had no idea what to do next.

Though he knew each second of delay must be stretching her overwrought nerves to the breaking point, he simply had to take a moment to drink in the sight of her. Thick, dark brown hair, a froth of curls escaping the pins at her nape and temples. Pale face that was all huge brown eyes over a straight little nose and trembling, plum-plump lips. High pert breasts made to fit into his hands; rounded hips made to fit against his body.

"What's your given name?"

She started. "V-Valeria."

Though she had nowhere to run now, he approached slowly. "By the blessed saints, you are beautiful, Valeria."

Her gaze never left him, yet still she jumped when he gently cupped her face in his hands.

And nearly destroyed his control by reaching up to clutch his fingers and whisper, "Please."

Only a direct hit by a lightning bolt could have stopped him then. He meant to merely brush her lips, as he had before, but when she opened her mouth at his touch, sparks of fire danced through him. He responded in kind, trapping the fullness of her lower lip and tongue against his teeth. His arms whipped around her shoulders to pull her close, while he nibbled the sweetness of her mouth, then delved deeper to explore the velvet wonders within.

He wanted to proceed slowly, but he absolutely had to

feel the weight and softness of her bare breasts in his hands.
Feverishly he unbuttoned her spencer and cast it aside, then
worked at loosening the fastenings of her gown.

She tried to help, her hands bumping into his in equal
haste, until at last he pulled the gown free to run his fingertips across the tightened nubs of nipple and around the
warm, satin globes.

He caught her gasp on his tongue and drank deeply as
his hands plied her breasts, her body shuddering at each
stroke. Her flailing fingers snagged his shirtfront, then,
awkward, tentative, began to insinuate their way inside.

He nearly lost control when one slim finger found bare
skin. Gasping in turn, he had to pull back. And he froze
as, with awe in her eyes, Valeria carefully unfastened the
shirt buttons and bared his chest.

She glanced up, as if seeking permission, and he gave a
curt nod. Reverently, as if he were a precious object, she
placed both palms against his flesh, then traced her fingers
over the muscles of his arms, his shoulders and down to
the nipples.

"Beautiful," she whispered.

His chest tightened with emotion almost as powerful as
the desire thrumming in his blood—the unique sensation of
being cherished.

"B-beautiful," he repeated, watching her.

With a hunger stronger than any he could ever remember, he craved complete union, the feeling of his body
sheathed in hers, the total possession of her whimsical,
greedy honesty.

Swiftly he spread a nearby saddle blanket, urged her
down upon it, stripping off her chemise and skirts as he
went, then shucking his own garments. Her eyes closed and
her head lolled back when, with lips and teeth and tongue,
he paid homage to the perfection of her breasts.

At first she stiffened when he slid his hand up the
smoothness of her inner thigh, until he soothed her with

more drugging kisses. Her nails bit into his shoulders when
he lowered his mouth to suck hard at the taut nipples, while
inch by inch his fingers crept up her thigh. And she cried
out when he at last delved inside, to find her wet and ready.

But though his need was now so acute that delay was
almost pain, he first wanted more. And so, crooning encouragement, he suckled harder, licked the moisture in the
valley of her breasts and moved his thumb around and over
her hidden pearl, deepening the pressure until she reached
her peak. With triumphant tenderness he watched a burst
of ecstasy light her eyes before robbing her of sense and
sight.

After a few moments, when her crazed breathing steadied, he nudged her legs apart. Though he craved a taste of
her, he knew with the small nugget of brain still functioning
that he couldn't last much longer. Still he staved off completion a bit longer, to rally her with kisses on her pleasure-
bruised mouth, until her breathing quickened and her pas-
sion-rosy nipples once again stiffened.

Only then did he position himself over her. But a mael-
strom of mind-melting sensation began swirling within him
as soon as he eased his needy member into her. The final
shreds of control dissolved and he drove hard, unable to
stop or even slow the explosion he'd staved off so long.

Even so, after the smooth glide of entry he noted unexpected tightness. His last conscious thought, before a wave
of pleasure carried him into the nearest thing to heaven on
earth, was the incredible realization that he was indeed Valeria's first lover. Her very first.

Drenched in sweat, her breath still coming in gasps, Valeria slowly struggled to consciousness.

She was lying in her hayloft. Naked. With a handsome
man half reclining on her chest, a man who had just transported her on what had been, except for the last painful bit,

the most excruciatingly intense, unforgettable adventure of her life.

A ferocious gladness filled her. Whatever happened now, she'd never regret this. Even the shameful knowledge that yesterday she'd almost dismissed her maid for the same indiscretion she'd just committed couldn't overshadow her joy.

She was smiling at the thought, heat still simmering in her veins, when the man who'd tenderly initiated her into the wonders of love play hauled her to her feet.

And stood, magnificently proud and naked, arms crossed, glaring down at her.

Eyes shocked wide open, she goggled at him.

Before she could even begin to figure out what made him suddenly so angry, he gestured toward the blanket.

A blanket, she discovered to her dismay, that was liberally stained with blood.

"Now, madam, might you do me the gracious favor of explaining just how it is you came to be a widow without having ever been a wife?"

"It must be my courses—" she began.

"Nay, don't think to fob me off. I've experience enough to know you had none, even though I've never before taken an untried lass."

Numbly she felt at the stickiness on her legs. "I'm b-bleeding?"

Some of the panicky surprise in her voice must have penetrated his rage, for his grim look lightened. "'Tis not uncommon the first time, I'm told, and 'twill likely stop soon." The momentary respite quickly ended, though. "So what were you about, woman? Surely you didn't think to catch yourself a husband!"

"Certainly not!" she exclaimed, aghast. "Even did I want one, I cannot imagine a less likely candidate for matrimony than you!"

The undisguised horror in her tone might have been

taken as an insult, but instead Teagan's face cleared. "Saints be praised, you recognize that truth! Here, then." He fished a handkerchief out of his coat pocket.

Suddenly recalling her own nakedness, she snatched the handkerchief with one hand and her discarded chemise with the other. Wrapping the latter around herself, she rummaged at the periphery of the rumpled blanket for the rest of her garments.

A touch at her shoulder made her jump. She looked over at Teagan, clothed now in his breeches. "Let me," he said, gently tugging on the chemise. "It's a fine lady's maid I make."

She allowed him to help her into the chemise, her nervousness returning now that the fire of passion had cooled. Embarrassment threatened as well, and she blessed her wisdom in choosing as a lover someone she'd need never see again.

But as he turned her around to face him, she couldn't help reaching once more to touch the satin steel of his chest, slowly stroking with the pads of her fingers each sculpted muscle.

He caught up her hand and kissed it. Then, when she reached for the gown he still held, he moved it beyond her reach. "Nay, I'm not leaving until you tell me why. Why me, today. And how any man breathing could have left so lovely a bride untouched. Unless you were wed by proxy?"

"No."

"Then why?"

He pinned her with that piercing, cat-eyed stare. Still too rattled to manufacture a lie, she blurted out the truth. "He never wanted me. Hugh was my brother's best friend. When he returned from Spain to tell me my brother had died, he asked me to marry him. I didn't figure out until later he did so only out of duty."

"When he left you on your wedding night?"

All the disappointment, humiliation and heartache of that night swelled up from memory, nearly choking her.

"Y-yes."

"But the story goes that he died in your arms. Was that a lie?"

"Nay."

"Then he must have come to—"

"Don't!" she cried, not wanting Teagan to probe into truths still too painful to be borne. And then, suddenly, she was furious with him for stripping her naked, not just to the skin, but to the soul.

"Oh yes," she spat out, "Hugh died in my arms. But not because he'd come to love his friend's poor orphaned sister. He died too delirious with fever to know in whose arms he lay. Aye, died with a woman's name on his lips— but it wasn't mine."

She closed her eyes and put shaking fingers to her temples, as if to squeeze shut the floodgates of memory.

After a few moments of silence, during which she recovered a modicum of control, Mr. Fitzwilliams said quietly, "He was a cad, then."

"Nay, you mustn't think that! He never betrayed me. The lady he loved had refused him some months before he married me, I later discovered. Hugh rejoined the army the day after our wedding and did not return until he was sent back gravely wounded."

She faced Teagan squarely. "So I was never a wife. But I longed to experience passion, to know what force it is that can drive men and women to such extremes of courage and folly. Situated as I am here, with little hope of ever moving in larger society, I thought you might be the perfect gentleman to show me. With, of course, no further obligation on either part."

He considered her. "You chose me as your tutor?"

She blushed. "I hoped you might be."

To her relief, for she half expected a revival of his anger, he made her a deep bow. "'Tis fair honored I am at your confidence in my…abilities. However, I fear I've not nearly lived up to that trust. Yet."

"Yet?" she echoed, her eyes widening. "There's… more?" Valeria couldn't imagine how those sweet sensations could possibly intensify without stopping her heart entirely.

He chuckled. "Many and wondrous are the ways to heaven, my lady."

Already the potent promise in his eyes, the smile dancing at his lips sent coils of anticipation spiraling to her now-quiescent core. She ought to finish dressing, send him on his way, and yet… "Show me."

He made a sweeping gesture. "Here? Now?"

"Neither Cook nor the butler ever venture to the barn, and I told my maid Mercy I'd ride long today. 'Tis the groom's day off and I sent Sukey Mae to town." Valeria hesitated, still shy of expressing her desires. "I've time, if…if you have."

"All the time in the universe," he whispered, and pulled her back to the blanket.

Then, at teasing length, he proceeded to reveal to her the full shattering beauty of ecstasy untarnished by pain.

Much later, as she lay in his arms, damp and sated, her mind floating in a sensual haze, the sharp bark of a dog warning of intruders jerked her alert.

"Heavens, that might be Sukey Mae returning. I must go."

She sat up, but as she reached for her chemise, he stopped her, bending to capture one nipple and worry it between his teeth.

The now-familiar warmth pooled at her center and coiled in her belly. She arched her neck, indulging herself one final moment in delightful torment. Then she gently pulled his head up to meet her lips.

She used her tongue as he'd taught her, wanting to con-

.vey not just her new knowledge but her thanks. A soul-deep thanks for this gift of pleasure he'd brought her—which mere words were hopelessly inadequate to convey.

Nonetheless, she would speak them. "Mr. Fitzwilliams."

"Teagan," he corrected. "Sure, and 'mister' is a bit too formal now."

She had to smile. It *was* ludicrous to fall back into the convention that did not allow the use of given names until after a formal, third-party introduction.

"Teagan. I must go, but first I would thank—"

"Nay." He stopped her with a finger to her lips.

"Should I not thank you?" She smiled slightly. "I'm sorry, I don't know what one—"

His hands flashed up to grip her arms so tightly she fell silent. "God forbid you should ever know," he said fiercely, and kissed her.

She'd feared it would be awkward, going about the business of dressing, tidying her hair. But once again, Teagan made it easy for her, commanding her to button up his shirt, alternating between straightforward lacing of her garments and teasing touches that let the sensual spell linger and slowly, slowly dissolve.

Ah, how swiftly she could come to crave his touch.

She dare not permit that. "When does your party expect to depart?"

"In a few days." He stopped fastening his waistcoat to study her face. "Will you ride tomorrow?"

She didn't pretend to misunderstand. "To fulfill a dream is splendid. But to try to live it again and again would be…dangerous." She swallowed hard. "It might then be very difficult to let it go at all."

He remained silent a long moment, his face unreadable, then nodded. "'Tis rare to find a lady as wise as she is beautiful."

A ridiculous hurt pierced her. What had she expected? That this handsome man, who probably had to turn away eager women wherever he went, would seek to persuade her?

Trying to reassemble the shattered bits of who she used to be, Valeria descended the ladder, then watched, already lost in bittersweet anguish, as Teagan prepared to ride away.

Before mounting the stallion, he walked over to give her one last kiss.

"Having plucked about as much as I can from the pigeons at Rafe's, I shall probably head back to London. If—if there should be some unexpected…consequence to this morning's pleasure, you will let me know?"

She gave her head a negative shake. "There won't be." She didn't wish to wound him by adding she could think of no one less qualified to assume the duties of fatherhood.

Nonetheless, he seemed to guess her thoughts. "Of course not. Whist, and what finer papa could a lad wish for than a shiftless Irish gambler?"

Before she could reply, he had hoisted himself into the saddle and swept her a bow. "Goodbye, Lady Arnold. God be with you."

"Mr. Fitzwilliams."

Wheeling the stallion, he set off across the stable yard toward the orchard. And did not look back.

A sinking feeling invaded her chest, as if her heart were a small pebble that had just been tossed into a very deep pond.

It was imperative that he ride away, she reminded herself.

A far greater danger than discovery stalked her. Were the fascinating Mr. Fitzwilliams to remain in the neighborhood, she was not at all sure she could prevent herself from attempting to seek him out. Her senses, awakened to delights of which she'd formerly had only the haziest conception, already clamored for more.

More of what the supremely skilled Mr. Fitzwilliams had

given her. What, she forced herself to acknowledge, he would in future give, with equal skill and thoroughness, to other ladies. She dare not read into their interlude, searing as it had been for her, any more than that.

Lud, though, 'twas a wonder women did not follow his carriage or throw themselves before his horse.

How ignorant she'd been when she'd blithely decided to satisfy the wonderings of her mind and the cravings of her body with one brief, blissful episode. Thinking she could then put it all behind her and go on unchanged, as men seemed to do so easily.

Only now, as her eyes followed the figure on horseback climbing the hill beyond the orchard, was the sober truth sinking in to her already-sorrowing mind and her already-needy body.

A woman couldn't give herself to a man without losing a part of her soul. And some irretrievable piece of hers was now disappearing down the ridge beyond Eastwoods in the possession of a wandering rogue she'd never see again.

Bemused as well as satisfied, Teagan guided Ailainn through the woods toward Rafe's hunting box. Faith, he still wasn't sure that he'd not just trysted with a goddess come to earth as a wood nymph.

Certainly Valeria—he let the music of her name play through his mind—had been nothing like any mortal woman he'd bedded, and he'd bedded a fair number. No, in a world where everything had its price and everyone who permitted the Jester close demanded his best performance, she had entreated only with her eyes and a whispered "please." Using no artifice to entice, intent not on punishing an errant husband or enlivening a selfish boredom, but on capturing wonder, she had, with her innocent yet powerful response, brought to passion a sweet majesty long since lost to him.

Could it be he'd encountered that rarest of all jewels—

a truly honest woman? One like his mother, who'd flouted her father's authority to follow the man she loved, faithful until the day she'd died—abandoned by that man.

The father whose irresponsible blood also flowed in Teagan's veins.

No, even if Valeria Arnold were gold, it was among dross that the Jester belonged, he reminded himself. With his pockets now well-lined with Rafe's and his friends' blunt, best to put this all-too-fascinating wood sprite out of mind and return to London immediately. After all, the winnings would last only so long. He must plan the Jester's next performance.

And extinguish this frighteningly intense desire to wheel Ailainn around and ride back to her.

Chapter Four

A week later Valeria pulled Specter to a halt before the barn. After giving the mare a final pat, she dismounted and handed the reins to the waiting groom.

Her cheeks warmed as she watched him lead the horse into the shadowed interior. She'd not been inside the structure since her tryst the week previous, an interlude so shocking, splendid and entirely beyond the scope of her normal staid existence that she now had difficulty believing it had really transpired.

Except for the constant, subtle hum of her awakened senses, the sharp and disquieting need that pulsed through her whenever, in some unguarded moment, her thoughts drifted back to that unprecedented morning. As all too often they seemed to do.

Firmly arresting the insidious longing to think on it again, she jerked her attention back to her conversation this morning with Gilbert, the farm's competent but rather taciturn foreman. Reviewing the laconic replies to her inquiries about the upcoming shearing, Valeria thought ruefully that Gilbert, having dealt with sheep all his life, seemed to commune with the beasts more readily than with two-legged beings. Given the state of her finances, however, it appeared Valeria would have a long, uninterrupted span of years in which to learn how to extract from him the information she needed.

Unless, out of boredom and despair, she finally accepted Arthur Hardesty's offer.

A shudder shook her frame. After that interlude in the hay barn, she would rather embrace the genteel poverty of Eastwinds.

She was trying, without much success, to raise her spirits out of the doldrums into which those dispiriting reflections had cast her when she spied Mercy, bonnet and apron blowing in the wind, trotting toward her.

Since the maid had suffered an injury to her ankle in India and normally avoided walking, Valeria felt an immediate frisson of alarm. "Is something wrong?" she called as the woman approached.

"I don't know," Mercy gasped, pausing to catch her breath. "There be a courier come with a message for you, sayin' he's to stay till you give him a note in return."

"A courier?" Valeria echoed in surprise. "From whom?"

"Wouldna say, Mistress. Nor would he even hand Masters the note, sayin' he was ordered to deliver it to you personal!" The elderly maid snorted in disapproval. "There's wishin' I was that your papa's batman were still about to give 'im a right proper set-down!"

"No matter," Valeria replied, falling into step beside the maid. "I expect we shall soon learn his errand."

When they reached the manor, Mercy halted. "Into the parlor with you now. I'll go round to the kitchen and fetch you up some tea whilst Masters tells Mr. Airs-and-Graces he can bring you the missive."

Within moments after Valeria had put up her whip and gloves and repaired to the parlor, Mercy entered the room with a tray of steaming tea, a young man in dark blue livery following in her wake. The maid jerked her chin at the newcomer. "Here he be, Mistress—whoever he be."

"Saunders, ma'am," the courier said, doffing his hat and offering a bow. "Sent to yer with this—" he held out a sealed letter "—by my mistress, Lady Winterdale."

Valeria scanned her memory. "The Dowager Countess of Winterdale?"

"Yes, ma'am. Begging yer pardon, Lady Arnold, if'n I disturbed yer house—" he glanced at Mercy, who gave an audible sniff "—but my mistress said as how I weren't to speak to no other but you, and was ta put this straight into yer hand. She also said I were not ta be quit o' this place till I had yer message in return."

"Very well, Saunders. I'll ring when it's ready. Mercy, would you escort him back downstairs, please."

After nodding a dismissal, Valeria deposited the vellum packet on the table beside her chair and poured herself a cup of tea, wondering what was so urgent that her husband's grandmother, a woman she had never met, thought it necessary to send the news by courier.

Word of some special bequest?

A thrill shivered through her before she laughed, dismissing so fanciful—if appealing—a notion. For one, Lady Winterdale was obviously very much alive, and besides, if someone had bequeathed her late husband anything of value, notice of it would surely come through a lawyer.

Seating herself, she broke the seal and began to read.

My dear Valeria,

   It was a great sadness to me that my indifferent health precluded my attending your wedding to my grandson at Portsmouth, and an even greater one that illness prevented my journeying to Eastwoods to see Hugh before his tragic demise.

   I have heard much of your devoted care to him dur-

ing his long decline. Now I beg you will show compassion for the grief of an old lady and come to London, that you might relate to me every detail of Hugh's
last few months.

    I've instructed my courier to wait upon your reply,
that I might know when I can look forward to your
arrival. Until then, I remain, yours…

After the usual expression of compliments, the note
ended with the dowager's signature in an impressive looping scrawl.

Valeria sat back in her chair, irritation and amusement
mingling with her surprise. Summon her to London, did the
countess, and with such arrogant assumption of Valeria's
instant obedience that she'd had her messenger wait upon
Valeria's reply!

Granddaughter-in-law or no, she was not a lackey to
spring to the countess's bidding. Though she had to admit
the idea of visiting the grand metropolis of London, a city
she'd never seen, was vastly appealing.

London, center of business and trade, of government, of
Society. London, where the members of the ton—that privileged world to which she belonged by birth but to whom
she had never been presented—would gather for the Season.

London, where one charming and unforgettable Irish
rogue was doubtless now residing.

A rush of excitement tingled her nerves. Don't be a
looby, she chastised herself. Even if she did not resent the
command thinly veiled beneath the politeness of the dowager's invitation, the cost of such a journey made it out of
the question. Much as she sympathized with the old lady's
evident need to cling to every memory of her beloved relative—a need with which Valeria was all too familiar.

Mindful of the waiting courier, she quickly composed a

reply, which, while honoring the countess's grief, was nonetheless firm in refusal. After sanding and sealing her note, she regarded it with a sigh.

London. Like so many other exotic lands and adventures she longed to experience, distance and poverty rendered this one just out of reach.

But one adventure she had claimed. A fierce gladness filled her that she had triumphed over modesty, upbringing and abject terror to seize the opportunity life had granted her. Especially since with the beginning of her courses, she now knew that stolen interlude had not left her a permanent and scandalous memento of her recklessness.

She suppressed a grin when Masters appeared practically the instant she rang the bell pull. No doubt her servants were as agog to learn the courier's message as they were insulted by his method of delivering it.

"Would you tell Saunders I have his message ready?"

"At once, my lady." However, Masters hesitated. "I trust nothing of an...alarming nature has occurred, ma'am?"

"No, Masters. My husband's grandmother merely wished to convey her sympathy on my recent loss."

The momentary crease of his brow told her Masters found that excuse for a courier-delivered message unconvincing, but he forbore further questioning. "I'm relieved to hear that," he said, and bowed himself out.

As she awaited the courier, Valeria mentally reviewed the list of small, dull, but necessary chores that would occupy the rest of her day. Another sigh escaped. Valeria Arnold, good soldier's daughter, would do what she must without further repining. Still, how exciting it would be to be reviewing instead the plans for departing to London!

A sharp knock at the door pulled her from her lapse into melancholia. "You may give your mistress this, with my compliments," she said, holding out the letter.

Saunders took it and bowed. "If'n I may be so bold, Lady Arnold, when can I tell my mistress ye'll be comin'?"

Taken aback, Valeria hesitated. It seemed odd indeed that the countess would have made her servant aware of her invitation. "I shall not be going to London," she replied.

"Then, begging your pardon, ma'am, my mistress said I was to give yer this—" the courier reached into his vest to extract another folded square of vellum "—n' this." From his trouser pocket he produced a fat leather purse.

Valeria heard the distinctive clink of coins as he transferred the articles to her outstretched hand. Her heartbeat leaped as her palm dipped under their weight.

For a moment she simply stared at him. "I—I shall require another moment, please," she said. After he bowed himself out, she hurried over to lay the money bag reverently on the desk, then ripped open the countess's second note and rapidly scanned the contents.

With numb fingers Valeria set the missive aside, loosened the pouch's drawstring and poured the coins onto the desk. Ten, twenty—there must be fifty golden guineas! No wonder the courier had been instructed to confide his message to none but the recipient.

Her mind still a swirl of disbelief, on knees gone suddenly weak she sank into her chair and, slowly this time, reread the countess's note.

My dear Valeria, I feared when my grandson went off soldiering, he would neglect his estates such that, with the barony's assets passing to Hugh's cousin upon his premature demise, he left you little beyond that wretched farm. Hardly a fitting repayment for your devoted care!

Lest a lack of funding prevent your accepting my invitation, my servant has been ordered to advance this sum and arrange your food and lodging for the journey. I shall live in happy expectation of meeting you shortly.

A rising excitement swamped any lingering vestiges of irritation over the countess's high-handedness.

Gilbert could handle the shearing without Valeria, and the small tasks awaiting her attention could just as easily be accomplished a month or two from now. Could she but persuade herself to accept the countess's largesse, she had no compelling reason to refuse the invitation.

Ah, to escape this dull backwater—and in London! Premier city of England, seat of government, finance and Society...residence of Teagan Fitzwilliams.

'Twas ridiculous how her breath fluttered at the very thought. Even should she go, London was a huge city. A half-Irish gambler of dubious reputation would hardly frequent the same circles as the Countess of Winterdale.

However, were Valeria to go, she should be able to steal a few hours in which to explore the fascinating metropolis Elliot had described to her so enthusiastically. The soaring heights of Westminster Cathedral and the perfection of Sir Christopher Wren's masterpiece, St. Paul's. St. James's Palace, surrounded by its vast park, and the grim silhouette of the Tower brooding over the Thames. The pleasure gardens of Vauxhall, illumined at night by thousands of lights; the docks by day crowded with ships unloading cargos from exotic lands she so longed to visit.

Awe at actually being able to view such glorious vistas scoured away the remnants of her resistance. Swiftly she withdrew more paper and sharpened her pen.

But as she rapidly composed her acceptance, a guilty excitement that had nothing to do with cathedrals, cargoes or commerce thrummed through her.

* * *

Three weeks later, Valeria sat beside Mercy in the comfortable carriage Saunders had arranged, anxious for her first sight of the countess's town house. Though in India she'd viewed sprawling cities and the opulent splendor of a nawab's palace, she still found the vastness of London impressive, and the classically designed and detailed dwellings of Westminster and Mayfair most beautiful.

Lady Winterdale's residence, she discovered as the carriage halted at last, was a three-story brick residence set on the lush green expanse of Grosvenor Square.

"'Tis lovely, is it not, Mercy?"

"As long as the roof don't leak nor the chimney smoke, I shall like it well enough," the maid replied prosaically.

"I expect you can count on that!" But as Valeria ascended the stone stairs, sudden nervousness afflicted her, and she smoothed her wrinkled pelisse with anxious fingers. The owner of such magnificence was certain to be pained by her outmoded, rather worn apparel.

The gesture didn't escape Mercy's sharp eye. "No use fretting yourself, Miss Val. Lady Winterdale knows how you're circumstanced, and if she don't, she ought to!"

True enough, Valeria reassured herself as she entered the vast marble foyer. It really did not matter whether or not the old lady approved of her. Valeria was here only to recount the episodes Hugh's grandmother had requested, and after that would be on her way back to Yorkshire.

The butler, a forbidding personage with a stiffly starched collar and expression to match, directed Mercy to meet the housekeeper, and bade Valeria follow him to a guest bedchamber.

"Lady Winterdale will receive you after you've refreshed yourself from the journey," the butler said. "Molly can assist with whatever you require."

An apple-cheeked young servant awaited her within a spacious chamber furnished in Chippendale mahogany and rose satin. After the butler departed, the girl confided that the countess had assigned her to be Valeria's personal maid for the duration of her visit.

Eagerness to remove the grime of the road and curiosity to meet her benefactress spurred Valeria to make quick work of repairing her appearance. After insuring every braided hair was in place and her dowdy gown as presentable as a few moments' ministrations could make it, she rang the bell pull.

The butler led her to a much larger bedchamber whose tall Palladian windows overlooked the gardens behind the town house. The figure reclining on the ivory brocaded sofa in the room's center looked up as she entered.

"Lady Arnold of Eastwinds," the servant intoned.

"Countess, thank you for your kindness in bringing me to London," Valeria said with a curtsy.

"Come closer, gel, and let me have a look at you," the countess said. "Jennings, bring us sherry."

The butler hesitated and cleared his throat. "Your physician recommends only tea, my lady."

The countess grimaced. "Impudent sawbones! If I can't have a glass of sherry to celebrate the arrival of my grandson's wife, I might as well cock up my toes now."

Valeria thought she heard a sigh escape the butler before he turned to her. "Tea for you, Lady Arnold?"

"If you please."

"Old retainers," the countess muttered after the butler left. "Never know their place. Now come, give me your hand. I shan't bite, you know."

Valeria approached as bidden and held out her hand. As the dowager took her fingers in a surprisingly robust grip, each woman silently appraised the other, Valeria searching for signs of the man she'd loved.

With her slightly hawked nose, broad brow and well-shaped lips, the countess must have been striking rather than handsome as a girl. Though the face and figure gave little testimony to the closeness of blood between this woman and Valeria's late husband, the sharp, piercing black eyes that watched her every step were so reminiscent of Hugh's that Valeria felt an automatic pang.

Just so had Hugh scrutinized her, when he'd first accompanied Elliot to her father's billet. An impetuous fifteen-year-old delighted by her beloved brother's visit and overwhelmed by his handsome friend, she'd pelted the two with pebbles as they rode up the lane, desperate to attract their notice. Caught in bittersweet longing for those long-ago days, she said, "Hugh had your eyes."

The countess's expression softened. "Aye. You loved him well, did you not?"

"Yes." *But he didn't love me.* Surprised by the acuteness of her lingering pain over that bitter fact, Valeria could think of nothing further to say.

"Sit." The countess indicated a wing chair next to her. "Aside from the several letters I believe he dictated to you, I know nothing of how Hugh fared after he was wounded. So, tell me everything."

"Of course." Pausing only long enough to sip gratefully at the hot tea the butler brought, Valeria described to his grandmother the shock of viewing Hugh's bloodied body, rigid with pain and incoherent with fever as he was unloaded from the transport ship. Then the desperate first weeks when he hovered between living and dying, the slight improvement that allowed him to be conveyed back to the small farm at Eastwinds where he'd grown up…and the final, slow decline.

"You were with him at the end?" the countess demanded.

"Yes, my lady."

"Did he have any last words?"

Lydia…Lydia?

The echo of Hugh's hoarse whisper invaded her ears, unleashing a cache of infinitely painful memories.

"H-he was not speaking very clearly toward the end," Valeria evaded. She didn't want to recall the anguish she'd felt at discovering her husband had never stopped loving the girl who'd refused his suit—anguish mixed with anger at his approaching death, and despair that she was helpless to prevent it. Or the stubborn, hopeless love that had prompted her to comfort despite the blow his words had dealt her.

"I'm here, my dearest," she'd whispered back.

"Kiss me, Lydia," he'd gasped. "One…last time."

And so she'd pressed her trembling lips to his hot, cracked ones, cradling his emaciated body close while her tears fell and evaporated off his fevered skin, her heart splintered by the knowledge that she could ease his final suffering only by pretending to be someone else.

Once more tears gathered. She swiped at them, angry with the countess for exhuming the ugly, hurtful truth.

She looked up to find the old woman staring at her. "He thought of her, didn't he? His precious Lydia."

For a moment Valeria could not breathe. Then, the habit of replying truthfully too ingrained for her to quickly dredge up a lie, she sputtered, "He…I…how dare you ask?"

"Don't trifle with me, gel! I'll have an answer. Or did you think to come to London and wheedle me with lies, mayhap claim some of the bounty that would have been Hugh's, had he lived?"

Valeria felt her face whiten, then suffuse with color. Slowly she rose to her feet.

"I have provided as full an account of Hugh's demise as I can. That being done, you can have no further use of me. Thank you for the tea, Lady Winterdale. You needn't summon your butler—I can find my way out."

Too furious even to consider how she was to manage the expense of the return journey, Valeria curtsyed and whirled around, intent upon summoning Mercy and quitting the house as quickly as possible. Only to find her wrist caught in the grip of one thin, clawlike hand.

"Here now, where do you think you're going, you silly chit?" the dowager said, tugging on the arm she'd captured. "Sit back down! I may be old and invalidish, but my sources among Society are excellent. You have no friends or relations here. A lady don't stay alone at a hotel, though if that wretched pig farm leaves you with more than a feather to fly with, I shall own myself astonished."

"Sheep. We raise sheep," Valeria replied through clenched teeth. "And Eastwinds is doing quite well. If you will kindly release my wrist, I wish to leave."

"Well, *I* don't wish it," the Dowager returned. "'Tis one of the few privileges of age, missy, to conduct oneself badly and get away with it. But I intend to explain myself, so climb down from the boughs and hear me out." When Valeria remained stiffly upright, the countess gave her wrist another shake. "Sit, I say!"

After briefly entertaining—and discarding—the notion of arm-wrestling her husband's elderly relation, reluctantly Valeria sat.

Waiting a moment, as if to make sure Valeria would not spring up and quit the room if she released her, the old woman let go of her wrist.

"Since you require it, I shall remain," Valeria said. "However, I shall not answer any further questions, nor do I possess any interest whatsoever in any bequest you might have intended for Hugh."

"If you haven't any interest in additional funds, you're a nodcock, girl, and not the intelligent lady I believe you to be! Not but that I don't think the better of you for being offended by my plain speaking. No sly-smiling, weasel-faced flattery from you, which just confirms the good I've heard of your character.'' The countess nodded approvingly.

Rendered off balance by the sudden shift from attack to praise, Valeria sat silently, a sliver of amusement piercing the defensive shield of her ire.

Before she could formulate a suitable reply, the countess continued. ''First, let me assure you I consider it the best of good fortune that the bird-witted Lydia Fontescue refused Hugh's suit! Oh, she claimed to love him—'' the countess paused to give a disdainful sniff ''—until she learned he meant to go fight with Wellington. Not for Miss Lydia to chance being left on the shelf, should her fiancé die in some heathenish land!''

The discomfort Valeria might otherwise have suffered at being forced to endure a discussion of the woman her husband had loved was blunted both by surprise at the countess's outspokenness and a grudging sympathy with the illwill the woman obviously still harbored toward the lady who had rejected her grandson.

Allowing Valeria no chance to insert a comment, Lady Winterdale continued. ''Lydia snagged herself the viscount she wanted. Already running to fat, Aylesbury is, with barely a thought in his head beyond the cut of his coat. And he ruined her figure, getting her with three puling imitations of his spavin-shanked self.'' The old woman shook her head in disgust. ''Still, Lydia wasn't the only lackwit, if by the time of his death Hugh hadn't come to appreciate the lady he did wed.''

''Please, Lady Winterdale, I don't want—''

''There now, girl,'' the countess said, patting her hand. ''You mustn't think too badly of him. You were married so briefly, and then him coming back more dead than alive... But he was ever a smart lad, and had the good Lord granted him more time, I'm sure he would have overcome that silly infatuation and learned to value you as he ought.''

His grandmother believed Hugh might have come to love her? Once again tears stung Valeria's eyes. How many long, lonely months had she hoped and prayed for that eventuality, until the final crushing disappointment?

Before she could master herself enough to reply, the countess sighed. ''Enough about the past, then. We must decide what's to be done with your future.''

''M-my future?'' Valeria stuttered, once again disconcerted by the dowager's abrupt shift.

''Of course, yours. My sources tell me that your papa, apparently as lackadaisical about what was owed you as my grandson, never gave you a Season. How are you to reestablish yourself in Society if you're not even out?''

''It is rather difficult to arrange a Season from Bombay, and then Papa was ordered straight from India to the Peninsula,'' Valeria retorted hotly.

''Ought to have sent you back home, even though your only relations are cousins several times removed. Still, your mama's people never stir from that medieval pile in Westmoreland and your papa's kin in Devon are just as bad. But we've matters of more import than abusing your relations, gel,'' the dowager continued, cutting off Valeria's protest. ''So you may cease looking daggers at me. Something must be done now. You've had sufficient time to mourn Hugh. You're still young, of excellent birth, and sufficiently attractive that your chances of remarriage are quite good. I mean to present you, missy.''

''Present me?'' Valeria echoed, both bemused and annoyed by this further evidence of the countess's highhandedness. ''My lady, I cannot conceive how—''

''True, you're a bit old,'' the lady continued, dismissing Valeria's interruption with an imperious wave, ''and though that lamentable farm will provide little enough dowry, once we've gotten you suitably attired, I have every expectation of bringing some respectable candidates up to snuff. My health don't allow me to go out, so I've arranged for my niece, Lady Farrington, to squire you about. Alicia will arrive tomorrow and escort you to the mantua-makers the instant her trunks are unpacked." The countess surveyed Valeria with a grimace. "You're not to stir from the house until your new wardrobe is delivered."

"Do I have no say in this whatever?" Valeria demanded when the countess at last paused for breath.

"You may thank me," she replied, the hint of a smile belying the tartness of her tone.

Valeria shook her head, trying to gather her disordered thoughts. Had she possessed sufficient funds, she probably would have chosen to come to London and enter Society after her year of mourning ended. Still, generous as the countess's plans were, she wasn't at all sure she should— or wished to—place herself under such obligation to her husband's imperious relative.

"'Tis all so unexpected. I must reflect—"

"What is there to reflect upon? You'd be a looby to refuse such an offer, and you know it. Now…" the countess turned her compelling, black-eyed gaze upon Valeria, and once again the old woman's resemblance to her grandson reverberated painfully through her "…there's naught to do but be sensible, thank me prettily and begin considering which new fashion will best become you."

"But I'm not so sure I wish to remarry," Valeria countered stubbornly. "Even were I fixed upon it, there's no guarantee, despite your generous support, that I would in fact attract an offer that would be acceptable to us both. I should not wish you to invest funds in an endeavor so uncertain of success."

"Perhaps you'd not find a suitor to your liking," the countess conceded. "But you must admit, Miss Contrary,

that you've a much better chance of finding a suitable candidate here and now than at any other time or place. I'm
not set on marrying you off, child. Should you end the
season unwed, I'll consider my duty to Hugh done, and
that's an end to it.''

Silently Valeria reconsidered the countess's proposal. As
the old woman said, should she ever wish to remarry—or
more importantly, to have children of her own—she would
be foolish to turn down this singular opportunity. And in
addition to that possibility were the attractions offered by
the city itself.

Ah, to have months to explore it, rather than a few days.
And after years of struggle, heartache and poverty, the prospect of simply enjoying the frivolity of Society life, garbed
in a wardrobe of fashionable new gowns, was wonderfully
appealing.

Reluctantly, Valeria tried to close her eyes to this attractive vista. 'Twas one thing for her to allow the countess to
pay her way to London, that she might render the old
woman some service, quite another to accept from this near
stranger the staggering sum Valeria suspected a Season
would cost. ''I must again thank you for the offer, but I
cannot feel I could accept such great largesse. Despite my
marriage to Hugh, I have no claim upon you.''

''Pft!'' The countess made an impatient sound. '''Tis all
well and good to be independent, gel, but don't whistle
away a golden opportunity out of misplaced pride.''

A pride she'd undoubtedly be forced to swallow over
and over, were she to remain here, subject to the whims of
this imperious and unpredictable woman. Perhaps her modest sheep farm—with Arthur Hardesty as a last resort—was
not so unappealing an alternative.

Her hawklike gaze on Valeria's face, the countess must
have seen the conflicting emotions mirrored there, for after
a long moment she sighed. The fierceness seemed to drain

from her and she sagged back against the sofa cushions. For the first time Valeria caught a glimpse of how truly ill the old woman was.

"My husband, children, grandchildren have all left me," she said quietly, her voice now subdued and weary. "Except for the foolish Alicia, who cowers every time I speak to her, I've no near relations still living. I like your spunk, my dear, your independence—and your devotion to Hugh. The doctors tell me I haven't long left. It would…comfort me to have you with me until the end."

The countess turned to look directly at her, and Valeria could read in her eyes how much it cost the proud autocrat to have to admit her weakness. "Would you not humor a sick old woman, and remain in London?"

Though her lips had been poised to utter a refusal, that sudden change from dictatorial to vulnerable touched something deep within Valeria. She, too, knew what it was to lose all those dear to her, to dine at a solitary table, sit before a solitary fire with only loneliness and memories for company. Neither wealth nor title could save the countess from the same fate.

Valeria could.

"I…I hardly know what to say."

Once again the dowager reached out to take her hand, her grip this time trembling, uncertain. "Say yes. You'll not need to suffer my company long, if the sawbones are correct. Can you really be so contemptuous of pleasure that you could not enjoy yourself in London for a few months? You need not remarry if you do not wish it. Stay, and let me repay the debt I owe you for nursing Hugh in spite of…everything."

"I loved Hugh," Valeria said. "No repayment is necessary."

"Then stay out of kindness for the grandmother who loved him, too. Please."

Crafty old beldame, Valeria thought, more than half convinced she was being cleverly manipulated. To refuse largesse was one matter, but how could one turn down a dying grandmother-in-law's last request?

"Very well, Lady Winterdale. I will stay."

The countess nodded. "Good. And you may call me 'Grandmamma,' as Hugh did. Now, if you will leave me, my dear, I fear I must rest."

Shaking her head at how brilliantly the countess had outmaneuvered her, Valeria curtsyed and walked away. But as she paused to open the door, she looked back to see the woman already asleep, something that looked suspiciously like tears seeping from under her eyelids.

Valeria paused, her cynical suspicions softening. Perhaps the old woman genuinely wanted her company—or at least a more worthy opponent with whom to clash swords than the apparently timorous Alicia.

As Valeria silently tiptoed out, a surge of excitement buoyed her spirits. She'd send her London maid out for a guidebook this very afternoon. Since it appeared she'd be treated to a several-month sojourn in the city, Valeria intended to profit from it—and not restrict her explorations solely to the handful of residential squares and business streets frequented by the ton.

No, she meant to discover all of London, even those less fashionable districts where she might chance encountering one handsome, charming half-Irish gambler.

Chapter Five

Though the early spring sunshine a month later did little to drive the chill from his chamber, the golden beam caressing his face was intense enough to roust Teagan from slumber. Rubbing a hand over the rough stubble at his chin, he squinted and sat up, a precipitous action that sent sharp pain lancing through his head. Groaning, he squeezed his eyes shut and leaned back against the pillow.

The cotton dryness of his swollen tongue and the bitter taste in his mouth must be relicts of the cheap brandy at the gambling hell Rafe Crandall had taken them to last night. The results of his evening's play were scarcely sweeter than the brandy residue.

Slowly this time, he eased himself to a sitting position and fumbled for the water pitcher on the bedside table. After cautiously opening his eyes just wide enough to pour a glassful, he shut them again and gulped it down.

Mhuire, but he was tired of drinking and dicing, the smoke and stink of stuffy, crowded rooms, the feverish eyes of brandy-soaked men caught in gaming's thrall, the endless charade of playing the reckless, jovial rogue. Laughing at coarse jokes he'd heard too many times, forced by necessity never to be able to turn down a wager over cards or a billiard cue, spending his nights in the company of men whose endless pursuit of superficial pleasures he cordially—but silently—despised.

He took another long draught of water and reached for the breeches he'd flung on the bedside chair near dawn this morning. After inspecting those pockets and the slim money pouch he extracted from the waistcoat dangling off the chair back, he reclined against the pillows once more.

Despite the brandy, his memory was only too correct. Though Teagan had not lost the entire stake he'd brought with him into the hell last night, his precious cache of coin had been severely reduced.

Sighing, he rose and walked to the washbasin. His landlady, Mrs. Smith, bless her, had the pitcher filled and a clean towel set out. For a moment he lost himself in the simple pleasure of scrubbing away the night's grit and smoke, reveling in the feeling of freshness despite the clanging set off in his head by the motion of bending over.

He would come about again, he told himself as he toweled his face dry and contemplated the effort necessary to shave. As a man whose whole income derived from gaming, he'd developed a strategy that for the last ten years had kept him, if not in luxury, at least one step ahead of the magistrate. Avoiding contests whose outcome depended solely on chance, he concentrated his efforts on games in which skill—a skill he'd worked hard to perfect—normally balanced out the capriciousness of pure luck.

Normally. But every so often, as if mocking his attempts to circumvent her, Lady Luck seemed to send him a succession of hands so bare of promise that even his experience and expertise couldn't manage to turn them to advantage. He'd just suffered a month of such hands, and the tidy bankroll of winnings he'd brought back with him from Rafe's house party had dwindled dangerously low.

A knock on the door interrupted his glum reflections.

"Thought I heard ye stirrin', sir!" His landlady entered with a bundle under her arm and a steaming tray. "And by the time it were when ye brought yerself home this morning, I expect ye could use a bit o' this."

The sharp tang of fresh coffee eased the queasy swirl left in the brandy's wake, and the aroma of fresh-baked meat pie made him realize that, having had no dinner the previous night, he was famished.

"Mrs. Smith, 'tis a blessing you are!" His mouth already watering, Teagan reached for his money pouch.

"Nay, put away yer coins," she said as she set down the tray. "I've just made the meat pies, and the coffee be fresh. Have 'em while they're hot."

Teagan took the mug and gulped a reviving draught of the coffee, then set about the meat pie. "Ah, sweet lady," he said after the first savory bite, "you're an *aingeal* flown straight down from heaven!"

Mrs. Smith chuckled. "An' ye're a lad with too honeyed a tongue! But a good tenant ye are for all that, always payin' me reg'lar, never pinching the maid nor bringin' in raff 'n scraff to brawl 'n gamble. I'd rather have yer plain "Mr." than half a dozen lordlings with fancy titles runnin' up their bills 'n sendin' their man bangin' on me door, hollarin' fer me to fetch 'em this 'r that."

"Why, Mrs. Smith, I shall have to change my new coat for an altar boy's robe, such a saint ye make me out to be," Teagan replied as he reached for another meat pie.

"Not a saint, I'll reckon," Mrs. Smith replied as she crossed the room, "but a true gentleman, fer all that ye carry on about bein' naught but a rogue." She deposited a bundle of folded linen on the bureau. "Maisy said to tell ye them new shirts iron up real nice. An' 'twas kind o' ye to give her an extra copper, her mum being sick 'n all."

"She does her work well," Teagan said, thinking of the young girl—she couldn't be much older than eight—with her thin shoulders and slender hands, sweat beading her face as she hefted the heavy iron and guided it across the endless stacks of linen shirts.

How could he not despise his aristocratic cronies who carelessly threw away hundreds of pounds on a single round of cards, when so many honest folk made do on so little?

"Ah, did ye not see the parcel what was delivered to ye yesterday? I set it here on the bureau. The boy what brung it said 'twas already paid for."

Teagan looked in the direction of Mrs. Smith's pointing finger to a small paper-wrapped package. After Oxford, he'd turned his back on the books he loved, but upon returning from Rafe's hunting box, winnings heavy in his pocket, he'd vowed to purchase a few of his favorites. Despite his dwindling resources, when he'd seen the small used volume of Herodotus in the shop window of the penny press, he'd not been able to resist it.

His spirits inched up a notch. Before he forced himself from his rooms this evening for another round of gaming, he would allow himself the pleasure of an hour in the intelligent company of that long-dead historian.

Mrs. Smith walked to the door, then hesitated. "There were a man come from that Hoby's yesterday, and one from that Mr. Weston as well. But I tol' 'em all the young gentlemen buy on tick, 'n ye'd always paid me sooner 'r late, and would pay 'em too, so's not to come round here bothering ye no more. That should hold 'em off a week."

Teagan looked over in surprise. "Thank you, Mrs. Smith. That was very kind."

Mrs. Smith shrugged. "The merchants' lads been comin' round here reg'lar since I bought this place caterin' to the Quality, fer it seems most o' the gentlemen never have a feather ta fly with. Spend it all on cards 'n spirits 'n women, with naught left to pay the duns." Mrs. Smith gave a sniff of disdain. "But I ain't forgot the favors ye've done me, and ifn I kin keep the collectors from botherfyin' ye till ye come about, I'm right happy to do it."

Surprised and touched by his landlady's intervention on his behalf, Teagan hardly knew what to say. "Ah, Mrs. Smith, I misspoke the truth earlier. 'Tis the very Queen of Heaven ye be, and a beauty besides!"

Laughing, Mrs. Smith waved a hand at him from the doorway. "More's the fool me, were I ta listen to yer pretty words! But go on, now, finish yer pies. There's ale in the kitchen—ring when ye're ready for it."

After she'd bobbed a curtsy and departed, Teagan chewed the rest of his meat pie and eyed the neatly wrapped package. After a few moment's struggle, he gave up, too eager to wait until after he'd finished shaving.

Quickly he unwrapped and drew out the volume. Though the cover's nicked and dented surface spoke of hard use and lack of care, nonetheless Teagan ran his fingers over it reverently. He opened the flyleaf, to find an inscription in fading black ink: "T. Williams, Oxford, 1808."

Oxford. In his head he heard Magdalene's bells tolling, surprising him with the lateness of the hour as he sat at the desk in his narrow room, immersed in the *Dialogues* of Plato. Close his eyes, and he could see the soft gold of the weathered stone of the university's halls and chapel glow in the early morning light as he strode to his professor's house.

A deep, barely conscious anger stirred, and he shut the cover with a snap. If the possession of a few ragged volumes, doubtless sold off at the first possible moment by university men more enamored of drink than scholarship, was going to sink him into a green melancholia over being torn from the one place he'd ever felt he belonged, he'd best resell the lot of them forthwith. That page of his life had been ripped out and trampled underfoot long ago.

After placing the book on the bureau, he strode to the washbasin and pulled out his shaving gear, trying to shake a lingering weariness. A ride would buoy his spirits, but Ailainn had thrown a shoe and was still at the smith's.

Teagan would make himself presentable, then go for a walk. Mayhap even spend a few precious pence to take a boat down to Hampton Court, that he might clear his mind and revive his spirits with a stroll through the gardens. And steel himself for another round of play tonight.

Perhaps he should look for another house party. The company would be more respectable and the players less fanatic than those who frequented the hells that, as he lacked entrée to the exclusive clubs of White's or Brook's, were his chief London haunts. He would be well fed for the duration, another plus, and there would be fields and woods through which he might race Ailainn, a pleasant change from the restrictive bridal paths of Hyde Park.

There might even be another lovely sprite of a neighbor.

At the thought, he slipped easily back into memories he'd reviewed all too often these past two months. What a marvel she'd been, his Lady Mystery, all wide-eyed wonder and desperate yearning, passionately curious, and yet wise enough to walk away when the time came. No, he concluded, his lips curving into a smile as he tucked the magical recollections back in their special place within his mind. There could be no other like his Lady Mystery.

But for the cost of a boat ride, there could be a temporary respite from the noise and clutter of London. For one afternoon he'd indulge himself in clean-scented air, blessed solitude…and sweet memory.

Several hours later, refreshed by his time away, Teagan strode into the Meridian, a modest gentleman's club off St. James's that had never quite achieved the cachet that allowed its former neighbor, White's Chocolate House, to transform itself into one of London's most exclusive establishments. The Meridian counted among its patrons a mix of clerks, neighborhood merchants and men of aristocratic birth whose connections were not sufficiently grand to gain them admission to the more select clubs.

Teagan noted Rafe Crandall already present, his small group nursing tankards of home-brewed.

Rafe raised a mug to him. "Ah, Jester, well met. Barkeep, a round for my friend."

As Teagan claimed a seat at an adjacent table, a young man rose from the back of the room and approached him.

"May I?" he asked, indicating the chair beside Teagan.

"Of course. A good day to you, Holden."

The young man smiled. "Much better than yesterday, thanks to you. Since you wouldn't hear me out last night, I had to find you today and—"

"Nor do I mean to listen now." Teagan cut him off, smiling. "'Tis the duty of one Oxford man to another to deflect the Captain Sharps out to fleece newcomers."

"Is it?" Insley glanced at Lord Crandall and his party. "Based on my experience, I would have concluded most Oxford men believe quite the opposite."

Teagan took a sip of the frothy ale just delivered by the barmaid. "You mustn't judge us all by the...dubious behavior exhibited by some."

"Why, Teagan," Rafe called over to them, apparently noticing the addition to their numbers. "'Tis the young bantling you've been bear-leading. Insley, ain't it?"

The young man inclined his head. "Lord Crandall."

"An odd role for you to play, Jester—rescuing innocents, rather than leading them astray," Rafe observed. "Or did his mama pay you to keep him out of harm's way?"

"Ah, Rafe, give the lad time. Even such a reprobate as you must have been green once," Teagan replied.

"Still don't think you should have won the infant's vowels back from that sharpster.'' Rafe shook his head. ''Dropping one's quarterly allowance at a gaming hell is practically a gentleman's...rite of passage. Why, an Oxford education's not complete until one has learned mathematics at the hands of the cent-per-centers.''

''For those who don't mind dishonoring their family name,'' Insley muttered.

Crandall sent the young man a sardonic glance and drained his glass. ''We're off to see what play there's to be had at White's. Care to join us? Ah, of course, how silly of me,'' he said, clapping his hand to his head in an exaggerated gesture of comprehension. ''Not likely to allow you into White's, are they, Jester?''

''Might be interesting to bring him as a guest, Rafe,'' another of Crandall's friends said. ''If his cousin the earl happened to be present, he'd likely go into apoplexy.''

Keeping tight rein on his temper, Teagan said lightly, ''Faith, and why should I wish to enter such portals? Nothing but a bunch of bloody Tories within, who'd as soon try to string up my Irish arse for sedition as look at me.''

''Shoot you for dallying with their wives, more like,'' Rafe returned. ''We're to try that new hell near Marlybone after dinner—Devil's Den, they call it. Play's said to be deep and the lasses comely. Join us, both of you—if Insley's mama will allow him out of the house tonight.''

Ignoring the jibe, the young man replied, ''I expect to play a few rounds later. My sister's come-out ball is tonight, and I must put in an appearance.'' Turning to Teagan, he added, ''Mr. Fitzwilliams, I'd be honored if you'd accompany me there.''

Rafe was moving with his friends to the door, but at that, he halted. ''Teagan? At a ton ball?'' He leaned his head back and laughed. ''You young cawker, don't you know Teagan ain't received? Not even by his own mama's family!''

"'Tis Lady Insley who'll be having apoplexy if you bring Teagan along!" one of Rafe's group added.

"Might have to toddle over and witness this spectacle myself," Rafe mused. "'Twould be quite entertaining— seeing the Jester get bounced out on his ear."

"Entertaining for certain," Teagan replied. "But not half so satisfying as a good dinner at White's."

Rafe appeared to ponder the alternatives. "Aye, Jester, you're right. As usual. But then, were you not usually right, in wagers and play, you'd have been clapped into prison for debt long ago, eh?" With a careless nod, Lord Crandall walked out, trailed by his sycophants.

"Ignorant ass," Insley said, watching them depart.

Teagan shrugged. "A bit worse than most, I agree. Though I've won a tidy fortune off him these last ten years, so I must not abuse his character too roundly."

"Would that you'd won enough to see *him* clapped in prison, and so spared us his company," the young man replied with some heat. "But no matter. I was quite sincere in my offer, by the way. Won't you take dinner with me at Crillon's and then go on to Marianne's ball?"

Teagan looked over in surprise. "That's kind of you, but however inelegantly he expressed it, Rafe was correct. My…presence is considered undesirable in proper ton circles, particularly if there are innocent maidens about."

"I can't understand why. From what I can discover, you've never debauched a maiden in your life, and have scarcely dallied with married ones the last few years."

"My behavior after being sent down from Oxford was a bit…less circumspect," Teagan replied wryly. "And once won, a bad reputation is easier kept than lost."

"Perhaps. But given the magnitude of the service you've done me, a service of which both my parents are aware, I'm sure *my* family would be pleased to receive you."

"'Twas a mere trifle."

"You may call it such, but I cannot. The horror that overcame me when I realized the extent of the vowels I'd signed, and knew that in order to make good on them I'd have to confess the whole ghastly business to papa…" Insley gave a reminiscent shudder. "Never again shall I be tempted to play beyond my means or skill. I *am* under obligation to you, whether you choose to recognize it or not, and I *should* be honored to acknowledge you, even at so public an event as my sister's ball."

The young man's declaration left Teagan at a loss, none of the usual light comments he kept at hand to deflect criticism or jibes being applicable. "L-let me accept the dinner invitation with pleasure, and leave it at that."

Insley offered a hand. "That will do…for a start."

Lady Farrington peered out the carriage window at the long line of vehicles waiting to discharge their passengers before the torchlit entry of the square's central town house and sighed. "I do wish you would have let dear Sir William escort us to Lady Insley's ball, Valeria. At least we would have had the benefit of that gentleman's uplifting conversation while we waited."

With what she considered true nobility, Valeria refrained from pointing out to her chaperone that had they departed at the hour first agreed upon, they would have arrived before this crush. "That may be true, Cousin Alicia," she replied instead, "but Sir William has already escorted us to three activities in the last two weeks. Though he is a good friend to Grandmamma, I should not wish to take advantage of his kindness."

Nor appear to be encouraging him to dangle after her, Valeria added silently to herself.

"To be sure, but 'twould be a very good thing if you could fix his interest. A truly noble gentleman, you must allow, learned and well spoken, as well as quite kind and distinguished. And at least ten thousand a year. Of course, I should not wish to imply that his income matters overmuch, but one cannot deny the possession of a handsome fortune must enhance his other fine qualities.''

''I will allow that Sir William is everything good and amiable. You have been exceedingly generous, introducing me to your friends, and bringing me along to so many delightful entertainments. But please remember, Cousin, I am in London only to keep Grandmamma company for a time.''

''Nonsense,'' Lady Farrington declared. ''I know 'tis only been a year since Hugh... But you're not getting any younger, my dear, and to whistle down the wind a gentleman like Sir William without at least making a push to—''

''Only look, I believe we're close enough to the entrance to step down. Do go first, ma'am, so Jeffers may hold the umbrella for you.''

With any luck, that would end the discussion of her erstwhile suitor for the evening, Valeria hoped, since the gentleman himself would doubtless soon join them. Surely even a lady as single-mindedly fixed on forwarding matrimony as Lady Farrington wouldn't attempt to advance a gentleman's suit with the man himself within earshot.

Valeria climbed down after Lady Farrington, wondering with some aspersion why that lady, if she were so enraptured of the wedded estate, did not expend her efforts on finding herself a husband and leave Valeria alone.

Her first month in London had been like dining on a diet of Gunter's sweet ices. But by now the time-consuming ritual of shopping for gowns, gloves, reticules, pelisses, shawls, stockings, bonnets, undergarments—it seemed every day Lady Farrington discovered another ''deficiency'' in Valeria's wardrobe that must be rectified by an immediate expedition to Bond Street—had grown tiresome. The exciting novelty of attending the apparently endless

round of at-homes, breakfasts, routs, card parties and balls
that made up the rest of Lady Farrington's existence, had
also paled.

Her chaperone's delight in introducing her new protégée
about was so obvious, however, that thus far Valeria had
refrained from begging off any of the invitations that Lady
Farrington eagerly accepted on their behalf. But her patience was wearing thin. She had about had her fill of overcrowded rooms, overdressed aristocrats and conversation
concerned solely with the latest fashions and the most scandalous on-dits.

They reached the entry at last and handed their evening
cloaks over to the butler. "Did I not tell you?" Lady Farrington said with a smile of pure delight. "Look there, at
the edge of the ballroom. Sir William awaits."

She sounded so enthused Valeria felt a little guilty for
having so little enthusiasm herself. Perhaps, she thought as
they awaited their turn in the reception line, if she'd been
able to see more of the city she'd feel less frustrated, but
it seemed that every time she tried to steal a moment to go
exploring, Lady Farrington or her grandmamma had some
objection.

That, Valeria decided firmly, would have to change. She
would simply have to make it clear to them both that she
must have more time to herself. More opportunities to venture beyond those areas in which the Upper Ten Thousand
lived, shopped and socialized.

For, if she were very honest, the fact that in the two
months of her residence she'd been nowhere that promised
even the chance she might see or hear something of Teagan
Fitzwilliams certainly added to the vague disappointment
she'd been feeling of late.

Not that she wished to actually meet him. Indeed, her
cheeks heated at the very thought. How could she look in
his face and not remember in scorching detail his lips on

hers, his mouth moving over sensitive areas of her body that a lady dare not even name? Or offer her hand without recalling the touch of those sure, knowing fingers?

But…to catch a glimpse of his handsome face in a crowd, to overhear the music of that lilting voice…to have tangible proof that the lover who had given her so incredible an interlude was flesh and not a chimera born of her lonely imagination…ah, that would be bittersweet joy.

By the time they'd finished greeting their hostess and her blushing daughter, Sir William had reached them.

"Ladies, how lovely you look this evening," he said with a bow. "Let me escort you upstairs."

He truly was an amiable gentleman, Valeria thought as she put her hand on his arm. Tall, with a lean, serious face, his dark hair touched with gray, Sir William Parham was a distant connection of Hugh's who had lost his wife two years previous. With three small daughters and no heir, he was known to be looking out for a second wife.

Valeria was more than a bit suspicious that Lady Winterdale had urged Sir William to consider Valeria for that role. Though she'd grown fond of the old woman and come to appreciate the concern behind the imperious facade, theirs still was a rather tempestuous relationship. Valeria, long mistress of her own establishment, did not take kindly to Lady Winterdale's managing ways.

In the matter of Sir William, she had to admit, apparently the old tartar was crafty enough not to try to force her choice on Valeria. Or perhaps she'd realized after their first few encounters that any attempt to bully her granddaughter-in-law, who could be just as obstinate and unyielding as Lady Winterdale herself, would most likely result in Valeria's doing the exact opposite.

Would she be attracted to Sir William, were it not for Lady Winterdale's interference? Valeria studied him covertly as, skillfully dividing his attention between the ladies on either arm, he turned to amuse Lady Farrington with a fulsome compliment. His manners were excellent, his conversation intelligent and his interests far-ranging. His attentions to Valeria were particular enough that she had no doubt of his intentions, yet not so familiar as to make her uncomfortable.

As Lady Farrington claimed, Sir William would make some fortunate lady an excellent husband. Valeria just wasn't sure an excellent husband was what she truly wanted.

Would her pulse race if he took her in his arms? Would his kiss make her blood quicken and her bones seem to dissolve…as a certain other gentleman's had done?

Would she look on him in a more favorable light if a charming rogue had not opened her eyes to pleasures far beyond what she'd imagined possible?

Having once tasted such pleasure, Valeria would never again consider binding herself to a man without it. Unfortunately, with an honorable gentleman who was considering making one a proposal of marriage, one could not discuss— or sample—the degree of pleasure obtainable without ending up with a betrothal ring on one's finger.

Valeria had not settled in her mind how she might solve that conundrum when they reached the ballroom. After escorting Lady Farrington to a comfortable chair beside her friends, Sir William bore Valeria off to join the dancing.

Just inside the entry of the Insley town house, Teagan paused to take a deep breath. Rafe had been right; allowing Insley to talk him into stopping by the ball was a mistake. He might well be ejected forthwith, and at the very least, would probably embarrass his earnest young friend or the lad's mother.

But before Teagan could tap Insley's sleeve to tell him he'd changed his mind, his eye was caught by one of the dancers at the edge of the ballroom above. A slender, grace-ful sprite of a lady, delicate as a butterfly in a gown of pale gold as she dipped and swayed through the movements of the dance on the arm of her dark-clad escort.

It couldn't be…and yet the shiver of awareness over his skin, the pull of connection that nearly impelled him to leave Insley's side and go to her, all clamored that it was indeed his Lady Mystery, somehow transported from the depths of Yorkshire to this London ballroom.

Trying to keep an eye on her, Teagan let Insley lead him forward, knowing it was now too late to retreat. Nor, de-spite the difficulties of finessing his way into Lady Insley's soiree, did he wish to leave.

He had no business intruding into the life of a respectable widow—and yet both the simmering desire the mere sight of her ignited in him and a deeper longing for something pure, honest and untainted by vanity drew him irresistibly.

That, and a natural curiosity to discover how a purse-pinched widow had ended up at this ton party in a stylish new gown.

He'd seek her out for a few moments—surely he could do that without irretrievably besmirching her reputation. Somehow he had to charm his hostess into permitting him to stay at the ball long enough to speak with Lady Arnold.

Chapter Six

After the dance ended, as Lady Arnold rose from the final curtsy, she happened to look down—straight at Teagan. Her eyes widening, the lady froze.

Teagan felt his lips curving into a smile so automatic and instinctive he was helpless to prevent it. Their gazes held, time halting in the power of that glance.

Then her eyes warmed with delight, and an answering smile lit her face—a smile that quickly faded as she must have realized the impossibility of publicly acknowledging him. But not before the heat of it rocked him to the core.

A tug at his sleeve brought his attention back to Insley. "There's Mama. Let me present you."

Teagan sucked in a deep breath. *Now for the difficult part.* Squaring his shoulders, he summoned up a smile and followed Insley, who came behind his mama to tap her arm.

"Holden, there you are at last!" she exclaimed, looking over her shoulder. "I should read you quite a scold, coming so tardy to your own sister's ball. But I'm sure Marianne will be glad to have you, late though it be."

"I've brought a friend, Mama." Insley stepped aside and beckoned Teagan forward.

Teagan made his hostess a deep bow. "A charming party, ma'am."

Lady Insley's smile died and she looked over at her son in unconcealed dismay. The fair skin of Insley's face reddened, but with a quick movement of his head he indicated that Teagan should stand his ground. "You'll remember Mr. Fitzwilliams, Mama. And remember also how indebted we are to him."

"Y-yes," she said, moistening her lips. "Indeed, but…I scarcely think Marianne's ball is the proper place—"

"To acknowledge a gentleman who has performed us a singular service? Then what would be proper, ma'am?"

Avoiding Teagan's eye, Lady Insley leaned toward her son, her voice lowered. "Holden, you cannot expect me…"

By now, a group of onlookers had stopped chatting and were watching with avid interest. Teagan hoped the humiliation twisting in his gut wasn't coloring his face. "Perhaps I'd best leave, Insley," he said quietly.

"If my friend is not welcome, Mama, then I will not stay, either."

"Holden!" Insley's mother reached an imploring hand toward her son. Stone-faced, he ignored it, waiting.

Before the small crisis could escalate further, another gentleman stepped from behind Teagan.

"Insley, Fitzwilliams," Lord Riverton said, offering his hand to each in turn. "Good evening. Lady Insley, your lord husband has just been telling me of the kindness young Fitzwilliams recently rendered the family."

His hostess goggled at him. "H-he has?"

"Indeed," Riverton replied. "I must say, I've known Mr. Fitzwilliams since Oxford, and always thought him a capital fellow. This latest incident just confirms that. But Lady Insley, we must not keep these gentlemen from the floor when young ladies are in need of partners. Let me procure you some refreshment." He offered his arm.

Lady Insley stood a moment, obviously torn between acceding to the direction of her son and this distinguished guest, and avoiding the probable outrage of the watchful mamas present should she allow this rogue of the first order to mingle among their innocent daughters.

Evidently lacking the mettle to withstand two determined gentlemen, with a sigh she capitulated. "M-Mr. Fitzwilliams," she murmured, giving him the barest nod of recognition. "I...I believe I should like a glass of punch," she said to Riverton, and latched on to his arm as if desperate to flee the scene of imminent disaster.

Though Teagan had indeed encountered the cabinet minister at Oxford and occasionally at subsequent social engagements, he couldn't imagine why Riverton should have come to his rescue. Whatever the reason, he was exceedingly grateful. He gave the older gentleman a quick nod, which Riverton acknowledged with a wink before leading his hostess away.

"I didn't know you and Riverton were friends," Insley said.

"Neither did I," Teagan replied ruefully. But his mystification over Riverton's unexpected assistance was quickly submerged in a rising excitement. Now all he needed was an introduction, and he could speak again with his Lady Mystery.

"Insley, did you notice the slender dark lady in the golden gown dancing the cotillion when we entered?"

"You must mean Lady Arnold. Lovely, isn't she?"

"Exceptional. Would you introduce me?"

"If you've the courage to brave her chaperone."

"Follow me," Teagan said, and led him to the stairs.

After a quick search, nerves dancing in anticipation, Teagan urged Insley across the crowded ballroom toward the far corner, where he spied Lady Arnold in conversation with an older lady and a tall gentleman.

He knew the instant she perceived their approach. The rigidly restrained anger that always smoldered in his gut flared briefly as he halted, silently damning his lurid reputation, for this time no welcoming warmth preceded the alarm that widened her eyes and drained the color from her cheeks. Something sharp and hurtful stabbed at his chest.

Well, 'twas only one way to reassure her. Teagan propelled Insley forward again.

Lady Arnold was even lovelier close up than she'd appeared at a distance. The soft canary-yellow of her gown set off her pale skin and the burnished richness of her dark hair, arranged atop her head in a charming confection of curls. The garment itself was a masterpiece of titillation, the tiny puff sleeves emphasizing her slender arms and elegant shoulders, the low décolletage instantly drawing his eye to the taunting swell of her breasts.

Silky bare skin, soft heavy mounds he had nuzzled and licked and kissed. Simmering desire intensified to a hunger that hammered him, sharp and urgent. For an instant he was captured by the absurd fantasy of carrying her off here and now, perhaps outside to the night-shadowed gardens or to some conveniently vacant adjacent chamber.

Distracted by the unprecedented ferocity of his need, eyes fixed on her downcast face like a mariner navigating to a lighthouse's beacon, Teagan at last reached her. Wanting to allay her alarm as swiftly as possible, he nodded for Insley to speak.

"Sir William, ladies, how nice to see you," Insley said on cue. "Lady Farrington, I've brought someone I believe your lovely protégée has not yet met. Please allow me to present my good friend, Mr. Fitzwilliams."

Ironic amusement curled Teagan's lip as Lady Farrington, consternation on her face, threw a panicked glance at the frowning Sir William. She obviously considered Teagan not at all the sort of gentleman she should allow her charge to meet, but since he was being presented by her hostess's son, she could find no polite grounds to refuse. After clearing her throat several times, she stuttered, "Y-yes, of course, Lord Insley."

The subtle insult of that long hesitation stung no less for being expected. But all Teagan's irritation faded as he looked back at Lady Arnold. After inhaling sharply, as if she'd been holding her breath, she smiled at him.

'Twas like basking in the first warm sunshine of spring after a long, frigid winter. His spirits lightening, Teagan bowed. "Lady Arnold. 'Tis utterly charmed I am to meet so captivating an addition to our London society."

"Mr. Fitzwilliams," she murmured, dropping a curtsy.

He yearned for that smile, the music of her voice, the warmth of her small hand resting on his arm. He simply had to capture her for a dance or a stroll before her conscientious chaperone found a way to dispatch him.

"This is your first visit to London, I understand," he asked, breaking the strained silence. "Won't you take a turn about the room with me, Lady Arnold? I should love to hear your impressions of our vast city."

Her smile faltered a bit. "I...I'm not sure—"

"Please," he added softly, holding out his arm.

After a short pause, during which his eyes implored hers in wordless entreaty, she took it.

The spark of contact sizzled through them. Teagan exulted as her breath hitched in a gasp, her hand clenched involuntarily upon his sleeve. Ah yes, that interlude in the hayloft had been no aberration. The passion running molten in his veins still scorched her, too.

While Sir William sputtered a protest, Teagan said to Lady Farrington, "Do not fear, madam. I shall restore her to you shortly," and urged Lady Arnold into motion.

For a few moments they walked in silence while, holding his inexplicably fierce desire in check, Teagan contented himself with devouring her with his eyes. After they'd distanced themselves from her party, Lady Arnold glanced up, and blushed once more.

"Really, Mr. Fitzwilliams, you must not look at me like that," she murmured.

Once again, her utter lack of flirtatiousness enchanted him. "And how is that, pray?"

"As if you wished to…" Apparently deciding it was best not to complete the thought, she continued with a touch of exasperation. "You know very well how you're looking at me."

"How else should I look at a beautiful lady?"

"Oh, do stop trying to put me to the blush. You'll make me cross, and then it will be very difficult to express the gratitude I owe you for not…giving way that we'd already met."

His amusement faded. "Ah, my singular reputation. Did you really fear I would embarrass you so?"

"Oh, no!"

Surprised—and gratified—by her immediate denial, Teagan nodded at her. "Thank you for that."

"It's just I had no idea what you *would* say, and feared I might not be able to fall in line quickly enough to avoid upsetting Lady Farrington's delicate sensibilities. Or arousing Sir William's suspicions."

Glancing back to the corner, Teagan found Parham watching them, lips set in a thin line, and instinctively he gripped her hand a bit tighter. *You'll not claim my Lady Mystery, you bastard,* he thought.

"Why, should anyone hint that there seemed to be some prior acquaintance, you need only say that we saw each other from a distance while riding in Yorkshire, but were never properly introduced."

She uttered a smothered choke of laughter he found totally charming. "You are the most complete hand!"

"You malign me, dear lady! Is that not perfect truth? The trick, of course, is in knowing how much to tell. Didn't you learn that in childhood? Or were you too much a paragon to need the knack?"

She laughed in earnest then. "Hardly a paragon! But much as a glib tongue might have proved useful, I'm afraid I haven't one. I found early on that Papa could always tell if I tried to 'adjust' the truth. The punishment was generally lighter if I simply owned up to my fault rather than— vainly, it generally turned out—tried to talk my way out of it. Now you, I'd wager—" she smiled at him "—can probably spin a tale with the best of them."

"Ah, yes," he replied, more than a hint of irony in his tone, "as everyone in this room is doubtless dying to warn you, I'm a pure master of the ability to deceive."

She glanced quickly around, as if suddenly conscious they were attracting no small amount of attention. "Ah. I take it your presence is not generally…appreciated at such gatherings as this?"

"No," he said shortly, regretting that truth for perhaps the first time since his Oxford disgrace. "However, Lady Farrington's credit is such that I believe your reputation can stand a single turn about the room in my company without suffering irremediable harm."

She shook her head in mild reproof. "Once again you would have me believe you are no gentleman, but you shall not succeed. Arranging a proper introduction tonight, as if we truly were meeting for the first time, as well as your…previous behavior, all give the lie to that claim. And I hope I'm not so pudding-hearted as to be afraid of a little gossip. Though the ability to dissemble well might be a useful skill. Perhaps one that, ancient though I've become, I should still attempt to master."

'Twas nonsensical that her defense of his character should move him, but it did. "Don't change, I beg you," he said more fervently than he'd intended. He tried to soften his vehemence with a smile. "Your honesty and innocence are all too rare."

Once again, his compelling gaze captured hers. After a moment, with a shaky laugh, she looked away. "What an odd notion you have of me indeed. I admit to honesty, but I'm hardly a saint, and no one growing up amongst the army in the wilds of India could be thought an innocent."

Lighten the tone, he chastised himself. Where had all his easy, practiced wiles fled? He must amuse her, lure her to linger on his arm. Make the most of what he knew, now fully conscious of Sir William glowering at them, might well be Teagan's only opportunity to speak with her.

"But I haven't asked you what I set out to discover. So, Lady Arnold, what brought you to London?"

She gave him a look that was almost—apologetic. "At the time we...met, I had no notion of coming here. Lady Winterdale, my late husband's grandmother, unexpectedly summoned me to visit her. She offered to frank my way, and I wished to see the city my brother had described to me with much enthusiasm, so here I am—under her niece Lady Farrington's chaperonage, as Grandmamma does not go out."

"And how are you finding our fine metropolis? Rather tame, I suppose, after the wilds of India."

"Well, Society is a bit...constricting, but the city itself is splendid! At least, what little of it I've managed to visit. I purchased a guide, but some of the sights my brother recommended I've not been able to get to. A lady cannot go about on her own, I've been told, but my old nurse has a bad ankle, and the maid Grandmamma assigned me does not care for walking." Lady Arnold sighed, a look of vexation crossing her face. "I'm afraid my chaperone considers nothing beyond the borders of Mayfair and the shops of Bond Street worth seeing."

"And what unfashionable locales do you wish to visit?"

She gave him a probing glance, as if wary of mockery.

Truly curious now, he prodded, "Come, you may confide in me. 'Tis the soul of discretion I am. Honestly."

To his delight, she smiled. "Very well, if we are being *honest*. But you must promise not to laugh."

"Cross my heart."

"I should like to see the West India docks and the Inns of Court. St. Paul's, but not on Sunday, so I might explore the building, even if 'tis not in a fashionable neighborhood any longer. Oh, the Tower, and Astley's, and old London Bridge." She sent him a challenging look. "There, I've just proved how truly unfashionable I am."

"'Tis the real London you wish to see, then."

Her wariness dissolved in a smile. "You *do* understand!"

"Sure, and I can—" he began. But they'd reached the end of their circuit, and before he could finish his sentence, Lady Arnold's arm was seized by her distressed chaperone, who looked as if she might at any moment succumb to an attack of the vapors, while the disapproving Sir William stepped forward to block Teagan's path, his tall form between Lady Arnold and Teagan's tainting presence.

A ridiculous sense of despair pierced him, as if light and hope were slipping through his fingers. Though he shrugged off the absurd notion, he could not prevent himself calling after her, despite knowing his invitation was certain to be spurned.

"I'm well acquainted with all parts of the city, Lady Arnold." Ignoring Sir William's muttered objection, he continued doggedly. "I would be happy to escort you to any of the sights you mention—"

"So kind of you, Mr. Fitzwilliams," Lady Farrington interrupted, "but I'm afraid Lady Arnold—"

"Is much too occupied," Sir William finished. "Besides, I'm available to take her wherever she wishes."

"Providing I have the time, of course?" Lady Arnold interposed sweetly. "Sir William, have you an interest in viewing the West India docks?"

"The docks?" he repeated with a grimace of distaste. "Certainly not! I cannot conceive what Mr. Fitzwilliams has been telling you about them, but I assure you the docks are no fit place for a gently bred lady."

"My brother Elliot disagreed, for he highly recommended them to me. And so," she said, with a glance toward Sir William and Lady Farrington, as if daring them to dispute her, "I should be delighted to accept your escort, Mr. Fitzwilliams."

"Valeria!" Lady Farrington all but shrieked. Lowering her voice, she continued in an earnest undertone, "My dear, I really don't believe that would be…prudent."

"Certainly not," Sir William echoed.

"Indeed?" The ice in her tone finally penetrated the abstraction of her two protectors, who fell silent. "Then would one of you please explain to me what possible impropriety there could be in my going out in broad daylight, my maid in attendance, with a gentleman who has just been presented to me by the son of my hostess?"

The clever girl had just outflanked them, Teagan realized with dawning admiration. To justify a refusal, Lady Farrington would have to either malign Teagan's character to his face—in itself a grievous breach of good ton—or even worse, assert that their hostess was not discriminating in her choice of guests.

"Well, I…that is…" the lady faltered.

"We shall speak of this later," Sir William interposed, throwing Teagan a dagger glance.

A mischievous look in her eye, Lady Arnold reached past Lady Farrington to offer him her hand. "Shall we say to-

morrow morning, Mr. Fitzwilliams? I'm staying with Lady
Winterdale, on Grosvenor Square. You know the house?''

''Y-yes, my lady,'' Teagan stuttered, hardly able to believe that Lady Arnold apparently intended to accept his
rash offer.

''Then I shall see you tomorrow.''

Teagan recovered his poise. ''I shall be counting the moments.''

That earned him a lift of her eyebrows and the hint of a
skeptical grin. ''Shall you, now?'' she drawled in a teasing
echo of his own lilting speech. And with a nod, she at last
allowed her two watchdogs to bear her away.

''I shall indeed,'' he murmured to her receding back,
only half surprised to discover he really meant it.

Oblivious to the whispers buzzing around him, Teagan
remained motionless, watching her slender figure disappear
amid the crowd of guests. Did she truly understand what
she had done? To contradict her guardian for interfering in
the conversation of a grown woman was one thing—but to
actually accept his escort?

Still marveling, he went in search of Insley. After locat-
ing his friend and paying his compliments to Lady Insley,
who looked vastly relieved to have Teagan depart before
spawning some social disaster beneath her roof, Teagan
escaped into the cool night. He parted at the street corner
from Insley, after turning aside the young man's offer to
share a hackney with a promise to meet him later at the
gambling club and walked off into the darkness.

He wanted time, before he resumed his gamester role at
the club tonight, to recall and savor the short exchange with
Lady Arnold. To muse over the strength of the attraction
that drew her to him, this slight, slender woman a disinter-
ested ton observer would account much less memorable
than most of the sophisticated, stylish beauties in the ballroom he had just left.

The potent physical connection between them he readily understood, but he wanted to pinpoint just what it was about Lady Arnold's character that so captivated him. Her independence, certainly—her insistence on choosing her own way. That honest, questing intelligence. Like the classical literature that had been his joy before the disastrous end of his Oxford career, she seemed both unusual and yet hauntingly familiar; set apart from her place and time; seemingly indifferent to the dictates of fashion. Timeless.

Then he threw back his head and laughed at his own whimsy. To be sure, he'd met Lady Arnold under extraordinary circumstances, magnified to even more epic proportions by his bemused remembrances and the depression engendered by his current run of ill-luck. Should he come to know her better, doubtless he would find she was little different than most well-born ladies—or gentlemen—he'd known: self-absorbed, rather shallow, interested in Teagan only so long as he could divert, amuse or distract her.

Something in his gut protested that cynical assessment, but he pushed it away. He'd fallen once, with his whole heart, for a woman who'd seemed to value his talents and opinions—and look where that had gotten him!

No, he would indulge this fancy only to the point of pursuing Lady Arnold until he'd plumbed to its source whatever intangible it was that attracted him. Which meant cutting short his gaming tonight so he might rise in time to present himself at Lady Winterdale's town house at the proper hour tomorrow.

A rueful grin creased his face as he changed direction and headed to the club. If Lady Winterdale's reputation as a stiff-necked, tyrannical stickler were accurate, the woman would have apoplexy at the very notion of her widowed granddaughter-in-law traipsing about London in the company of one of the ton's most notorious rakes.

Still, boldness had carried him this far, and should Lady

Winterdale's butler shut the door in his face, he'd weathered snubs before. He would call on Lady Arnold tomorrow, as promised.

Even though by morning, either the lady herself or her relation would probably have talked her out of the folly of pursuing a closer acquaintance with the totally ineligible Teagan Fitzwilliams.

Chapter Seven

Over the sound of Lady Farrington's sobs, Valeria heard the countess's tart voice emanating from the darkened hallway outside the sitting room. "How can a body be expected to sleep in the midst of this caterwauling?"

Already almost at the point of wishing to shake her prostrate chaperone, Valeria tried to keep the exasperation from her voice. "Cousin Alicia, you must calm yourself! You've awakened Grandmamma!"

That produced a momentary respite from the sobbing. "It's all the fault of that Awful Man!" Lady Farrington said tremulously. "My poor nerves cannot support any more. You must prevent Aunt Winterdale from—oh!"

Occupied in chafing Lady Farrington's chilled fingers, Valeria looked up to see the countess glaring at them, then back to discover that her chaperone had fainted dead away.

"What's happened now to put that silly fool into such a taking?" the dowager demanded as she entered the room.

Caught between dismay at the lady collapsed on the couch, concern for Hugh's grandmother and irritation at the farce the evening had turned into, Valeria said, "Grandmamma! It's much too late for you to—"

"Stuff and nonsense," the old lady interrupted. "I sleep

away half the day, anyway. Call Alicia's maid to deal with her and tell me what's going on.''

Valeria paused, reluctant to abandon her unconscious chaperone. ''Should I not look for her vinaigrette?''

Lady Winterdale made a contemptuous noise as she jerked on the bell pull. ''Let her be. Alicia swoons over something twice a month. Darcy will see to her.''

Valeria bit her lip. Not only had Lady Farrington inflamed an episode that the ton might have otherwise considered only mildly gossip-worthy, she had roused the countess, who despite her feisty words had suffered such a spell of weakness two days ago that her doctors had confined her to bed for a week. ''Please, ma'am, return to your chamber, and I will come report to you as soon as we get Cousin Alicia settled into bed.''

''Where, you're about to tell me, I belong also?'' the countess retorted. ''Very well, I shall retire. But only if you promise to bring some sherry when you come in.''

The old woman's face assumed a mulish expression that Valeria knew, from a month's experience, might very well result in her refusing to budge if Valeria did not submit. ''As you wish, Grandmamma,'' she replied with some asperity, ''but only because I'm being blackmailed.''

Leaning heavily on her cane, the dowager moved toward the door. Valeria knew better than to offer her assistance. ''Least I can still do *that*,'' Lady Winterdale muttered.

And so, after helping Lady Farrington's dresser to revive her mistress and assist her to her own chamber, Valeria snatched the sherry decanter from the sideboard and headed for the dowager's room, two glasses in hand. After the events of this evening, Valeria felt the need for fortification as well.

She found Lady Winterdale settled on her favorite sofa by the fire. At her entrance, the lady pointed an imperious finger at the wing chair beside it. "Sit now, and pour me a glass. Then explain what's going on."

Valeria took the chair indicated and tarried as long as she could in pouring the smallest amount of sherry she dared into each glass, pondering what to reply.

'Twas probably best to relate the whole. For one, given Lady Winterdale's extensive contacts among the ton, she would most certainly receive a full account from her cronies tomorrow. And as Valeria had confessed to Teagan, she wasn't very good at evasion.

She handed Lady Winterdale her sherry. "At the ball tonight, I made what Lady Farrington believes to be a very unfortunate connection."

"'Unfortunate' enough to have Alicia enacting Cheltingham tragedies in my upstairs parlor, obviously! Don't speak in riddles, child. What 'connection'?"

"I was introduced to Mr. Teagan Fitzwilliams, a gentleman who is not, as Cousin Alicia expounded to me at length on the way home, a fit person for me to know."

"The Fascinating Fitz?" The countess gave a bark of laughter. "I should think not! What maggot did Lady Insley take into her head, inviting him to her ball?"

"As to that, ma'am, I cannot say. However, Mr. Fitzwilliams was presented to me by Lady Insley's son, and seemed to be perfectly charming."

The countess snorted. "Of course he's charming. How else could he coax women who should know better out of their skirts? He's a rogue of the first order, missy! Which, of course, is why he ain't received. Lord, that I'd been there to witness what a dust-up he must have caused." For a moment the countess seemed to contemplate the vision with amusement, before fixing her gaze back on Valeria. "Did that widget Alicia swoon right there at the ball?"

"No, ma'am, fortunately not. However—" Valeria could not prevent the aggravation that entered her tone "—after-

ward, she was so overcome with…emotion that she nearly
collapsed in the refreshment room. Sir William and I had
to practically carry her to a chair, which I fear attracted no
small amount of attention. I suggested she retire to the
lady's withdrawing room to compose herself, but she insisted we leave the ball at once. If Mr. Fitzwilliams does
have a scandalous reputation—"

"And he does."

"Then I fear that by making such a to-do over the matter,
Cousin Alicia drew more notice to my meeting him than
would ever have occurred had we simply remained."

With a grimace of distaste, Lady Winterdale nodded.
"Blast Alicia! She was ever a nodcock."

The old woman settled back to sip her sherry. Just as
Valeria was hoping she'd satisfied Hugh's grandmother
with that brief summation, the countess spoke up again.

"What happened after you were introduced? Surely the
rogue hadn't the effrontery to ask you to dance!"

"N-no, we took a turn about the room. His conversation
was quite unexceptional. Having learned it was my first
visit, he merely inquired how I liked London."

"'A turn about the room.' And did he take a turn with
any other of the ladies present?"

Valeria took a small sip from her glass. "I cannot say.
Immediately after we bid him goodbye, Cousin Alicia had
her…episode and I was preoccupied."

"So one of London's handsomest rogues insinuates his
way into a ball, finagles an introduction and strolls about—
only with you?"

"As I said, Grandmamma, I do not know. He may have
talked and danced with a number of ladies."

"Not if I know Lady Insley. No matter that that pup of
hers was escorting him about, she'd have managed to show
Teagan Fitzwilliams the door as quickly as possible, or risk

outraging every marriage-minded mama present with an innocent daughter's good name to protect.''

The countess fell silent and fixed a considering look on Valeria, who willed her face not to flush.

"No, gel, something ain't right here,'' Lady Winterdale said after a moment. "Teagan Fitzwilliams is known for squiring only the flashiest of Diamonds. Not that you're an antidote, but I can't see him being so struck by your looks that he'd use the few moments' entrée Insley provided to beg an introduction to you, not when I know for a fact there were half a dozen Incomparables present. Unless he was *renewing* an acquaintance. Do you know him, child?''

Valeria felt a sinking in the pit of her stomach. *Don't be ridiculous,* she told herself angrily. She was a woman grown, after all, and accountable to no one.

Then she recalled Teagan's words, and snatched at them. "We were not precisely acquainted, ma'am. He attended a house party in the neighborhood of Eastwinds earlier this year, and I saw him while out riding. But we were never formally introduced.''

The countess studied Valeria's face, no doubt observing the heat she felt creeping into her cheeks. "Well, you're a widow, and what you've done is your own affair. No, I don't wish to know! But foolishness that may pass unnoticed in the country won't do in London, where everyone knows everyone else's business. Acquainted or not, if he has the audacity to show his face here, you must refuse to receive him.''

Valeria felt her cheeks warm in earnest now. "I'm afraid I cannot do that, Grandmamma.''

"And why not?''

"After I'd told Mr. Fitzwilliams that there was much of London I'd not yet been able to see, he kindly offered to escort me about the city, and I accepted his offer. He is calling for me tomorrow morning.''

A long, ominous silence followed, during which Valeria prepared herself for an outburst once the countess absorbed the full meaning of her words.

"Are you daft, child? Do you wish to ruin your reputation practically before you've established it?"

"Really, Grandmamma! As you've noted, I'm a widow, not some innocent virgin. Mr. Fitzwilliams could have embarrassed me tonight by revealing a prior acquaintance. Instead, he very properly sought an introduction. And if he were the villain everyone seems to delight in painting him, when I previously encountered him, riding alone and unprotected, he might easily have taken advantage of me. Instead, he acted the perfect gentleman."

"I can imagine," the countess said dryly. "Come now, puss, I'm not so old that I can't remember the sort of...fascination a man like Teagan Fitzwilliams can exert over a woman. But there's more at stake here than the excitement of a few afternoons spent with a dashing rakehell. You must consider your future. How can you hope to fix the interest of a man like Sir William if you're wasting your time trifling with a gazetted ne'er-do-well?"

With difficulty, Valeria held on to her temper. "First, though I readily admit Sir William is a superior gentleman, I am by no means assured that he wishes to fix his interest on me, nor am I sure I would encourage him if he were. I've heard nothing that persuades me I should cut the acquaintance of a man who was introduced to me in perfectly acceptable circumstances, who has always conducted himself in my presence with utmost courtesy, and about whom the only ill that has ever been voiced is a vague innuendo based on no evidence whatsoever."

"Vague innuendo, is it? Then let me offer you some facts. Truth, missy, not rumors! While at Oxford, he seduced the wife of his Oxford mentor's son, and nearly convinced the besotted woman to run off with him."

"So I understand. But he must have been very young then—sixteen or seventeen? And the lady much older? Having once or twice observed similar cases among the army in India, I suspect it was much more likely that a bored matron seduced a handsome young man. And only the young man paid the consequences."

The countess lifted an eyebrow. "Perhaps. But any possible sympathy one might have had over that unfortunate episode was quite ruined by the blatant way he conducted his subsequent affair with Lady Uxtabridge. Strolling into Covent Garden with that woman on his arm, both of them somewhat in…disarray, and then kissing her on the lips as he seated her next to her husband in Uxtabridge's own box!" Lady Winterdale shook her head. "Shocking bad ton."

"Foolish, certainly. Of course, Lord Cranston and Lady Fellowes are much more discreet," Valeria replied, naming a young aristocrat and the married lady he'd driven out in Hyde Park the last three afternoons running. "And Sir Alewynd and Lady Lydia are merely convivial friends," she added, indicating a couple, both married to other partners, whose touching and nuzzling, followed by their mutual disappearance for a good hour or more, had caused no end of scandalized speculation at a ball the week previous.

Lady Winterdale frowned, obviously displeased to have had her arguments rebutted so neatly. "Fitzwilliams is of dubious parentage, and a gamester besides."

"He can hardly be held accountable for his parentage. And I have it on the authority of my neighbor, a collegemate of his, that turning to gambling was more necessity than choice. What other occupation is open to a landless gentleman whose family disavows him? The army requires the funds to purchase a commission, and of course, the church was not a possibility."

"A gentleman would have found another way," Lady Winterdale insisted.

Valeria raised an eyebrow. "Perhaps. But I suspect that Mr. Fitzwilliams is really guilty of no more than being half-Irish, having an unfortunate affair with one woman and a too-obvious one with another. Unless you can inform me of some other venality he's supposed to have committed. Seducing and abandoning an innocent maiden? Murder? Theft or embezzlement? Cheating at cards?"

"Not that I've heard," the countess admitted.

"Well, then. Papa told me the army taught him to value a man's actions over his parentage and prior record. I, for one, do not intend to condemn a man based on his having once committed mistakes for which the grandson of an earl not possessed of an Irish father would have long since been forgiven."

"Very well, I'll allow Mr. Fitzwilliams may have been ill-used. But life ain't fair, missy, as you should well know. 'Tis a rogue's reputation he bears, whether deserved or not. 'Tis also the way of the world that if one plays with pitch, one gets blackened fingers. For all your noble talk of treating a man by his actions, are you prepared to risk sullying your own reputation? Ruining your chances of a decent marriage?"

"Other than your kind sponsorship, Grandmamma, I cannot see that I possess anything that would entice Sir William, or any other ton gentleman, to offer for me. To be sure, you've tricked me out in fashionable garments and had Cousin Alicia introduce me around, but the fact remains that I'm a widow of no particular beauty, somewhat stricken in years, with naught but a barely profitable sheep farm."

"Don't be buffleheaded, child. Surely you know I didn't bring you all the way to London just for a Season. I mean to leave you my fortune."

Her lips already parted to continue arguing, that announcement caught Valeria entirely unawares. She paused in mid-breath, stunned. "Y-you are going to—!"

The dowager waved a hand. "Now you've made me bolt from the gate. I hadn't meant to confirm it to you yet—don't want it puffed about, lest all the rakehells and fortune hunters in London descend on you like a flock of vultures." She gave Valeria an exasperated look. "All the *other* rakehells and fortune hunters."

"Dear ma'am, I hardly know what to say," Valeria replied, still astounded. "Surely you have blood kin—"

"Don't you be telling me who I can leave my money to and who I can't! Alicia's got her own fortune, which is a mercy, since she's too great a widget to attract a gentleman of sense, and my great-nieces and -nephews are naught but a passel of idle, ignorant fools. Which I'm delighted to say that you, girl, are not."

Valeria had to smile. "A high compliment indeed."

Lady Winterdale chuckled. "Mind your manners, child. Ah, 'tis been a delight having you here, a debater worthy of my wit, someone who doesn't toady or shrink away every time I look daggers at them. But after the…last few days, I can't pretend I have forever. I'd like to see you settled. And if not in wedlock, I'd like to die knowing you'll be happy." Looking away, the countess added in a gruff voice, "Happy as you've made me these last weeks."

A lump in her throat, Valeria reached over to grasp the dowager's thin, veined hand. "Thank you, Grandmamma. I've been happy here with you."

"Then you'd best stop acting the fool," the countess replied, the tart tone back in her voice, as if regretting her momentary softening. "Which means that when he calls, you mustn't receive Teagan Fitzwilliams."

She held up a hand to forestall Valeria's protest. "Don't waste your breath assuring me you're immune to his charm.

I've known the boy since they sent him down from Oxford, and even at my age, I can't image a woman receiving the full attention of those mesmerizing eyes and keeping her senses—or her chemise—in place! Damnation, child, I didn't bring you to London after having your heart broken by a good man to watch you get your heart broken again by a bad one.''

"I have no intention of risking my heart."

"No, and I'm sure you don't, but even women of sense tend to turn idiotish when a devil as handsome as Fitzwilliams comes calling. But enough of this. I don't mean to deny him the house. You'd only sneak out to meet him then, just to spite me."

"I hope I'm not so small-minded," Valeria said primly.

"You're an unbroken filly too apt to take the bit in her teeth," the countess replied, and gave a crack of laughter. "Ah, but you remind me of myself at your age! All I ask is that you consider carefully. Sir William's a fine man. He'll give you companionship, comfort, children to occupy that restless spirit, and a permanent place in Society. Don't throw all that away for a man who'll dazzle you for a week or a month and then leave you alone with your regrets the rest of your life. You will think on it?''

Once again touched by the countess's concern, Valeria replied quietly, "Yes, Grandmamma. I'll think on it."

"Good. Leave me now, child. I'm fatigued."

A frisson of fear shook Valeria. "Are you all right, ma'am? Should I summon your physician?"

"Lord, no! There's nothing that incompetent will do but leech me, and I've had enough of bleeding. I'm not ready to stick my spoon in the wall yet. Go to bed, child. And try not to be a fool."

Valeria kissed the old woman's hand. "I'll try, Grandmamma. Good night."

Valeria slipped from the room and walked across the hall

to her own chamber. What a contradiction the countess was—gruff for the most part, which only made her very occasional softening the sweeter. Valeria realized that over the last month, the manipulative, combative old lady had managed to steal into her heart. Suddenly the fact that she would soon lose the countess's companionship and counsel filled her with sadness and a deep regret that she had not come to know Hugh's grandmother sooner.

So what did she mean to do about Teagan Fitzwilliams? The countess was wise in advising caution. It would be all too easy to be "dazzled" by the man.

However, Valeria did very much want to explore London. She had to admit that she'd feel safer, once beyond the confines of Mayfair, if she were to have a gentleman to escort her, and Sir William had already indicated his disdain for her chosen destinations. As she'd told the countess, she did not mean to eschew the escort of Teagan Fitzwilliams merely because he'd acquired what was, in her opinion, an undeservedly scandalous reputation.

Surely she was sensible enough to spend a few mornings in his company without losing her wits entirely—and tumbling back into his bed.

Attractive as that prospect might be.

A shaft of desire stabbed her at the very notion.

No, an affair with Mr. Fitzwilliams wouldn't be wise. Though she wasn't sure she wished to remarry, she also wasn't sure she did not. As the countess warned, squandering her reputation in a flagrant affair with a well-known rogue would effectively eliminate that choice.

A fraternal relationship in which she merely explored the city with him, in daylight hours with her maid to chaperone, should not. Any prospective suitor who trusted her so little that he doubted her word about the nature of her relationship with Mr. Fitzwilliams would obviously not be worthy of becoming her husband, anyway.

Husband of the *rich* Lady Arnold. A rich woman who, unlike a widow struggling to survive, would be free to marry—or not marry—as she chose.

Elation filled her as the full implications of that seeped into her mind, and she laughed out loud. She would be truly free—free from worry over want, free from the necessity to marry for security, free to pursue her own interests and desires.

That decided it. She would meet Mr. Fitzwilliams in the morning and, if he were amenable to the limits she set on their relationship, tour London with him.

As Valeria settled back into bed, she tried to damp down the glow of anticipation. 'Twas only a visit of the city. She mustn't make the mistake of seeing in Teagan Fitzwilliams either a potential suitor—or a friend.

And be he ever so dazzling, surely after what had happened before, she was too intelligent to risk handing her heart over to a man who could have no interest whatsoever in it.

At the Devil's Den a few hours later, Teagan laid down the last card of his winning hand, and to the groans of the other gentleman, drew over a stack of guineas. While scooping them up to place in his purse, he called to a passing waiter to have the butler bring his coat and cane.

"What's this, Jester? Leaving us already?" Rafe Crandall peered at Teagan through the haze of smoke.

"Merely taking pity on you, my lord," Teagan replied. "I've won enough for one evening. 'Tis time to let you other gentlemen have a go."

"I do believe our Jester's reforming his ways," Rafe announced to the group, which included Teagan's friend Lord Insley, as well as Crandall's usual cronies, Markham and Westerley. "First he visits a debutante's ball—though how he managed that feat without being tossed out on his rear I still cannot fathom—and now he means to retire to his bed before dawn! Damme, Teagan, what's about? Not trying to turn respectable on us, are you?''

''Wouldn't do him no good,'' Markham observed. ''His family won't touch him. His cousin, the earl, would rather spit on 'im than look at 'im. Told me so himself at White's t'other day.''

Teagan gritted his teeth at the casual insult and forced his usual bantering tone. ''Whist, and should I ever be in danger of earning the earl's approbation, I should have to quit England forthwith.''

''Aye, he's a dull dog, your cousin,'' Rafe agreed over the ensuing laughter. ''Probably despises you because he knows the ladies prefer your energetic and talented performance to his money and title.'' Then Rafe straightened, spilling some of the brandy in his glass. '''Od's blood, that can't be it, can it? Jester, you're not sniffing up the skirts of an honest woman, are you now?''

Careful, Teagan warned himself. Despite his constant state of inebriation, Rafe Crandall was no fool. ''Faith, and what would I want with the likes of an honest lass?''

''True, true.'' Westerley wagged the wine bottle he held. '''E's got no money to get leg-shackled. 'N anyways, no ton mama worth 'er salt would let 'em next 'r nigh some innocent virgin. Rich merchant neither. If he'd a mind to marry, Jester'd have to find 'imself a widow.''

''A rich one,'' Markham said, flicking a cigar ash off his florid brocade waistcoat. ''Dressin' well's expensive.''

''And one poorly chaperoned,'' Rafe observed. ''Very well, I concede.'' He threw up his hands in a gesture of surrender. ''Any female with money enough to tempt the Jester would have to be long in the tooth and ugly besides, not to have already been snatched up by some other fortune hunter.''

"And Jester's too discriminating to settle for an ugly woman, be she ever so rich, eh?" Westerley asked.

"Now wait a moment." Rafe frowned and closed his eyes, as if making a diligent effort to concentrate. "Isn't the beauteous Lady Arnold, my lovely neighbor from the far north, presently visiting poor old Hugh's grandmamma in London? I believe I remember m' mother nattering on about it when last I visited the family manse. And don't I recall the Jester taking a ride in her woods?"

Teagan hesitated, knowing he must choose his words with caution. After so carefully guarding the secret of their first meeting, he certainly didn't wish to say something that might inspire Rafe Crandall and his drunken cohorts to bandy Lady Arnold's name about.

Insley shot Teagan a quick glance. "Gentlemen, if you are to retain any pretensions to the name, you really must cease discussing respectable ladies in such terms."

"I believe our plain talk offends young Insley," Rafe sneered.

"Perhaps we should send for his mama to escort him home," Westerley sniggered.

Teagan gave an elaborate yawn. "If you gentlemen persist in discussing so dismal a topic as marriage, I shall certainly leave." After making them an elaborate bow, he walked with unhurried steps from the room.

Insley followed him. Once outside the club, Insley stopped Teagan with a hand to his elbow.

"No word of what happened at the ball will be spoken by me. But I expect your presence there—and the story of the lady whose introduction you sought—will be one of tomorrow's on-dits. What," Insley said hesitantly, "do you mean to do about Lady Arnold, if I may ask?"

In his mind's eye Teagan saw the image of a polished mahogany door shutting in his face. "Probably nothing."

Insley offered Teagan a hand. "'Tis your own business, to be sure. Good night, then."

After shaking the young man's hand, Teagan turned to walk pensively into the lightening dawn. Insley was correct; Teagan's impulsive claiming of Lady Arnold's acquaintance earlier in the evening would certainly become fodder for the gossip mills. When Rafe Crandall heard of it, as inevitably he would, the suspicions he might voice would fly through the ton. The ensuring speculation was certain to be far more damaging to Lady Arnold's reputation than Teagan had ever envisioned when he'd permitted himself that innocent stroll across a ballroom with her.

A sinking sense of dread dulled the rush of anticipation that had buoyed him since leaving the Insley ball. He'd erred, allowing a selfish desire for her company to lead him to defy the social ostracism he usually accepted without question, thereby calling down on her head the avid notice of the ton.

The idea of Lady Arnold's name being involved in scurrilous innuendo sickened him. And if it became known that he was squiring her about the city, the rumors would only grow worse.

His Lady Mystery deserved better than that of him.

Perhaps he would do her a greater service by not keeping their appointment, after all.

Chapter Eight

Before nine the following morning, Valeria's maid did up the last tiny button on her favorite of the new morning gowns, a deep peach sarcenet. After instructing Molly to take her pelisse downstairs so she might be ready to set out as soon as she'd offered Mr. Fitzwilliams refreshments, she picked up the guidebook and crossed to the wing chair near her window overlooking the garden, where crocuses and daffodils were just now awakening from their winter sleep.

Excitement bubbling in her stomach, she opened the guidebook and tried to concentrate on choosing the sites for their first expedition.

Bullock's Egyptian Hall at Piccadilly, the guidebook said, offered an excellent collection of objects gathered from Africa and the far Americas, including an extensive exhibit of animals and insects. She wrinkled her nose at the idea of tropical insects, having encountered more than she ever wished to see again while living in India.

But viewing the relics from the land of the Pharaohs would be interesting, or perhaps they could stop by Astley's Royal Amphitheatre, whose equestrian displays her brother, Elliot, an avid horseman, had pronounced "spectacular."

Mr. Fitzwilliams, himself a fine rider, would probably enjoy the show.

Valeria pried her mind from contemplating the admirable figure Mr. Fitzwilliams presented while mounted on his fiery black and tried to direct her attention back to the guidebook. For the first time she wished her window overlooked the front entrance instead of the back garden.

Idiot, she chastised herself. Time would pass even more slowly were she to sit watching the street. And she certainly didn't wish for Mr. Fitzwilliams to ride up and find her with her nose pressed to the glass, as if she had nothing more urgent to do than wait for his arrival.

Though that was the truth. *Read,* she told herself again, and picked up the guidebook.

But after another half an hour, during which she lost her place a dozen times within the same paragraph, she shut the book in disgust. A glance at the mantel clock revealed the hour not yet struck ten.

With a sigh, Valeria put aside the volume and stood up. She'd walk in the garden, she decided. Jennings could summon her from there easily enough, and she could more profitably occupy herself comparing the plants now peeping out of the ground with the slower progress being made by those in her garden farther north.

Suitably attired with shawl and mittens, she set off across the rose walk. But even after she'd made a slow inspection of each of the three garden rooms, there was no news of a visitor.

Valeria sat down on a bench and lifted her face to the soft, early spring sun. Surely the hour was late enough. They *had* specified this morning, had they not?

Perhaps something had come up to delay him. But if so, why had he not sent her a note of explanation?

She took another circuit of the garden, more quickly this time. But by the end of that transit, she could no longer avoid acknowledging the bitter truth: after she had given him that oh-so-public invitation in the ballroom, Teagan Fitzwilliams was not going to call.

She should be insulted. Instead, her chest tightened with an inexplicable sense of loss.

'Twas foolish in the extreme to be so disappointed. It just pointed up the uncomfortable fact that she, at least, had been far too eager to see him again.

An eagerness he plainly didn't share.

Perhaps he'd just been toying with a woman who was obviously anxious for his company. That lowering thought revitalized her flagging spirits as nothing else had, and anger flickered.

She was being just the sort of fool her grandmother had deplored, investing with far too much importance an excursion for which her intended escort couldn't even be bothered to make an appearance. Perhaps he'd chosen to speak to her on a lark, to see how much he could induce the little country bumpkin to blush, and never had any intention of calling.

Her ire truly roused now, she raised her chin. Teagan Fitzwilliams might not find a jaunt about London interesting enough to tempt him from other pursuits, but Valeria Arnold was not to be put off so easily. She wished to visit the city, and visit it she would.

She would send Molly out for a suitable map, she decided, and ask the maid which of the footmen she considered stout enough, and agreeable enough, to act as their escort. Then she'd figure how to wheedle Lady Winterdale into excusing the servant from his duties long enough to accompany them.

She sprang up, ready to march back to house and summon Molly, when a footman hurried down the path to her. "Beggin' your pardon, ma'am," he called. "You've a caller awaitin' in the parlor."

Her wrath cooled as if doused with ice water, leaving her with a mix of surprise, delight and trepidation.

"W-who is it?"

"A gentleman, ma'am. Jennings didn't give his name."

Don't be a looby, she told herself as she followed the footman. *It might not even be Mr. Fitzwilliams.*

But her pulses, already fluttering, leaped as she walked into the parlor. By the window, golden hair glinting in the noonday light, stood Teagan Fitzwilliams.

He turned when the butler announced her, a slight smile on his face, his eyes that mesmerizing kaleidoscope of gold and amber.

"Lady Arnold," he said, and made her a deep bow.

Oh, Grandmamma was right. Teagan Fitzwilliams was all too dazzling.

Valeria sucked in a breath and ordered herself to produce coherent speech. "Good morning, Mr. Fitzwilliams. Jennings, would you bring us tea?"

After the slightest flicker of a glance toward her guest, the butler bowed. "As you wish, my lady."

Valeria made herself walk calmly toward him, wishing the butterflies in her stomach felt less like sparrows flapping bony little wings against her ribs.

She should be cool and distantly polite. After all, he was late. Very late. He owed her an explanation, and it had better be a good one.

"Won't you sit down, Mr. Fitzwilliams?"

He stepped toward her, raised a hand as if to take hers, then closed it into a fist and drew it back. "N-no, I shouldn't. I should just stand and deliver the apology I owe you for being so frightfully tardy. Actually, I had convinced myself that I ought not to come at all."

Despite her rallying speech in the garden not a quarter hour previous, Valeria felt a ridiculous sense of hurt squeeze her chest, displacing the thumping sparrows.

"If you have changed your mind and do not wish to accompany me, of course I—"

"No! No, you mustn't think that. I should love to escort you!" He gave her his full smile then, that curve of dimpled cheek and slight narrowing of eyes that somehow only made their outrageous sparkle brighter. "But," he continued, the smile dimming, "after much reflection, I concluded it would be…wiser if I did not. Indeed," he added with a lift of his brow, "I'm fair astonished you even received me. I'd rather expected to have Lady Winterdale's butler bar your front door against my encroaching person."

Valeria knew he meant the remark to be amusing. But suddenly she was pierced by the image of a golden-haired orphan, then a man, standing on the front steps of a succession of houses while a lifetime of doors slammed in his face.

She pushed the disturbing vision aside. "And why is that? I've not been long in the city, but I thought it was customary for a gentleman to call on a lady to whom he'd been properly introduced the previous—"

His wry chuckle startled her into silence. "Whist, and you did roll them up, horse, foot and guns! A clever stratagem, my lady, but a sophist's trick, as we both know. As I'm sure your guardian has explained to you at length, mine is not an acquaintance you ought to pursue."

Valeria lifted her chin. "I'm not a green girl, to be told who I should see and who I shouldn't."

"'Tis not a bad thing to attend to those who have your best interests at heart. Which is why, in the end, I decided to come this morning. That, and the belief that your kind defense of me deserved better than the rudeness of my not keeping our appointment at all."

His face had grown serious, and Valeria felt the spirits sent soaring when she beheld him standing by the parlor window once again sink.

"So…you're *not* going to escort me."

He looked away, as if the hurt she hadn't been able to keep out of her voice was reflected also on her face.

"It was inexcusably selfish of me to seek you out last night. You *are* new to the city, so you may not know, but I assure you every spiteful cat and idle dandy in the ton is speculating over their morning chocolate today about why the notorious Teagan Fitzwilliams sought an introduction to a shy country widow. And given his temperament, when my Yorkshire host, your neighbor Lord Crandall, hears of it, he will certainly draw conclusions detrimental to your reputation that, I'm afraid, he will be only too happy to broadcast to the largest possible audience."

Teagan paused, his face grim as if envisioning the uproar. "Fortunately," he continued, "the ton, though malicious, has a short memory. If we have nothing further to do with each other, some new scandal will soon occur to displace the rumors. So regrettably, I must withdraw my offer. After the…kindness we have shared, I cannot permit an association with me to tarnish your sterling character."

Valeria stared into his eyes, but could detect neither irony nor falsehood. Though Mr. Fitzwilliams wished for her company, he would eschew it…to protect *her* reputation.

A tiny knot of gratification and wonder grew in her incredulous chest. And the ton believed him no gentleman!

Valeria couldn't help the smile that sprang to her lips. "As it happens, after hearing the account of our 'introduction,' Grandmamma drew the same conclusions."

Mr. Fitzwilliams had turned toward the window, but at that he whirled to face her. Surely that wasn't…a blush beginning to color his cheeks?

"She believes that I…that we—?"

Valeria nodded, still smiling.

He blew out a gusty breath and ran a hand through his hair. "I wonder she didn't have me shot on sight."

"She did warn me that the 'foolishness' a widow might indulge herself with in the country would not be possible in London, where members of the ton seem to do nothing but spy on and gossip about all the other members of the ton."

"She's a wise lady, your grandmamma."

"Yes. I agreed that such…reckless conduct would be out of place here. But I also informed her that I refused to allow the prejudiced opinions of the fashionable world to dictate my actions. As I myself find nothing to reproach in your behavior toward me, and since you know all of London well—by the way, you do, don't you?"

"Y-yes, but—"

"Then, if you are still agreeable, I see no reason not to have you escort me as we discussed. We shall explore in the mornings, as I'm obligated to make calls with Lady Farrington most afternoons, and my maid will accompany us to preserve the dictates of propriety. Though I must say, I consider her presence a nonsensical requirement, and hope she will not expire from boredom. Now, I've been going over my guidebook all morning. I fear it's too late to set out today, but perhaps tomorrow—"

"You cannot be serious! My little innocent, though you may persist in your fantasy that I'm a gentleman, I assure you that the ton speaks of me in very different terms. Broad daylight and accompanying maids won't matter a ha'pence. 'Tis a fragile thing, a reputation—a woman's even more so than a man's. You may think that by associating with me you are only being fair and impartial, but the world will not see it so. They will say I intended to seduce you, lead you to ruin. And ruined you will be."

When Valeria uttered a dismissive laugh, he continued. "'Tis no joking matter. Surely your grandmother is presenting you in hopes of finding you another husband. Rumors that you are conducting an affair with me would destroy any chance of attracting a respectable suitor, and close the doors of the best of polite society to you.''

He rounded on her, the intensity of his gaze holding hers. ''You cannot conceive what 'tis like to be cast into permanent exile from decent company, to have your name always linked to slander or spoken with sly innuendo. You would rue the loss of your good reputation till your dying day. Which is about as long as you would hate the man who caused you to lose it.'' His impassioned tone softened. ''Please, Lady Arnold, let us be able to part as friends.''

The conviction in his voice shook her to the marrow. Before she could prevent herself, she asked, ''Rue the loss of my good name, as you have rued the loss of yours?''

For an instant he froze. Then, almost as if he were physically donning a mask, she watched him wipe the earnest expression from his face, shake his head and summon up a smile. ''Me? Whist, and when had an Irish beggar's brat any good name to lose? Nay, dear lady, 'tis your own fair self that concerns me.''

''Yes, being a beggar's brat and a seducing rogue, you always worry about the reputation of fair ladies.''

The smile slipped a little. ''Nay, I haven't always.''

Despite the teasing expression still on his face, for an instant Valeria saw such bleakness in the depths of his eyes that she had the absurd desire to gather him into her arms. Mercifully, before she rashly did something that would have embarrassed them both, the look vanished.

Rattled by the intensity of that compulsion to embrace him, she could think of nothing to say.

Then a wave of awareness swept through her, some wordless sense of connection that drew her irresistibly to Teagan Fitzwilliams with an attraction that went well beyond the physical. She had known, as he had, an orphan's fate, the terror of losing all that was beloved and familiar. Known the anguish of being rejected by one she thought would love her, and left to make her way alone in an indifferent world.

They stood motionless, bound in place by the strength of what was flowing between them. A bond she *knew* was mutual just as clearly as she knew he would never acknowledge or act upon it. In order to protect her.

With the only soul she now cared about having only weeks left to live, Valeria didn't want to give up this profound, inexplicable link. Somehow she must convince him that parting ways wasn't necessary.

Jennings's knock at the door startled them both.

"You must at least take tea before you leave," Valeria said, gesturing to the settee before busying herself with the tray the butler left before them.

Her caller hesitated, obviously debating the rudeness of refusing against the prudence of an immediate departure.

"Sugar, Mr. Fitzwilliams?" She dropped her gaze to his cup so he could not catch her eye to make his excuses.

She heard him sigh, followed by the soft slide of superfine against brocade upholstery. "If you please."

Silence fell while Valeria worked to prepare their tea and her arguments. "Though I appreciate your experienced view of London society, Mr. Fitzwilliams," she said a moment later, handing him his cup, "there is another factor of which you are not aware. Although it is not yet generally known, Lady Winterdale intends to settle her fortune on me."

She risked glancing at him. The surprise on his face appeared genuine.

"That is excellent news. My congratulations."

"Now, I will allow that if country-nobody Lady Arnold dallied with a rogue, Society might well delight in shredding her reputation. However, much will be excused the heiress of the rich Lady Winterdale. I doubt I would be left completely friendless.''

He nodded. ''Aye, the glitter of gold makes an excellent cleanser. But unless you remain completely above reproach, some of the more discriminating would still cut your acquaintance. 'Tis a risk you need not take.''

''Perhaps not. But, as we've both noted, I'm not a ton lady, nor, given what I've seen of them thus far, am I sure I wish to be. Oh, I've enjoyed Grandmamma's hospitality, but I suppose I've been a soldier's daughter too long. Having lived among men who in the course of their duties put their lives at risk daily, I rather doubt I'd ever feel at home in a society whose time is spent mostly in the frivolous pursuit of pleasure.'' She smiled wistfully. ''I'm not sure where I belong.

''But,'' she continued before he could comment, ''the imminent possession of a fortune frees me from having to worry about Society's good opinion. I need not remarry unless I choose to. And I certainly would not marry a man who would believe Society's evaluation of me rather than make his own assessment of my character.''

''Such a man would certainly not be worthy of you.''

She smiled. ''Precisely. So you see, if you still refuse to honor your promise of escorting me, I am forced to conclude that your concern for my reputation is merely a pretext to avoid my company.'' She took a deep breath, steeling herself to ask, ''Will you make me conclude that?''

Mr. Fitzwilliams stared at his teacup, thumb rubbing the thin china stem, as if engaged in some inner struggle. ''I should affirm it. In truth…Lord forgive me, but I cannot. Neither, though, can I countenance harming you.''

Euphoria filled Valeria, sent a smile bubbling to her lips. ''You won't. You are merely a knowledgeable friend acquainting me with the attractions offered by your city.''

''The ton will never believe that.''

She shrugged. "The ton can believe what it likes."

For a moment he said nothing. Then, with a deep sigh, he looked up at her. "So be it then."

"Naturally, there will be no repetition of the...foolishness my aunt deplored."

His changeable eyes grew alert, their sparkle intensifying. Slowly he scanned her from her forehead down her face, her neck, to linger at her breasts before returning to focus on her lips. Heat scoured Valeria in the wake of that glance.

"Whist, will there not?" he murmured. "Is it sure you are?"

Watching the dimple that creased his cheeks and the roguish gleam in his eyes, she was not sure at all. "Certainly," she lied. "You will conduct yourself as the perfect gentleman I have pronounced you to be. So, do we have a bargain, Mr. Fitzwilliams?"

He raised his teacup to her in salute before placing it back on the table. "A bargain it is, Lady Arnold."

Her pulses leaped in joyous expectation. With a calm Valeria was far from feeling, she carefully deposited her own teacup and rose to hold out her hand. "Until tomorrow then, Mr. Fitzwilliams."

He came over and kissed it. "Until tomorrow."

Scarcely breathing, Valeria watched him walk out, her fingers burning where he had held them, her hand tingling where he had kissed. Legs turning shaky, she collapsed back into her chair.

Oh, my, this was definitely not wise. And she was going to do it anyway.

As he walked back to his lodgings, Teagan found himself breaking into a whistle.

He shouldn't be feeling this surge of energy, as if every sense had been heightened. He should be castigating himself for not having talked Lady Arnold out of the foolishness of seeing him again.

But oh, with a ferocity so deep-seated it almost frightened him, he wanted to see her. And so he'd given in, let the lady have her way.

How unique she was with her mix of innocence and worldly wisdom, her lack of concern for presenting a fashionable facade. She possessed a perception that was almost painfully acute and a straightforward manner entirely bereft of guile. Her wit delighted him, her honesty charmed him, and despite his acquiescence in the matter of seducing her again, her mere presence enflamed him more than the practiced wiles of the most voluptuous society matron.

'Twas a conflagration he'd hold at a low burn, though. He'd given her his word.

Unless, of course, *she* chose to break the agreement. His mouth dried and his body hardened at the prospect.

Even the weariness with which he faced another night's ritual of gaming faded in the face of his anticipation. For the first time in recent memory, Teagan could not wait for it to be tomorrow.

Her mind wandering, but with a polite smile on her face, Valeria served tea to the guests who stopped by Lady Farrington's afternoon at-home. She was performing the hostess's duties alone, however, her chaperone having taken to her bed again upon being informed that Valeria had not only received Teagan Fitzwilliams this morning, but was insisting she meant to go driving with him tomorrow.

Valeria sighed. She was sorry to distress Lady Farrington, who had shown her every kindness, and she hoped that her behavior would not cause undue embarrassment. But she would not allow her chaperone's opinions to over'urn her own.

Given the contretemps at the Insley ball, their at-home

was attracting a larger number of guests than usual. Despite Valeria's lack of fortune, Lady Winterdale's sponsorship had been sufficient to attract to her the interest of half a dozen courtiers, though Sir William Parham had been the most assiduous. Many of Valeria's dance partners from the previous evening as well as a number of acquaintances, their avid curiosity barely concealed under an exchange of polite conventionalities, crowded into her drawing room.

By the time she had fended off for the tenth time the same probing questions about her meeting with Teagan Fitzwilliams, some of them phrased in terms so insulting to that gentleman that she was hard put to reply civilly, she was ready to trade so-called ''polite society'' for a clan of Aborigines that very afternoon.

She wasn't sure whether to be pleased or annoyed when Sir William lingered after the other guests departed to beg her company for a stroll about the gardens. Knowing she might not be able to respond courteously to the warning she feared he meant to deliver, she hesitated a long moment before finally taking the arm he offered.

''Thank you for allowing me to remain,'' he said once they'd reached the rose walk. ''I wanted to apologize, which I wasn't able to do last night before Lady Farrington or this afternoon in a drawing room full of guests.''

''Apologize?'' Valeria repeated, defenses on alert.

''Yes. I hadn't meant to belittle the attractions you wished to see in London, nor disparage your brother's advice. Although the West India docks are an...unusual site to capture a lady's interest.''

She found herself bristling. ''I'm an unusual lady.''

He smiled. ''You are indeed.''

Instantly suspicious, Valeria looked up at him. But in his hazel eyes, quite fine if not as uncommonly brilliant as Mr. Fitzwilliams's, she read not censure, but sincere appreciation. She allowed herself to relax a bit.

"I found myself wondering if Mr. Fitzwilliams kept your appointment."

Valeria stiffened once again. "Excuse me, but I do not think that is your concern."

"It is presumptuous of me to inquire. After all, you're an independent lady who's been mistress of her own establishment for years, quite capable of deciding on your own whose company you will keep. However, I—"

"Please, Sir William, you may spare yourself warning me that Teagan Fitzwilliams is a rascal whose escort will lead to my utter ruin. My chaperone has already fully covered that topic. Therefore, you—"

Sir William began to chuckle. Thrown off stride, Valeria fell silent.

"Yes," he said, controlling his mirth, "having witnessed Lady Farrington's reaction last night, I'm sure she has harangued you—at much greater length than you wished to hear! Actually, my intention was quite the opposite. If you are in fact determined to go through with your plan, I wanted to reassure you that I do not believe Teagan Fitzwilliams will cause you any harm."

This was so completely opposite what she'd expected to hear from him that Valeria was left momentarily speechless.

"It's good of you to reassure me," she managed.

"My younger brother was at Eton with him and quite admired him, actually. He kept the lads amused, winning their pennies with his card tricks and sleights of hand. Which I suppose was fortunate, since Rob says his family frequently neglected to bring him home during term breaks, so he must have needed those funds." Sir William sighed. "However, to be honest, I have to admit I cannot be happy about your spending time with him. His rogue's reputation among the ladies is well earned."

"I see. And naturally he is the only single gentleman among the ton who has ever dallied with a willing matron."

Sir William flushed at her blunt words. "He is not, of course, and you are correct in inferring that he has perhaps been unfairly maligned for behavior forgiven in others. That was not precisely what I meant."

Sir William paused and put his hand over the gloved one she had rested on his arm. "Y-you cannot be insensible of my regard for you."

Valeria was glad he'd given her an opening to speak frankly. "Sir William, I know Grandmamma must have spoken to you on my behalf, and I wish to assure you in the strongest terms that despite your fondness for Lady Winterdale, you must not feel compelled to—"

"No, it's not like that. Well, I admit, at first I called on you mainly because of my sympathy for the…circumstances she'd described."

Mortifying fear shot through Valeria. "Indeed? And just what did she tell you that inspired such compassion?"

"You will say she should not have spoken to me of your deepest feelings, and perhaps you are correct. But she knew I, of all men, would understand. I, too, lost a spouse whom I loved almost beyond reason, and…" He stopped and swallowed hard. "I…I know how difficult it is to go on. Lady Winterdale was concerned for your future, and I knew it was time that I, too, move on with my life. She hoped perhaps we might…help each other."

Remorse filled Valeria. Until this moment she had thought of Sir William only in terms of being Lady Winterdale's willing pawn, considering neither that gentleman's reasons for calling on her—nor his feelings. "I am sorry for your loss," she said, patting his hand.

He captured her fingers and held them. "Thank you. Although initially I called at Lady Winterdale's behest, I now enjoy your company for its own merits. Indeed, I had hoped we might soon reach an...understanding. Which is why I cannot help being dismayed by your introduction to Mr. Fitzwilliams. After all, he's not called 'Fascinating Fitz' for naught. Ladies seem to find the handsome rogue nearly irresistible.'' He smiled wryly. ''In comparison, I'm a rather dull dog.''

His modesty touched her. ''I think you're a very fine gentleman.''

He laughed with self-deprecating humor. '''Fine,' I believe, is an adjective a lady uses when she can't think of something more dashing. Dull or not, I'm hoping there will still be a chance for me...for us—'' He broke off, flushing. ''Forgive me. I'm putting this badly.''

Valeria looked at his averted face. No, he hadn't the mesmerizing handsomeness of Teagan Fitzwilliams. But there was strength in those broad shoulders, kindness and a deep sense of honor in his character that led him to commend even a gentleman he obviously saw as a rival. And courage to speak of his feelings when she had given him no real reason to believe they would not be summarily rejected. A most admirable gentleman, in sum.

Sir William's a fine man. The countess's words echoed in her head. *Don't throw a chance to fix his interest....*

''Let me return the courtesy of speaking frankly, Sir William. I'm not sure *I* am ready to remarry. But should I become so, I recognize that Teagan Fitzwilliams is not a likely candidate for husband. I admire you all the more for your honesty today, I value our friendship...and certainly do not dismiss the possibility that it could become more.''

Sir William kissed her hand. ''That, dear lady, is all I ask. Except perhaps that you will also allow me a chance to squire you about the city. Unfortunately, I must leave this afternoon to resolve a pressing problem at my estate.'' He sighed. ''I cannot regret enough the necessity to depart at this particular moment! But when I return, if you will

permit me, I promise to escort you wherever you wish—
no matter how 'unusual' the place.''

Consider carefully…and try not to be a fool, the countess had counseled. "I should like that."

Sir William smiled, the pleasure lighting his eyes more
fervent than Valeria would have wished. "Excellent. I'm
afraid I must depart now to prepare for my journey. Shall
I bring you back to the house?''

"Thank you, no. I'd prefer to remain a bit longer in the
garden.''

Sir William glanced quickly around, then leaned toward
her. At about the instant Valeria realized he meant to kiss
her, he halted. Cheeks flushing slightly, he raised her hand
and brushed his lips over her knuckles instead.

"I shall leave you now. Your most obedient servant,
Lady Arnold.''

Valeria bid him goodbye, not sure whether she was relieved or disappointed he'd changed his mind.

And knowing she was even more foolhardy to wonder
how his kiss might have compared to the expert caresses
of Teagan Fitzwilliams.

Chapter Nine

Two weeks later, Valeria went in to breakfast with Lady Winterdale. Having never fully recovered from the spell of weakness that had sent her to her bed, the countess tired after walking more than a few steps. Since she absolutely refused to be carried up and down the stairs, she now received her friends and took her meals in the sitting room adjacent to her chamber.

Watching with a worried eye as the countess picked at her toast, Valeria filled her plate from the assortment of dishes Cook had sent up to tempt her mistress's flagging appetite. It pained her to see Grandmamma growing steadily weaker, but having received one of the worst scolds of her life yesterday for attempting to cajole Lady Winterdale into eating, Valeria knew it was useless to speak about it.

Nor could she help feeling a ready sympathy. Choosing—or not choosing—to eat was one of the few things over which the once indomitable countess still had control.

"Abandoning me again this morning, eh, missy?" Lady Winterdale said over her teacup. "Always gallivanting about, with never a minute to spare for an old lady."

"Pooh, Grandmamma, that horse won't run. You know

very well if I did stay, you'd dispatch me on an errand as soon as your friends arrived for a good gossip.''

"Wouldn't bother me to have you lurking about.''

"No, but you know it inhibits the others. *They* have too much delicacy to shred the character of their adversaries and meddle in the lives of all their relations with a witness present.''

The countess chuckled. "Impertinent chit! You've been out five mornings already with that Fitzwilliams rogue. Can't image what else of interest you'd have left to see in London. Alicia told me that there's been no gossip about your excursions, so you're still receiving invitations aplenty.''

Valeria smiled ruefully. "No gossip yet, although I expect there will be sooner or later. I suppose thus far either no one in the ton has been up early enough to see us, or none venture into such unfashionable locales.''

"Alicia's gone to some trouble to introduce you. I don't want you neglecting your social duties with her.''

"I won't, Grandmamma. We are to go to King's Theatre tonight with Sir William, who's just arrived back in town.''

"And none too soon," Lady Winterdale muttered. "Well, and what do you think Sir William will say to all this racketing about you've been doing in his absence?''

Valeria didn't pretend to misunderstand. "Actually, he stopped by before he left London to reassure me that Mr. Fitzwilliams would make a very safe escort.''

The countess raised an eyebrow. "Did he? The boy's downier than I gave him credit for. Where do you go today?''

"Spring Gardens. Knowing my interest in foreign travel, Mr. Fitzwilliams recommended Mr. Wigley's Royal Promenade Rooms, which house a splendid panorama of St. Petersburg and thirty other cities. And there's also Monsieur Maillardet's exhibition of moving mechanical figures, which include a lady playing the harp and a bird that moves and sings. I can't imagine how they work, but perhaps Mr. Fitzwilliams can explain them.''

''What would a rake know about mechanics?''

''He's amazingly knowledgeable, Grandmamma. When we went to see the marble statues Lord Elgin brought back from the Parthenon, Mr. Fitzwilliams related the myths of all the gods portrayed, along with a general history of the entire Peloponnesian Wars.''

The countess snorted. ''Sounds dry as dust.''

''On the contrary, I found it fascinating!''

Lady Winterdale groaned and raised her eyes to the ceiling, as if imploring the deity. ''First she insists on seeing a certified rogue, now she's talking like a demned *bluestocking!*'' The countess looked over to shake a finger at Valeria. ''Child, you are past praying for.''

Valeria gave her an apologetic smile. ''I'm afraid I shall never be fashionable.''

''You'll return after viewing these mechanical toys?''

''N-not today.'' Feeling a bit guilty, Valeria explained, ''You see, the weather has been inclement for the last week, but today promises to be fair and warm. I've decided to take a water taxi to the Tower—''

''Where the erudite Mr. Fitzwilliams will no doubt regale you with the entire history of the kings and queens of England.''

''—and if the weather holds, go on after nuncheon to view the West India docks. A locale, I know, that is even more unfashionable, but which I am most anxious to see!''

Valeria knew her eyes must be shining with an excitement she had difficulty subduing, even in her Grandmamma's presence. She looked forward this morning to not just a few hours, but an entire day of unsullied pleasure in the company of the most interesting, congenial companion she'd known since she lost her brother.

Like Elliot, Mr. Fitzwilliams seemed to take an avid interest in almost everything, and like Elliot, he never seemed to mind the questions she peppered him with. They'd had the most stimulating discussions about English law while visiting the Inns of Court, about the intricacies of investment and finance during their tour through the City.

She'd been surprised by the keenness of his mind and his obvious breadth of knowledge. And he'd adopted toward her an easy, avuncular manner that reminded her so much of her brother that within an hour of their first excursion she felt they were the best of friends.

Except for the acute awareness that simmered always just below consciousness. And occasionally bubbled to the surface in pulse-quickening moments, like when he took her arm to help her in or out of the carriage. Or once, when she slipped on a rain-slick cobblestone coming out of the shed in which Lord Elgin lodged his marbles, and Teagan caught her shoulders to keep her from falling.

Each time, they'd stood immobile, gazes locked, held as if by some inescapable force. Each time Valeria had felt a powerful urge to lift her lips to his, so tantalizingly close, to tangle her fingers in the thick golden silk of his hair.

Each time he had moved away first.

She would have thought such episodes would have spoiled their camaraderie, made her feel shy and awkward. Instead, they seemed to enhance and deepen the bond between them. When near him, Valeria felt a shivery expectation, such as long ago in India when Papa's relations had sent her a package not to be unwrapped until the holidays. Each day of waiting, speculating over the delights soon to be revealed, had enhanced the anticipation.

Though, as he'd promised, Mr. Fitzwilliams had never gone beyond the line of friendship. True, at every outing he made some teasing comment about her lips or eyes, his tone more than the words themselves conveying that he'd not forgotten the long-ago interlude in her hayloft. Twice he had followed the remark with the suggestion that she abandon convention and come back with him to his rooms.

But the offer was always delivered in such an outrageously flirtatious manner that Valeria could never be sure just how serious he was. Fortunately for the sake of her reputation, he had never persisted in trying to persuade her to cross the bounds she had set. But still…

She came back to herself with a start, to find Lady Winterdale's eyes fixed on her. Realizing she must have been gazing into the distance, a dreamy expression on her face, Valeria felt her cheeks heat.

"Excuse me, ma'am! I've been woolgathering."

"Child, I'm afraid for you," the countess said.

Valeria knew the old woman was concerned with much more than her lack of fashionable aspirations.

She took Lady Winterdale's hand and squeezed it. "I'm being careful, Grandmamma. I promise."

Lady Winterdale shook her head and sighed. "Ah, but can you be careful enough?"

A knock at the door, followed by Molly's entrance, saved her from the necessity of a reply. "Mr. Fitzwilliams is here for us, my lady."

"Thank you, Molly. Fetch the picnic basket Cook made up, and tell Mr. Fitzwilliams I'll be down in a moment."

Avoiding her grandmamma's gaze, Valeria leaned to kiss the old woman goodbye. "I'll stop by later and tell you all about my adventures."

Lady Winterdale nodded. "See that you do."

Valeria exited the room, hard-pressed to keep herself from skipping. She knew she was smiling, but such a joyous expectancy filled her, she felt like gathering the whole world in an exuberant embrace. The sense of setting out on a grand adventure buoyed her, as it had when she'd stepped onboard the vessel that had carried her family to India.

She knew Lady Winterdale worried about her barely concealable enthusiasm for her excursions with Teagan Fitzwilliams. Mercy, too, was suspicious enough that she'd nearly insisted, despite her bad ankle, on replacing Molly as Valeria's chaperone on the last two outings. Not wishing her nurse's glowering presence to dampen the delight of her limited time with Teagan, Valeria had with difficulty persuaded her to remain at home, though not before Mercy delivered a sharp warning against becoming too fond of so handsome and ineligible a gentleman.

In the back of her mind, Valeria knew her rapidly growing attachment to his company ought to worry her, too. Each day they explored, the list of sites still to visit dwindled, and soon their pretext for being together would vanish.

What she would do then, she had no idea. But with the conviction of one who had spent more than enough of her life in loneliness and grief, Valeria resolved for the present to put aside doubt, fear, or caution. She would focus instead on enjoying to the fullest the about-to-be-unwrapped gift of today.

Having dispatched Molly, as well as James, the footman Lady Farrington had insisted on adding to Valeria's party, to buy meat pies from a nearby vendor, Mr. Fitzwilliams spread their picnic cloth on Tower green.

"There, milady Valeria. Your throne, established in the driest bit of greensward I could discover, awaits."

"Thank you, gallant sir!" Valeria seated herself and, after arranging her skirts, patted the place beside her. "Sit, and I'll unpack the bounty Cook provided. We probably have no need of additional meat pies."

"Ah, but Valeria-love, how else was I to have a few minutes alone with you? Since you are so disobliging as to always refuse to steal back to my rooms with me."

"Oh, Teagan, do stop," she replied, chuckling. "You've already practiced your wiles on Molly. I believe she's more than half in love with you, which is making poor James quite jealous."

Teagan, with the quick wit she'd soon noticed in him, had skillfully taken advantage of Lady Farrington's addition to their group, realizing that, with the footman to escort Valeria's maid, he could safely dispatch the two on small errands.

'Twas a kindness to both couples, he told Valeria, the twinkle in his eyes belying the seriousness of his tone, for it prevented Molly from becoming bored by giving her a handsome young footman to flirt with, and allowed Teagan and Valeria to converse with much more freedom and privacy than might have otherwise been possible.

He'd also induced her to dispense with cumbersome titles. As Teagan pointed out, 'twas a bit ridiculous for two who had shared such intimacies to address each other as "Lady Arnold" and "Mr. Fitzwilliams" during private chat.

"You have a talent with people," Valeria observed, watching her maid and the attentive footman walk away.

Engaged in pulling the cork from their wine, Teagan made a short bow over the bottle. "Sure, and a rogue must needs charm the ladies."

"True, 'twould be hard otherwise to maintain one's reputation. But you talk just as easily with James, and can always find something to interest him, no matter how unlikely the locale. You persuaded the Tower guard to give us an extended tour after I'd just overheard him telling another group of visitors the rooms were closed."

"'Tis my Irish tongue. Faith, but it can be very persuasive."

"Can it, now?" But as she echoed his teasing tone, the memory of what that tongue had persuaded her to do invaded her mind in a hot rush of sensation. Ordinary hunger forgotten, suddenly she was starving for the taste of him, the banquet of responses he could evoke with his knowing hands and lips. Her eyes lifted to his mouth, her fingers itching to reach out and pull him the small distance that separated her greedy tongue from his.

He must have sensed her need, for his smile faded and his hands clenched on the wine bottle. His golden eyes blazed with an answering heat. "Valeria," he whispered.

"We got six meat pies. Think ye that'll be enough?"

Molly's cheerful voice jerked Valeria back to the reality of where she was, sitting on a blanket on Tower green, brightly garbed guards within sight, curious visitors wandering the grounds all about her.

"M-more than enough, thank you," she answered in a voice that wobbled only slightly, thinking how wise she'd been to provide herself with a multitude of chaperones.

Molly insisted on unpacking and dividing up the provisions, she and James then removing a short distance away to devour their meal.

"So, what did you find most remarkable this morning?" Teagan asked, handing Valeria a wineglass.

"I thought the mechanical figures most ingenious, particularly the man dancing on a circus tightrope. But I am somewhat sorry we visited the menagerie."

"Why is that? Do you not like animals?"

"On the contrary, I like them very much. I felt so sorry for the beasts, though—and pity is not an emotion I'd ever envisioned feeling for a tiger! We encountered ferocious ones in India, where they sometimes carry off livestock and even threaten the inhabitants. But those poor creatures! Stolen from their homeland, trapped in an alien place, pacing their narrow cages with no hope of breaking free…"

"Aye. 'Tis no wonder they roar with the pain of it."

The odd tone of his voice caused Valeria to look up, into

the sparkling depths of Teagan's golden eyes. *Like you,* she thought, and knew he was thinking the same.

"Is there no way out?" she asked softly.

He remained silent, staring off into the distance. Valeria began to fear she'd breached the trust between them, articulating an insight to which she ought not have given voice, when Teagan spoke.

"Sometimes I dream of using Ailainn to begin a stud farm, such as I used to run in the summers for my grandfather. A simple place in the country I can purchase when the dibs are in tune, and manage like a proper gentleman farmer. But the dibs are never in tune long enough." His wry smile took on a bitter edge. "I suppose I could try to entice a rich woman into marrying me. But I pray heaven I'll never be that desperate or that deep in my cups. What a treat for the lady, to take to husband a man who'll sooner or later abandon her, as dear Papa did us."

Before she could think what to reply, Teagan put down his glass. "Let Molly help you pack up. There's much to see at the docks, and we must view it all before four of the clock. After that, the guildmaster locks the great gates and not even the king himself could gain entry."

He sprang up and walked away, leaving her still at a loss for words to ease the ache she heard in his voice.

By the time he returned with the hackney, the light-hearted sparkle was back in his eye, and conversation grew general. And once they arrived at their destination, Valeria forgot the incident in her wonder over the long avenue of brick warehouses set on stout stone foundations, the crowd of ships straining at anchor in the swift-flowing river, awaiting their turn to disembark their cargoes.

Before her awed eyes she saw flags from a dozen nations, men in sailor's garb, in factor's suits, in flowing Eastern robes. A forest of stout posts lined the quays, bearing huge hoists and winches by which means the sailors were levering a diversity of cargoes out of the holds of their ships.

Eager for a closer look, Valeria begged Teagan to take her to the quay of the easternmost warehouse. Molly and James declined the treat, preferring to wait with the hackney.

"It's said ten thousand tons of shipping is unloaded on these docks in a year," Teagan told her.

"How do you learn such things?"

"I've often had occasion to play cards with merchants and factors. Most men like to speak of their work, if you give them the opportunity."

Valeria edged closer to the water. "See the ropes strain! What is it they're hauling up now?"

"Why, 'tis a fine Queen Anne chair and a beautiful balustrade. Or it will be, when the carvers finish it."

"Ah, 'tis a block of mahogany! Where would that come from, do you think?"

"The forests of Asia, probably, though I believe some grow in the Americas as well."

Valeria stood on tiptoe and leaned forward to get a better look at the rich, red-hued wood glistening in the afternoon sun. "How beautiful it—oh!"

Her words ended with a small shriek as one of the hoist ropes snapped and the huge block teetered, then tumbled out of the cargo net toward the dock below.

Before she could think to move, Teagan seized her and half carried, half dragged her away. As the mahogany crashed onto the quay where she'd been standing a few seconds earlier, he pulled her into the safety of a small alley bordering the warehouse.

The foreman directing the winch-handlers ran after them. "Cor, ma'am, is you all right?"

Teagan set her down and steadied her against him. "Unhurt, sir. A bit frightened, perhaps."

"Lord be praised," the man declared, and trotted back to the quay to deliver to the workmen a loud and, to Valeria's ears, completely incomprehensible harangue whose angry tone alone she could understand.

"You are unhurt?" he asked, still cradling her against his chest, his panting breaths warm against her face.

"Perfectly fine," she answered. "It all happened too quickly for me to be afraid."

"Well, I'm glad you weren't," he muttered. "I was terrified." As if to emphasize those words, he hugged her.

Surprise soon gave way to sweetest pleasure. She loved the strength of his arms cradling her to his chest, the faint scratchiness of his chin pressed to her temple. The feel of his body against hers from chest through torso, her legs brushing his, sent sparks through every nerve.

Her mind instantly recalled that other time she'd felt him full-length against her, the sultry pressure of his body touching hers intimately, while his tongue, slow and languid, spiraled her to unimagined bliss.

Fire ignited within her, kindling her bones, melting conscious will and molding it to new purpose. She felt the tremors of an answering explosion vibrate through his body.

Valeria pulled her chin from the spot he had tucked it, in the hollow of his shoulder. Slowly, as if reluctant to lose even one small area of contact, he allowed her to back off. His breathing ragged, he looked down at her.

"Please, Teagan," she whispered, and raised her lips.

This time he did not move away. Making a sound deep in his throat, he brushed his mouth against hers gently, his touch soft and almost unbearably sweet. Clutching his shoulders, Valeria traced the tip of her tongue over the lips she'd wanted so long and so badly to taste.

As if a wall of restraint had been breached, with a growl he hauled her closer, crushing her breasts against his chest.

His tongue parted her lips, delved deep into her mouth, teasing, stroking, fanning the flames within to a conflagration that burned away any thought of where they were or why she had waited so long to come into his arms.

She wasn't sure whether she'd been kissing him an eternity or an instant—whichever was not long enough—when he broke away, gasping, and pushed her unsteadily aside.

Had he not fended her off, Valeria would certainly have claimed his mouth again. She stared up at him in confusion as the fog of need began to clear.

"Ah, sweeting," he murmured, raising one shaky finger to touch her kiss-reddened lips. "We cannot."

Running footsteps approached.

"My lady!" Molly's panicked voice called across the sudden stillness. "There be a courier come from the house. 'Tis Lady Winterdale! We must return at once!"

Chapter Ten

Apprehension making it difficult to breathe, Valeria scrambled from the hackney. Jennings opened the front door before she could touch the handle, and to her surprise, Lady Farrington hurried out from the parlor, a damp handkerchief in her hand.

"Valeria, at last! She's been asking for you, and I so feared you might not return in t-time!"

Dread slammed into her chest. A queasy mix of fear, anguish and angry protest, too reminiscent of another time, another sickbed, churned in her gut. "I'll go up at once."

She fumbled with the fastening of her pelisse, felt rather than saw Teagan brush her fingers away and undo the ties, then hand it to the butler. "Go," he said quietly.

She gave him a quick nod and ran for the stairs.

Teagan watched her ascend, an echoing sadness in his heart. Though to hear her speak of her dealings with the countess, it appeared the two argued more than they agreed, Teagan knew she cared deeply for the old woman. The news brought by the courier who'd summoned them back had been alarming, and the face of Valeria's chaperone even grimmer.

Lady Farrington stood near the base of the stairway, looking up. "If she'd been at home where she belonged, Aunt Winterdale wouldn't have become so distressed."

At first Teagan didn't realize her remark was intended for him.

"I'm sure she never meant to distress her grandmother, or you, my lady," he belatedly replied.

"Well, she's home now." Lady Farrington did not turn to address him directly. "And she will have no further need of your services, Mr. Fitzwilliams." Still showing him her back, Valeria's chaperone walked to the stairs.

Before Lady Farrington had taken two steps, Jennings had the massive entry door open. "Good day, sir," he said, pointedly standing aside to allow Teagan to exit.

He was being ejected. Though the butler made no move toward him, Teagan suddenly noticed a brace of footmen standing by silently, as if to assist in his departure should he prove uncooperative.

Chagrin heated his face. With the butler's disapproving eyes burning into him, Teagan stepped mechanically toward the door. A panicky awareness washed over him when he crossed the threshold and the portal slammed closed behind him.

Not until this moment had he realized how much his access to Valeria depended upon the goodwill of an old woman who might very well be dying.

As he stood motionless on the front porch, a carriage careened down the street and slowed before the town house with a screech of brakes. Before the vehicle even stopped moving, Sir William Parham leaped out and came up the steps at a trot, giving Teagan a quick nod as he passed.

As it had for Valeria, the door opened for him before he could reach it. In the entryway beyond, Teagan saw Lady Farrington hurry down the stairs to seize the newcomer's hand. "My dear Sir William, thank you for coming! I very much fear Valeria will n-need you—"

The mahogany portal closed behind Sir William, cutting off the rest of Lady Farrington's sentence. Numbly Teagan descended the rest of the stairs.

Valeria will need you.

He clenched his teeth and slammed one fist against his thigh, fighting an upsurge of humiliation, anger, fear—and a pathetic burst of jealousy.

She's my Lady Mystery, you bastard, he silently raged at Sir William, who even now was being led into her presence, probably gathering her into his arms, comforting her against his chest.

For one ridiculous moment, Teagan wished he were a rich, well-respected gentleman worthy of courting a gently bred lady, able to offer her a home and children, able to vow to keep her in love and comfort the rest of her days.

But then, he thought as he trudged blindly back toward his lodgings, Lady Mystery had never truly been his. She was no more than a sweet illusion, a fleeting shaft of sunlight and warmth that had briefly brightened the gray sameness of his days. A searing memory of a morning in a hayloft he could now scarcely believe had been real.

Valeria hurried to the large canopied bed where the countess lay propped up against the pillows, taking shallow panting breaths.

"Late, girl," Lady Winterdale scolded as she fixed her still-fierce gaze on Valeria. "Nearly too late."

"Nonsense, Grandmamma," Valeria whispered, grasping the thin chilled hands between her warm ones. "I'm sure you'll improve. You're too ornery for St. Peter to want you yet."

A ghost of a chuckle exited thin lips already turning

waxy. "Can't cheat death forever. Do something...for me?"

"Of course," she answered, blinking back tears.

"Leaving you money. Winterdale Park, too. Go there afterward. Consider carefully...what you want to do. Promise me?"

"I promise."

"Good." The countess squeezed Valeria's hand, the faintest bit of pressure. "Remember...not to be a fool."

"I shall try. I love you, Grandmamma."

The countess smiled faintly. "My darling girl."

Then Lady Winterdale closed her eyes and softly exhaled her last breath.

And Valeria put her face in her hands and wept.

With the grim efficiency of one who had organized the ritual three times before, Valeria consulted with the vicar and sent notes to Lady Winterdale's cronies about her grandmamma's funeral service. She sat beside Cousin Alicia's bed, putting cold compresses on that afflicted lady's temples and bathing her forehead with lavender water while she wailed with a grief Valeria expressed, after her first bout of tears, only in stoic silence. She supervised the draping of the mirrors and doorframes in black, the ordering of mourning apparel for herself, Lady Farrington and the servants, and steeled herself to meet the flood of visitors who called to express their regrets.

She received Lady Winterdale's lawyer and man of business, hearing with perfect indifference the news that she now possessed cash and property that would make her wealthy beyond imagining.

An indifference that remained unbroken until the afternoon she and Molly went shopping for black lace crepe, ribbons and feathers to adorn their mourning bonnets.

At the first establishment they entered, the customer being waited upon, Lady Evelyn—an earl's wife with an expensive younger son to maintain—stopped in mid-sentence and insisted that Lady Arnold be served first. With profuse expressions of sympathy, she latched on to Valeria's arm and begged to be allowed to assist her.

Uncertain how to get rid of Lady Evelyn without appearing rude, Valeria allowed her to accompany them to the next shop. While they walked that short distance, two strolling gentlemen joined them, one a widower with five children and the other a fashionable dandy with a strong preference for the green baize tables of Pall Mall, the two gentlemen disputing with the earl's wife as to who should take Valeria's arm.

Had she not needed the black crepe and ribbons that very day, Valeria would have abandoned the shopping excursion and called for her carriage forthwith. By the time she'd purchased the few items she considered truly essential, a small crowd had gathered, the babbling group tripping over each other to try to carry her parcels, advise on the best shop to patronize, and persuade her to allow them to take her to Gunter's for some refreshment.

After finally extracting her arm from Lady Evelyn's grip, persistently refusing all invitations and having Molly yank the packages back from the hands of her too-willing assistants, she and the maid at last escaped back into their waiting carriage.

If this, she thought as they regained the blessed quiet of Grosvenor Square, was a sample of what she could expect in her new life as the rich Lady Arnold, Valeria wanted no part of it. As soon as Lady Winterdale's services were concluded, Valeria intended to honor her benefactress's wishes and leave London for Winterdale Park.

Protected in a cocoon of numbness, Valeria attended the funeral several afternoons later. Even the necessity of assisting Lady Farrington, who collapsed at the churchyard and had to be carried back to her carriage, did not penetrate that soothing fog.

With her cousin tucked up in bed and her own maid dismissed, Valeria sat alone by the flickering light of a single brace of candles in her grandmother's sitting room.

Her sitting room now.

Her tightly knit calm was unraveling in a tangle of emotions, all of which she'd experienced before. She hadn't had enough time. Though she'd come to love the crusty old lady who'd adopted her, she hadn't expressed those feelings often enough. And though she'd deluded herself into believing she was prepared for her grandmother's death, she now found she had no adequate defense against the stark loneliness that clawed at her.

In one respect this loss was better than the last, she told herself, attempting to rally her depressed spirits. She knew the countess had grown to care for her, and however poorly she'd expressed it, Valeria knew the countess had realized she was loved in return.

Valeria wandered to the bed and trailed her hand across the pristine linen, hardly able to believe her grandmother's frail frame but valiant spirit would no longer occupy it. Could it have been only a week ago that she'd rushed here to clasp those thin gnarled fingers?

From the one person she truly wished to see, the one whom she felt would appreciate her grief and whose mere presence would ease her sorrow, she'd heard nothing.

Perhaps, having been exiled from his family so young, Teagan Fitzwilliams had no experience of proper mourning protocol, and thus had not thought to call or write.

Still, she'd hoped she might catch a glimpse of him, mayhap receive an encouraging glance, during the service to which Sir William escorted her in compassionate silence.

But there'd been no sign of Teagan's handsome face or distinctive gold hair among the large crowd of mourners.

Now, alone in this empty, echoing room, she had to conclude that Teagan Fitzwilliams, probably surmising correctly that her grandmother's death would leave her too busy for sightseeing excursions, had dismissed her to go on with his life.

Would he care that she'd determined to leave London? If he knew, would he have called to bid her good-bye?

Would he have pressed her to stay?

Suddenly she couldn't bear the thought of quitting the city without making some final contact with him. She would pen him a farewell note, she decided—and realized with chagrin that she didn't even know his address.

No matter, she thought. She'd send James with the message. The servant's grapevine knew everything, and surely he would be able to track down Mr. Fitzwilliams.

Swiping away a tear, she went to find pen and paper.

As Teagan left his lodgings to walk through the drizzling gloom of the London night toward Jermyn Street, his thoughts, as they had so often this past week, returned to Valeria.

Within a day of Lady Winterdale's death, rumors began to circulate that her granddaughter-in-law, the quiet little widow Lady Arnold, had been named her sole heiress, making her very, very rich and catapulting her in the eyes of the ton from country nobody to socially prominent in the breath it took the speaker to describe her bequest.

Valeria wouldn't care about that, he knew. She'd lost a friend, not a benefactress, and though she'd been bereaved before, having already experienced what she must face again wouldn't make enduring the grief and sudden shock of loneliness any easier. Teagan had ached to be with her and offer whatever help and comfort he could.

Realizing with angry resignation that he would almost certainly have been refused entry had he tried to attend the funeral services this afternoon, he'd merely stood under the portico of the building facing St. George's, Hanover Square, and watched as Valeria was hustled from her carriage into the church and then back out again.

He'd sent her a note the day of Lady Winterdale's passing, but had received no reply. Suspecting her chaperone had not allowed it to be delivered, he'd called and been turned away three times by a stone-faced Jennings. Finally he'd come by way of the mews to the servant's entrance and asked for Molly. James had intercepted him instead, taking him into the shadows of the garden and begging him not to put Molly's employment at risk by asking her to smuggle a message to her mistress.

Lady Farrington's doing, he knew. Valeria's personal dragon of a protector would do whatever was necessary to ensure the unworthy Teagan Fitzwilliams never succeeded in intruding his polluting presence upon her cousin again.

Every man of birth and address in London now hanging out for a wife, as well as a miscellany of fortune hunters and ne'er-do-wells, would be flocking to her, the already-blessed Sir William at their head. The kindest, most intelligent and wittiest ones might even be worthy of her.

Teagan might as well face the fact that his sunlit, laughter-dappled interludes with the now rich and socially prominent Lady Arnold were over for good.

He turned the corner and looked up wearily at the light blazing from the windows of the gaming hell where tonight's play would take place. There could be no more fitting metaphor of his world of separation from Valeria, he thought with bitter amusement, than the large, beautifully appointed marble mansion she now owned and this smoke-and-tobacco stained, brandy-redolent establishment he was now bracing himself to enter.

He had never felt more alone in his life.

Mercifully, as he entered the game room at Devil's Den, Teagan found neither Rafe Crandall nor his cronies present. Relieved to be spared the necessity of summoning up a lighthearted banter he was far from feeling, Teagan settled into a quiet round of whist with a rich merchant.

He had amassed a modest stack of winnings when the door opened and the occupants of the room stirred. Teagan looked up to see Jeremy Hartness, Earl of Montford, cross the threshold, his noble lip curled as if in disdain at the assembled patrons, most of whom would never have been allowed to set foot on the stairway leading up to White's.

The wealthy, powerful Earl of Montford. Teagan's first cousin.

For an instant Teagan sucked in a breath and closed his eyes. *Not him, not tonight,* his beleaguered spirit protested.

The earl usually avoided locales in which he might encounter his disreputable cousin, which suited Teagan. When they did chance to meet, normally Teagan was poised and ready to wield his rapier wit, countering the innuendo and outright insult the earl always flung in his direction.

Montford would certainly try to abuse him now, but tonight, Teagan had no heart for a fight.

He bent his head and studied his cards. Perhaps Montford would simply pass by and leave him alone.

Teagan's downcast eyes caught the reflection off the highly polished evening shoes that halted beside his table.

"Well, well, what have we here? It appears the normal level of scum inhabiting this sorry hell has sunk even lower. Unless I'm mistaken, 'tis that infamous Irish Captain Sharp, Teagan Fitzwilliams."

Slowly Teagan looked up. "Why, I believe 'tis my illustrious cousin, the Earl of Montford. Faith, and what would bring you out of your citadel at White's? Surely you don't wish to gain firsthand knowledge of the ills you so love to deplore in the Lords.''

''Still playing the buffoon, I see. Gentlemen, shall we offer this broken-down exile the opportunity to earn a little coin? As a gamester lamentably lacking in skill, he seldom knows where his next meal is coming from. Perhaps we ought to show the lower orders a little compassion.''

The gentlemen accompanying Montford looked at each other uneasily. Among them Teagan recognized several of the earl's boon companions: Rexford, second son of a duke and married to the sister of Montford's wife; Wexley, a wealthy but amusing fribble of good birth; and Albemarle, whose estates marched with Montford's.

''I...I expect we could play a few hands,'' Rexford said, still looking uncertain.

''Nay, Cousin, can you not see they're uncomfortable among such rough company? Faith, and I'd hate to tax the gentlemen's wit or relieve them of their fat purses.''

''Small chance of either,'' Montford replied with a sneer. ''Come, gentlemen, have a seat. You, there—out!'' The earl waved a hand at the merchant, who, to Teagan's disgust, scrambled to give up his chair to the new arrivals.

What was Montford up to? Teagan wondered as the earl and his friends called for wine and a fresh deck of cards. Jeremy Hartness had hated him from the moment Teagan's six-year-old foot had touched Montford land twenty-two years ago. It could not be coincidence the mighty earl had appeared at a gaming establishment he'd normally not deign to enter. Montford would never seek Teagan out without a reason, and it wouldn't be a pleasant one.

The earl insisted on piquet, and Teagan drew the obviously nervous Albemarle as a partner. His cousin was reasonably adept, and they split the first two rubbers. The lack of love between the two being well known, word of the match spread, and by the time they began the third rubber quite a crowd had gathered.

Standing at the edge of it, Teagan was surprised to note, was Lord Riverton. Still grateful for the earl's intervention on his behalf at the Insley ball, Teagan gave him a quick nod. Somehow, surrounded by this hostile group, Teagan felt better just knowing Riverton was there.

After the commencement of the third rubber, Teagan's partner began to make a series of such ill-judged plays that they went down heavily, nearly wiping out Teagan's small stack of coins.

So that was the ploy. Well, he'd have none of it.

"Much as I hate to leave so convivial a group, I fear I have a previous engagement. Gentlemen," Teagan said, preparing to gather up his remaining coins.

Montford put a hand out to block Teagan's reach. "What, leaving so soon, and after such a paltry reverse?"

"I've little enough left, and nothing else to stake, as you can see. And I'm expected elsewhere."

"Your penny harlot can wait. Let's have another rubber."

Teagan searched for the proper words to extract himself without slighting his partner. He'd not allow Montford to lead him into a verbal row his cousin could then point to as evidence of Teagan's bad breeding.

"I generally prefer to game on my own, without a partner," he said at last.

"Well, that's easily arranged. We'll make it whist—just you and I. And double the stakes."

Should he lose the first round, doubling the stakes would leave Teagan without a coin to his name. "Another time, perhaps." He started to rise from his chair.

Montford uttered a scornful laugh. "Always knew you were a coward. But then, one couldn't expect proper be-

havior from a man whose mother betrayed her breeding by
running off with her Irish groom like a common strumpet.''

Teagan froze. Someone gasped, and the hubbub of voices
in the room dwindled into silence.

Rage filled the icy void he'd wandered in for the past
week, rage at the tormentor who'd never lost an opportunity
to belittle him since the day a lost, frightened boy had approached the lad introduced to him as his cousin—and got
punched in the gut.

Leaning across the table, he slapped the earl's face.
''Name your seconds.''

In the fraught silence that followed, the earl slowly raised
his fingers to rub at the red mark Teagan's hand had left.
''Nay, dueling is a custom reserved for gentlemen. I'll not
accept the challenge of a worthless guttersnipe. If you want
to try to defend the honor of your whore of a mother, sit
down and play. And the game's not over until *I* say we're
done.''

Icily lucid in his rage, Teagan had to acknowledge his
cousin was clever. His own prowess with both sword and
pistol were such that fighting his cousin was almost tanta-
mount to the earl's murder. But after the earl had offered
him such an insult, Teagan couldn't withdraw, no matter
what form was chosen to settle the business.

Teagan sat back down. ''Deal the cards.''

''Very well. Let's make it more interesting and triple the
stakes. Ah, have you not sufficient coin?'' the earl interrupted when Teagan started to protest. ''Save your worthless vowels for the tradesmen—I'll have none of them. But
you do have one item I'd not mind collecting. Let's add
that stallion of yours to the stake.'' Montford turned to his
friends with a laugh. ''Horseflesh is the only thing of value
the damned Irish have ever produced.''

Ailainn. Ailainn, almost as much friend as mount. Teagan would rather shoot the stallion than see him go to the earl. But truly, he had nothing else.

"So be it," Teagan replied through gritted teeth.

The earl smiled, a curve of the lips that held no warmth. "Done. Now, gather round, friends! Watch me send this blot on the family escutcheon back to the Dublin gutter where he belongs."

Chapter Eleven

Ruin. His total and irreversible ruin. That was what his cousin intended, Teagan realized.

Having hated him for years, why had Montford chosen this precise moment to strike?

The earl must have been keeping a closer watch on his detested half-Irish cousin than Teagan had imagined, for after the disastrous reverses of last month, his finances were at the lowest ebb they'd been since he'd begun his career as a gambler. Already pledged on the table along with Ailainn was the entire stake he had remaining.

Though his luck had improved of late, he'd curtailed his play the last few weeks, content to quit after only modest winnings, so as to rise early enough to escort Valeria Arnold about London. A small reserve remained back at his rooms, scarcely enough to cover this month's rent, and far less than he'd need to pay his other bills.

Should he lose tonight, word of it would begin to circulate practically before the last card hit the table. By next morning, every merchant to whom he still owed money would be at his door, with the constable on their heels if Teagan couldn't make good on his debts.

Prison. Disgrace.

If he could shake off his anger and play with all the skill he possessed—a skill he knew to be superior to his cousin's—he'd be able to stave off that catastrophe.

As long as capricious Lady Luck did not despise him as much as the earl his cousin.

"Sad as I am to disappoint you, Montford," Teagan said as the earl shuffled the deck, "you'll ne'er be the breaking of me. Should you carry off my blunt—a most improbable event—I can always take the king's shilling."

"About time you should. 'Twould end for good and all your pretensions to being a gentleman. Instead of preventing you, Grandpapa should have assisted your joining the rest of the gutter-born thieves and criminals in the army years ago. Now I, the grandson of his own blood, his heir," the earl continued, his voice growing strident, "he maligned for not wishing to purchase a commission. But his harlot daughter's only son? Oh no, *his* life was too precious to be risked fighting savages in the Americas."

As his cousin's words echoed in Teagan's incredulous ears, he scarcely noted their biting scorn. His thoughts whipped back to his searing final interview with his grandfather after his Oxford debacle. After excoriating him for bringing dishonor on his mother's name, the old man had refused Teagan's plea to purchase him a commission. He'd not inflict upon the army a cowardly Irish beggar's brat, the old earl had railed, adding that if Teagan tried to enlist as a common soldier, even under a false name, Lord Montford would have him found and cashiered out. After which the old man had had him ejected from the house.

Teagan had stalked away, vowing never again to ask his mother's family for anything.

Had his grandfather refused his request—as his cousin's words seemed to suggest—not out of contempt, but from fear of losing his only link to his beloved daughter?

"Why, gentlemen, he's so frozen with terror," Montford's mocking voice recalled him, "he can't even pick up his cards."

Teagan jerked his thoughts back to the present and examined his hand. Inattention now could force him to flee London, perhaps require him to join the army in truth.

Yet despite the dire choice he'd face were he to lose this round, the roiling mix of shock, doubt and disbelief, threaded through with a thin, tentative joy, forced him to voice the question churning in his head.

"You thought Grandpapa favored me? Is that why, though you've always known you would have everything— the title, wealth, power—you've always hated me?"

A sudden rage blazed in his cousin's blue eyes and he leaned close, his clipped, furious words pitched for Teagan's ears alone. "Aye, you. Spawn of a penniless Irish scoundrel. Everyone else knew what you were from the moment you arrived in England—why could Grandpapa never see it? How could he think a few paltry achievements would ever make you superior to me? 'Why can't you ride like Teagan?'" he said, mimicking an old man's tones. "'Why can't you shoot like Teagan?'"

With a growl Montford pushed away and slammed the first card down on the table. "Thank God the old fool died soon after your disgrace, before he was able to recall you. Though I doubt he'd be so proud of you now, were he here watching you be reduced to the stews from which you came. If," the earl added, smiling at Teagan as he took the first trick, "you don't get clapped in debtor's prison first."

Reeling from that second revelation, Teagan struggled to focus on the game. His grandfather had been on the point of recalling him? The old man had possessed a fearsome temper, and though Teagan had never known him to apologize for words or acts uttered in anger, he sometimes quietly attempted to make amends. Had he wished to be reconciled with his only daughter's son?

Perhaps it had been fear of having Teagan restored to the old earl's favor, rather than dislike, that had caused Jeremy Hartness to bar Teagan's entry into the Montvale townhouse that long-ago day. When, having heard his grandfather had been stricken and was not expected to live, he had put aside his pride and come back to see the old man one last time.

The horsewhip his cousin had brandished wouldn't have kept him out. Jeremy's assertion that another confrontation with Teagan would perhaps fatally tax their grandfather's rapidly failing strength had.

Montford smiled again as he won a second trick. *Focus on the present,* Teagan rebuked himself with disgust. If he weren't more careful, the earl would very soon have no need of skill to accomplish Teagan's ruin.

Had that been the purpose of Montford's unprecedented candor? To rattle Teagan out of his customary sangfroid?

The flicker of a glance at his cousin's impassive face told him nothing. Renewed fury settled Teagan's disordered thoughts. *Whatever ploys you use, you've chosen my ground, and you shall not win on it,* he silently vowed.

The room remained quiet, the attention of everyone present riveted on their table. Teagan narrowed his mind to calculating the statistical probability of the cards he needed being still in the deck, and predicting from his cousin's play the cards he held.

Teagan rallied to win the first hand, then lost the second. The earl, he had to admit, had gotten much better at analyzing his opponent.

Still, after Teagan drew for the decisive third hand, the tightness in his chest began to relax. Given what he held, he was reasonably sure of winning at last.

With cool confidence he laid down an ace—only to have his cousin trump it. To his surprise, the earl then led back with another off—from the one suit in which Teagan had only a single low card. To his growing dismay, with un-erring accuracy his cousin took control of the game, leading each play with a superior trump or a higher card in the suit, as if he had deduced the whole of Teagan's hand.

Teagan was going to lose.

As if from a great distance, he heard his cousin's shout of triumph as he threw down the last card.

"Done—and done in!" Montford crowed. "Make sure to send the horse before you slink out of town."

Weighted down by the enormity of the impending disaster, Teagan sat stunned, watching the face card his cousin had just played spin on its edge.

Like a runaway stallion, his mind raced pell-mell through the consequences of his impending loss. A lightning-fast, covert trip to his rooms to recover his few remaining coins before the news got out and the vultures descended, cutting off any escape but prison. Shame that he must betray his landlady's confidence in him by leaving her unpaid. A detached calculation of whether his coins would take him far enough from London to escape the magistrate. And if he made it away, whether he'd still retain enough to stake a renewed round of gaming.

The quixotic conclusion that perhaps he would have to enlist, after all.

But while those dark thoughts went swirling through his head, a darker shadow on the edge of the falling pasteboard suddenly captured his attention. While his cousin accepted the congratulations of his friends, Teagan leaned forward to seize it.

Even after he examined it more closely, he had difficulty believing the stunning conclusion. No wonder his cousin had been so confident of winning. The cards they'd been playing with were marked.

His cousin was rising, the other gentlemen slapping him

on the back. Teagan rummaged through the deck, finding on other pasteboard edges the same subtle indentations.

Idiot! He cursed his inattention, for though the marking system was not one he'd seen before, he should have found the earl's unexpected skill in this hand suspect early on, had he not allowed his cousin to rattle him by resurrecting old ghosts.

And then a sense of imminent triumph swelled his chest. 'Twas not Teagan who would be ruined tonight, but his duplicitous cousin.

Much was permitted the favored few who possessed wealth, title and privilege. A man might humiliate his wife by openly flaunting a mistress. Might beat his spouse and children, abuse his servants and retainers, neglect his lands, beggar his estates. But a gentleman never, ever cheated at cards.

To do so would mean expulsion from every club, social ostracism for both the offender and his kin, a shame that would dishonor his name for generations. Even the ignominy of a ruined gamester's suicide was less damaging to his family than the dishonor of his being found a cheat.

All those years of slights, insults, persecution were about to change on the edge of a spinning card.

But even as he opened his lips to proclaim his discovery, Teagan hesitated. His cousin could descend to the fiery pit with Teagan's fervent blessing. But this disgrace would ruin not just Jeremy Hartness, but his entire family.

His wife, a bland society matron of whom Teagan knew no ill except she—or her relations—had displayed the poor judgment to have her wedded to his cousin. Their young son now at Eton where, as Teagan well knew, the boys were even crueler than their elders to one they judged unfit.

And Jeremy Hartness's crime would besmirch the name of the grandfather who had apparently loved Teagan, the name of the mother he still cherished.

What good has being grandson of a Montford ever done you? he asked himself mockingly. But even as he gazed down at the evidence in his hands and chastised himself for being twenty varieties of a fool, his mind was already considering other options.

His cousin's fall would be a mighty one, but few would notice the final ruin of a man clinging to the edges of gentility. How could the ignominy attached to his name be worse? There were compensations, he thought with a bitter twist of the lips, for having no reputation left to lose.

If he could escape with his modest reserve, he could make his way somewhere else. Begin over again. Even join the army, if matters grew too desperate.

Would anyone mourn his disappearance from London? Surely not the brandy-reinforced occupants of such hells as Devil's Den. No one except the landlady he would, he vowed, at some point manage to reimburse.

And perhaps one sweet lady whose grief might be deepened to discover the man she'd insisted on believing a gentleman was in fact only the impecunious gambler everyone had claimed him to be.

Pain twisting in his chest at that thought, Teagan looked up. From across the table, amidst a cacophony of voices, cheers and catcalls, he saw Lord Riverton.

A frown on his brow, the older man met his gaze and jerked his chin toward the cards.

Riverton knew.

Teagan drew in a sharp breath. Before he could speak or move, Riverton reached out to snag the elbow of the earl, who'd just called for his coat and cane.

"Not so quickly, Montford. There's a small matter of the cards…" Lord Riverton let his words trail off.

Had it been Teagan who'd hailed him, his cousin probably would have brushed him off and walked away. But as a cabinet minister and one of the most highly placed men in England, Lord Riverton could not be ignored.

A cabinet minister renowned for his penetrating intellect, as well. As Montford turned to the older man, the triumph faded from his face, to be replaced by uneasiness. "The…cards, my lord?"

A calm sense of inevitability came over Teagan. *For you, Mama.* Giving Riverton a minute, negative shake of the head, Teagan rose. "The cards fell for you, Cousin."

Riverton returned a sharp look. Teagan met it steadily. Finally the older man nodded. "So it appears."

Relief washed over Montford's face. "Indeed. Good evening, my lord." Giving Riverton a deep bow, Teagan's cousin turned to leave.

"A word with you, Montford, if you please." Lord Riverton's quiet voice cut through the hubbub. While the earl froze in midstep, the cabinet minister turned to the friends who waited near the door. "Go along, gentlemen. Montford will join you later."

The earl looked back at Riverton, hesitating as if he wished to refuse but was unable to devise a sufficient excuse. Finally, summoning up a brittle smile, he faced his friends. "Get a table at White's and order up a bottle, if you please, Wexley. I'll be along shortly." His face paling beneath the smile, he turned to Riverton.

The cabinet minister motioned him to a table in the back corner of the room. "Over there, where we can be private. Fitzwilliams, you will accompany us."

For a few long moments, the earl stood motionless. Teagan had the grim satisfaction of watching a sheen of sweat appear on his cousin's brow. His fingers trembling slightly, the earl reached up to pull at his neckcloth, as if the material had suddenly grown too tight.

Then, carefully avoiding Teagan's gaze, he said, "My pleasure, Lord Riverton."

Teagan followed them to the table and sat where Riverton indicated. Though Teagan himself had chosen not to expose Montford, if Lord Riverton wished to reveal the bastard's perfidy, so be it.

A forced cheeriness in his tone, Montford began, "My lord, how can I be of..." At Riverton's unflinching stare his words trailed off and he swallowed hard.

After a long, tense silence the minister seemed content to prolong, Riverton said quietly, "You miserable little muckworm. Were it not for the respect in which I held your grandfather, I would have ordered that deck to be examined."

As the earl sputtered a protest, Riverton interrupted with icy contempt. "Spare me your excuses. And listen well. You beat your cousin at cards tonight, nothing more. If you or any of your friends spread tales of bankruptcy or ruination, I shall be compelled to reveal what I know. And though Society, hypocritical as it is, might dismiss an allegation coming from Mr. Fitzwilliams, I assure you the ton would take very seriously any such accusation made by me. I trust I've made myself clear?"

The earl moistened his lips. "My lord, I assure you—"

"Good. Remove yourself from my sight. And remain out of it." Riverton waved his hand toward the door.

The minister watched impassively as Teagan's cousin hurried off, then focused his penetrating regard on Teagan.

"A costly bit of honor, Mr. Fitzwilliams."

"Ah, milord," Teagan replied, exaggerating the lilt, "as anyone can tell ye, an Irish gambler has no honor."

Riverton lifted his brows, but made no reply. "A fine animal, your stallion. I shall offer to buy him from Montford. Naturally, he will sell the beast to me, so you needn't worry about his welfare."

A small sop, given the enormity of the catastrophe about

GET FREE BOOKS
and a
FREE GIFT WHEN YOU PLAY THE...

LAS VEGAS
GAME

Just scratch off the gold box with a coin. Then check below to see the gifts you get!

DETACH AND POST CARD TODAY! ▶

YES!
I have scratched off the gold box. Please send me my **4 FREE BOOKS** and **gift** for which I qualify. I understand that I am under no obligation to purchase any books as explained on the back of this card. I am over 18 years of age.

H4JI

Mrs/Miss/Ms/Mr	Initials	

BLOCK CAPITALS PLEASE

Surname

Address

Postcode

Worth TWO FREE BOOKS plus a BONUS Gift!

Worth TWO FREE BOOKS!

TRY AGAIN!

Visit us online at

www.millsandboon.co.uk

Offer valid in the U.K. only and is not available to current Reader Service subscribers to this series. Overseas and Eire please write for details. We reserve the right to refuse an application and applicants must be aged 18 years or over. Offer expires 30th April 2005. Terms and prices subject to change without notice. As a result of this application you may receive offers from Harlequin Mills & Boon® and other carefully selected companies. If you do not wish to share in this opportunity, please write to the Data Manager at the address shown overleaf. Only one application per household.

Mills & Boon® is a registered trademark owned by Harlequin Mills & Boon Limited. The Reader Service™ is being used as a trademark.

The Reader Service™ — Here's how it works:

Accepting the free books places you under no obligation to buy anything. You may keep the books and gift and return the despatch note marked 'cancel'. If we do not hear from you, about a month later we'll send you 4 brand new books and invoice you just £3.59* each. That's the complete price - there is no extra charge for postage and packing. You may cancel at any time, otherwise every month we'll send you 4 more books, which you may either purchase or return to us - the choice is yours.

*Terms and prices subject to change without notice.

THE READER SERVICE™
FREE BOOK OFFER
FREEPOST CN81
CROYDON
CR9 3WZ

NO STAMP
NECESSARY
IF POSTED IN
THE U.K. OR N.I.

to overwhelm him, but Teagan felt perversely comforted. ''Tis most grateful I'd be, milord.''

Amusement flickered in Riverton's eyes, and Teagan had the uncomfortable feeling that the older man knew his feckless gambler's pose for the sham it was. "Given the consequences, I have no doubt your cousin will keep mum about the events of this evening. Which should give you a few days' grace to gather your things and depart London before word of your…pecuniary difficulties gets out."

The heightened alertness that had sustained Teagan through the game began to ebb, and he felt suddenly weary. "Aye, my lord. Thank you for that, too."

Lord Riverton studied him. He seemed about to say more, but after a moment's hesitation, merely nodded. "Good night, Mr. Fitzwilliams."

Bidding Riverton goodbye in turn, Teagan rose and made his way into the night. His footsteps on the dark street seemed to echo like the muffled beat of the drums before an execution. Though Riverton was undoubtedly correct about the silence his cousin would maintain concerning the events of the evening, Teagan's long and intimate acquaintance with the less elevated strata of society told him that any one of a dozen other witnesses—waiters, footmen, the doorman—would quickly spread the titillating tale of this verbal duel between their betters.

By tomorrow, every tradesman in town to whom he owed money would be on Mrs. Smith's doorstep, probably followed by the constable. If Teagan wished to avoid the very real possibility of being clapped into debtor's prison, he'd best clear out his things and leave London tonight.

And go where?

Dark memories he normally succeeded in suppressing flashed through his mind. Clutching the fingers of his dying mother long after she'd gasped her last breath, as if his six-year-old hands could keep her from death's icy grip. Fear and blows and desperate hunger, replaced by wretched sickness on the heaving packet that had carried him across the Irish Sea. The kindly face of the clergyman who'd found him starving and half-frozen on the Dublin streets, assuring him the unknown relations to whom he was sending Teagan would welcome him home.

And what a welcome. His hopeful dream of joining a family had not long outlived the moment when the cousin of like age to whom he'd just been introduced—Jeremy, now Earl of Montford—punched him in the stomach.

A more recent memory, even more bitter, replaced that vision. Standing before his grandfather in the late earl's study, the old man's face contorted with rage as he uttered the last words Teagan ever heard him speak: ''Get out of my house and take your black Irish arse back to the devil that spawned you!''

He could go there, Teagan thought with macabre humor as he slipped upstairs to his rooms. Fearful that rumors might even now have begun to circulate, by the light of a single candle he quickly packed his few possessions and checked the pockets of all his waistcoats to augment the pitifully small store of coins he'd removed from his desk.

He paused a long moment in front of his books. Then, with a sigh, he mended a quill, pulled a bill from the stack in his drawer and penned a note on the back of it, instructing Mrs. Smith, with his apologies for the inconvenience, to sell the volumes and accept the money thus obtained in lieu of the rent he owed her.

In the bottom of the desk he came across his old dueling pistol. He checked the box and smiled without humor. He had only a few shots left, but if it came to that, one would be enough.

After adding the pistol to his other belongings, Teagan slung the saddlebag over his shoulder. He paused, taking a last look about his room, his eyes lingering on the copies of Homer, Virgil and Plato.

Not all his memories of this London sojourn would be bitter. He'd spent some quiet afternoons recapturing those lazy Oxford days when his life had been lived through the pages of his books, his future seeming securely pledged to the pursuit of scholarship.

And he'd spent some joyous mornings in the company of an intelligent, spirited, inquisitive beauty who'd challenged his mind, tantalized his body and touched his soul. His lovely Lady Mystery, whom he'd once halfheartedly tried to lure to these rooms. One of the very few people he'd met to whom his past and his family background truly seemed to mean nothing, who had taken Teagan as she found him—and seemed to like what she saw.

Desolation settled in his chest. Please God, he prayed, as he crept back down the stairs into the night, let it take several days for word of his ruination to spread to the ton and forever destroy her good opinion of him.

Chapter Twelve

Before quitting London, Teagan made one more stop, at the stables where he boarded Ailainn. The horse lifted his head and whickered as Teagan silently approached.

"It's good ears you have, my beauty," Teagan whispered, stroking the stallion's velvet muzzle. "I must leave you now, but Riverton will make you a good master. A blessing, that, for if I thought you were to go to a rider as ham-fisted as Montford, I might have to use one of my last shots on you, and then where would I be?"

The horse snorted and tossed his head, as if disagreeing.

"Ah, 'tis sorry I am to abandon you, my lovely, but I've no choice. Though Lord Riverton might forgive the theft, you're too striking to pass unnoticed, and the duns would find us too easy to follow."

Giving the stallion one last bit of sugar, Teagan stepped away, resisting the burning in his eyes. *"Taim i' ngra leat,"* he whispered.

Blindly he walked away, forcing his thoughts to the bargain he must strike at a livery stable on the outskirts of the city. He'd need a mount less flashy than Ailainn, and priced accordingly, to get him surreptitiously away.

As he exited the stable, a prickling of apprehension penetrated his depression. Instantly alert, he halted, sensing more than seeing a form in the shadows.

"Don't be reaching for your popper, now." A man's voice came out of the darkness. "I mean ye no harm. In truth, 'tis a proposition to yer benefit I've got for ye."

"Who are you?" Teagan demanded. "Step out where I can see you."

The man moved cautiously closer. In the dim light of a neighboring gas lamp Teagan could just make out the broken-nosed profile of a one-armed man, the buttons of his ragged uniform coat glinting in the gloom. The maimed rifleman he'd seen begging for coins in the meaner neighborhoods by the West India docks.

Teagan relaxed a little. "What do you want, soldier? I'm afraid I've no blunt to spare tonight."

"Boot's on t'other leg, sir! As it happens, I heared ye might be of a mind to earn some yerself."

Teagan smiled without humor. "Ah, how swiftly the news of disaster blows on the wind."

The soldier grinned back, a single tooth gleaming. "Aye, it rightly does. And knowin' how's you might not be wantin' to leave the city, with that purty little lady ye've been squiring about still residin' here and all, there's a gent I knows what thinks ye might be ripe for an occupation to get ye back in the ready."

"Which 'gent'?" Teagan asked, still marveling at the speed with which word had spread from Devil's Den.

"A gent with money in his pockets, and 'tis all ye need to know about him."

A job offered by a gentleman who wished to remain nameless was a dubious prospect, but Teagan wasn't in a position to be overly choosy. "What sort of occupation?"

"Nothin' too hard for an enterprisin' gallant like yerself what knows his way about the streets and the parlors, if ye take my meanin'. Ye've only to drop by the house of a government mort and pick up a case from his stables. If somewhat was to see ye nosin' about, ye can claim to be payin' a visit, which is the beauty of it, ye see. Take the case and fetch a horse from the livery I shows ye, and ride yer bundle to a barkeep in Dover. And keep your trapper shut after. Easy enough, eh? Do it right and quick, with no questions asked, and there'll be a bagful of guineas in it, with a promise of more.''

''And what's in the 'case' I'll be delivering?''

The soldier shrugged. ''No need of you knowin'.''

''Pick up a case—documents, probably—from a government official's house and carry them clandestinely to Dover,'' Teagan mused aloud. ''From which port they'll be smuggled over to France? I'm to be a spy, then?''

The solder pointed to his empty sleeve. ''Done gave me arm for bloody England at Badajoz, and what thanks did I get for it? Me mum was run off the land, me wife and baby starved, and 'tis no one wantin' to hire a one-armed bloke now. Nor has dear ol' England smiled on ye neither, eh?''

What *had* his mother's country—or her countrymen— ever done for Teagan? Why should he feel any loyalty to a land whose inhabitants, since the very day of his arrival on English soil, had despised him as Irish and inferior?

''Well, does ye want the job or no?''

A few midnight rides. The passing on of a handful of anonymous dispatches that would probably never do anyone any harm. And no one would ever know.

He would earn enough to stave off his creditors and stay in the city, build up a stake and resume gaming. Remain in London, where he could devise some way to outflank Lady Farrington and see Valeria Arnold again.

And grasp some small, satisfying revenge on a society that allowed men like his cousin to flourish, while maimed soldiers and honest Irishmen struggled to survive.

But even if no one else ever learned of it, Teagan would

know. And betrayal, even of a nation to whom he owed no loyalty at all, was still dishonor.

It would make him no better than the cousin he despised—make him unworthy of the trust Valeria Arnold had so gallantly and mistakenly placed in his character.

"Tell your 'gent' I'm not his man."

"Is ye sure of it? 'Tis easy blunt to earn for a bruisin' rider like yerself. Iffn' I could ride with this arm, I'd be doin' it meself."

"I'm sure. Now, I'm sorry, but I must be out of London by first light."

To his surprise, the soldier smiled once again. "Aye, if ye be set on the straight 'n narrow, I expects ye must." After giving Teagan a salute with his remaining arm, the soldier melted off into the shadows.

Teagan turned up his collar against the light rain that had started to fall. Already the dense gloom of night was lightening in the east. He wasn't sure how far north his coins would carry him, but if he wished to escape at all, he must get himself to that livery stable forthwith.

A chill rain was spattering the London streets as Lady Winterdale's luxurious traveling carriage bore Valeria away from Grosvernor Square at dawn. A warm brick at her feet and a thick fur wrap across her lap to keep out the damp and chill, Valeria leaned against the padded squabs and numbly watched the now-familiar streets pass by.

So driven had she been to leave by morning, she'd instructed Molly to remain in London to assist Mercy in packing the large barouche with the rest of the belongings the housekeeper had informed her Lady Winterdale always carried when she removed to Winterpark. Hanging on to the shreds of her rapidly disintegrating patience, Valeria had then attempted to soothe the butler's scandalized horror over the fact that she would be traveling without even a maid.

Her early departure also spared her further meeting with Lady Farrington, who had nearly fallen into another spasm when Valeria stopped by last evening to bid her goodbye. Protesting that Valeria was too distraught to make so important a decision wisely, Lady Farrington begged her not to leave. But determined to slip out of town before the ton—and helpful "friends" like Lady Evelyn and the gentlemen from her shopping excursion—learned of her intent, Valeria refused to delay. Her grandmamma's final wish was that she remove to Winterpark, and go she would.

She'd been up late supervising the final packing. But despite her fatigue, after finally reaching the haven of her bed, she'd found sleep eluded her.

It wasn't grief, or nervousness about the challenges awaiting her at Winterpark, that kept her from claiming a few hours' rest before beginning her long and doubtless tiring journey. No, pathetic fool that she was, the watchfulness that had her starting at every small sound, stirring to every servant's muffled footfall, came from the idiotish hope that James had located Teagan Fitzwilliams and was bringing a reply to her note.

Of course, the fitful sleep into which she finally fell was not disturbed by any such event. Mr. Fitzwilliams probably hadn't yet returned to his rooms, if James had indeed managed to locate them. Even had Teagan received her missive, there was no reason to believe he'd feel moved to make immediate reply.

Such foolish behavior only proved, Valeria concluded, watching the drizzle turn to a steady downpour that obscured everything along the road north behind a damp gray veil, that Grandmamma had once again been wise by suggesting she leave the city—and its proximity to the all-too-fascinating Mr. Fitzwilliams. She badly needed the perspective time and distance could provide.

The great wealth that would allow her the freedom to choose her future was now hers—but at the cost, she thought with a renewed ache of sadness, of the one whose sagacity might have guided her in that choice.

What did she want?

The extremely rich Lady Arnold would be forgiven for claiming the escort of Teagan Fitzwilliams on jaunts about the city. Should she arrive at a ton function on his arm, or invite him to her own, however, she would almost certainly subject him to being snubbed, or worse. The great wealth to which she owed her own acceptance would not be sufficient to purchase his social redemption. In fact, her seeming to take up with him now that she *was* rich would confirm, rather than rehabilitate, his reputation.

He would never be thought a respectable suitor, even if he were interested in such a role. 'Twas most unlikely his haphazard youth or his erratic life since leaving Oxford had provided him either experience in or a desire for so permanent a relationship as wedlock. But as a lover…?

The almost tactile tension that simmered between them whenever they were together suggested he would be quite willing to renew the promise of passion they'd forged in the hay barn. Would an undoubtedly glorious but probably fleeting affair with him be enough?

And how would one affect her other choices? A fair-minded gentleman like Sir William might tolerate her friendship with a rogue. Hypocritical as it might be, however, though a widowed *gentleman* might set up a mistress without prejudice to his eventual matrimonial intentions, a matron who took so notorious a lover would likely forfeit any chance of later marrying a man of character. Which would also mean giving up the possibility of an ever-broadening circle of children, friends and grandchildren—

that community of kinship and comfort Valeria forfeited when her parents, her brother and now Lady Winterdale died.

Was a passionate affair, no matter how glorious, worth accepting permanent loneliness for the rest of her life?

Or would she do better to think seriously of accepting the offer Sir William had all but formally made? He'd been a steady, sympathetic presence all through these days of loss and strain. Never once had he intruded upon her grief, nor had he sought to use his privileged position as a close family friend to further his suit.

And she knew beyond doubt *he* was not interested only in her newfound wealth.

If his kisses, thus far untasted, should not stir in her the intensity of reaction of Teagan Fitzwilliams', they would at least have the advantage of permanence. And though no instantaneous, visceral attraction drew her to him, she found his tall, well-made figure attractive, and could easily envision progressing from friendship to a more intimate relationship.

As the miles rolled past in a continued bleak downpour, the same arguments circled around and around until her tired temples ached. Finally, with a burst of anger, she put all such thoughts aside.

Sir William was ensconced in London, and heaven knew when or if she would ever see Mr. Fitzwilliams again. With increased appreciation for Lady Winterdale's perspicacity, Valeria vowed to throw all her energy into mastering her new position as mistress of Winterpark.

Fatigue finally driving the whirling thoughts from her mind, Valeria was dozing in the early dusk of the rainy late afternoon when the coach jerked to a sudden halt, nearly throwing her off the seat.

She righted herself and scrambled to the window, but

could see nothing through the steady rain but a thick stand of trees. "Wilkins, what is it?" she called out.

"An oak be blockin' the road, my lady," came the reply. "The Crown and Kettle's not but a few miles ahead. I've sent Robert to bring back a lad to help us clear it. Don't you worrit none, we'll make the inn afore nightfall."

The coachman doffed his cap and walked over to soothe the restive horses. Valeria settled back on her seat, impatient with the delay and already anxious for the warm fire and hot food awaiting them at the inn.

After a surprisingly short interval, she heard the clatter of approaching hoofbeats. Wilkins appeared by the coach door, his brow creased in a frown.

"Perhaps we be closer to the inn than I thought, for—"

The loud report of a pistol drowned out the rest.

His face a study in dismay, the coachman scrambled for the box. A rough voice shouted, "Reach fer that blunderbuss, laddie, and ye're a dead man."

Wilkins froze.

"Hands over yer heads, now, nice 'n easy."

They were being robbed? Indignation coursed through Valeria, followed by a burst of exasperation. She'd traveled by coach from Bombay to Calcutta with her papa, the pistols he'd taught her to use when she was but twelve years old never far from her hand. But so befuddled had she been while packing last night, she'd neglected to get them from the trunk in which they'd been stored in London.

While she frantically considered how she might turn any of the commonplace objects within the coach into a weapon, a burly man in a frieze coat, his face obscured by a muffler, appeared beside the vehicle. Pointing a nasty-looking pistol at Wilkins, who quickly raised his hands above his head as ordered, he motioned the coachman aside.

"I'm gonna open the door slow, little lady. 'Tis a filthy

night, so don't be botherfyin' Mad Jack aweepin' or afaintin'. Jest hand out yer baubles, and I'll be off.''

In the next instant Valeria heard the report of another pistol, followed by an anguished wail. As she ducked away from the window, a figure hurtled out of the darkness and slammed into the frieze-coated man at knee level, knocking him off balance.

His pistol discharged skyward as he went down. From her position pressed against the door panel, she heard scuffling, gasps of breath and muffled curses, then the crack of bone against bone.

Was the newcomer rescuer or accomplice? Had the cry of a man injured come from her coachman—or another attacker?

Bracing herself in a crouch, hands gripping the only weapon she could devise, Valeria waited.

A second later, the coach door was thrown open to frame a mud-spattered man, his thick hair dripping rain. ''Are you unhurt, ma'am?'' he asked.

Valeria stared into familiar golden eyes whose expression of concern turned to a shock as keen as her own. Her grip slackened on the brick she'd been about to heave.

''Teagan?'' she gasped.

Chapter Thirteen

Wilkins appeared behind Teagan before he could answer. "Cor, didn't recognize ye at first, Mr. Fitzwilliams! Thank the lord ye happened upon us when ye did!"

"You are unharmed, Lady Arnold?" When Valeria nodded, Teagan turned back to the coachman. "'Tis thankful I am as well, Wilkins! Help me immobilize this brigand before he can attempt any more mischief."

As she watched the two men begin to secure the robber with a bit of rope Wilkins produced, Valeria felt suddenly dizzy. With more speed than grace, she sat back on the padded seat. "Allow me to offer my own thanks for your timely intervention, Mr. Fitzwilliams," she called down.

Occupied in knotting ropes about the wrists of her still-unconscious attacker, Teagan nodded. "'Twas my privilege, Lady Arnold."

Her other groom trotted up. "Splendid shot, sir! Winged through the shoulder the one what was guardin' me, and sent the bastard bleating back into the woods—beggin' your pardon, ma'am," he finished, flush-faced.

"I disremember ever seein' a move like how ye took this bounder off his feet, neither," Wilkins chimed in. "A right pretty hook ye dealt 'im!"

"Thank you, gentlemen. The streets sometimes prove a more useful training ground than Gentleman Jackson's. Harness our 'guest' to the back of the coach, please."

While the two servants dragged off the robber, Teagan turned back to Valeria. His eyes widened, and with a wry smile, he extracted from her unresisting fingers the warming brick she still held. "A bit crude, isn't it?"

"Perhaps, but 'twas the best I could contrive, considering I was too totty-headed to bring my pistols."

"Quite enterprising! But since you are safe, let me leave you and help these fellows get your coach underway. Wrap back up, now, before you catch a chill."

He lifted one hand, his eyes warming, and for a moment Valeria thought he meant to touch her cheek. But abruptly the glow faded and he backed away.

"Mr. Fitzwilliams!" she called after him. "When you have finished, please rejoin me! I should like to hear your account of the attack."

Another shouted "halloo" told her Robert must have returned from the inn. Pulling the fur wrap up to her chin against the damp, Valeria settled back on her seat. Her mind busy with speculation, she scarcely heard the distant murmur of voices as the men moved the obstructing tree.

How had Teagan Fitzwilliams ended up on the Great North Road? She'd had no indication he meant to leave London. Of course, she'd not seen him for over a week.

Had he received her note before his departure? Surely...surely he hadn't been following her!

She immediately dismissed so ridiculous a notion. But why had he left, and by what means? She'd seen no horse.

Impatient to learn more, she had to clench her hands in her muff to keep herself from climbing out to check the coachmen's progress. Finally, as the gray afternoon dissolved into black, Mr. Fitzwilliams returned.

"You're now ready to proceed. I'm honored to have been of service." He made her a bow.

Surely he didn't mean to simply…leave! "Please ride with me, Mr. Fitzwilliams. You've not yet relieved my curiosity about the attack and how you came upon it."

For a moment she thought he'd refuse. Then, with a short laugh, he shook his head. "Sure, and any other lady would have fallen into palpitations. Whereas you, Lady Arnold, likely wish to know the make of the pistol the brigand used and just where I wounded his accomplice."

She smiled back. "And how you managed it. Please, do ride with me at least as far as the inn."

He eyed the padded seat dubiously. "'Tis soaked through I be, and muddy besides."

Which meant he must also be chilled to the bone, she realized. He ought to be out of the rain. "My dear sir, had you not fortuitously happened upon us, I would have lost my jewels and my purse, if not much more! I believe I can forgive your leaving a bit of damp in my coach." She patted the seat beside her. "Please."

Still he hesitated. "How could I refuse so gracious a lady?" he said at last.

The words, the smile were as they should be, but the timing and tone of them, the odd hesitations in his speech ever since she'd recognized him, sent a message of alarm to all Valeria's senses. Something was not right with Teagan Fitzwilliams, something beyond the odd coincidence of so unexpectedly encountering him on the road.

As he eased himself into the coach, Valeria noted that under his sodden cloak, he still wore evening dress. She'd lit the coach's lamps while the men moved the tree, and in their light she could see his mud-spattered face was unshaved, his eyes red rimmed, as if he'd not slept in many hours. It appeared he had left London this morning without even having changed his clothes.

He sank back against the squabs and closed his eyes. An air of strained exhaustion surrounded him, as if he had reached the very limits of his physical and mental reserves. She did not think his intervention in the robbery could be the sole reason for it.

What had happened? She opened her lips to ask, then closed them. Tread cautiously, instinct told her.

"Since we can now be private, I shall avail myself of your first name, as we did in London. How did you come to be in this vicinity, Teagan? I did not see your horse."

He opened his eyes. "The animal pulled up lame some miles back, I'm afraid. I was leading him when I heard the first pistol shot."

She noted he did not answer her first question. "Not your fine stallion, I hope!"

"No, I—" He stopped abruptly, and some fleeting emotion passed over his face before he continued. "I left Ailainn back in London. 'Twas a job horse, poor beast."

"You heard the shot, and then…?"

"Grabbed my pistol and crept to the clearing. Downing a tree to block the road is an old robber's trick. Seeing there were but two of them, and the coach door not yet opened, I knew 'twould be safe for me to…interrupt."

"Safe to—" She gasped. "You might have been killed!"

He shook his head. "With the weather so foul, they weren't expecting outside aid, and I was able to approach quite close. Clipping the accomplice was mere target practice, and once I knocked down the brigand at the coach door, I knew with your groom and coachman, it would be three of us against their two."

"I think you're incredibly brave. Most men would have kept to the shadows and hoped to remain unnoticed."

At her fervent tone, he seemed almost to…wince. "I'm no hero, Valeria," he said quietly.

Once more the feeling invaded her that something awful had occurred, and once more she had to restrain herself from asking what. "You have certainly shown yourself one to me. You are...traveling north?"

"To Harrowgate, I expect."

"Then you must be planning to break your journey at the Crown and Kettle, since Wilkins tells me it is the best hostelry for miles. Won't you join me for dinner? 'Tis the least I could offer you, as my rescuer."

She waited for the smile, the polished reply full of teasing innuendo that the charming Mr. Fitzwilliams would normally have returned. Instead, he clenched his jaw and looked away. Her alarm deepened.

"Teagan?"

He looked back, his smile forced. "I suppose I'm in no position to refuse your kind offer."

"I would enjoy your company," she said softly. "I've...missed the chats we shared in London."

He straightened abruptly. "Excuse me! I have not yet expressed my sympathy on your recent grievous loss. That is, I expect you didn't get my note."

He had written? Joy made her heart leap. "No! When did you—"

"No matter. Doubtless you left before it could be delivered. I *am* sorry, Valeria."

"Thank you. I grew to be...very fond of her."

She fell silent, a silence that stretched between them, a silence the always witty, ever entertaining Mr. Fitzwilliams would normally have broken with some clever question or teasing inquiry.

Finally Valeria said, "I...sent you a note as well. Last evening. To tell you I was leaving London for Winterpark, Lady Winterdale's country home. 'Twas her last request that I go there immediately."

He nodded. "I'm sorry, but I did not receive it. I—my landlady—was not in when I last stopped by my rooms."

"Do you make a long visit in Harrowgate?"

"Perhaps. I'm not yet sure." He sighed deeply and ran a hand through his sodden hair. "Ah, Valeria, I might as well confess what you've no doubt already surmised. I lost badly last night, so badly I cannot meet my obligations in London. I had to quit the city forthwith."

Leaving behind even his beloved stallion? "I see," she said, choosing her words with care. "And you go to Harrowgate on a repairing lease?"

"Yes. I really ought not to dine with you this evening. There's certain to be dice or cards in the taproom, and…and I ought to begin that repair immediately."

His funds must be limited indeed if he dare not wait even a single night before attempting to recoup his fortunes. Small wonder she sensed about him such an air of weary desperation.

Suddenly she realized how truly alone he was. Even in her darkest days at Eastwinds after Hugh's death, though bereft of her beloved family, she still had duties to perform, retainers who were also friends, and a home to call her own.

Since he had no family worthy of the name, perhaps a friend could help. Yet because they *were* friends, how it must gall his pride for her to see him in such dire straits. If she wished to assist him, she would have to go about it indirectly.

"Having journeyed all day," she said at last, "I'm both fatigued and famished. Robert will have ordered up rooms and a meal when he stopped at the inn for assistance, so I expect to dine right after arriving. Would you not spare me the fate of eating alone? Since I'll be retiring immediately after, you would still have time for a full evening's…activities."

Once again he made no quick rejoinder, added no flirtatious offer to assist her in retiring. Instead, a slight smile curved his lips. "You are kind, Lady Arnold."

Her concern deepening, she cast about for some means to dispel the grim resignation that clouded his countenance and colored his voice.

"I believe the inn is a several-mile journey. Shall we continue the discussion we began at Tower Green about Mary, Queen of the Scots? Is it true the Irish would have supported her, against Elizabeth?"

"Sure, and the Irish have always rallied round any who oppose England," he replied, a flicker of interest stirring in his exhaustion-glazed eyes. "Though I've no doubt, had that lady been more astute and ended up on the throne, the lads across the sea would have opposed her as well."

For the remainder of the short drive, Valeria engaged him in a discussion of English politics, and Teagan gradually recovered some of his normal, easy manner.

His reserve returned when they reached the inn. As he handed her down from the coach, however, the front door of the establishment opened and the landlord hurried out, followed by a plump, red-faced lady and half a dozen men.

"Welcome, Lady Arnold!" the innkeeper called. "And a hearty welcome also to the gallant gentleman who foiled Mad Jack! Mr.—"

"Teagan Fitzwilliams," that gentleman replied with a bow as the men from the taproom shouted and clapped.

"Joey, my stable boy—he helped move the tree that blocked your carriage, my lady—rode on ahead and told us of the ambush," the landlord said as he advanced toward her. "Lucky ye be that Mr. Fitzwilliams came upon ye, Lady Arnold! Mad Jack's a fearsome customer, and has given the local magistrate the slip for weeks now."

The landlord reached her side and bowed. "Such a frightening experience! My wife has your room and a hot posset ready, if you'd like to retire immediately, and will send supper up in a trice. Mr. Fitzwilliams, allow me and the neighborhood to offer you dinner and a round.''

The landlord's expression of sympathy provided Valeria a perfect opportunity to crystallize the sketchy plan she'd been formulating. ''Thank you, sir,'' she replied, trying to sound faint and anxious. ''My nerves are sadly overcome.''

Ignoring Teagan's start of surprise, she continued. ''Although I had intended to remain here until my maid and baggage catch up to us, this episode has so distressed me I am most uneasy about the rest of the journey. Mr. Fitzwilliams,'' she said, turning to him, ''I expect you plan to set out tomorrow. I will advance my own departure, if I can impose upon you to escort me the rest of the way to Winterpark. It would greatly ease my mind, and I'm sure my servants would appreciate your support.''

''Indeed, sir,'' Wilton called down, doffing his cap. ''James done told us you was a right'un. The boys 'n me'd be honored if ye'd travel on with us.''

The landlord's wife stepped over to pat Valeria's arm. ''You poor, poor dear! 'Tis a wonder you didn't swoon dead away! I certainly hope the kind gentleman can delay his journey long enough to assist you.''

Teagan looked over at Valeria, eyebrows raised at this sudden attack of nerves. She lowered her lashes demurely.

''If it will make the lady easier in her mind, of course I must do so,'' he replied, subtle irony in his tone.

The assembled crowd murmured their approval.

''Thank you, Mr. Fitzwilliams,'' Valeria replied. ''I am now even more deeply in your debt. Mrs....''

''Gowan, ma'am,'' the innkeeper's wife answered.

''Mrs. Gowan, will you pack us a basket of victuals and fetch me in the morning when Mr. Fitzwilliams is ready?''

''Certainly, my lady.''

''Then with thanks to all of you, gentlemen, I shall retire. Until the morning, Mr. Fitzwilliams?''

For a long moment Teagan fixed her with a quizzical gaze, as if trying to determine just what sort of rig she was running. Then he bowed and took her outstretched fingers to kiss. "Until morning, Lady Arnold."

Amid clapping and cheers from the onlookers, she followed the innkeeper's wife into the building.

Though regretting the loss of Teagan's company during dinner, Valeria was pleased at the success of her stratagem. If she could just keep him occupied on the journey until he lost that frighteningly desperate air…

Perhaps she might even persuade him to remain for a few days at Winterpark. A blast of warmth entirely unrelated to her gratitude for his rescue blazed through her at the thought.

His belly full of the best dinner he'd had in weeks and his head woozy from the drinks raised in his honor, much later that night Teagan walked unsteadily up the stairs to the bedchamber the innkeeper had insisted he take for the evening. To cap off the night, jingling in his pockets was a small stack of coins he'd won off the local magistrate, who'd been happy to lose his blunt to the man who'd relieved him of the problem of Mad Jack.

From its beginning, with Teagan reduced to the most desperate conditions he'd experienced since being cast out of his grandfather's town house ten years ago, this day had improved beyond imagining. When his job horse had pulled up lame, leaving him soaked, stranded and near penniless by the side of the road, he'd tethered the poor beast in the woods, pulled out his pistol case and loaded the weapon, nearly convinced that the Almighty was trying to tell one Irish drifter it was time to return to his celestial home.

Then he'd heard the pistol shot, and the rest had been automatic. In his comings and goings in the meaner neighborhoods, he'd seen too many petty thugs like Mad Jack to stand by and allow him to abuse a lady, even an arrogant English aristocrat who probably deserved whatever punishment the brigand had intended to mete out.

And then to discover the carriage belonged to Valeria! It seemed odd that she would have rushed out of the city, despite the folderol about following Lady Winterdale's last request. Surely it would have made more sense to remain in London, attended by the solicitous Sir William and the hordes of other suitors who would find ways to entertain the newly rich widow, despite her being in deep mourning.

And why had she practically compelled him to escort her to Winterpark? With a humiliation that made his face burn in the darkness, he knew she was too intelligent not to have understood far more about his true circumstances than he'd admitted in his one cryptic utterance. Did she mean to bid him begin his "repairing lease" at Winterpark?

The notion of a few days' respite was all too attractive. He couldn't remember the last time he'd slept a whole night through. The very idea that he must begin gaming again with his reserves so slim that every coin must be counted, every wager carefully calculated in order to avert disaster, made his stomach churn with revulsion.

He remembered only too vividly his original precarious climb out of penury. Endless nights of slowly building a stake, followed by the terror of unexpected reverses that could wipe out a month's worth of gains in an evening. The constant uncertainty, the distasteful necessity of cajoling drunks, deflecting the malicious and forcing himself to win from lads too green and green-faced to be able to count the cards in their hands.

Teagan reached the landing and stumbled into his room, then began pulling off his still-damp garments. One coin from tonight's precious winnings he'd expended to have the innkeeper's wife extract a change of clothes from his soggy saddlebags to air out and press for tomorrow, and another for the hot water to bathe and shave with in the morning. It seemed an eternity since he'd last felt clean and dry.

Stripped down, he dropped wearily onto the softness of the bed. *Mhuire,* but he hated the necessity of beginning again. Ten years ago, the indignity of it had been blunted by rage and heartache over Evangeline's duplicity, the ruin of his career and the unfairness of his exile. Fueled by anger and grief, he'd careened through the first few months almost unaware of what he did.

And made mistakes he now regretted. But that excess of emotion had burned itself to cinders long ago. This time he had no inclination to mask the bitterness of his descent with sweetly false matrons and quantities of strong drink.

What choice did he have but to continue gaming? He leaned back against the headboard, supporting his aching head on his hands. 'Twas amusing, really. Even were he finally ready to concede victory to his cousin by relinquishing his last pretensions to gentility, having been raised as a gentleman, he knew no trade by which he could make a living.

There was gaming, the army—or marrying a rich woman like Valeria Arnold.

Valeria, who'd been both friend and lover. The mere thought of her in the barn at Eastwoods still had the power to speed his pulses and harden his body in an instant.

The blaze of attraction that had ignited in Yorkshire still smoldered between them every time they met. In London Teagan had teased her about it, daydreamed of its fiery potential. Had hoarded the possibility of once again claiming her, with the greedy pleasure of a small child hiding a sweetmeat, delighted by knowing it was his, to devour whenever he chose. With little effort, Teagan knew, he could persuade her to become his lover again, and under the potent spell of passion, probably bewitch her into wed-lock.

Thereby solving his financial woes forever.

The idea of using her like that revolted him.

With a bitter bark of laughter, Teagan sat back up. A fine, proper rogue he was. Too proud to enlist in the army, too principled to perform a possibly treasonous task, too squeamish to seize the solution that would set him up for life. Bleating and moaning about having to dirty his hands once again with gaming, the only other option open to him.

Of course, there was always the pistol.

An equally disturbing idea suddenly struck him.

Perhaps Valeria Arnold had a very different reason for coercing his escort.

Since he'd last seen her, the balance between them had shifted. Lady Arnold was no longer owner of a barely prof-itable sheep farm, a fellow orphan and shabby-genteel out-sider tolerated at the edges of the ton. Possessed of great wealth and the influence that accompanied it, she could now command a leading role in Society.

If she invited him to linger, would it be as the friend who had explored London with him? Or as other rich ma-trons had before her, would she offer him the bounty of her home in exchange for his performance in her parlor and her boudoir, until the novelty of his attractions paled?

Destroying the magic of what they'd shared by turning it into a transaction driven by lust and power?

His mind rebelled at the thought. The honesty, purity and intelligence his Lady Mystery had displayed at every meet-ing were not a sham. She'd not insisted on seeing him just to spite her chaperone, had not been merely toying with him all those mornings they explored London, sharing ideas and laughter. From initial attraction, they'd come to know and like each other. She respected him—had she not dem-onstrated that on numerous occasions?

But she'd not then been a rich English matron.

Was it in fact Lady Farrington who'd rebuffed his calls and notes after Lady Winterdale's death? Or, with her position assured, had Lady Arnold decided it was no longer politic to be seen with Teagan…at least not in London?

Not for many years had someone from English society seemed to reach out to a lonely Irish outcast, to solicit his opinions, admire his ideas and value his person. He must not forget how that interlude with Evangeline had ended.

Indeed, every hope he'd ever cherished had turned out to be false: finding a family, winning Evangeline's love, pursuing a career as a scholar. 'Twas idiocy to let himself believe that Valeria Arnold, now that she possessed wealth and position, would treat Teagan Fitzwilliams in the same manner as when she'd been the impecunious Lady Arnold.

Wasn't it?

His eyes burned and his head ached dully. *Mhuire,* he'd think no more on it. Tomorrow he'd escort Lady Arnold to Winterpark as promised.

He only wished his chest didn't ache with apprehension that his beloved image of Lady Mystery, like every other illusion he'd cherished save that of his mother's love, was about be shattered by reality's iron fist.

Chapter Fourteen

Late the following afternoon, Valeria gazed out the window of her coach at the gatehouse beyond the tall iron entry portals of Winterpark. Her new home.

She took a deep breath and tried to stifle the nervousness fluttering in her belly. For the first time, she wished she had waited at the inn for Mercy and her baggage. Through all the many changes in her life she'd had her old nurse at her side. Coming now as mistress to the new household whose respect she must win, she sorely missed the comfort of her friend's presence.

Part of her unease stemmed from her uncertainty over what to do about Teagan Fitzwilliams. The slight relaxation in his manner during their drive yesterday had disappeared once they reached the inn, and his behavior today had been even more distant. He'd declined her offer to accompany her in the coach, preferring instead to hire another mount and ride beside the carriage.

She'd heard him trading quips and conversation with the coachman—and had been ashamed by the pang of envy that provoked in her. Though Teagan had politely accepted a share of the lunch Mrs. Gowan had packed for them, he'd chosen to tie his mount behind the coach and climb up on the box beside Wilkins to eat it.

The remote and silent stranger he'd become was so far removed from the engaging Teagan she'd thought she knew that she was no longer sure whether he needed or would accept anything more from her. However, as she girded herself to take up her new duties, she decided she would still extend to him the hospitality of Winterpark. Good breeding alone dictated that, since he'd been gracious enough to delay his plans in order to escort her home, she should invite him to remain as long as he wished. He could then accept or refuse as he chose.

The idea of him cooly declining and riding out of her life without a backward glance, as he had once before, was so dismaying she thrust it from her mind.

The carriage was now traveling down the wide graveled drive Wilkins had described, which after about a mile circled in a large arc around the front lawns of Winterpark Manor itself. Stilling another anxious tremor, she focused her thoughts on planning how best to greet her new staff.

In the fading light of the late spring day she noted the drive was well kept, the parkland stretching out from it neatly scythed. Of course, she'd expected that Lady Winterdale's favorite property would be perfectly maintained, ready at any moment should that exacting lady pay an unannounced visit. As the carriage began to round a wide curve, Valeria thrust her head out the window to get her first glimpse of the house, and caught her breath.

Centered on a tall rise, the dark bulk of what must be forestland behind it, the building glittered in the distance with a summer firefly twinkling of lights. With its dignified grandeur and the beckoning glow from its myriad of mullioned windows, for an instant it seemed to Valeria as if the spirit of Lady Winterdale herself were present to wel-

come her. Her chest tightened with a bittersweet mingling
of gratitude and grief.

As the carriage halted beside a large brick portico, a
liveried footman ran over to let down the steps. "Welcome
to Winterpark, my lady," he said, assisting her out.

Valeria murmured her thanks and looked over at the
handful of retainers who had trotted up to greet Wilkins,
tend the horses and begin unstrapping the baggage.

Teagan dismounted and handed the reins to a waiting
groom. "'Tis a lovely new home you have, Lady Arnold."

"Yes," she replied, nerves once again on edge. "Shall
we go in?"

He nodded and followed her up the entry stairs. An aus-
tere personage in black livery, the butler by his manner and
carriage, opened the massive front door to admit them.

"Lady Arnold," he said with a bow as they entered. "On
behalf of the staff, may I welcome you to Winterpark. I
trust your journey was a pleasant one?" His glance slid to
Teagan. "You've brought guests, my lady?"

"Yes. Giddings, is it not? Mr. Fitzwilliams, an acquaintance from London, assisted me after my carriage was at-
tacked yesterday near Dade's Run."

Amid the exclamations of distress from the butler and
the two attendant footmen, she continued. "No one was
injured, thanks to this gentleman's timely intervention, but
my nerves were sorely shaken. Wishing to reach Winterpark as quickly as possible, I prevailed upon Mr. Fitzwilliams to escort me immediately. My maid is following with
the rest of the baggage."

Giddings gave Teagan another bow. "Our thanks to you,
sir, for rescuing our mistress! The housekeeper, Mrs.
Welsh, is supervising the preparation of your bedchambers
and will wait upon you shortly, my lady."

"Thank you, Giddings. Given the lateness of the hour

and my fatigue, I should prefer to see only you and Mrs. Welsh today and meet the rest of the staff tomorrow.''

''As you wish. When should you like dinner served?''

Valeria stole a glance at Teagan. He stood silently studying her, a sort of guarded expectancy in his eyes.

Perhaps he was merely exhausted. He could not have had much sleep the last few days, and had been in the saddle since early morning.

''Mr. Fitzwilliams, after your many kindnesses, please forgive my being such a poor hostess, but I should really prefer a tray in my rooms tonight.''

The butler bowed. ''Of course, Lady Arnold. Shall I show you both to your chambers?''

''I would like a brandy in the parlor first,'' Teagan said, avoiding Valeria's glance.

''Certainly. Robbin?'' The butler nodded at a footman, who sprang to attention. ''Show Mr. Fitzwilliams to the parlor and pour his cognac. Robbin will convey your dinner order to the kitchens whenever you are ready, sir.''

''I shall bid you good evening, then, Mr. Fitzwilliams,'' Valeria said. ''I remain greatly in your debt. Although I shall be much occupied the next few days assuming my duties here, please feel free to remain at Winterpark as long as your plans permit. I'm sure Giddings and the staff will extend to you every courtesy.''

He raised an eyebrow, as if doubting her words. ''Your offer is most kind. Perhaps I shall take you up on it.''

His tone, too, seemed almost…mocking. Uncertain what to read from it, Valeria hesitated. Finally, conscious of the waiting butler, she said merely, ''Good night, Mr. Fitzwilliams.''

''My lady,'' he replied with a deep bow.

Valeria followed Giddings to the stairs, conscious of Teagan's gaze still fixed upon her back. Whether he chose to stay—or leave—was up to him. But after his puzzling behavior of the last two days, she could not help feeling a distressingly acute sense of…loss. Evidently the friendship she thought they'd forged in London had been only an illusion of her overhopeful imagination.

He'd outflanked her first offer, if such it had been, Teagan thought as he fought to hold open his eyes and finish the brandy he'd ordered. With him being shown to his rooms well after she retired, if she had intended to convey, by word or gesture, her willingness to have him join her in her suite, she'd now have no opportunity.

Would she have extended such an invitation?

He still couldn't quite believe she would. But after deliberately keeping his distance all day so as to avoid having her say or infer something that might confirm his worst suspicions, he hadn't been able to prevent himself from ordering the cognac. Thus guaranteeing that his faith in her honesty could remain unbroken at least one more day.

She would be occupied with her new responsibilities, she'd said. He should avail himself of the hospitality of Winterpark for as long as he wished.

Was that truth, or merely polite words meant for the servants' ears?

He'd put it to the test, Teagan decided. He would rest here a few days, continue to avoid her company so she might be free to "assume her new duties." And see how long it took before Valeria Arnold shattered his last illusion by having her unobliging guest evicted.

He was wrapped in a large, warm cocoon, with crisp clean linen beneath his cheek, his head cradled against a softness like eiderdown—or a woman's breasts.

Valeria.

But as he snapped his eyes open, Teagan discovered himself alone in what turned out to be a very large canopied bed with hangings of rich blue satin. He looked around in bewilderment, the sunshine filtering through the lace veiling the tall windows setting dust motes dancing and making him squint against the brightness.

Was he back in his grandfather's chamber at Montford?

Consciousness, and with it, memory, returned with a jolt. No, not Montford. He was at Winterpark. Valeria Arnold's newly inherited manor, where she'd invited him to tarry as long as his "plans permitted."

Plans she must know were nonexistent.

Before he could assemble his still-muddled thoughts and decide whether he would in fact tarry, or call for his horse and ride off without seeing her again, a soft tap sounded at his door. A red-haired, freckle-faced young girl in maid's uniform entered immediately after, a bowl of fresh flowers in her hands.

She halted in surprise as she noticed him staring. "Ah!" she exclaimed. "'Tis awake ye are at last, sir! Mrs. Welsh was after thinking ye'd sleep the week through."

Teagan pulled the sheet to his chin and eased up against the pillows. "How long have I been asleep?"

"Two nights and most of two days, sir," she replied, depositing the arrangement of golden daffodils and pink tulips on a side table. "'Tis afternoon now."

He must have been more exhausted than he'd realized, he thought in shock. At that moment his stomach growled, protesting its long neglect. "No wonder I'm so famished," he said ruefully. "Would there be any chance of getting a cup of ale and some cold victuals from the kitchen?"

"Oh, better than that, sir! Mistress gave orders that we weren't on no account to disturb ye, but to have a hot meal waiting whenever ye awoke. Oh, and I'm to summon Nichols to assist ye when ye're ready to bathe and dress. He's just a footman—our late mistress being a widow so long, we've no gentleman's gentleman about—but Nichols's uncle is valet to some fancy London gent, and he's always wanted to take up the trade... But now me tongue's runnin' on like a fiddlestick, and here ye be, fair starving!''

The maid rushed over to give the bell pull a vigorous tug, then turned to make him a curtsy. "I'm Sissy, sir, and we be ever so pleased to welcome ye to Winterpark.''

Undisturbed rest. A hot meal. The services of a valet— or almost a valet. If Valeria Arnold were trying to entice him to stay, she was certainly making the terms of whatever bargain she eventually wished to strike attractive.

But after a long rest that left him more energized than he'd felt in months, with sunshine to warm his face in a beautifully appointed room where he was being waited upon with such solicitous attention, Teagan found he was no longer so bitterly suspicious. And it was impossible not to respond to the little maid's loquacious cheerfulness.

"Is that Irish I hear in your voice, Sissy?''

"Aye, sir. Lady Winterdale, God rest her soul, had an estate near Killarny, and after her last visit brought me mum back here. I understand ye're from the fair isle yerself! Which explains how ye come to be so uncommon brave.'' The maid's eyes widened with awe. "By the saints, 'tis but natural ye were worn to a nub! Wilkins says ye vanquished those robbin' brigands all by yerself!''

So he was being touted a hero, as well. Teagan couldn't help grinning. "How many of these brigands did I dispatch? 'Twas rather dark, and I couldn't see well.''

"Oh, I disremember—'twas so excitin', the way Wilkins told it! Despite the rain and gloom, he says ye shot one of 'em from long range clean through the shoulder, and disarmed another afore he could move! 'Tis no wonder our new mistress feels so beholdin', ye savin' her baubles and rescuin' her person from—'' the maid halted, her freckled cheeks pinking ''—a-an Awful Fate! 'Tis grateful we all are to ye, sir, for protectin' Lady Arnold. She's not so grand as the old mistress, but she's ever so kind, and—ah, here I go ablatherin' again. I'd best be gettin' back to the kitchen afore me mum takes a birch rod to me. Yer food will be up directly, and ye're to ring for Nichols when ye're ready.''

With another curtsy, the little maid bustled out.

Teagan stretched back in the soft bed and stared at the intricate patterns on the mullioned ceiling. If one were going to have one's illusions shattered, as least it eased the sting to have the carnage take place in such luxurious surroundings.

But perhaps, for once, he had encountered someone who truly was as honorable as she appeared. Even given the beauty of these splendid surroundings, that would be the most wonderful awakening of all.

An hour later, fed, bathed and groomed nearly as well as Ailainn by the eager ministrations of his would-be valet, Teagan left his luxurious chamber.

Lady Arnold, he was told when he inquired of the servant leading him on a tour through the house, had ridden out to inspect some of the tenant farms. In her absence, however, the mistress invited him to avail himself of the fine table here in the billiard room, or select from the assortment of instruments there in the music room, or take out a weapon from the gun room, should he wish to try the hunting in the home woods. When the young man opened the door to display the next grand chamber, however, Teagan knew he need explore no further.

Having been told all his life he was destined for the fiery pit, Teagan had never given much consideration to what heaven would look like. But as he stood on its threshold, the thought suddenly occurred that for him, this room would be its very image. Inhaling sharply with awe and delight, he walked into Winterpark's library.

Except for the fireplace wall and a mullioned window

overlooking what appeared to be a rose garden, the large room was entirely given over to bookcases. A small fire burned in the grate to ward off the afternoon chill, adding a piquant hint of wood smoke to the familiar odors of leather binding and aged vellum.

Excitement swelling his chest, Teagan dismissed the footman and hurried to the nearest bookshelf, which, he soon discovered, housed what appeared to be a complete selection of Shakespeare. From there he wandered around the circumference of the room, trailing his fingers reverently over the best collection of fiction, poetry, philosophy, natural science and ancient literature he'd been privileged to gaze upon since leaving Oxford.

Behind the fretwork doors of a secretary near the window, he found some of his dearest friends: Plato, Horace, Virgil, Homer. Drawing out a volume, he sank down into the leather wing chair beside the secretary, and with the joyous thankfulness of one who, after a long, dangerous journey, at last reaches safe haven, began to read.

Some time later he looked up, startled to note that the daylight by which he'd begun had been replaced by a golden glow of candles he didn't remember lighting. His stomach once again protested his inattention.

He cast a glance at the large clock ticking on the mantel; 'twas nearly time for dinner. He would have to put up the book and return to his rooms to dress. After having abandoned his hostess for two entire days, he should try to be at his most entertaining tonight.

But as he walked to the desk to search for a marker, his hands stilled on the page. Buttressed by unpleasant memory, his suspicions returned with a rush.

Since he was traveling in the same direction, he'd offered to escort home the rich widow who'd befriended him at the house party they'd just attended—and been unexpectedly invited to sojourn there. Having lost heavily that week, he'd gratefully accepted....

Enough, he thought, pushing the degrading images away.

He turned to leave, then halted. Having reached one of his favorite passages, he really did not wish to abandon his book and go to dinner. Perhaps he would request that a tray be brought to him in the library.

If he did, would Lady Arnold come in later, her slender form displayed in a tantalizing cloud of low-cut silk, her dark brows creased in annoyance, her voice subtly shaded with the inference that he owed her his company at table...and elsewhere? As had that other matron in another library, at another needy time in his life?

And should he refuse her unspoken command, would he find himself shown the door, dismissed as precipitously as he'd been that long-ago evening?

Carefully Teagan marked his place and walked to the bell pull. He'd have his dinner here at the desk.

And discover this very night whether Valeria Arnold was indeed a treasure like finest gold—or merely another of the brassy imitations he'd been encountering all his life.

As if from far away, the sound of persistent tapping gradually intruded upon Teagan's consciousness. Someone was knocking at the library door, he realized.

Before he could brace himself for an encounter with a possibly indignant Lady Arnold, Giddings entered.

"Will there be anything else tonight, sir? My mistress instructed you were not to be disturbed, but 'tis late and I wish to retire." A trace of unbutlerlike aggravation altered his normally impassive expression.

Teagan glanced at the mantel clock—and was shocked to find it after midnight. "N-no, nothing, thank you, Giddings. I hadn't realized the time. Please send the footmen to bed, as well. I can find my way unassisted."

"Thank you, sir, and good night. I'll have Robbin bring you additional wine and candles." The butler bowed and turned to leave.

"Giddings!" Teagan called after him.

"Sir?"

"Has…has your mistress retired yet?"

The butler stiffened. "Several hours ago. I should be loath to rouse her, sir, as she begins her duties—"

"No, I didn't mean that you should." The staff seemed properly protective of its new mistress—a testimony to how quickly Lady Arnold had taken over the reins. "I wished to know her…whereabouts, that was all," he finished lamely. "Good night, Giddings."

The butler gave him a wondering look, which Teagan supposed he deserved, and bowed himself out.

Teagan glanced from the mantel clock about to chime the astonishing hour of one, to the remains of his dinner, to the door through which the butler had just disappeared.

The door through which Valeria Arnold had not entered.

His spirits leapt and a smile blossomed on his face.

Perhaps his Lady Mystery wasn't an illusion, after all.

After Robbin brought in his supper tray earlier this evening, Teagan had sat tensed, ears tuned for the sound of footsteps as he ate, only one eye on his book. But as the mantel clock ticked away and no lady in an evening gown and an aggrieved attitude appeared to interrupt him, the words of Homer worked their usual magic. His mind slipped back to the vicissitudes of Odysseus's journey, both his dinner and his dilemma forgotten.

As if summoned by his thoughts, Robbin reappeared with a tray bearing wax tapers and another decanter of wine. Thanking him for both, Teagan bade him good-night.

He listened as the servant walked back down the hall, his muffled footfalls gradually fading into a silence broken only by the occasional creak of several-hundred-year-old

Elizabethan beams and the soft scuffling of the nocturnal creatures in the garden outside the window.

Leaving him once more alone in a dwelling filled with peace and beauty, free to enjoy an activity far different from those transpiring in the overcrowded rooms he would normally occupy at this hour. Where, by rights, he ought to be seated now, stomach churning from too little food and too much cheap liquor, nerves taut as he counted cards and calculated wagers, eyes burning from smoke and liquor fumes, ears assaulted by raucous laughter and loud voices. A seat he *would* be occupying, had he not met Valeria.

Oh yes, she'd realized the full import of his circumstances practically from the moment she recognized him after the attack on her carriage. With the empathy of a kindred soul, and a keen sensitivity for his self-esteem, she'd quietly, generously given him this opportunity to rest and refresh his badly battered spirit.

Teagan tried to remember another place and time he'd been offered shelter, food and diversion, for which some service had not been exacted in return.

His mother's family had begrudged him the very air he occupied and the morsels he consumed, making him pay with slights, insults and blows endured for every day of charity they'd resentfully provided. At the dubious haven of Eton he'd had to beguile his schoolmates with quips and tricks to earn the pennies that kept him from starving between terms. At Oxford…he still could not bring himself to think back on the devastation of Oxford.

And in the years since, the charming rogue's persona he'd perfected in the wake of his banishment had been welcomed at gaming rooms, dinners and house parties only as long as he entertained while plying the cards of his trade.

The last crusty scab of suspicion peeled away, leaving a fragile, tender new skin of faith. Awe welled up in him, as

it had at Oxford when he'd discovered that within the world
of scholarship, he could not only belong, but excel.

Shame succeeded it.

By doubting her honesty he'd wronged Valeria and
shown himself unworthy of the unwavering purity of
friendship she'd extended.

The desire to make amends consumed him. Suddenly he
couldn't wait to see her again.

Carefully he closed the volumes on the desk and blew
out all but one branch of candles. Taking those, he exited
the library and took the stairs to his room.

Beginning tomorrow morning, Teagan Fitzwilliams
would seek every possible way to demonstrate his appreciation for the truest friend he'd ever had.

Chapter Fifteen

Following directions given by the helpful Nichols, Teagan found his way to the breakfast parlor early the next morning. A rising excitement tempered with no small amount of nervousness tightened his chest and brought a smile, unbidden, to his lips.

He paused on the threshold, still seeking the best words to frame an apology, should Valeria have taken offense at his missing dinner last evening. But as he scanned the chamber, he discovered not the dark-haired Lady Mystery he sought, but a tall, thin older woman who turned to him, a forbidding expression on her shrewd face.

Valeria's nurse Mercy, he recognized from several previous meetings, who appeared to be gathering up her mistress's sewing things.

Damping down a sharp disappointment, he entered.

"Good morning, Mistress Mercy. How was your journey from London? Less distressing than Lady Arnold's, I hope."

"Tolerable."

That response not being amplified by further comment, after a moment's hesitation, Teagan proceeded to the sideboard. Having filled his plate, he tried again.

"You arrived yesterday, Mistress Mercy?"

"Yes."

"With no lingering threat of highwaymen, I trust?"

"Highwaymen?" She sniffed in disdain. "We're here, and you're here, and enough said, young man. I'd suggest you eat your breakfast before it turns cold."

Teagan could not help grinning. "Ah, Mercy-lass, ye know ye're fair bursting to converse with so charming a gentleman as meself."

The maid's glacial look thawed somewhat. "Aye, you're a rogue good and proper! I've seen your like too often in the army, sweet-talking lads with more flash than merit."

Teagan touched his chest with a theatrical gesture, as if wounded. "Upon my word, Miss Mercy, did I not know better, I might believe you don't like me overmuch."

"You're handsome as you can stare, with the devil's own tongue to boot, and you may work your wiles with my blessing—as long as you don't work them on Miss Val."

Teagan sobered abruptly. "Surely you know I'd never bring harm to your mistress."

Mercy raised her eyebrows. "Nor threaten to?"

Half amused, half appalled, Teagan said, "Whist, but ye're not implying *I* set up that ambush at Dade's Run!"

"Perhaps not," Mercy conceded, "but you must admit, 'twas devilish convenient, you popping out of the woods just in time to save her. And thereby making her feel beholden enough to change her plans and invite you for a cozy stay—when you should be going on about your business.

"Nay—" she waved him to silence when he would have protested "—mayhap I do you a disservice with my suspicions. But this I know for truth. Miss Val has a weakness for you, and I'll not have you taking advantage of it. That poor lass lost her whole family, survived a husband too addled to realize the treasure at his feet, then found a grand-mamma only to have her taken almost the moment the lady grew dear to her. She don't need more heartache in the form of a fast-talking rogue who'll try to seduce her for the amusement of it.''

Teagan met Mercy's accusing stare. ''On several occasions, your mistress has stood my staunch friend. I've had few enough of those in my life that I'd risk ruining the relationship by trying to take advantage of her.''

The two of them exchanged glare for glare. Finally, as if satisfied, Mercy gave a short nod. ''See that you do not. I promised the late colonel, her papa, I'd watch after her, and so I will. Remember that.''

''Lady Arnold's welfare is of great concern to me,'' Teagan replied. ''Remember that.''

''Words be easy,'' she retorted. '''Tis deeds win the battle. Good day, sir.'' Clasping the sewing basket to her bosom like a shield, Mercy marched to the door. Just before exiting, she paused to look back at him.

''I'm instructed to tell you there be horses aplenty in the stables that need exercising. You can have your pick.''

''And where is your mistress today?''

The nurse hesitated, as if debating whether she might withhold the information. ''She's driven out to visit more of the tenants,'' she said at last, her tone grudging. ''We don't expect her home before tea.''

''Thank you, ma'am. I'll endeavor to do nothing to earn the hostility you've graciously accorded me,'' he replied, grinning.

With another darkling look, the nurse quit the room.

Despite the residual sting of having to ride a horse other than Ailainn, Teagan decided to avail himself of the stables. He'd enjoy the exercise as much as the beast, and perhaps on his ride he might encounter Valeria.

Some hours later, disappointed at not having met her, he

was returning to the manor along a trail the head groom had recommended—through the open woodland in the hills above Winterpark—when he spotted a small gig driving toward him. He was delighted to discover Valeria at the ribbons, a soberly dressed older gentleman riding a tall gray gelding alongside the vehicle.

As Teagan approached, she pulled up the gig. "Good afternoon, Mr. Fitzwilliams. I see you found a horse to your liking. Are you enjoying your ride?"

"Very much, Lady Arnold. The woodlands about Winterpark are lovely. If the farms are in equally good heart, 'tis a fine estate."

"The farms are very well kept, thanks in large part to this gentleman. Mr. Fitzwilliams, may I present Lady Winterdale's estate manager, Mr. Parker."

The two men exchanged bows. "Can I escort you back to the house, Lady Arnold?" Teagan asked.

With an expression of regret, she shook her head. "No, I have several farms yet to visit. Though I should enjoy your company until our paths diverge."

"Shall I ride on ahead, then, my lady?" Mr. Parker asked. "If I can inspect the equipment I mentioned at the Barrows farm before you arrive, we shall finish our rounds more quickly."

"Of course, Mr. Parker. Left at the next crossroads?"

"Yes, Lady Arnold. The Barrows farm is but half a mile farther. Pleasure to meet you, Mr. Fitzwilliams."

At Valeria's nod of dismissal, the estate manager put spurs to his horse. Valeria set the gig moving, and Teagan motioned his horse to keep pace.

"You are looking rested, Mr. Fitzwilliams."

He grinned over at her. "As well I should be!"

She chuckled softly, and it struck him again how much he'd missed her engaging gurgle of laughter, the warmth of camaraderie they had shared in the city.

"I must apologize once again for being such a neglectful hostess," she said. "No doubt I shall master them in time, but the duties here are more wide-ranging than any I have shouldered before."

Teagan remembered the maid's enthusiasm and the butler's protective concern for his mistress. "From what I've seen, your staff is much taken with their new lady."

She laughed again. "I expect they're relieved to discover I'm not nearly the tyrant their former mistress was! Though she trained them well. The household runs so smoothly, it scarce needs my guiding hand."

"They have certainly been most accommodating. Indeed, 'tis rather I who should beg *your* pardon for being so disobliging a guest! As if sleeping through most of two days was not impolite enough, I became so engrossed in my book last evening that I missed dinner, though I do appreciate the tray Robbin so kindly procured me."

"I had hoped you would enjoy Lady Winterdale's magnificent library. Ah, but here's the turning. The farm isn't far, and the view is much prettier if you continue along straight. Please, don't let me detain you."

Teagan didn't want to leave her, didn't want their too-short conversation to end so abruptly, but her words seemed so clear a dismissal he felt a shaft of dismay. Perhaps she *was* angry with him for neglecting her, after all. "You will be returning for dinner?"

"I'm not sure. There are mills and fences and some sort of mechanical plow I must inspect, apparently. Perhaps I shall see you later."

She signaled the horse to turn at the crossing. Unable to conjure up a reason to make her linger, Teagan was forced to halt his mount and let her pass.

She glanced up and smiled as the gig turned—the same shy, uncertain smile he'd found so irresistible that first morning in her barn.

The thought triggered memories that set his pulses racing. For a crazed instant he thought of seizing the gig's traces to stop the vehicle, carrying Valeria to the nearest croft or shelter where he might once again use his hands and lips and expertise to turn those dark eyes smoky with desire, make her slender body writhe with passion.

Not here, not yet. He gripped the reins so hard their leather bit into his fingers and forced himself to let her go.

And then laughed at his own absurdity. Had he not just last night felt the righteous horror of an outraged virgin at the notion of her as a calculating seductress sweeping into the library to have her way with him?

Whist, but he was an idiot of an Irishman to have resented any opportunity to be once more transported to that heaven.

Anticipation fanned his ever-smoldering hunger into a fire that flashed through his veins. Every sense energized, he spurred the stallion to a gallop.

May the God who watches over fools and gamblers send Lady Arnold to the library tonight, he prayed. Whatever proposal she had a mind to offer, whatever the reason behind it, tonight he had no intention of resisting.

Several hours later, Valeria peeped into the library. The scene within brought a smile of delight to her lips.

Cravat askew, booted ankles crossed, a glass of wine in his hand, Teagan Fitzwilliams reclined in his chair behind the library desk, a book propped on one knee. Before two brilliantly lit, double-branched candelabras, a half-consumed dinner sat neglected on a tray pushed to one side, while the rest of the desk's broad surface was strewn with a haphazard assortment of volumes large and small.

Still smiling, Valeria noted that the doors of the nearby mahogany secretary stood open. Having taken an exhaustive tour of the library her first afternoon at Winterpark, she knew the secretary housed Lady Winterdale's impressive collection of ancient literature. Mr. Fitzwilliams was a lover of the classics, it appeared.

He straightened, and Valeria darted back. But he merely readjusted the volume on his knee, nodding as if in agreement with the long-dead author, and then repeated a sentence she supposed must be Greek. "Ah, yes!" he said, and smiled down at the book.

Valeria's chest tightened. *Yes, indeed,* she thought, taking in his intent but relaxed stance, the vitality his figure conveyed even when motionless, the obvious pleasure evident in that smile. His appearance this afternoon had not been an aberration. Gone entirely was the tense, brooding, exhausted man who'd briefly shared her carriage en route to the Crown and Kettle.

Fierce gladness filled her that, despite her misgivings upon their arrival, she'd persevered to offer him this gift of time and solitude. However temporary a reprieve it might prove from the harsh reality of his circumstances, his three days at Winterpark appeared to have succeeded in revitalizing him, body and spirit.

Although he did seem to be avoiding her, she thought, her delight dimming a little.

Small matter, that. He was a man, after all, and it might be more than a man's pride could suffer to admit he'd needed the respite she'd given him. Too lowering to reaffirm that he must soon depart and remain out from London until he could sufficiently recoup his finances.

But if he did leave with only a short courtesy of a farewell, she would at least know she'd offered a refuge when he'd needed it most. And with absolute conviction, she believed that whether or not he could bring himself to express it, he had recognized and appreciated that gift.

And that, she told herself, squelching the forlorn hope

that now or someday they could share more, might well
have to be satisfaction enough.

"Lady Arnold!"

Valeria jumped guiltily, heat pinking her cheeks at the
knowledge that he'd caught her spying on him. "M-Mr.
Fitzwilliams! Please, don't let me disturb you."

"Have you dined yet?"

"Yes. One of the tenants was kind enough to regale me
with an excellent rabbit stew." She smiled wistfully. "The
meal reminded me of my campaigning days in India with
Papa and my brother Elliot."

Teagan fixed on her those glittering golden eyes she
found almost impossible to resist. Her body began to tingle
and her willpower to dissolve even before he spoke.

"Will you not join me for a glass of wine? I can assure
you it is excellent."

In the suddenly small confines of the library, he radiated
a masculine presence that sang a siren's song to every nerve
of her body. Even knowing the shoals ahead, she doubted
her ability to steer clear if she approached any closer.
"It…it is rather late."

His smile faded, increasing her guilt. "Could you not
spare a moment? At least long enough for me to thank
you."

She didn't pretend to misunderstand. "Friends…assist
one another, Teagan. And don't need to be thanked."

"Then would you do something for me—as a friend?"

Agreeing was a bad idea. A very bad idea, when she
hungered with the ferocity of a starving beggar invited to
a banquet to touch his hair, his body, to feast once more
on those lips.

My house. My library. No one need ever know.

"Would you?" he repeated, both a command and an
appeal.

She shook her suddenly woozy head. "W-would I what?"

His smile deepened and his eyes fixed on her lips. She could almost feel the warmth of his breath on them. Shivers skittered across her stomach.

"Stay and talk with me." He tapped the volume at his knee. "About this, if you like. A wonderfully written book is a glory in itself, but even better when it's shared. Please." He gestured toward the sofa before the fire.

'Twas embarrassing how intensely he affected her, alarming—as well as arousing—how much those naughty little suggestions darting through her mind magnified his allure.

She should be sensible and go up to bed.

But that would be ungracious, would it not? He might believe that, finding herself now a wealthy woman, she had no more use for his company. Though she thought it unlikely, given his experience with the female sex, that he could be unaware of his potent effect on her.

Still, she ought to be courteous. She could manage sitting by the fire on the sofa while he sat behind the desk and they discussed a common love of literature.

As if bound to him by some unspoken accord beyond her mind's control, her feet had carried her halfway across the library before she realized she'd entered the room.

Teagan smiled at her, wondering if she realized how adorable she looked, her face flushed, her fluttering hands betraying the nervousness that seemed to pull her at once to go and to stay, as it had in the barn at Eastwoods. To his relief, after a long hesitation she walked in and took the place he indicated on the couch.

"I must warn you," she said as she arranged her skirts, "I'm an indifferent scholar. Living in India much of my youth, where both distance and climate argued against

Englishmen maintaining well-stocked libraries, resulted in rather large gaps in my knowledge of literature and philosophy. I see from the selection on the desk that you prefer the ancients. Is that what you studied?''

How had he survived almost two weeks of her absence? It was all he could do not to walk over and draw her into his arms. He was almost positive she would welcome the embrace. Almost.

What had she asked him about? His studies, of course. He felt a bit dizzy, and shaking his head to clear it, he tried to focus on the conversation.

''Y-yes. While most of the lads at Eton struggled with languages, I found I had a gift for them.''

''Dear me, how unfashionable!''

''Aye, but since I could also put a bullet through a wafer at twenty paces and mill down upperclassmen who out-weighed me by several stone, I was spared any indignities being attempted on my person.''

Although the intense attraction she exerted over him did not lessen, as the conversation progressed Teagan relaxed a bit. How strange, that he could feel such a strong desire and yet at the same time chat with her so easily, friend to friend.

He looked back up to find her grinning at him. ''You know, you lose that Irish lilt when you speak of your books. Which is a shame. I rather like it.''

''I'll not believe that,'' he replied. ''Surely, like the rest of your countrymen, you despise all things Irish.''

''I met many fine Irishmen with the army. Perhaps some a bit too fond of grog, but good soldiers all—skilled, loyal and ferocious. The kind of ally one would wish at one's back in a battle—or when facing down highwaymen.''

Teagan laughed. ''I hear I've become a legend.''

''Thank Wilkins.'' She rose and walked over to the desk, where he still stood. As the distance between them narrowed, the very air between them grew charged. Once again he had to struggle to focus on her words rather than her nearness.

"Are these works your favorites?" she asked, pointing to the volumes he'd set out on the desk. When he nodded, she continued. "What is so inspiring about them that a young lad would struggle to master an antique tongue, merely for the privilege of reading them?"

"For one, every question of philosophical significance was first posed by Plato and Aristotle, and all analysis since is based on their work. But to read them in the Greek—ah, the precision and clarity of the language, the poetry of its form, make it well worth the mastering."

"A master of Greek? My, you *are* accomplished! I wonder you did not make a career at scholarship, given that—" He must have winced, for she stopped abruptly. "I-I'm sorry. That is none of my affair."

"You needn't apologize." His knew his smile had a harsh edge. "A scandal that was the talk of the ton hardly qualifies as confidential. 'Tis true that playing the gamester wasn't my *original* plan."

"But after...what occurred, you had no other choice," Valeria said quietly. "Life is so often unfair. You forfeited your future, but I've not heard anything to suggest the lady involved suffered accordingly."

She obviously wished to know the whole, and there was no reason not to tell her, Teagan supposed. For the first time, he even felt a willingness to share the bitter truth.

The sympathy in her glance was almost...painful, however, and he looked away. "I'd penned her enough rash testaments of my devotion that, once the affair became known, it was no piece of work to fix the blame. I even wrote one note—by the saints, what a fool I was!—begging her to run away with me. As if any woman with a particle of sense would have eloped with a stripling who possessed barely a shilling and no possible means of support.''

Though he shook his head mockingly, he knew Valeria's discerning ear had probably read in the timbre of his voice how desperately the love-besotted university lad had suffered from an older woman's rejection, more keenly even than from the wreckage of his career.

He looked back at Valeria, a wry smile on his face. ''I can scarcely believe I'm burdening you with sorry details that, I assure you, I've never before revealed.''

''Friends trust each other with their confidences,'' she said softly. ''I am honored you would confide yours to me.''

Warmed by her sympathy, he tried to lighten his voice as he continued. ''She did succeed in recapturing the full attention of her often-neglectful husband, which was perhaps her intent all along. In fact, I later came to suspect she arranged our last meeting so that we *would* be discovered.''

As the full meaning of that revelation penetrated, Valeria's pensive expression turned almost—ferocious.

''That selfish, calculating bitch!'' she cried. ''She *used* you, then!''

At first startled by her vehemence, Teagan began to chuckle. ''My dear innocent, lest you have any doubt, let me assure you I used her, too—thoroughly and often.''

''But to deliberately betray you, with no regard whatsoever to what that must mean to your position at the university! Why, she cannot have cared for you at all!''

Teagan's face sobered. ''No, I don't expect she did.''

''Well, I think she should have been flogged in the main street of town!''

Teagan watched her, so small and fierce, and the teasing reply he'd meant to utter failed him. So fierce—on his behalf. Bristling to right the wrongs done him.

"Whist, such a bold champion ye be," he said unsteadily. "Ready to charge into battle."

"Well, someone should have!" she retorted.

A sparkle of more than ordinary brilliance filled her dark eyes. His throat constricting, he reached out, to catch on his finger one crystalline tear.

She was weeping—with outrage at his pain.

Suddenly, the faint odor of a dimly remembered perfume washed over him, the feel of gentle hands lifting him to his feet, brushing off his knees and hugging him close. The reassuring certainty that whatever distress he'd suffered would be dissipated in the security of that embrace.

He came back to the present to find his fingers still resting on Valeria's cheek. She stared up at him, motionless, as if in thrall to his touch.

Teagan's chest tightened until it was difficult to breathe. A light-headed, falling sensation made him dizzy. To steady himself, he reached out and drew her, unresisting, into his arms.

"Ah, sweet lady," he whispered into the silk of her hair, "don't weep for me."

She moved away, and, panicking at the thought of letting her go, he tightened his grip. But she merely drew back far enough to angle her face up to his.

Gentleness ignited into conflagration at the first brush of their lips.

She made a small, impatient sound deep in her throat and dug her fingers into his shoulders, urging him nearer. Except that he'd already tightened his arms to crush her close, starving for the feel of her against his chest, desperate to taste her lips, her tongue, her teeth, to inhale the essence of her and transport them to a place where separate entities dissolved and they became one.

His blood was boiling through his veins, his pulse frantic to keep pace. Her fingers tugged aside his loosened cravat,

stroked the skin beneath, slid lower to scratch at the buttons
at his neck.

With the last shred of his rapidly disintegrating sanity,
Teagan realized that if she succeeded in wrenching open
his shirt and running her greedy, knowing fingertips over
the bared skin of his chest, he'd be catapulted beyond control, driven only by the raging need to disrobe and possess
her. Here, now, beside the desk or on the sofa, in a public
room where at any moment a servant might walk in.

Disengaging from that kiss was the hardest task he'd ever
performed. With a mewling sound of protest she resisted
his retreat.

"Valeria, don't!" he gasped. "Touch me again, and by
the saints, I'll be taking you right this minute, in your own
library. You can't want that!"

Her eyes unfocused, her breathing ragged, she stared up
at him as if his words made no sense. "I—I can't?"

"No, sweeting." Unable to let her go, he left his hands
loosely cupped over the softness of her shoulders, and by
a ferocious force of will kept her at arm's length.
"You...wanted us to be friends. Just friends."

"Friends?" she repeated, swallowing hard. "D-did I? I
seem to be having difficulty remembering."

The entreaty in her passion-glazed eyes made it difficult
for him, too, to recall the reasons why they must resist what
they both wanted. "So do I," he admitted.

"Teagan, could we not be...closer friends?"

Another wave of heat scalded him at her inference. "*Mo
muirnin,* that's what you want?"

"Yes," she whispered faintly, and then louder, "yes."

So be it, he thought, and abandoned the thankless battle
to be noble. "You'll let me come to you later?"

"Come now."

With hands that trembled as much as his own, she reached to pull his head down for another fierce kiss. "Hurry!" she said, and gathering up her skirts, fled from the room.

Chapter Sixteen

Teagan gave Valeria a half hour to prepare for bed and dismiss her maid, then he blew out the candles and headed for the stairway. He climbed the risers almost without seeing them, his breath coming fast, his heart tripping a rapid beat as if he'd been running rather than maintaining the decorous pace of a guest retiring for the night.

He entered his room and leaned back against the door. How much longer must he wait until he could be reasonably sure of not encountering any servants in the hall? Restless, he fingered the buttons at his waistcoat, then decided not to strip to his shirtsleeves. He wanted Valeria to relieve him of his garments…one by one.

Greedily he envisioned it, the images sending a dizzying rush of heat and need through his already needy body. How he loved her touch, that endearing mix of eagerness and hesitancy as her fumbling fingers struggled to detach a button from its mooring. The catch in her breath when garment gave way to skin; the shuddering inhale as, with the pads of her fingers, she explored the contours of his body, avid, eager, yet reverent.

Cherishing.

His skin grew damp with a moisture she soon would take

on her tongue, giving back of her own. And suddenly he could not wait a moment longer.

Forcing himself to move calmly, like a proper guest on a nocturnal search for wine or candles, he proceeded down the hallway into the master wing. And then he was before her door, the handle turning noiselessly as he grasped it.

He slipped in, and caught his breath. Evidently she'd not heard him enter, for Valeria stood near the window, her back to the door, her hands clasping and unclasping behind her. Pale moonlight silhouetted the dark outline of her figure within a halo of silky golden fabric that reflected the glow of the candles on the bedside table.

"Valeria," he whispered.

With a small exclamation of surprise she whirled to face him. Before she could move, he covered the distance between them, took her hands and kissed them.

"You're trembling! I'm sorry I frightened you."

"No, I'm not frightened." Her wide dark eyes devoured his face, uncertain still. "It's…just that it's been so long— and I want you so badly."

Tenderness invaded his chest and he smiled at her. "I'm here, *mo muirnin*."

He drew her into his arms. She slid her hands into his hair, tangling them in its strands, and pulled his mouth to hers in a fierce, hard kiss that left him gasping. While her eager tongue danced with his, their bodies bumped at chest, waist, hips in a series of torrid collisions that made him realize she wore nothing beneath the fine silk of her robe.

When at last she broke the kiss, his knees were rubbery. She swayed as well, and he put his hands on her shoulders to brace her. "Ah, sweeting," he said with an unsteady chuckle. "We've no need to rush. I want to carry you to the luxury of that great soft bed and come to know you again one slow inch at a time."

She shook her head vehemently, her eyes pleading. "Not slow! Not this time. Now, Teagan. Please!"

Inhaling a deep breath, she gently pushed away his fingers, loosened her robe and shrugged it off her shoulders. Bereft of speech or movement, Teagan watched as the filmy material drifted to the floor, leaving her naked and vulnerable to his gaze.

"Now," she whispered.

Transported to paradise, where does one start? At the hollow above the smooth curve of her collarbone, which cried out for his tongue? The plump breasts whose erect nipples beckoned him to taste and touch? The satin round of belly he could almost feel skimming beneath his fingertips, gliding under his lips? Or the tight curls below, springy softness concealing velvet folds whose hidden pearl yearned for the completion of his kiss, the caress of his thumb?

The tightness of his breeches approached pain, but he would stave off fulfillment. The first time they'd come together, months ago, had been his. This, the first time they'd lie together after so long a wait, would be hers.

"What do you want, Valeria?"

"What do—?" She broke off, confused. To his delight, comprehension sent a rosy blush to her cheeks. "I...I want you to...take me."

"How shall I take you? Tell me."

"I..." She moistened her lips. He bent to capture her tongue, drawing it between his lips to stroke and tease, but preventing her from pressing her body against his.

He released her mouth. "Say it, Valeria. The very words as you describe it will give me pleasure."

"I...want your hands...on my breasts."

"Like this?" He cupped his hands under them, rubbed his thumbs across the nipples.

Her gasp was his answer.

"What now?" he whispered.

She wobbled, her grip on his arm unsteady. "B-bed."

Hands still caressing, he helped her pliant body recline on the sheets, propped pillows beneath her head.

"Your mouth…" She urged his chin downward.

"At your nipples?"

"Ah, yes," she said, then groaned as he gently raked one taut tip with his teeth.

Eyes closed, for timeless moments she held him there, to pleasure first one breast, then the other.

Finally she moved him away. "Please…I want…you," she said between gasps, "here." One hand flailed toward her slightly parted thighs. "Within me."

Her skin was sheened with dampness, small rivulets of it pooling between her breasts, in the valley of her navel. Teagan knew she could not be far from completion. And much as he yearned to join her in one flesh, he craved even more to relive the dream that had titillated him all these months—the slow torture of his body inflamed, while her fingers freed him from his clothing one agonizing button at a time. He didn't want this to end too soon, in a frantic pop of fasteners, a ripping down of his trouser flap.

Besides, the means of sweet deliverance were so temptingly close. He nudged at her thighs, which she hastened to part wider. Then, before she could realize his intent, he moved a finger within those hot silky folds while he bent to suckle the sensitive nub above.

Her back arched; her nails bit into his shoulders. Moments later she uttered a muffled cry as the waves of pleasure he unleashed washed over her.

Afterward, she lay limp and spent. Still completely clothed, he eased up to recline beside her.

When at last her dazed eyes opened, he leaned to gently kiss her cheek.

"You cheated," she accused.

"I deflected."

A lazy smile grew on her lips, a wicked twinkle in her eye. She traced a finger down his shirtfront, slowing as she descended, inching past his waistband, creeping down the superfine of his breeches, until she stopped with the barest pressure of her fingertip against the pulsating bulge beneath his trouser flap.

He stifled a groan.

"Now," she murmured, "I want slow."

Much later, Teagan awakened against the damp pillows to find Valeria asleep in his arms. A sense of awe filled him as he gazed at her relaxed figure, her head cradled in the hollow of his shoulder, her breasts at his chest, her soft belly and warm thigh pressed against his thoroughly satisfied member, one long sweep of leg entwined with his.

Powerful emotion surged through him. He drew her closer and wrapped his leg more tightly around hers. He'd been wrong about the library, he decided. *This* was heaven.

He couldn't remember ever sleeping close to anyone before. He'd been exiled to the garrets growing up, and for protection's sake had never attempted to lie beside any of the lads while at Eton or university. Even if he'd had the inclination, given the nature of his relationship with the ladies with whom he'd previously trysted, there'd been good reason not to linger once the coupling was done.

He almost shook Valeria, wanting her to wake and share with him this sense of euphoria and peace, then chuckled at his foolishness. She'd be up betimes to care for the Winterpark flock. Not being able to make out the time on the mantel clock above the dying fire, he wasn't sure how much longer before he must leave her.

Though he wished the night might never end. The strength of his will had been nothing against the ferocity of his need, and though they'd avoided torn buttons and ripped clothing, even the second loving had not been slow enough. But the third—ah, that was a sensual ballet of point and counterpoint, arched arms and the curve of leg over leg…hands skimming down a shiver of skin…lips dipping to drink and drink again…the final melding of limbs into a long-delayed, sense-stunning climax.

He was smiling into the darkness, reliving it all over again, when Valeria stirred.

"Teagan?" she breathed.

He kissed her forehead. *"Mo muirnin."*

She smiled. "I hope that means something good."

"My darling."

Her smile softened. "You have made me feel cherished, and I thank—"

He put a finger to her lips. "Whist, and what did ye tell me earlier? No thanks needed between friends. Especially not very close—" he kissed her eyelashes "—very special—" he kissed the tip of her nose "—friends." He claimed her lips.

She parted them for him, met his tongue in a waltz that was long and slow and sweet, until the member he thought totally satisfied began to stir once more.

But there was no more time now, he knew, so best to stop this before it began. He broke the kiss and pulled her up to sit beside him.

"Do you visit tenants again today?"

"Yes. Would…would you like to accompany me?"

"I should be delighted."

"I shall be leaving very early.

"I'll find you."

"I'll have Cook pack a lunch."

He nodded and made himself ease from the bed, to keep himself from blurting that the food didn't matter; he could nourish himself on the sight of her face, drink in the timbre of her voice and the sound of her laughter.

But then he'd sound like the besotted moonling he was.

The fire had died to embers and he shivered a bit in the chill. "'Tis cold. You *could* help me dress."

Her teeth gleamed in the darkness. "No. This friend is better at assisting you to *un*dress."

Suddenly he wasn't so cold. "I shall remember that."

After donning his clothes, a mundane procedure made unexpectedly erotic by knowing that she was naked, watching him, Teagan came back to the bed.

He leaned over to fill his hands with her bare breasts while he nibbled at her lips. "Until later."

"Aye, *mo muirnin.*"

Valeria hugged herself and watched Teagan's silent exit. 'Twas still before dawn, but she had no desire to sleep any longer. Besides, it would be best if she were to make her preparations and depart even earlier than usual. Before her new household she might don her clothes and her respectable widow manners with impunity, but Mercy knew her too well. One look, and the maid would guess everything.

This interlude with Teagan was a madness that could not long endure, but for the few precious days that it lasted, she meant to throw aside caution and enjoy every moment. She did not wish to hear—or heed—the warnings of disaster her old nurse would feel compelled to deliver.

All her life Valeria Arnold had followed instructions, done her duty, made the best of whatever fate dealt her. And when Teagan Fitzwilliams rode out of her life again, as she knew he would, she would doubtless need every bit of her fortitude and endurance to survive.

But for the first time in her life, she was with a man who not only could bring her to a level of pleasure she hadn't dreamed possible, but one who stimulated her mind and evoked her laughter as readily as he stirred her senses. No love she'd before experienced, certainly not for her father or Elliot or even for Hugh, had made her feel so closely bonded to another human soul.

If only to herself, Valeria admitted she had committed the unpardonable sin of falling in love with Teagan Fitzwilliams. She knew the catechism of punishment well enough to realize she would probably soon be suffering the torments of the damned. But for now, she intended to drain every honeyed drop in the wine of this short-lived, unexpected gift. And let the future worry about itself.

She'd managed to keep herself from asking how long Teagan meant to stay, knowing any answer shorter than "forever" would be impossible to bear, knowing she dare not count on her increasingly feeble pride to prevent her begging him to remain longer.

He would be here until he rode away, she thought as she climbed out of bed. And he would not ride away today.

The Lord be praised for Wilkins's busy tongue, Teagan concluded as his brown gelding trotted beside Valeria's gig. He'd feared when he recklessly invited himself along today that his presence might be met with wary hostility or, even worse, give rise to immediate suspicions about their relationship. But the story of his dashing rescue had apparently spread about the countryside, for he was greeted wherever they went with almost as much curiosity and acclaim as Valeria herself.

'Twas quite a novelty, being welcomed as a hero.

His enjoyment of that notoriety did not approach the pleasure of spending a whole day in Valeria's stimulating and knowledgeable company. He'd managed his grandfather's stud farm over several summers, and was impressed by the breadth of her acquaintance with agricultural procedures. As was the estate manager, Mr. Parker, who accompanied them and often sought her opinion.

But what enchanted Teagan most was simply contem-

plating the contrast between the decorously gowned Lady
Arnold conducting estate business with her retainers—and
the naked, candlelight-dappled enchantress who only a few
hours ago had acted out his most erotic fantasies.

The proper decorum they had to maintain before the estate agent and the various tenants, rather than frustrating
him, seemed to enhance the power of their wordless com-
munication. The lingering glances, hands that almost but
not quite touched, the brush of his sleeve against her skirts
as he helped her down from the gig—each revived a bit of
the magic of that midnight interlude. Who would have
thought propriety could be so arousing?

As the hour approached noon, Valeria pull up the gig.

"Mr. Fitzwilliams and I will lunch by the river, Mr.
Parker. You are welcome to join us, or since we are near
your sister's farm, you might wish to visit there."

Mr. Parker's face brightened. "That is most kind, Lady
Arnold. If you are perfectly sure you will not need me, I
should like to stop at Susan's."

"Please go, then, and give your sister my regards."

"Of course, Lady Arnold. Thank you again."

Teagan's pulses sped as the estate agent departed. "Freeing us from our chaperone, my lady?"

Valeria gave him a demure look from under her lowered
lashes. "Mr. Parker fair dotes on his nephews, and never
misses an opportunity to see them. And with you to carry
the basket, I don't expect I shall need his assistance at
luncheon. Unless you would like to recall him?"

"Certainly not. I am here to serve your pleasure," Teagan said, taking the basket she indicated.

"I hope so," she murmured. "Follow me, please?"

Bemused, Teagan followed, not sure what his Lady Mystery had in mind. But after they crossed a field and penetrated beyond a screen of trees, he stopped short. "Ah, 'tis
lovely!"

Valeria turned back to him, his awe mirrored on her face. "Is it not beautiful?"

Down a steep, wooded incline he saw a sun-dappled clearing beside a swiftly flowing, crystalline river, its far bank protected by a thick copse of oaks.

"Mr. Parker showed me the place on my first tour of Winterpark," she told him as they picked their way down the trail. "'Tis where all the lads swim in summer, he said."

Teagan noted the river's shallowness and seclusion. "It looks ideal for that. And for a picnic." He chose a wide oak at the clearing's edge and set down the basket. "My lady, your banquet awaits."

She offered her hand, and he eased her to a seat on the blanket she'd spread, then sat beside her, her hand still in his. The afterglow of intimacy shared, the promise of passion to come, shimmered in the air.

Teagan stared at her lips, already thirsting to kiss her. "This," he said, "is going to be a very long day."

"And I thought you were enjoying yourself!"

"Your company is a delight. But after last night, I find myself impatient to be your *close* friend once more."

Her lips curved into a smile. Slowly she lowered her eyes to his neck cloth.

Best redirect this conversation, lest he forget Mr. Parker would soon be rejoining them. Shifting uncomfortably, Teagan released her hand. "Whist, my naughty sprite, how you set me ablaze with only a glance! But tell me, are *you* enjoying yourself here? Winterpark looks to be a heavy responsibility. Will you stay here to manage it, or leave it in Mr. Parker's capable hands and return to London? If rumors of Lady Winterdale's wealth are correct, you have the freedom to do whichever you like."

Valeria looked up from the package of cold chicken she was unwrapping. "Perhaps I shall stay here...I'm not sure as yet. I've never had a settled home. Given Papa's numerous postings, we never stayed long in one location.''

Nor, shuffled from one unwilling relative to the next, had he. He could well understand her uncertainty.

She offered Teagan the meat and cheese, then accepted the glass of wine he'd poured. ''Having experienced the whirlwind of a Season once, I've little desire to return to London and live among Society. Once I have Winterpark settled, perhaps I shall travel.''

''And where would you go, Miss Adventurer?''

''I've always envied gentlemen, who, if they had the funds might journey wherever they wished. Now that *I* have funds, perhaps I shall become one of those eccentric ladies who tour exotic foreign lands. Before I resign myself to a lifetime of Ladies Aid Society meetings and parish charity work, there is so much left to see!''

She made a sweeping gesture toward the river near their feet. ''I'd like to barge the Euphrates and pole down the Nile. Cross the Alps and climb the foothills of the Himalayas. Sleep in the shadows of the Pyramids, and walk barefoot on the sands of Cadiz!''

Her ardent enthusiasm brought a smile to his face. But recalling the wealth that would enable such travels led him to the unpleasant truth that so rich a widow was most unlikely to end up an eccentric explorer. A surge of indignation rose in his chest at the thought of his Lady Mystery being cajoled by some gentleman into giving up control of her estates—and her dreams.

And suddenly he felt compelled to ask, ''Would you take no companion on those adventures?''

She grew still, then looked up at him. ''I might.''

He grew still as well, trapped by the yearning in her gaze. Helpless, he leaned toward her. She met him halfway, just a gentle nuzzle of lips, sweet and impossibly arousing.

"Perhaps we should have kept our chaperone, after all," Teagan murmured unsteadily.

"And why is that?"

"With no maid to attend you and no ironing girl in sight, I cannot proceed where I'd like if we're to emerge from this glen with your reputation intact."

A sparkle danced in her eyes. "A dilemma, but..."

His temperature shot up at that small hesitation.

"'Tis true," she said in a musing tone, as if calculating a problem in mathematics, "that I cannot remove or replace so fashionable a gown without proper assistance—quite an argument against fashion, I must say! Nor is there a way to conceal a neck cloth wrinkled beyond repair. But—" she reached for the top button of his waistcoat "—even if your cravat remains tied, I see...possibilities."

His heartbeat sped to a gallop and his mouth dried. "D-do you?" he stuttered.

"The army teaches one to be very resourceful," she murmured, freeing the two top buttons of his waistcoat and one in the shirt beneath.

"Praise the Lord for army training."

He reached for her, but she batted away his hand. "We've already established that Lady Arnold must remain pristine. You, my dear *close* friend, are easier to tidy."

By the saints, she had learned her lessons well. She pushed him gently back against the tree trunk and slipped one more button free, her fingers dipping beneath the cloth such that the edge of her nail just grazed his nipple.

A moan escaped him. "Valeria, love—"

She shushed him with a finger to his lips, and he abandoned any attempt to speak. One button at a time, she bared his chest from collarbone to waist, all the while watching him, just watching, eyes avid and plump lips pursed. Slower still, she freed the fastenings of his breeches, careful now to touch only fabric.

The soft breeze brought shivers to the intimate skin she exposed, further hardened his aching fullness. Though almost completely clothed, he felt more naked now than he'd ever felt undressed.

"Valeria, torturess, what are you doing?" he groaned, when for long charged moments she neither stroked nor kissed, touching him only with her eyes.

She smiled. "Admiring the…scenery. But I suppose you should find it difficult riding in that state?"

The mere thought dragged from him another strangled moan, which apparently was answer enough, for she nodded. "Then I shall have to correct that. So, *mo muirnin.*" She dropped her voice to a whisper. "What would you have me do?"

The cool air caressing his nakedness seemed to fan, rather than mitigate, the inferno scorching his heavily clad back, legs and shoulders. As did her naughty, knowing look while she awaited his answer. Imagining what she might do with her cool satin fingers and hot velvet mouth nearly brought him to climax.

Not being at all shy, he had no trouble voicing his preferences. And with a hungry intensity that suggested she'd been saving him for dessert, she hurried to comply.

By the time, a heart-stopping interval of supreme bliss later, he had revived sufficiently to recover sight and breath, Valeria was gathering the remnants of the picnic food. She took the last sip of wine and conveyed it from her mouth to his.

"Don't," she ordered when he moved his still-shaking hands to try to rebutton his garments. "I shall attend to those directly."

And so, while he sat there bemused, she proceeded to put up food, glasses, napkins, plates, pausing at intervals to cast lingering, provocative glances at the unclothed portion of his anatomy. After finishing with the picnic things, she knelt beside him, once more making a leisurely exploration of his mouth while refastening his garments with soft, glancing touches, until he was nearly ready to begin all over again.

"That," he pronounced after she'd dismissed with an airy wave of her hand his protest at being informed they must now return to the gig, "was definitely cheating."

She made a little moue of her lips, prim as a nun. "No more so than you were last night."

"Ah, but last night we played more than one hand. Whereas you've just called the game to a halt."

"There's always tonight, isn't there?"

He caught her by the shoulders and pulled her to him, claimed her lips in a quick assault that within seconds splintered her facade of matronly composure.

"Yes, sweeting," he whispered, bracing her shaking body against him, savage satisfaction filling him at the intensity of the response he evoked in her, "you can wager on tonight."

Chapter Seventeen

With a whistle and a spring in his step, Teagan entered the breakfast parlor. Valeria was not present, but he hadn't expected her to be. Given the paucity of rest they'd had last night, he wouldn't be surprised if, her duties requiring her to remain at the manor today, she slept until noon.

However, awakened by the bright sun streaming in his window, despite his scant two hours' slumber Teagan had never felt more alive, more energized. Since, having crept back to his own room in the predawn stillness, he could not doze with Valeria in his arms, he'd decided to rise and dress. He was, he'd realized with a grin, quite famished.

As if she'd been watching for him, a moment later Valeria's nurse Mercy walked in. Even the dour look on the woman's face as she gazed at him could not dent his high spirits.

"And a lovely good day to ye, Mistress Mercy," he sang out, strolling over to fill a plate at the sideboard.

"Mr. Fitzwilliams," the nurse responded.

"Do you bring me a message? Or is it just that, it bein' such a beauteous morning, ye're wishful of conversin' with me today."

"I bring no message…from my mistress."

Grinning, Teagan continued. "Sure, on such a day a stroll in the gardens would be just the thing. Or, as I remember ye're not much for strollin,' perhaps later I could take ye and your mistress for a drive."

"My mistress, having work to do, has departed."

Teagan looked up in surprise. "I thought she wasn't to ride out today."

"Parker summoned her early. An accident at the mill. She went to assist."

Teagan halted in the midst of buttering his toast. How early? he wondered with a spurt of unease. He recalled her bedchamber as he'd left it in the misty predawn—sheets in disarray, her night rail flung on the side chair, the lingering odor of lovemaking potent in the air.

Mercy would have gone to awaken her.

He glanced over to find the nurse staring at him, accusation in her eyes, and felt a flush mount his cheeks.

She watched him steadily while the attending footman poured him coffee, waiting until the servant left the room.

"'Tis I who have a message for you, Mr. Fitzwilliams," Mercy said quietly after the man's exit. "Don't do this to her. 'Tis crime enough that you'll shatter my poor mistress's heart when you go. Winterpark can be a haven for her, with work to help her heal. Go now, before 'tis too late. Don't leave her to deal with the shame of a bastard brat."

Before he could think what to reply, she walked out.

His high spirits vanishing with his appetite, Teagan stared at his chilling toast and cooling coffee.

He knew Mercy had disapproved of their London excursions together. For the first time, he saw his sojourn here through her eyes as well.

A feckless, indigent gamester with no money and few prospects. Valeria's irresponsible lover, taking advantage of her goodwill, living off her largesse.

The image sickened him.

Though he'd never sunk to accepting the hospitality of a lady to whom he was not sincerely attracted, he had on several occasions dallied with women who supplied him with comforts for the duration of their liaison. Those females weren't fit to mention in the same breath as Valeria.

Their time together, from the very first meeting at Eastwoods, had been far more than a meaningless tryst based on lust and mutual convenience. Regardless of how it might appear to Mercy—or any other uninvolved outsider.

Surely Valeria knew the truth of that, didn't she?

For a moment the need overwhelmed him to run to the stables, ride out to find her, assure her...of what?

That he loved her? That a half-breed Irish gambler of no income and dubious reputation begged the honor of the pure, lovely, *rich* Lady Arnold's affection?

What did he know of love, beyond the hazy memory of a six-year-old in his dying mother's embrace? But if it meant the mere sight of her filled him with gladness, her wit and intelligence drew him so strongly he wanted to be nowhere else but at her side, and her touch had the power to melt him where he stood, then love her he did.

Buttressed by the hope of asking for her hand, he could steel himself to a new round of gaming, and having redeemed his debts, could return and ask her to marry him.

But though that would protect her from the dishonor of conceiving a bastard, it would do little to preserve her reputation. In fact, he thought, remembering with humiliation and chagrin the tarnish still clinging to his mother's name, it might well expose her to permanent derision for being, like Lady Gwyneth, foolish—and wanton—enough to cast herself away on an Irish wastrel.

If he truly wished to protect her, the best thing, as Mercy urged, was to leave her. Leave, and never come back.

The very idea of it made him want to howl with anguish.

Only then did he realize how completely Valeria's essence had seeped into every pore of his being, so that the thought of living without her seemed no life at all.

He might as well choose the pistol.

Mercy was right, though; he should leave soon, before the servants began to murmur about his nocturnal wanderings. Before the full significance of the energy flashing between himself and Valeria became apparent to more than her faithful nurse. Before her credit and her credibility suffered in her household and her neighborhood.

How much longer was safe—a day, maybe two? And even that, if he touched her, would risk the possibility of a child. How could he manage to stay without touching her?

The enormity of impending loss sucked the energy from his body, left him too listless even to rise from the table. After Robbin, brow creased in concern, asked him for the third time if he wished more coffee, Teagan forced himself up and drifted down the hall, feeling already like a sacrificial offering about to be stripped of his soul.

Without remembering how he'd gotten there, he found himself in the library. Mechanically he began to reshelve the volumes he'd left strewn on the library desk—a task so reminiscent of his exit in disgrace from Oxford that he had to choke down a bitter laugh at the irony.

But then indefatigable determination of the sort that must have led his mama to escape her relations and set off into the unknown with her Irish lover built back up in him, sparking a new idea rife with possibility.

The solution to this dilemma might be the one he'd rejected ten years ago. Young and hotheaded, at his grandfather's final insult he'd stormed out, vowing never to ask a Montford for anything again. But as ten years without one had demonstrated with painful clarity, all the things he valued most—honor, dignity, the hand of the woman he loved—depended on his occupying a respectable position in society. A position that, by English social code, could be conveyed on him only if he were once again received by his mother's family.

The idea of crawling on his belly to beg his cousin for reconciliation made him gag. But to salvage a life with Valeria, he would crawl and he would beg.

He might not have to abase himself totally, he thought with a grim smile. Should Jeremy prove resistant, a word in Riverton's ear might make the earl more receptive to receiving his disreputable cousin with better grace.

He'd reinstate himself with the family and press them to find him some respectable position—assistant to a government official or secretary to a nobleman. To limit the inevitable gossip among the ton, it would be in the family's interests to find him such a position quickly.

He was quick-witted, hardworking, and as Valeria had said, good at ingratiating himself with people at all levels of society. Once in a position, he would excel.

Having reconciled with the Montfords and taken that post, he could then return, confess his love and beg Valeria to marry him as soon as he'd worked himself to a level in which the world would not consider their union quite so dreadful a misalliance.

Valeria would marry him…wouldn't she?

Mercy, who knew her better than anyone, had said he held her heart. Her fierce, continual concern for him surely demonstrated a deep emotion. And her passionate response to him, as powerful as the response she evoked in him— surely that was love translated into touch.

He smiled a little, thinking of the delicious things she'd done to him and for him in the magical stretches of the night. A fierce satisfaction filled him at knowing he was the only man who had ever touched her thus.

The smile faded. She damned well better marry him. He'd gut any other man who dared touch her as he had.

But a plan to salvage their future did not change the bitter fact that he must still leave her now. And soon.

Though he need no longer worry about the possibility of a child. Should she conceive, he would simply marry her sooner. If not for the distress it might cause her to have to marry in that way, he'd welcome any reason that shortened the time before he could return to claim her.

Would she understand why he must go? She was too intelligent not to comprehend the danger they courted. But if he confessed his love and his hopes for their future, surely any hurt his leaving might cause would be offset by knowing that as soon as he could, he would come back.

Sure, and what did he have to offer her now but fine talk? he thought, frowning. The most derelict drunk in the parish could boast of the grand feats he would perform— tomorrow or next week or next year.

If she did love him, being Valeria, she might well press him to disregard the opinion of Society and marry her immediately. She might not understand his need to prove himself—in his own eyes and the world's—a man worthy of her love. She might even think his plan an excuse to evade marrying her, and doubt the strength of his affection.

Which would surely wound her more than leaving now with his vows of love unspoken.

"Words be easy. 'Tis deeds win the battle," Valeria's nurse had said, and she was right. Teagan would not speak to Valeria until he'd translated plans into action and action into accomplishment.

Which meant when he departed, he might express only his fervent vow to return.

The thought of leaving still too painful to contemplate, he turned his mind to planning, and another prospect flashed in his mind. Perhaps he need not approach the earl, after all. His mother's maternal family included a duke and claimed influence even superior to the Montfords'.

One of the few pleasant interludes he could remember from childhood was visiting Lady Charlotte Darnell, his mama's first cousin. That lady—she'd urged him to call her "Aunt Charlotte"—was now a widow residing in London.

Lady Charlotte it would be, then. But before he figured out how to approach her, he must solve a much more difficult dilemma—finding a way to say goodbye to Valeria.

Perhaps he should simply pen her a note and leave now, before she returned and the magnet of her presence could draw him away from his resolve to depart. But that was the coward's way, and after all she'd given him, she deserved better than a letter left with the butler.

Besides, remaining until tomorrow would mean they'd have tonight. One last night.

Only the last for now. For when he'd built a new life worthy of her, he would come back to reclaim her—and all the other nights of their lives.

Though exceedingly weary, Valeria was not able to return to Winterpark Manor until late afternoon, when the fire at the grain mill had at last been put out, those wounded in the dust explosion that caused it cared for and returned to their families.

A smile curved her lips as she walked up the entry stairs. Ah, what a joyous reason for fatigue! Perhaps she could rest before dinner. Teagan would be departing all too soon, and she had no intention of wasting the few nights she had left with him in slumber.

He must have been watching for her, for he appeared in the hallway immediately after Giddings took her wrap.

"Valeria, welcome back. I trust the situation at the mill is now resolved?"

"Yes. The building shall require repairs, but no one was grievously injured, thank goodness."

"I'm glad to hear it. If you are not too exhausted, would you join me in the library for a moment?"

Ah, the library. Sparkles danced across nerves she'd thought too tired to respond when she recalled what had begun the last time she'd been in that room with him.

"Yes…my very close friend," she murmured, smiling.

A smile he didn't return. Alarm banished fatigue in an instant.

He neither looked at her nor touched her after she followed him in. Her stomach commenced a downward spiral.

He was going to tell her he was leaving. He would smile, and kiss her hand, and express his appreciation for her kind hospitality…then announce his imminent departure.

Out of the whole of a long, bland, passionless lifetime, could she not have just a few more days of bliss?

She took a deep, shuddering breath. If this were the end, let her manage it with dignity. No tears, no argument, no begging him to remain just one more day.

Head held high, she walked to the sofa and seated herself. "What is it, Teagan?"

He paced to the window, then turned to her. His face looked as strained as she knew hers must be.

"There is no easy way to put this, so I'll just say it outright. I must leave Winterpark, Valeria."

Even with her expecting them, the words still struck like a blow. She gripped the sofa arm to steady herself. "When?"

"Tomorrow."

So she had one more night. Or did she? Had the time they'd shared, so unparalleled in splendor for her, been merely one more of any number of similar interludes for him? One which had now lost its luster? No, she could not believe that.

"I see," she managed to reply at last.

"You cannot think I *want* to go!" He strode over to seize

her hands and kiss them. ''There is nothing I would love more than to remain here with you, as lost in our own private world as we have been these two days past. But as Mercy pointed out to me this morning, we both know that cannot be. The unusual circumstances of my arrival have allowed us a few days' grace, but if I linger much longer, malicious gossip about the real nature of our relationship is sure to erupt. I will not stay and cause your new staff and neighbors to turn against you.''

He paused as if he would say more, then closed his lips. Unable to trust her voice, she merely nodded.

''I will come back, Valeria. 'Tis time for me to get my affairs in order, as I should have done long since. But once I do, nothing under heaven will keep me from you.''

''Get…your affairs in order?''

''I mean to approach my mother's family and see if they will permit a reconciliation. Gambling was never to be more than a temporary support, and it's past time for me to find a more respectable occupation.''

A wistful smile touched his lips. ''I'd like to become a man you can be proud to acknowledge as your friend. A man people will not feel obliged to warn you against.''

''I am proud already to call you my friend.''

He swallowed. ''Ah, lass, 'tis the beauty of ye,'' he said, his voice rough. ''Ye see good where there is none.''

''Nay, Teagan. I see what everyone else has overlooked.''

His jaw tightened, and as if unable to restrain himself longer, he pulled her up from the sofa and into his arms, crushing her against his chest.

''Ah, *mo muirnin,* I shall miss you every day and every hour. And thank the lord at the end of every night, for it means one less day remains until I see you again.''

He would come back.

He sought her lips, and Valeria gave them eagerly. His

kiss, deep, urgent, almost frantic, seemed to say he, too, needed to affirm that this bond they shared would endure the trials of separation to come.

Then he released her, pushed her gently back to a seat. "If I am not to ruin all yet, I shall have to be more discreet than that for the rest of today."

"Surely...we will still have tonight?"

"You'll allow it?"

"Yes! Oh, yes."

"Saints be praised," he said fervently, making the sign of the cross. "I don't think I could face the purgatory of leaving tomorrow if I did not know we still have the heaven of tonight."

With a quick sideways glance, as if afraid someone might oversee them, he kissed Valeria on the forehead. "Go rest, then, *mo muirnin*. We've but one more night, and I promise to make it one you will never forget."

A gentle rain was falling at dawn the next morning as Valeria walked Teagan down the path to the stables. He'd slipped to the kitchen to pack himself some meat and cheese for the journey so he might be off at first light, the better to reach London as soon as possible.

"I'll leave the horse at the posting inn. One of their ostlers will return him."

She nodded, biting her lip to avoid asking if he had sufficient funds for the journey, knowing that, even if he did not, his pride would not allow him to accept any from her.

She waited while he entered the stable, saddled a mount, sent the sleepy groom he'd awakened back to bed.

The drizzle had stopped and the new sun had just begun to peep over the eastern hills as they walked toward the carriageway out of Winterpark, both silenced by the heavy weight of imminent separation.

Out of sight of both house and stable, he wrapped his

mount's reins around a tree and took her in his arms. For a long, precious moment he simply held her, while Valeria memorized the sound of his heartbeat and breathed in the scent of his skin.

The passion they'd shared last night had been rough and frantic, slow and gentle by turns. The kiss he bent to give her now was the latter, long, lingering, tender. Despite her best intentions to be strong, she felt the hot sting of tears behind her closed eyelids.

He broke the kiss and she lowered her head to his shoulder, not wishing to look up so he could say goodbye, hoping with all her strength that he would say instead the words he'd hinted at but never spoken, the three words she so badly wanted to hear. Freeing her to say them, too.

But he said nothing. At last he lifted her head, framing her face in his hands, the golden cat eyes that had enthralled her from the first commanding her gaze.

"On my mother's grave and by all the saints, I swear I will come back, Valeria. Do you believe me?"

"Yes," she replied, disappointment battling with the hope that urged her to trust his words. "I believe you."

"Goodbye, then, *mo muirnin*," he said roughly, brushing his lips against her forehead. "Dream of me."

He pushed her gently away. Without looking back he strode to his horse, untied the reins and leaped into the saddle, kicking the stallion into a trot.

Numbness, like the shock after a mortal injury during which one does not yet feel pain, held her motionless as he rode away. Valeria wasn't sure how long she stood there, the sun of a new day dappling her hair, a soft breeze wafting bird calls to her from the trees beyond the flower border. All the signs of a normal morning, as if half her soul and all her joy had not just been wrenched from her to disappear down the road to London.

She turned toward the house—and found Mercy approaching her. "Child, child," the nurse sighed, her eyes scrutinizing Valeria's face, "what have you done?"

"What I wanted, Mercy," she replied fiercely. "And I will not regret it."

"Ah, Miss Val," the nurse murmured, holding out her arms and gathering Valeria close. "I surely hope not."

Chapter Eighteen

A week later, Teagan presented himself at the Mount Street town house of Lady Charlotte Darnell. Once he'd set out from Winterpark, his entire mind and will focused on what he must accomplish, as often happened with fickle Lady Luck, the cards that had fallen so badly the previous month suddenly realigned themselves in his favor. A few nights' concentrated effort at inns along the road back to London had amassed him sufficient funds to be able to return to his rooms and stave off the threat of the magistrate.

Dressed now in the best Weston and Hoby could offer, trying to keep his nervous fingers from rearranging his cravat, he stood in Lady Charlotte's anteroom while the butler went to determine if his mother's cousin would receive him. If ever Teagan needed the Jester's glib tongue and charming manners, 'twas now.

Please, Mama, he prayed, *let Lady Charlotte remember me with kindness.*

A few moments later the butler returned. "My mistress is in the morning room. If you will follow me?"

He never heard the butler announce his name. A shock pulsed through him the moment he beheld the tall, golden-haired lady who sat on the brocade settee, her clear blue eyes examining him avidly.

In the small study of the rambling manor at the stud farm Teagan had managed for several summers, he'd come upon a miniature that the friendly cook informed him was of Lady Gwyneth—apparently the sole remaining portrait of the earl's disgraced daughter. A portrait that bore so uncanny a resemblance to Lady Charlotte that for an instant he'd wondered if it were his mother come back to life.

"You are the image of Mama!" he blurted. Then, remembering the imperative to make a good impression, he swept her a deep bow. "Excuse me! 'Tis good of you to receive me, Lady Charlotte."

His mother's cousin continued to study him, her serene face impassive. Desperation making sweat pop out on his brow, he held her glance and tried to smile.

She shook her head slightly. "Teagan, Teagan," she said, advancing toward him with both hands outstretched, "why have you stayed away so long? And it's 'Aunt Charlotte,' you will remember."

So dizzy with relief he thought he might faint, Teagan sent a silent prayer of thanks to his mama and all the other saints in heaven before bending to kiss her fingers.

"What a handsome devil you've grown to be! And you are correct—your mama and I looked so alike many thought us sisters rather than cousins. But come, sit with me." She waved him toward the settee. "I'll have Martin bring us tea—or shall we make that champagne? A reunion after so many years demands a celebration!"

While the butler brought wine and refreshments, Lady Charlotte chatted about his mama and their growing up together. Once they'd disposed of the refreshments and sipped the promised champagne, she said, "But enough of ancient days. Tell me how you are and what you've been doing! I can't believe you've committed half the sins gossip

lays at your door—no more than I believed the tales the
Montfords told about you when you were growing up."

Teagan smiled ruefully. "I expect in both cases much of
the talk is deserved. Since I learned early on that Mama's
family would attribute blame to me regardless of how I
behaved, it seemed only prudent to earn the thrashings I
was going to receive anyway."

"And in more recent years?"

He shrugged. "I've been an honest man, if a gambler
can be described as such." He paused, his face heating.
"The affair with Lady Uxtabridge I regretted almost from
the moment it began, but at the time I was still too angry
and bitter to heed the harm I caused. After that...despite
what rumor claims, my dealings with the ladies have been
no more reprehensible than any other bachelor's."

She chuckled. "If Society were to ban every gentleman
who committed youthful follies, the ton would be thin of
company indeed! I don't know what happened at Oxford—
and no, you needn't tell me! But I thought it dreadfully
wrong of the family to break with you over it. Of course,
Uncle Montford was ever a hot-tempered, harsh discipli-
narian. Indeed, I never forgave him for what he did to
Gwen, forcing her to choose between her home and the
man she loved. And I still blame Uncle Montford for her
death."

A fierce expression briefly creased her forehead before
she continued. "At the time of the Oxford...incident, my
husband agreed with the earl, and absolutely forbade me to
interfere. Sometimes when one is handling a forceful gentleman, as with a feisty stallion, 'tis best to let him have
his head until he settles down. I hoped you would contact
me, send me some word. But you seemed to go off in a
different direction altogether, which only confirmed Darnell's view that your grandfather was right, and made it
impossible for me to approach you. By the time my hus-

band died last year, I was not sure you would care to be approached, after so long a silence. I am so very glad you decided to seek me out at last.''

She paused and gave him a searching glance. ''So, why did you decide to seek me out?''

''Perhaps because I am finally past the period of youthful follies. I have had enough of gaming, Aunt Charlotte, of living on the fringes of decent society. I came to ask if you would be willing to assist me in finding proper employment and…and help me redeem my reputation.''

To his surprise, she leaned over and gathered him into a swift embrace. ''Oh, my dear Teagan,'' she said as she released him, ''that has been my fondest wish ever since the dreadful interview with your grandfather turned you against us all! Of course I shall help you. Perhaps, when we have achieved your aims, I shall feel less guilty.''

''Guilty, Aunt Charlotte? Whatever for? You must know I would never have wished to come between you and your husband. You shouldn't take yourself to task for not intervening with Grandfather.''

''It's more than that, Teagan.'' Her smile faded and a look of grief came over her lovely face. ''Your mama was not just my cousin—she was my dearest friend. When she ran off, I felt bereft, and when she died, it was as if I had lost a part of myself. When that clergyman found you in Dublin and sent you home, I felt a merciful God had given something of Gwen back to us. I…I wanted to take you. I *should* have taken you.''

Tears gathered at the corners of her eyes. ''Had our situations been reversed, Gwen would have found a way to do that for my son,'' she asserted, her voice fervent. ''No grandfather's contention that he belonged with the Montfords, or husband's insistence that she safeguard her strength for a babe of her own, would have stopped her.''

The lady's distress seemed so deep Teagan felt moved to protest. "You mustn't blame yourself. I'm sure you—"

"I haven't yet told you the whole. Do you remember the one visit you paid me, soon after you came to England?"

"It is one of my most pleasant childhood memories."

She squeezed his hand. "I was in a…delicate condition at last. I begged my husband to let you come, and since he wished to keep me happy, he asked Montford to send you to us. But I became ill, and they returned you to your grandfather. I…lost that child, and took many months to recover. After that episode, Darnell wouldn't hear of your returning. You were too rough and ill-behaved—I would tax my strength. I knew from your short visit how you were being treated, but I put my hopes for a child of my own over the welfare of my dearest friend's s-son."

Lips pressed together, Lady Charlotte fell silent.

She had wanted him, Teagan thought with a sense of wonder. Surely it could make no difference after all these years, yet somehow the knowledge that his mother's cousin would have taken him in, had she been allowed to, still had the power to warm some cold, lonely place in his heart.

And she had suffered from her failure to help him. Teagan put a sympathetic hand on her shoulder.

Wiping her eyes with an impatient gesture, Lady Charlotte turned back to him. "By the time I conceded that my hopes of a child would never be realized, you were nearly grown. Then came Oxford, and once again I let others overrule the judgment of my heart. Again, I failed both you and Gwyneth. I tell you all this not to assuage my guilt by asking for forgiveness—nothing will make amends for the errors of the past—but so you will understand why I assure you there is nothing I will not do now to help secure your future.

So," she patted his hand, then rose and crossed to ring the bell pull, "let me write some notes. Several of Darnell's friends still hold positions of influence. Surely one of them will know just the posting to meet your needs. Shall I ask them to join us for dinner tonight?''

Taken aback by the swiftness of her action, Teagan stuttered, ''I—well—y-yes, tonight would be fine.''

''That is…you do not have any previous engagements?''

''No, my lady. I am entirely at your disposal.''

''Excellent. I must go write the necessary letters.''

Teagan rose and bowed. ''How can I thank you enough, Aunt Charlotte?''

She hesitated. ''There is one thing.''

''If it is within my power to perform, it is yours.''

She smiled, so tentative and uncertain that he was instantly reminded of Valeria, and a pang of longing pierced him, marrow deep.

''Would you consider…staying here with me? I know the offer comes twenty years too late, far too late for you ever to allow me to claim you as the son I never bore, but having the ton know that you are residing with me would advance your cause, and—and I should like it very much.''

Teagan came over to kiss her hand. ''I should be honored to reside here. Honored to be considered a son.''

Once again tears glistened in Lady Charlotte's eyes, and once again she brushed them away. ''T-thank you. That means more than you will ever know. Please excuse me while I prepare the letters, before I turn into a watering-pot like one of those vaporish females I so deplore.''

She linked her arm in Teagan's and walked with him to the parlor door. ''I'll instruct Martin to have a suite of rooms prepared, to be at your disposal whenever you choose to make use of them. Now, bid me goodbye like a dutiful son,'' she ended, smiling as she held out her hands.

Teagan saluted them in the elaborate French manner. ''My very dear Aunt Charlotte, I am forever in your debt.''

''Nonsense. 'Tis rather I who am in yours! Perhaps now,

when I meet her in the hereafter, I shall finally be able to look your mama in the eye."

Late that afternoon, Teagan returned to Lady Charlotte's town house, the sum total of his earthly possessions bound up in two small trunks and one string-wrapped bundle, the latter given him on his way out of his lodgings by his tearful landlady, Mrs. Smith.

After bidding him wait a moment, she'd scurried off and returned with a parcel in which he recognized the used copies of Herodotus, Plato, Homer and Virgil he'd left with her to pay off his debt. "Knowin' how much store you put by 'em, I couldn't bring meself to sell 'em," she told him. "'Specially with me being right sure you'd be acomin' back. Best of luck to ye, now." Depositing the books on top of his other effects, she'd pushed him toward the door.

The sense of awe and excitement he experienced upon crossing the threshold of his new home recurred as Martin, with a deference Teagan thought almost excessive, ushered him into the suite of rooms Lady Charlotte had allotted him. The bedchamber with its Chippendale mahogany furnishings was nearly as grand as Valeria's chamber at Winterpark, and the attached sitting room offered a pair of comfortable leather armchairs and a study desk flanked by bookcases, as well as a large window overlooking the back garden.

Martin informed him that, though the late Lord Darnell's valet had already obtained another position, Martin had a nephew who'd just finished his training as a gentleman's gentleman, whom Martin would be happy to recommend to Mr. Fitzwilliams.

The situation was so reminiscent of Nichols at Winterpark that Teagan had to smother a grin. Informing Martin he would consider it, he dismissed the butler.

His grin returned as he gave the elegant bedchamber a

slower inspection. The only thing that would make this long-delayed homecoming sweeter, he decided, would be if he could look forward to sharing that large canopied bed with Valeria tonight.

Bittersweet longing dimmed his excitement. What would she be doing at this moment? Riding out to meet her tenants? Sitting in the estate office consulting with Mr. Parker? Clipping herbs in the kitchen garden with Mercy?

Missing him, as he was missing her?

He'd just, with another silent thanks to the loyal Mrs. Smith, arranged his meager collection of books on the bare shelves of the nearest bookcase when a tap sounded on the door, followed by the entrance of Lady Charlotte.

She stopped in the center of the chamber and gestured around. "You like the rooms, I hope?"

He walked over to kiss the hand she offered. "They are splendid, Aunt Charlotte. Indeed, they seem to have cast upon me such a reflection of glory that, since the moment I entered them, Martin has been practically begging me to allow him to be of service."

Lady Charlotte laughed. "As well he might. They are the master's rooms, after all."

His teasing smile faded as the significance of her gesture penetrated. "Aunt Charlotte, are you sure—"

"Hush," she said, putting a finger to his lips. "I wished you to have them. After the part Darnell played in keeping you away so long, it only seemed fitting, somehow. But I really came to see if I might steal you away for a time. Rather than writing a reply, one of the gentlemen to whom I directed a note has called in person. He's been a particular friend for years, so I'm delighted he is eager to meet with you. He's waiting below, if you can forgo your settling in long enough to receive him."

Teagan's heartbeat quickened. This, now, was the second test he must pass—convincing a man of sense and breeding that he could fulfill the requirements of whatever position the gentleman wished to offer him.

"Of course. I shall be right down."

"Excellent. I'll tell him you are coming and wait with him below." After a slight hesitation, as if uncertain how he would receive such a familiarity, she leaned up to kiss his cheek.

Teagan watched her walk out, then lifted a hand to his face, warmed by her lips. He couldn't remember the last time he'd received a kiss of affection completely devoid of carnal overtones. It felt odd—and strangely comforting.

So startled had he been by her gesture, he'd neglected to ask the name of the gentleman awaiting him. Well, no matter. Aunt Charlotte would introduce them soon enough.

Taking a deep breath, he strode back to the bedchamber to check his reflection in the pier glass, making sure his cravat was neatly tied, and brushing a nonexistent bit of lint off the dark blue lapels of his coat.

He must be polite, respectful, not too charming. Make a favorable impression and appear to be a credit to his aunt. Uneasily, he wondered just how much the unknown gentleman knew of him and his reputation.

Then, shoulders back and spine ramrod straight, he walked down to meet Lady Charlotte's friend.

Quietly he entered the room where his aunt sat beside her guest, a gentleman whose back looked vaguely familiar. Two steps later Teagan halted in surprise. "Lord Riverton!"

The gentleman turned to him, ironic amusement in his gaze. "Mr. Fitzwilliams."

His aunt looked from one man to the other. "I see there's no need for introductions. I shall leave you two to converse, then. You will return for dinner, my lord?"

"I should be delighted, Lady Charlotte."

Lord Riverton stood and bowed as Lady Charlotte, giving Teagan a quick wink of encouragement, walked out.

"Won't you sit, Fitzwilliams? Although I suppose it is presumptuous of me to invite you to be seated in your own drawing room." Riverton raised an eyebrow. "My compliments. You are more resourceful than I'd thought."

Not sure whether Riverton's comment was sincere or mocking, Teagan replied, "It is Lady Charlotte's drawing room, my lord. I am but her guest."

"And her kinsman as well, are you not?"

Teagan nodded. "Lady Charlotte, out of affection for my late mother, has agreed to help me obtain a responsible position. Do you…have such a post to offer me?"

"Actually, I've had a post in mind for you for some time. Please, sit, and let us discuss it."

Teagan took the chair indicated, spirits quickening at the inference that his next goal might be within reach. He liked and respected Riverton, and whatever the earl had to offer, he'd do his utmost to satisfy his requirements.

"By the way, that stallion of yours is doing well. A bit of a handful when he's fresh, but quite a sweet goer."

"Then you've removed him from Montford's care. Thank you for that, my lord."

Riverton nodded. "As I mentioned, I've been observing you for quite some time. Were you aware of it?"

"N-not exactly, my lord. I did notice you seemed to turn up in locations I would not normally have expected you. And assisted me on several occasions, as well."

Riverton chuckled. "Crandall's doxy fair at the hunting box. An…interesting affair, to be sure. You occupy a rather unique position, Fitzwilliams. Though of the gentry, your need to survive after Oxford forced you to mingle with, and develop a broad acquaintance among, the lower orders. I could use a man with such contacts."

"In what way, my lord?"

"Actually, I've already approached you about it. Through an intermediary, of course." Riverton fell silent, watching Teagan's face.

Teagan scanned his memory, trying to recall a time at which he'd been contacted by anyone on a matter of employment. Then the connection slammed home and he whipped his glance to Riverton.

"That night in the stable after I lost everything to Montford—*you* were the one who sent the soldier?" he demanded, incredulity mingling with horror.

"Yes. But before you draw your pistol, let me assure you that I represent the opposite of what you are now presuming. The world knows me to be a member of the privy council. But only a few—including your aunt, whose late husband previously occupied this post—know that I also hold a hidden portfolio to investigate and pursue men who attempt to subvert the interests of our nation."

"You are...a spy?"

"I prefer to view myself as a protector of the liberties and privileges all Englishmen enjoy. I'm assisted in that aim by a number of men at all levels of society, in and out of government. Such as Sergeant Wilkerson, who approached you that night."

"Then why—" Teagan began, but Riverton waved him to silence.

"I shall explain. You were quite justified in assuming, by the manner in which the job was presented to you, that what you were being offered that night was a treasonous assignment. Particularly after that episode with your cousin, I was reasonably sure what caliber of man you are. But before I could ask you to assist me, I needed to be absolutely convinced of your honor. Given the straits to which you were reduced, I knew if you would not stoop to betrayal then, you were incapable of it."

Teagan sat back in his chair, trying to sort out all the revelations. "I...I'm a bit taken aback."

Riverton laughed softly. "As well you might be. I'd known for some time you must be a man of intelligence. You'd not have survived solely by gaming otherwise. It remained only to determine if the caliber of your character matched that of your wits. Now that I am convinced it does...would you be interested in assisting me?"

A covert fighter protecting English society against treason and corruption. Teagan grinned. Quite an extraordinary position for a half-breed Irishman.

"What would you have me do?"

"Actually, the assignment offered that night was genuine—if the opposite of what you were led to infer. I've been watching a minor government official whom, lamentably, we believe is selling copies of secret documents to the French. We know dispatches are being sent from his home to Dover. We need to know the identity of the person or persons who are receiving them and carrying them to France."

"And I would determine that, under guise of being the runner paid to transport the packets?"

"Yes. We want a full description of the recipient, plus any information you can glean on where he comes from, whether he carries the messages to France personally or turns them over to a different agent, and by what means the messages themselves leave England. Information that might be gleaned from conversation and observation by a gambler flush with a new stake, while he plied his luck at cards in a Dover tavern."

Riverton paused. "I would be remiss if I did not warn that 'tis dangerous work, Fitzwilliams. With the financial rewards so great and the consequences of discovery so dire, men would kill to protect their investments and cover up their involvement."

"'Tis not that part that troubles me, my lord." Teagan frowned, his excitement dimmed. "If I understand you correctly, in the job you envision I would continue to play the Jester? A man living by his wits and the roll of the dice? 'Tis precisely that life I wish to escape."

"I think we might be able to accommodate both our aims. You want to be readmitted to the Polite World. For that, only two things are essential—the correct backing, and money." Riverton gave him a sardonic smile. "Though it pains me to admit how shallow our privileged world can be, once it becomes known you have Lady Charlotte's support, and once you begin spending the funds I will make available to you, I believe you will find Society pleased to accord you a very warm welcome back!"

Teagan took a moment to absorb the import of Riverton's words. "Even if I appeared still to spend my life gaming, among company of rather dubious reputation?"

Riverton shrugged. "I offer you Lord Crandall, Westerley, and any number of similar fribbles."

Teagan laughed without humor. "Point taken. You are sure I would be of more use to you as the Jester than, say, as a respectable secretary or assistant?"

"You would be of nearly irreplaceable value in such a role. Men who can move easily—and when need be, invisibly—among all levels of society are extremely rare. You would be performing an invaluable service for me—and your country. A service that would have to remain unacknowledged, of course. But there would be a handsome monetary reward, quite enough to support rumors of newly acquired wealth. So…will you assist me?"

Teagan sat silent, considering. He would be restored to Society, have an income that forever freed him from fear of want. But…in the eyes of everyone, he would still be the irresponsible Teagan Fitzwilliams, gambler and rogue.

Not the responsible man with a respectable position beside whom Valeria could stand with honor.

"I trust the lady will have you, anyway."

Teagan's gaze jerked back to Riverton. "How did you…"

The minister smiled. "Fine spymaster I'd be if I didn't know where my operatives were at all times, eh, Fitzwilliams? She's lovely, and I wish you the best of luck winning her hand. Though, by what I saw at the Insley ball, and by Wilkerson's news from the docks, I suspect her heart is yours already." His face sobered. "This is not precisely what you envisioned, I realize. But the work of combating England's enemies is constant, and vitally important. Can I count on you?"

I am already proud to call you my friend. Valeria had been ready to stand by him, even as an indigent gamester. Still…Teagan wanted so much for her to know he was now doing something of which she could truly be proud.

"Would I be able to tell her the truth?"

"In vague generalities, perhaps. 'Tis not wise for any of us to divulge specifics to our loved ones. As you can understand, not only would we risk inadvertent disclosure, such knowledge would place them at risk."

Teagan extended his hand. "When do I begin?"

Smiling, Riverton shook it. "Shall we discuss it further tomorrow? When I bring back your stallion. Consider him the first payment on what England owes you."

Chapter Nineteen

A month later, grubby and bone-weary, Teagan rode Ailainn back to his aunt's town house in Mount Street. The report he had just delivered to Riverton, painstakingly gathered over many evenings of gaming and not a few heartstopping nights trailing a man he'd observed with the barkeep to whom he'd given his packets, should lay the groundwork for breaking up the ring that was marketing the stolen dispatches. Riverton had commended him on his work, Teagan recalled with a novel sense of satisfaction.

Riverton also told him that while he was away, Aunt Charlotte had been staging his reintroduction to the ton. He should expect several months of dinners, balls and receptions, during which Lady Charlotte would manipulate the social connections necessary to guarantee his permanent acceptance. After that, Riverton warned, Teagan's worst problem would be avoiding the schemes of matchmaking mamas who, assured of his restored status, would be almost as devious as their government traitor in attempting to trap the handsome, newly rich Mr. Fitzwilliams into marriage.

Recalling how Lady Insley had nearly fainted at the idea of admitting him to her ball, Teagan had difficulty believing the warning. But he'd gladly run a gauntlet far more dangerous than girlish sighs and matchmaking stratagems in exchange for the stature that would allow him to court Valeria Arnold with honor.

He'd debated penning her a note…but Riverton was correct. 'Twas better not to invite speculation by writing from Dover, nor could he reveal what he was doing there. Instead, he'd concluded, he'd wait until he could journey to Winterpark and speak with her face-to-face…and ask for her hand.

'Twas early evening by the time he'd returned Ailainn to the stables, ordered up hot food and water from the kitchen, and proceeded up the stairs to his rooms.

He sank into one of the leather armchairs, too weary to move, wanting nothing more than a warm bath, a warm meal and sleep. A knock at the door made him look up.

"Aunt Charlotte!"

"Welcome home, Teagan!" She walked over and bent as if to hug him, but he fended her off.

"I'm all over mud and smelling of horse."

She gave him a quick hug nonetheless. "As if I care for that! I'm so relieved you are safely back. I know you cannot tell me where you were or what you were doing, but I do know it was most probably dangerous."

Teagan gazed up at her anxious face, his respect for her rising another notch. Suddenly he remembered Riverton informing him that the late Lord Darnell had formerly held the position Riverton now occupied. She must have lived with similar uncertainty for years.

"No wonder you are so circumspect! And no wonder that your husband did not wish to add to your worries by seeing you saddled with an ill-behaved, half-Irish brat."

A look of sadness dimmed her face. "That was at least part of his reasoning, I suppose. I never managed to convince him it would be a blessing, not an imposition. But," she said, her expression clearing, "I disturbed you only to ask if, after you've bathed and dined and had a chance to rest, you feel you could accompany me this evening. There's a rout hosted by some friends of Lord Riverton at which I should like to present you.''

Teagan had to laugh. ''Lord Riverton warned me you'd begun your campaign for my rehabilitation. I suppose we must begin, then. But would your hostess not be inconvenienced by so late an addition to her guest list?''

''Not at all. I told our hosts, the Earl and Countess of Beaulieu, I would bring you along if you'd returned.''

A niggle of foreboding arose, and Teagan had a vivid image of walking through a throng of richly dressed aristocrats, all of them with heads averted, pointedly ignoring his presence. He'd weathered such humiliation before, but he dreaded having Aunt Charlotte witness—and be grieved by—such a spectacle.

''Are you certain 'tis a good idea to begin tonight?''

''Are you too fatigued?''

He could hide behind that excuse, but he owed it to her to express his reservations honestly. ''I am sure your friends would greet me kindly, but I am…somewhat concerned about the welcome I'll receive from their other guests. I…I don't want to embarrass you, Aunt Charlotte.''

Lady Darnell took his hand, mud and all. ''Teagan, do you trust Lord Riverton's strategies and expertise?''

''Absolutely.''

''Then you mustn't doubt mine in my own arena. I possess a great deal of social power, and I've been wielding all of it on your behalf.'' She gave a self-deprecating smile. ''I've little enough else to show for my life. For weeks now, I have regaled every person of prominence, from Prinny on down, with my delight in having persuaded my dear cousin's son to take up residence with me. They know I have settled an income on you and named you my heir. No one who wishes to safeguard a position in the ton will dare show you less than extreme cordiality, for all London knows any individual foolish enough to incur my displeasure might as well slink back to whatever provincial backwater from which they sprang. In fact, I rather fear you will be flattered and toadied to a most uncomfortable degree.''

His mind still worrying over the prospect of his gracious aunt being wounded by slights directed toward him, it took a moment for the information she'd just delivered to register. "You n-named me your heir?'' he echoed.

"Yes. The solicitors completed the paperwork last week. And though I am sure Riverton will see you well compensated for your recent efforts, the income I mentioned is now available for you to draw upon whenever you wish.''

Surprised and moved, Teagan hardly knew what to say. "You are too generous, Aunt Charlotte. I will be well paid for my work—''

"Nonsense. I have a large income in my own right from my grandfather the duke, in addition to the very comfortable legacy Darnell left me. Besides, the family owes you that and more. Uncle Montford should have settled an income upon you when you went to Oxford, if he hadn't been so disagreeably ill-tempered and controlling. You cannot imagine how I regret all those lost years I might have been indulging you in ponies and sweetmeats and all the treasures young lads enjoy.''

"You would have spoiled me outrageously.''

"Indeed I should have. Besides, I understand you may soon be wishing to set up a household of your own. No— I shall not tax you about the lady. I do hope you will bring her to meet me soon, though. So will you not accept the income? It would give me so much pleasure.''

Teagan put his hand to his chin, as if giving her question serious thought. "Now, let me see. Whist, and shall I whistle a fortune down the wind and grieve the heart of a kind lady who's shown me naught but affection since the moment I turned up, like a bad penny, on her doorstep?''

Lady Charlotte burst out laughing. ''My, but you sound like your papa when you do that!''

Teagan's merriment vanished. ''You...knew my father?''

''Of course! You're his very image. Impossibly handsome he was, magical with horses, and so charming I vow he could coax the birds into song. Quite frankly, I envied your mama.'' Lady Charlotte's smile faded. ''Gwyneth knew what she wanted from the moment she met Michael Fitzwilliams, and he felt the same. 'Tis tragic a love as deep and mutual as theirs ended as it did. But here is Harold with your dinner and your bathwater, so I'll leave you. Can you be ready by nine? Riverton is calling.''

Teagan pushed away a vague sense of unease. ''Let the games commence,'' he said, reaching for the dinner tray.

Lady Charlotte laughed. ''Let them commence indeed! And I have no doubt that you will bring home the laurel wreath of social victory!''

After his aunt departed, Teagan began eating while the servant set up the hip bath by the fire. But the meal he'd been so hungry for suddenly seemed tasteless.

Though Lady Charlotte seemed to blame his grandfather for the tragedy that had overcome his parents, Teagan believed a man was accountable for his own actions. Whatever his reasons, Michael Fitzwilliams had abandoned his dying wife and penniless son.

All his youth his Montford relations had drilled into him how much he resembled his irresponsible wastrel of a father. Having Aunt Charlotte, who had actually known the man, confirm the resemblance disturbed him more than he wished to admit.

A few hours later Teagan stood with Lord Riverton at the foot of the stairs, waiting for his aunt to descend. As she appeared on the landing, he heard Riverton's intake of breath and smiled. In her gown of frosted lavender silk, which brought out the blue of her eyes, Lady Charlotte did indeed look magnificent.

With the dignity of a queen, she slowly descended the stairs to take the hand Riverton offered. "Charlotte," the earl said, gazing into her eyes. "How is it you contrive to look younger and more beautiful every time I see you?"

Blushing a little, his aunt laughed. "Really, Mark, were we not such old friends, I would accuse you of flirting. At the least, 'tis bald-faced flattery."

"'Tis the Lord's own truth," Riverton responded. "To me, you still look every inch the beauty who took the ton by storm at her come-out ball."

"Stuff and nonsense," she reproved, tapping him with her fan. "I vow you don't even remember that night."

"Do I not?" Riverton replied. "You wore a gown of celestial blue satin over an open robe of white, with a wreath of white rosebuds in your hair. I thought you the most exquisite creature I'd ever beheld."

The teasing look on his aunt's face faded. "Y-you do remember," she faltered.

"Every moment," Riverton affirmed, his voice intense.

So that is how the land lies, Teagan thought, his smile broadening.

A blush tinging her cheeks, his aunt turned toward Teagan. "I expect we mustn't keep the horses standing. Teagan, you will give me your arm?"

"Of course, Aunt Charlotte." He threw the older man an apologetic glance as his aunt, after according Riverton a rather nervous smile, passed him to take Teagan's hand.

Teagan thought he heard the earl sigh, and then they were descending the stairs to the carriage.

"Are you acquainted with our hosts this evening, Teagan?" Lord Riverton asked as they entered the vehicle.

"Lord Beaulieu," Teagan said, trying to place the name. "Ah, he's the 'Puzzlebreaker' who founded that club devoted to the solution of mathematical problems?"

"Yes. An interesting and intelligent man," Riverton replied. "Also an associate of mine."

Teagan glanced up at Riverton, who gave him a slight nod. Another member of Riverton's network, he surmised.

"His wife is a lovely lady, formerly widow of Viscount Charleton," Lady Charlotte said. "I was particularly glad you were able to join us this evening, for this will be her last public entertainment. She's in a delicate condition and is about to leave London for her confinement."

"First child," Riverton said with a laugh. "Beaulieu is so nervous, you'd think he were about to give birth."

"As well he should be nervous," Lady Charlotte replied sharply. "So many things can go wrong."

She averted her face, and Lord Riverton reached over to touch her hand. "I'm sorry, Charlotte," he said quietly. "That was poorly said."

She shook her head slightly and turned to the window. "Ah, we've arrived. What a crush of carriages!"

Teagan had seldom seen his imperturbable employer so at a loss for words, and felt a sympathetic pang. With a hopeless shrug at Teagan, Riverton turned to help Lady Charlotte descend from the carriage.

Then they were caught up in the throng and borne along to the receiving line. Lady Charlotte again took Teagan's arm, presenting him to her acquaintances as they waited.

Had it not been so bitterly ironic, Teagan might have laughed out loud. His aunt's prediction had been only too correct. Gentlemen who a month previous would scarcely have accorded him a glance, much less a word, lingered to shake his hand, two of them insinuating they would be delighted to introduce his name as a prospective member of their club. Matrons who had shunned his gaze and crossed the street to avoid subjecting their innocent offspring to the contagion of his proximity now flocked around him as if he'd discovered the secret location of the fountain of youth, their blushing daughters in tow. Before he'd met his hosts, he'd been pressed to sign a dozen dance cards.

All this courtesy was being extended, he thought with faint contempt, to a man who had reportedly just returned from a spate of gaming at the spas along the coast. Wealth and sponsorship were indeed splendid launderers of character, it appeared.

After being kindly greeted by the earl and his countess, he was borne off by Lady Charlotte, who insisted on claiming him for the first dance.

As he returned her afterward to Riverton's waiting arm, Holden Insley called a greeting.

"Mr. Fitzwilliams, may I join the multitude—" Insley waved at the eager crowd already pressing up to them "—in congratulating you on your recent good fortune!"

"Thank you, Holden. I must admit I'm finding the change a bit…overwhelming."

"I cannot think of anyone more deserving of good fortune. I had best release you, though," he said with a chuckle, "before some impatient matron with a daughter to present stabs me to death with a quill from her ostrich plume headdress."

He walked off, leaving Teagan to parry the enthusiastic greetings of several such matrons. After signing yet another dance card and extracting himself from the lady's clinging hand, he attempted to head toward the refreshment room, where he'd seen Riverton disappear.

"Well, well, Jester! If you've not landed on your feet like the proverbial tomcat."

Teagan looked up to see Rafe Crandall blocking his path, swaying slightly, the equally inebriated Wexley behind him. "Stap me, if I didn't damn well nearly swallow my teeth t'other day when Winslow—family's all to pieces, y'know, and three daughters to marry off—put up your name for membership at White's!" He raised a champagne glass to Teagan, slopping some of the contents. "I shall try to win some of that new blunt off you, eh? Though I do think it blasted unfair, don't you, Wexley? Doxies already hang over Jester. Now that he's rich, all the hothouse flowers in London'll be rubbin' their petals up against 'im, too."

"Unfair," Wexley echoed, shaking his head and almost losing his balance.

"Watch out. Those virginal buds'll be wantin' to lure you not to pleasurin', but to the parson's mousetrap!"

Had he really spent most of the last ten years in such company as this? Teagan thought with a grimace of distaste. "Thanks for the warning, Rafe. I'll be on my guard."

"See that you are." Crandall wagged a finger in Teagan's face before moving out of his way. "Bad enough t'see you redeemed. If I heard you was to be leg-shackled, 'twould be enough to make a fellow lose his lunch."

As the evening progressed, however, Teagan began to wonder if he might not prefer Rafe's company, after all. He'd lost count of the effusive matrons who'd greeted him and the profusion of tongue-tied maidens who'd been thrust before him, with whom he'd attempted to carry on a stilted, mostly one-sided conversation.

No wonder Valeria wanted no part of this, he thought. For a moment, the urgent desire to gaze on her lovely, intelligent face, hear her musical voice and her witty commentary, filled him with a wave of acute longing.

The strong sense of being watched pulled him from his

reverie. He glanced up to find the Earl of Montford staring at him, a sardonic look on his face.

Teagan stiffened. "Cousin," he said, nodding.

Montford didn't return the courtesy. Before Teagan could summon up a properly piquing comment, yet another eager matron rushed up to introduce her daughter and solicit his signature on her dance card.

Montford watched until the pair walked away. "My, what a spectacle. But I'm not as easy to gull. Blood will out. I'll wager those little fillies making eyes at you wouldn't be so eager to jump into harness if they knew how quickly your dear papa abandoned your mama. You may have induced Lady Charlotte to cover your sins and endow you with funds—or should I say 'seduced'?—but—"

Riverton seemed to materialize out of nowhere, to clamp a hand on the earl's arm. "Montford," he interrupted in a low, steely voice, "if you want to keep all your teeth, I advise you not to complete that sentence."

Montford gave Teagan a resentful glance, but fell silent.

"I expect you to treat your cousin, if not with friendliness, at least with courtesy," Riverton added.

After a long moment, Montford turned to give Teagan the minutest of bows. "Cousin. Since you've brought your watchdog, I suppose I must comply."

"You would be advised to remember what this watchdog watched," Riverton said, his tone still menacing. "Recall also that I possess fewer scruples than your noble cousin. Indeed, I must insist that you stroll with me. There seems to be a small matter of which you need reminding."

Riverton swept a gesture toward the door. After an irresolute moment, Montford nodded. Giving Teagan a look of loathing, he followed the cabinet minister.

While Teagan stood watching them, a heavy woman in

a puce gown, her headdress rising several feet above her elaborate coiffeur, bumped into him.

"Why, Mr. Fitzwilliams," she cried in shrill tones, latching on to his arm. "How nice to meet you again. Lady Amesbury, you'll remember! You must come take tea with us tomorrow, must he not, Marianne?"

She jerked forward a thin, plain brunette with the frightened expression of a cornered rabbit. "Y-yes, Mama," she replied in a barely audible voice.

"Marianne has been in raptures over you, Mr. Fitzwilliams! Now, surely you cannot wish to disappoint a lovely young lady, eh? Do say you will come tomorrow."

A scarlet flush mounted the girl's pale cheeks. "Please, Mama," she said in an urgent undertone.

"Pish-tosh, Marianne, sometimes a girl needs to take the lead—and a gentleman don't mind knowing he's appreciated, does he, Mr. Fitzwilliams? You will be there, won't you?" Her grip on his arm tightened, as if she did not intend to release him until she'd obtained his consent.

Her daughter had turned pale, and she looked as if she were about to expire on the spot from mortification. Vulgar and encroaching as Teagan found the mother, he could not help but feel sorry for the girl.

"Should you like me to call?" he asked Miss Marianne.

She goggled at him, as if astounded he'd actually deigned to address her. "I, ah, y-yes," she stuttered.

Already regretting his momentary chivalry, Teagan could do nothing but bow and agree to present himself the following day. Shaking free of Lady Amesbury's arm, he made his way toward the refreshment room, determined to find his aunt and beg her to let them depart.

As it was, he had to endure several more dances before he at last made his escape. His head pounding more painfully than with the worst of cheap brandy hangovers, he sank thankfully into a corner of the coach.

"Aunt Charlotte," he groaned, "I believe I was mistaken. I don't wish to be reinstated, after all."

Riverton chuckled. "You've only begun, my friend. You do realize you are expected to call tomorrow upon every one of the young ladies with whom you danced tonight."

Teagan groaned again. "Do you not have some urgent assignment for me, sir—preferably to the Outer Hebrides?"

"You'll be wishing it were to the Straits of Magellan once you've taken tea with Lady Amesbury," his aunt said.

"I felt sorry for the daughter," Teagan admitted.

Riverton grinned. "By the time tea is concluded, you will doubtless have confirmed the old adage that no good deed remains unpunished."

The carriage slowed before the Mount Street town house, sparing Teagan a reply. As the hour was late and he'd been in the saddle for nearly the whole of the day, he excused himself from having brandy in the parlor with his aunt and Lord Riverton. Though as he mounted the stairs, he could not help throwing a speculative glance back at Riverton, his dark head bent over Lady Charlotte's blond one.

Fatigue was only partly responsible for Teagan's need for solitude. The degree of attention he'd been accorded was, as he'd told Insley, unsettling, and made him speculate that except for the stain it cast upon his reputation, his banishment had perhaps been more boon than bane. Certainly he'd had more intelligent and stimulating conversation in half an hour with Valeria than in that whole evening with a mansion full of people.

Valeria. His thoughts returned to her like a lodestone to the north, but for the first time since he'd left her, worry clouded the purity of his longing to end their separation.

His aunt's and cousin's words echoed in his head.

His parents' love had been deep and mutual, Aunt Charlotte said. Certainly his mother had believed Michael Fitzwilliams's vows of affection, abandoning her privileged place in English society to run off with him.

And then had been left by him to die alone and destitute in a Dublin hovel.

How could his father have loved Gwyneth Hartness— really loved her, as Teagan loved Valeria—and disappear, leaving her ill and penniless, with a young son to care for? Had time and proximity and poverty degraded that deep emotion? Or had he not been capable of love that endured?

Teagan was his father's image, as even Aunt Charlotte had told him. If he persuaded Valeria to pledge him her love, how could he be sure he too did not possess some flaw deep within his character, a weakness that might lead him to one day leave her as well, heartbroken, if not penniless?

Every instinct protested. He loved Valeria with all the strength his soul possessed, and would gladly lay down his life for her.

But could he *live* a lifetime with her?

What, after all, did he know of love or permanence? His sole previous grand amour had endured a mere matter of weeks, and the casual relationships he'd had with women since weren't worthy of mention.

An excruciating memory, perhaps the most devastating of his life and one therefore that he rigidly suppressed, forced itself into consciousness. The look on the face of his Oxford mentor when he'd walked in to find Teagan in flagrante delicto with his son's wife: horror succeeded by sorrow—and deepest disappointment.

Teagan would rather shoot himself than ever bring such a look to the face of Valeria Arnold.

How could he know for sure he would not? Until he could convince himself he could never subject her to that abomination, he must not return for her.

Chapter Twenty

Valeria sat in the estate office trying to force herself to concentrate on the ledger before her. Sighing, she reached over to sip Mercy's special chamomile tea, beside which reposed a basket containing two of Cook's best jam tarts fresh from the oven. Adding their sweet scent was a vaseful of summer's first roses, just delivered by Sissy.

All the staff were so solicitous, trying to cheer their list-less mistress, that she would have to at least nibble at a tart, although it seemed her appetite had vanished with her enthusiasm weeks ago. One drizzly morning that was turning to sunshine as Teagan Fitzwilliams rode away.

For a fortnight after his departure she had been so ill she could not eat at all. Half defiant, half terrified by her folly, she had shared Mercy's unspoken fears. Yet with the relief that came with her courses had also come an unexpectedly deep sense of disappointment.

She had not conceived his child. She would not carry within her a part of him that would belong to her forever. She did not have reason to call him back.

Though that latter thought had occurred only to be con-temptuously dismissed. Teagan had promised to return, and she would wait for him to honor that pledge. She would never stoop to trapping him with a woman's oldest trick. Once had been more than sufficient to give herself in marriage to a man who didn't really want her.

Would Teagan return? In more than two months, she'd received not the briefest of notes. Though he had not promised to write, somehow she'd expected...something. Some contact that assured her that what they'd shared still meant as much to him as it did to her.

Had he won enough to make it back to London? Was he able to reconcile with his family? Was he seeking a position, or now embarked in a new post, and if so, where in England had that taken him? Was he even now making preparations to return to her, buoyed with confidence at the success of his plans?

Or had his family rejected his overtures, leaving him trapped in a gambler's uncertain life, mired in a role he believed made him unworthy to approach her?

Oh Teagan, why have you not written to me? she thought, suppressing the tears that seemed of late to come so easily. Even the worst news would be easier to bear than this uncertainty.

At a soft tap, she looked up, to see Mercy entering.

"We have visitors, Miss Val. No—not him."

Heat burned in her cheeks, followed by anger. Rage at the foolish hope that still caused her heart to leap every time Giddings came in with a tray that might bear a letter, or when she chanced to hear hoofbeats or the rattle of a carriage approaching up the drive.

Mercy came over to place a sympathetic hand on Valeria's shoulder. "I'm right sorry, chick, but 'tis even worse. Sir Arthur and Lady Hardesty are awaiting you."

"The Hardestys!" she exclaimed with a groan. "Whatever brought them here?"

"Lady Hardesty says they were journeying to London, and Winterpark being but half a day's travel off the main road, she felt she simply must stop to see you.'' Irony colored the nurse's tone.

"How did she even know I resided here?'' Valeria grumbled. ''Ah, yes. Maria Edgeworth, the town crier. Which means she must know all about Grandmamma's bequest, and be even more convinced that I should make the perfect wife for her son. I don't suppose you could say I'm out?''

"I could, but 'twould only delay her.'' A grim look came into Mercy's face. ''She was hinting that they expected to be avisiting near on a week.''

"A week!'' Valeria said, her voice rising to a squeak. ''I shall be ready to do murder within a day!'' An even more unwelcome memory intruded, and she groaned again. ''Tis worse than her ploy to bring me to Hardesty's Castle. I should not be surprised if she intends to remain until she manages to throw Sir Arthur together with me in some 'compromising' situation that, she will insist, requires us to marry in order to preserve my reputation.''

Valeria paced to the window. ''I shall see them now. Then, while Lady Hardesty rests later this afternoon, I can figure out some means to detach them from Winterpark.''

Smiling with gritted teeth, Valeria entered the parlor to greet her unwanted guests. ''Sir Arthur, Lady Hardesty. How...unexpected to see you.''

"Dear, dear Valeria, how could we be so close and not stop to express our condolences over your grievous loss?'' Lady Hardesty exclaimed, as if they'd come for a morning call instead of from a distance of several hundred miles. ''Besides, traveling is so injurious to my delicate health, I must interrupt my journey at frequent intervals.''

Valeria cast a skeptical eye over Lady Hardesty's stout figure and glowing cheeks. Sir Arthur, however, did look pale and uncomfortable. Not entirely, she suspected, from the motion of the carriage.

Taking pity on him, she extended her hand. "Sir Arthur, you appear fatigued."

He kissed her fingers. "But you, Lady Arnold, are, as always, kindness and beauty personified."

"Oh, Arthur is always in perfect health!" his mother said. "Now *I* am feeling rather faint. Perhaps some tea and cakes would restore me. That is, assuming the cook kept here by Lady Winterdale is superior to the creature you employed at Eastwoods. And Valeria, dear, why are your entryway and mirrors not still draped in black?"

"It has been more than three months since Grand-mamma's passing," Valeria replied, ignoring the first remark and trying to rein in her temper.

"Well, one must not be remiss in observing the proprieties! Appearances are important, especially before the servants. At least you are still wearing your black. Although you must tell your maid—I trust you now have someone more skilled than that elderly nurse—to be more careful how she irons the bombazine. I believe I see a shiny spot on your skirt."

"You must excuse me while I go see about refreshments," Valeria said, fearing for her temper—or the nearest china vase—if she did not make an imminent escape.

"Very well, if you cannot trust your butler to make the arrangements. After we've eaten you can take Arthur for a walk in your gardens, which my guidebook tells me are excellent. A walk is so beneficial for the constitution."

Valeria wasn't *that* sorry for Arthur Hardesty. "Then he should escort you, Lady Hardesty. 'Twill help you recover from your journey."

Her smile disintegrating into a grimace, Valeria stalked out of the room and leaned back against the closed door with a sigh.

Giddings approached, concern creasing his brow. "Is something wrong, my lady?"

"N-no, Giddings. My...guests are a bit trying."

"Please send in tea and cakes." A thought occurred, and she added, "Ask Mercy to prepare me a pot of the chamomile, as well."

There was nothing humorous about the Hardestys lingering at Winterpark.

She couldn't endure a week of Lady Hardesty's tactless manipulation. She must find a way to speed their departure, she thought as she reentered the parlor.

She found Lady Hardesty examining the jade figurines on the mantel.

"Antique, are they?" her ladyship inquired, as if inspecting the possessions of one's hostess were part of the normal protocol of an afternoon call.

"Ming dynasty, the registry reports," Valeria replied, her temper once more aflame. "If you would be seated, Lady Hardesty, tea should be here momentarily." Turning to Sir Arthur in an attempt to redirect the conversation away from his mother, she inquired, "How goes the farm work at Hardesty's Castle? Was the shearing successful?"

"It went splendidly," Lady Hardesty replied for him. "Arthur, you must tell dear Valeria about the several days you spent overseeing the shearing at Eastwoods. Arthur takes particular interest in insuring your property is correctly managed."

I'll bet he does, Valeria thought acidly.

"Masters appeared more frail than ever when I visited last week," Lady Hardesty continued. "And your housemaid, Sukey Mae, the one I often recommended you dismiss, has proved herself the trollop everyone knew she was. Ran off with the squire's groom—and no wedding before that trip!"

"Ah, here's the tea," Valeria said, as Giddings came in bearing the massive tray. A merciful space of time was occupied fixing cups and dispensing the jam tarts.

"The small pot contains my herbal brew," Valeria informed Lady Hardesty, who was avidly emptying her plate. "My own health has been indifferent for weeks, and I've had to resort to herbal infusions to settle my stomach. Indeed, my throat has been rather raw and I fear I may be developing a cough. I was…reposing when you arrived."

"Valeria, dear, you work too hard. Managing an estate this size is too arduous a task for a gently bred lady. You need a husband to take the burden from those slender shoulders—don't she, Arthur?" Lady Hardesty cast an arch look at her son, who choked on his tea.

To wrest control of an estate as wealthy as Winterpark, Lady Hardesty was apparently prepared to risk her oft-proclaimed delicate health—which was not so delicate that it prevented that lady from consuming an impressive number of jam tarts, Valeria noted.

"Oh, and speaking of bad breeding…I've just received the most amazing news! It seems that blackguard I warned you about last winter is now running the most astounding rig on another supposedly genteel lady of the ton!"

"Mama, really," Sir Arthur objected. "Lady Charlotte Darnell was first cousin to Teagan Fitzwilliams's mother."

Valeria's heart skipped a beat and she almost dropped her teacup. "T-Teagan Fitzwilliams?" she stuttered.

"So-called 'aunt' she may be, but I still say there's something havey-cavey going on. As unrepentant a gamester as ever, and out of the blue, here he is living in Lady Charlotte's home, being introduced by her to Society and, rumor has it, even named her heir!"

"Perhaps he has finally reconciled with his mother's family," Sir Arthur said. "In that case, we should commend both sides for settling their differences."

"Well, I think a woman of her mature years should know better than to have been taken in by such a rogue!"

"Apparently she's not the only one so taken in," Sir

Arthur persisted, some irritation in his tone. "Your friend Maria said in her letter that not only is Lady Charlotte introducing him about, he is being everywhere received by the first families. She even wrote that several young ladies have already set their caps at him."

"Set their caps at him and the Darnell fortune," Lady Hardesty retorted. "More fools, they! That squabby little Marianne Amesbury he's said to be courting has neither wit nor beauty. Ha! Offspring of a nobleman and a vulgar Cit's daughter! If she does manage to snare Fitzwilliams, I predict she'll end up abandoned just like his mama, Lady Gwyneth."

"You have ever been prejudiced against poor Mr. Fitzwilliams!" her son exclaimed. "As I've often told you, Mama, I knew him well at Eton, and *I* found no vice in him."

For the next few moments mother and son squabbled over the merits of Teagan's character, requiring no comment from Valeria. Which was fortunate, for she did not think she could have managed a coherent word.

By the time an uneasy truce finally brought momentary silence, she had recovered herself enough to quickly insert, "How fatigued you must be, Lady Hardesty. Please, allow Giddings to show you and Sir Arthur to your chambers. I myself intend to seek my bed." She rose and walked swiftly over to yank on the bell pull.

"You do look rather unwell, Lady Arnold," Sir Arthur observed. "Mama, I believe we are tiring our hostess."

Snatching up the last of the jam tarts, Lady Hardesty allowed her son to hoist her to her feet. "You'll be able to change to half-mourning soon, Valeria dear, which will not make you look as haggard as that black. Very well, Arthur, I'm coming. We shall see you for dinner."

Valeria marched over and yanked open the parlor door,

causing Giddings, who'd apparently been leaning into it while he turned the handle, to nearly fall into the room.

"Please convey Sir Arthur and Lady Hardesty to their chambers," she said, wild with impatience to be rid of them so she might sort out her shocked and conflicting emotions.

"This way, Lady Hardesty, Sir Arthur," Giddings intoned, and at long last led them away.

She needed silence and solitude. Without even waiting to find a wrap, Valeria half-ran to the library, jerked open the terrace door, and fled into the gardens.

She should be thrilled for him. Apparently Teagan had succeeded in obtaining a rapprochement with his family, although according to Lady Hardesty's informant he had not given up gaming. His reputation must also be a fair way to being mended if he was being received not just by his own family, but by households with marriageable daughters.

Were the young ladies tossing their caps at him?

Was he in fact courting one in particular?

The pain of that thought cut so deep Valeria's knees were suddenly weak, and she had to sit down abruptly on the nearest garden bench. No, she could not believe the vows of constancy he'd uttered with such fervent conviction could have been forgotten so quickly and completely.

Besides, Maria Edgeworth was the worst sort of gossip, whose tales could not be depended upon to contain more than a modicum of truth.

But if he had reconciled with his family and nearly restored his good name, why had he not come back for her? Or at least written of his progress?

Perhaps he was still arranging employment, though if she could believe the report of his being made the heir of his mother's wealthy cousin, he'd have no need of it.

Or perhaps Valeria was an even greater fool than the Cit's daughter who thought to capture Teagan and the Darnell fortune. Perhaps she, too, was merely another woman he'd bewitched, pleasured well and left behind.

Even as her heart cried out against that painful assessment, the sound of footsteps crunching on the gravel pathway caught her ear. She looked up to see Giddings approaching. "A letter for you, my lady," he said.

He had written, after all! Her bruised spirits rebounding with a joyous leap, Valeria thanked the butler and took the folded paper from his hand. Fingers trembling with eagerness, she unfolded the missive.

And found at the bottom of the page of sloping masculine scrawl the signature "W. Parham."

Disappointment struck her like a blow to the chest. She shut her eyes against the tears that threatened, her rigidly clenched fingers crumpling the paper.

She would not weep. She'd vowed over Hugh's grave never to waste another tear on a man, and she had no intention now of breaking that vow.

Some time later, when she felt she could open her eyes without the vista beyond them blurring, she smoothed the paper and read Sir William's letter.

My dear Lady Arnold, I hope this finds you recovering your spirits after the pain of your recent loss. I certainly wish it may, for London seems very dull without you, and I impatiently await your return to the city.

The Season continues much the same, though you will probably be pleased to learn your friend Mr. Fitzwilliams has reconciled with his family and is presently residing with his mother's cousin Lady Charlotte Darnell, a most influential Society hostess. He's become quite the darling of the young ladies, as one might expect of a gentleman of his charm and address.

Please know I stand ready to lend you whatever assistance it is within my power to afford. I should be

honored to come to Winterpark and escort you back
to London whenever you are feeling sufficiently recovered to undertake the journey. Your friendship has
been my most particular joy, and it remains my fervent
wish that it might continue to grow and deepen.

In hopes of seeing you again soon, I remain…

Senses dulled to a low throb of agony, Valeria refolded
the letter and stared sightlessly at the garden.

So most of what the Hardestys had reported was true.
Teagan was restored to favor. She must be glad for that.

But if he had not felt compelled to inform her of so
important a development, he could not hold her in the same
degree of regard and affection she did him. While she worried and wondered and pined away at Winterpark, he had
been disporting himself with the eligible ladies of London.
In all likelihood, he was never coming back.

The conclusion cut like a sword slash to the bone. She
had to breathe in and out slowly, cautiously, until the pain
was bearable.

If Teagan Fitzwilliams was not coming back, what was
Valeria Arnold to do with her life?

At least part of Lady Hardesty's assertion was true. Including Winterpark, the London town house, Eastwoods,
and several other minor properties she'd not even visited
yet, her estates now required more work than she wished
to take on alone. And having tasted the delights of passion,
she did not wish to live the rest of her life celibate.

After secretly hoarding for several weeks the suspicion
that she might be with child, she now found the idea immensely appealing. She would, she concluded, very much
like children of her own.

Which all suggested that, as Lady Hardesty would no
doubt be delighted to point out, Valeria ought to seriously
consider the idea of remarrying.

Not Arthur Hardesty, of course. But Sir William Parham, who'd been her quiet support through the trial of Lady Winterdale's funeral, who'd both generously alleged Teagan Fitzwilliams's honesty and with self-deprecating modesty expressed his own wistful desire to win her affection, might be the very man.

Quiet, dependable, well-respected. A skillful husband of her new estate and a kind husband to her person. A good provider who would be a fond father to her children. Perhaps even a man with whom she could share a mutually enjoyable passion, if not one as mindlessly intoxicating as that which she'd experienced…elsewhere.

It suddenly occurred to her that in Sir William's letter she had the answer to all her dilemmas.

She would not have to outwit or displace the Hardestys. Nor did she need to remain passively waiting for a man who could not even be bothered to pen her a letter. She would simply announce to her erstwhile guests that she'd received an urgent summons to return to London immediately.

Of course, she would assure them, they were welcome to rest at Winterpark until Lady Hardesty recovered fully from the rigors of their previous journey. Since circumstances compelled her to travel at a pace far too fatiguing for one of her ladyship's delicate constitution, Valeria would have to deny herself the pleasure of their company on the road.

Once there, she would see if, from the ashes of heartache and disappointment, she might be able to build a new relationship. One whose virtues of friendship, mutual respect and permanence compensated for its lacking heart-stopping extremes of ecstasy and despair.

Teagan Fitzwilliams is in London, her heart whispered.

London is a large metropolis, answered her head. And she had no desire whatsoever to see him.

*   *   *

In the late morning ten days later, Teagan reclined in the leather armchair in his sitting room, trying to summon up some enthusiasm for the masquerade ball Aunt Charlotte wished him to escort her to this evening.

The patina of social acceptance had quickly worn thin. 'Twas amusing, Teagan thought, that this former social pariah who'd been banned as a threat to virginal heiresses, was now, as heir to a sizable fortune, in danger from them.

The Marriage Mart of London society must be negotiated by a single gentleman of means with the caution of a Castlereagh, he'd discovered. He must not pay undue attention to any one maiden lest he give rise to expectations he had no intentions of fulfilling. And he must be ever mindful of the circumstances and chaperones attending any maiden with whom he found himself, so as to avoid potentially compromising situations.

Such as had been the case with the Amesbury chit. A moment of compassion had led him to ten days' worth of intricate social ballet in order to extricate himself short of a declaration, but with honor intact.

And though he pitied the poor girl, his sympathies ended well short of offering marriage. The contrast between her painfully young and diffident character—unfortunately all too typical of the tender maidens to whom he'd been introduced—and Valeria Arnold only made the intelligence, wit, independence and passion of that lady more striking.

The lady to whom every night he made love in his dreams, every morning awoke disappointed not to find in his arms. With his social position firmly secured, he ached to return to her.

If only he could banish the doubts that spawned nightmares that woke him, bathed in sweat, wracked by visions of a woman dying alone and abandoned, a woman with his mother's body and Valeria's face.

He had betrayed a trust before, he thought, recalling with a wrench of pain his Oxford mentor's sorrowful face. What made him so sure he would not do so again?

His father's son...cast in his father's image. Flesh of flesh, blood of blood—and heart of deceitful heart?

He slammed his fist down on the table in despair. Somehow he must decide soon...before he lost everything by making Valeria lose faith in his vows to return.

"Teagan, may I come in?"

He started at the sound of his aunt's voice. "Of course, Aunt Charlotte."

She entered a moment later, a small wooden box in her hands. "While up in the attics searching for my costume, I found this. 'Tis something I'd always intended to give you someday, but had forgotten I still possessed."

She held it out. Curious, he took it.

"It contains your mama's letters. The clergyman who found you discovered these at the rooming house in which you'd been living when Gwyneth died. Uncle Montford was going to burn them, but Gwen's old governess, knowing how close we had been, spirited them away and sent them to me. I kept them, thinking one day you might like to have them."

"Have you read them?"

"No. Most of them were written by your father to Gwen, and I felt they were too private for my eyes. But I hoped perhaps they might help you better understand the man your mother loved so much."

Teagan was not so sure he wished to read them, either. "Thank you, Aunt Charlotte. That was very kind."

She smiled. "I must help Charity finish my costume, so I'll leave you to them." Dropping a quick kiss on his forehead, she slipped back out.

Teagan put the box on the table and stared at it.

Why should he wish to read the letters of a man who

had so bewitched his mother that she'd followed him to her death, in heartbreak and penury?

His grandfather was right; they ought to be burned. He carried the box to the hearth.

But as he removed the first letter, the faded, spidery script of the missives written nearly thirty years ago by the man whose blood coursed through his veins, but about whom he knew so little, cast an irresistible spell.

Teagan walked back to his armchair, set the box on the table beside it and began to read.

The notes were arranged in roughly chronological order. Apparently once Lady Gwyneth's parents became aware of her attraction to a totally ineligible Irish groom, the young lady was packed off to her cousin's and the groom banished to the stud farm at Langdon—the same one Teagan had later managed, he realized. The two had then established a clandestine correspondence.

The bulk of the letters expressed their love and longing, their search to find some way to bridge the social chasm that separated them. And when the lady's parents threatened to put an end to her infatuation by marrying her off to a more acceptable suitor, Teagan found a note planning an elopement.

Despite his initial disdain, he was caught up in the drama of his parents' love and separation, which paralleled in some ways his own with Valeria.

But it was the final two letters that riveted his attention. The first, written by his father from the port of Galway, sent love and encouragement to his wife and young son in Dublin, and adjured them to stay at the boardinghouse where he'd left money for them during his journey to the Americas. Once he'd settled and bought property, he would send for them to begin a new life in a land where no one would think twice about an earl's daughter marrying an

Irish groom. A land where a man's character and achievements, not his pedigree, determined his worth.

The last letter, from a shipping company in Galway, dated just a few days before his mama's death, regretted to inform Mrs. Fitzwilliams of the demise of her husband aboard the brigantine the *Merry Alice,* lost with all hands in a violent storm off the Irish coast.

Teagan sat motionless, the letter clutched in his fingers, as the full implications of his father's correspondence gradually filled his mind.

Michael Fitzwilliams had loved his wife and son until the day he died. He'd left them to travel to the Americas where he, a man possessed of sufficient funds to buy both overseas passage and property upon arrival, intended to build a new life for them.

Not a wastrel. Not irresponsible. Not a careless bastard who'd abandoned his own son and the woman who'd loved him to die in penury.

Carefully Teagan refolded the letters and tucked them back in the wooden box. His one legacy from the father who'd loved him.

Then an even more arresting conclusion captured him.

If his father had honored his love and trust until death, then Teagan need no longer fear to go to Valeria.

The box forgotten, he ran to find his aunt.

He tracked her down in the sewing room and begged for a private moment. Obligingly, she dismissed her maid and beckoned him to a chair.

"What is it that has put that starry light in your eyes, my dear?"

"I shall tell you all about it later. But for now I need to inform you I cannot escort you tonight. I must leave London as soon as I can pack a bag."

"In such a rush? May I ask your destination?"

"Winterpark, a country estate that is now home to Lady

Arnold, the late Dowager Countess of Winterdale's grand-daughter.''

His aunt's delighted smile faded. "Lady Arnold?" she repeated, distress in her eyes. "Are you telling me Valeria Arnold is the lady for whom you've been pining?"

"I shall pine no longer," he said, excitement bringing a smile to his lips. "In fact, if I am very lucky, I shall bring her back to introduce to you—as my affianced wife. Give me a kiss, and I'll be off."

He bent down, lips pursed. She ducked her head to avoid his salute. "Lady Arnold is not at Winterpark."

Teagan paused. "You must be mistaken. I know she retired there after Lady Winterdale's death."

"Yes, but she returned to London about a week ago."

Valeria here? Then why had she not contacted him?

"Are you sure?" he demanded.

"Absolutely. She paid me a call yesterday. Oh, Teagan, there were a number of ladies present, and I'm afraid they were gossiping—about you."

Teagan grew very still. "And what were they saying?"

"Lady Jersey and Mrs. Drummond-Burrell and Princess Esterhazy were here, and the princess commended you for your recent exemplary behavior. Then Sally asserted that there is nothing so engaging as an almost-reformed rake. When I protested that assessment of you, she pointed out as proof all the young ladies whose mamas have been pressing invitations on you, and the Amesbury chit everyone says you've been courting. Then...then Lady Arnold asked me if it were true that you were courting her, and I said I wasn't sure, but that you had called there quite often and were not the sort of man to trifle with a girl's affections."

Teagan groaned and closed his eyes.

"Oh, Teagan, I'm so sorry! I had no idea—"

"No, how could you? But I must seek her out at once, before my case is irretrievably lost."

"Does she have any idea of your true feelings?"

"An idea, but I never confessed my love openly."

Lady Charlotte gave him a push. "Then you've not a moment to spare. Sally Jersey told me after Lady Arnold left that Sir William Parham had confided to her he meant to propose this very afternoon!"

Chapter Twenty-One

Valeria sat by the window in a pool of early afternoon sunshine, waiting for Sir William to arrive. He'd begged leave to call upon her at one. She was reasonably sure he meant to make her a proposal of marriage.

She was not at all sure what she would reply.

Deny it as she may, she'd been secretly hoping ever since her arrival a week ago that, some morning or afternoon, Molly would run in to announce that Teagan Fitzwilliams had called. She'd held her breath at each of the evening entertainments she'd attended, usually on Sir William's arm, half hoping, half dreading to meet Teagan.

He hadn't called. She hadn't met him.

Ever since arriving, she'd also debated the wisdom of writing to inform him of her return. But what would she say? "Dear sir, I have come back to London to see if the passionate love you made to me at Winterpark was indicative of a lasting affection, and to discover if you truly meant your vow to return."

She'd concluded 'twas impossible. Surely he would soon discover that she had returned. If he wished to make good his vow, he would seek her out.

But when days passed with no word of him, in desperation she'd actually called at his aunt's house, almost expiring with fear that he might be in the parlor with his aunt when she arrived. Mercifully, he hadn't been, but what she'd learned there had been almost as heartbreaking as being treated by him with casual courtesy as an acquaintance with whom he'd once explored the city.

According to the ladies present, including his aunt, Teagan was in fact courting the Amesbury girl. Even more damning, Lady Charlotte had answered all her questions with a cordial openness that made painfully clear she had no notion that Teagan was even acquainted with Valeria.

If he had not so much as mentioned her to the lady who had opened her home to him and made him her heir, Valeria could not fool herself any longer that he'd ever harbored toward her any truly serious intentions.

He'd only promised to come back. She did not doubt the intensity of the passion they'd shared, and was certain if she offered herself, Teagan might oblige her by continuing their affair. But he'd never spoken of love, never offered marriage. Only her imagination had filled in those gaps.

Whereas Sir William was about to pledge her both. Was she ready to abandon her consuming, painful, hopeless infatuation with Teagan Fitzwilliams in exchange for the solid reality of Sir William's care and comfort?

She heard murmuring in the hallway, and a moment later Jennings opened the door to announce Sir William.

He walked toward her smiling, warm affection in his eyes. She allowed him to kiss her hands.

"Valeria, I expect you know why I asked if I might call on you today. It cannot come as any surprise that I—"

"Please, Sir William, go no further!" she exclaimed. "If I am not being too presumptuous in assuming a proposal is your intent, I beg you will not."

Surprise and distress replaced the glow in his eyes. "You find me so distasteful? But I thought—"

"You know I do not! You are everything that is fine and caring and admirable. It's just...I am not sure yet whether I can return your sentiments with the fervency you deserve. For a time, I harbored a...prior attachment, from which I have not yet entirely recovered."

He regarded her gravely. "I see. Does the...object of this attachment not reciprocate your affection?"

"N-no. Oh, you mustn't fault the gentleman—'twas mere foolishness on my part. But I would not insult the purity of the sentiments you've expressed by leaving you in ignorance of my...circumstances."

He smiled wryly. "You haven't yet given me time to express my sentiments," he pointed out.

She felt her cheeks flush. "N-no, I suppose not."

"Valeria, do you think there is a chance you might...recover from this prior attachment?"

She returned his serious regard. "'Tis possible."

"You are correct in assuming that I wish to hold the whole heart and loyalty of the lady I ask to be my wife. But as long as there is still a chance your affections may become as fully engaged as I would wish, I must be content with that." He gently tipped up her chin with his finger. "Not happy, you understand. But willing to wait until you are ready to offer more. Have we a bargain, then?"

"I...suppose so," she murmured, watching a hotter light spark in his eyes before his gaze lowered to her mouth.

And then he swiftly bent to kiss her.

'Twas a mere brush of his lips, which he made no attempt to prolong or deepen. Yet when he straightened, his breathing was uneven and the hand at her chin shaking.

"Yes, I am entirely ready to hope for more," he said.

Valeria wasn't sure what she was ready for. Sir William's kiss had certainly been pleasant enough, but she'd felt—disloyal. As if betraying a trust.

"I brought my traveling carriage," he said, stepping

back, "in hopes that, had I received a favorable reply to the question you prevented my asking, I might have conveyed you to meet my mother. But since you haven't precisely refused, either, I should still like you to accompany me. 'Tis a fine afternoon, the drive is quite pleasant and my mother is an admirable lady with whom I think you would enjoy becoming acquainted. Will you come?"

Would Sir William attempt more liberties in a closed coach? But if she were contemplating marriage, Valeria ought to take this opportunity to know him and his family better—and to learn how she truly felt about his taking liberties.

"Yes, Sir William. I should like that very much."

Two hours later Valeria sat beside Sir William as his coach traveled past the lightly wooded fields just north of London. He had not attempted to take more liberties, engaging her instead in easy conversation, and much of the constraint she had initially felt upon being closeted alone with him in the coach had dissipated.

They had just begun a discussion about poetry when a shout, followed in rapid succession by the loud report of a pistol, brought the carriage to an abrupt, jolting halt.

The incident at Dade's Run coming instantly to mind, Valeria drew in an alarmed breath. But before she could move or speak, the carriage door was flung wide and a one-armed figure in a uniform coat too grimy and tattered for her to be able to identify the regiment pointed a pistol at them. "Stand 'n deliver!" he ordered.

Keeping the pistol trained on them, the soldier angled his head back. "Always wanted to say that," he informed someone behind him.

"Get them out of the coach," a muffled voice said.

"You 'eard the guv'ner—out ye go, me pretties. Arms up and no funny business, neither."

"Please, sir, be calm and stop waving that pistol," Sir William implored. "I'll step out if you wish, but let the lady remain in the coach."

"Don't worrit yerself, we don't mean no harm to the lady. But out 'e says, so out ye goes." The soldier motioned with the pistol. "Now, be quick about it."

Indignation had begun to replace Valeria's initial shock. "You, sir, have taken the king's coin. How dare you disgrace your uniform by becoming a common thief?"

"Feisty one, ain't ye?" the soldier said with a chuckle, waving Valeria past him.

Reluctantly she climbed down. Outside she saw two more armed men, pistols trained on their coachman and groom. Then, as Sir William stepped out, a tall figure dressed all in black, a scarf obscuring his face, came from behind the coach and knocked him to the ground. When she cried out in protest, the one-armed soldier turned his pistol on her, forcing her to stand by helplessly while the highwayman swiftly bound the struggling Sir William's wrists behind his back and gagged him.

After the dark-clad bandit finished trussing up Sir William, he nodded to one of his accomplices, who lay down his pistol and came over to bind her wrists as well.

"You will all hang, you know," she said furiously.

The dark-clad man forced Sir William's strenuously resisting body into the coach and shut the door, then turned to her. "Will we now?" he said in an all-too-familiar lilt before clapping a gag over her mouth.

Incensed, she kicked and struggled as he picked her up. "Drive home, easy," he instructed Sir William's coachman, who hastened to obey. Then, hefting her to his chest, he carried her to a waiting gig.

He deposited her beside it and waved a hand at his accomplices, who lowered their weapons and trotted toward horses tethered in the woods beyond the highway. Before she could attempt to scramble away, an awkward business with no hands to brace herself, the bandit once more clasped her to his chest.

Not until Sir Williams's coach was well away and the horsemen nearly out of sight did her abductor remove the gag. Jerking her head, she managed to nip one of his fingers.

He yelped and waved the injured digit. "Sure, and is that any way to reward me for removing the cloth?"

"Teagan Fitzwilliams, I'm going to murder you!"

Grinning, he pulled the mask from his face. "Ah, 'twas certain I was that I'd fooled ye, lass."

"For a few moments only. But what maggot did you take in your head, abducting me off a public highway? And how dare you tie up Sir William? I expect he shall shortly call you out for that affrontery!"

"Whist, but the man's lucky I only tied him up. I should have gutted him for trying to run off with ye. But he's welcome to go a round with me at Gentleman Jackson's, if 'twill soothe his injured sensibilities."

"He wasn't 'running off' with me. We were making an afternoon visit to his mother."

"He had the effrontery to ask to marry ye, didn't he?"

"I cannot see how that is any of your concern."

"Not my concern! Did I not ask ye to wait for me? Did I not vow on my mother's grave I'd be back for ye?"

"Yes—months ago. And not a single word did I hear from that morning to this. Until my former neighbors happened to stop at Winterpark, I had no idea whether you'd even reached London. And when I did hear of you—accepted by your family, embraced by the ton, pursued by the ladies—what was I to think? Even your aunt believed you to be courting Miss Amesbury."

"Actually, I was doing my very best *not* to court her.

You have no idea how complicated it can be for a gentleman who's turned respectable to avoid marriage.''

"It seems you've been doing quite an admirable job."

"Ah, Valeria-love, I'm sorry for that. After Aunt Charlotte accepted me, and it become apparent that my reputation could be salvaged, all I wanted to do was come for you. But…but then I began to doubt myself. After all, what had I ever known of constancy? All my life, I've been told I am a wastrel just like my father. The only person besides you who ever offered me acceptance and respect, who seemed to believe I possessed honor and character, I repaid by seducing his daughter-in-law and betraying his trust. I worried that some flaw within me might someday cause me to do the same to you…and I couldn't bear taking that risk."

"Oh, Teagan, you would never serve me thus."

"I now believe that, too. I've just read the letters my father wrote to my mother. He didn't desert us, Valeria. He was lost at sea on his way to build a new life for us in America."

In his expression, in his voice Valeria could read how much that fact meant to him. "I'm glad for you, Teagan. But if you wanted to propose to me—I'm assuming this elaborate charade is a proposal?—why did you not simply call? There was no need to play highwayman. And I would be very obliged if you would remove the ropes binding my hands. They chafe dreadfully."

"Since you've no place to run now but back into my arms, I suppose it's safe," he agreed, untying the cord and then rubbing solicitously at her wrists.

"The highwaymen was Mercy's idea—well, indirectly," he continued. "And I did call. But Molly told me you'd gone off with Sir William, to his mother's. And my aunt had informed me earlier that Lady Jersey knew Sir William intended to propose today. So naturally I assumed—"

"Incorrectly, as it turns out."

"—that he'd proposed, and you'd accepted. I couldn't let you make a mistake like that."

"A mistake? Marrying a good, responsible, upright man who, when he wants to propose, makes a proper call at a proper hour in a proper parlor?"

"You wouldn't be happy living with so stuffy and predictable a husband."

"Oh, would I not?"

"Come now, Valeria-love! You're more a rascal than I ever was. What proper matron would seek out and seduce a known rogue—in her hay barn? Or defy convention to befriend him in London? Or leave her proper suitor dangling and conduct an affair with him under the noses of her new household? Or pleasure him in an open field in broad daylight?"

"Perhaps," she conceded. "But I do want some proper things. A home. Children. A place to settle down."

"Ah, Valeria, your home is here." He put her hand to his chest. "Within the heart of a man who is terrified to promise you forever, but cannot envision life without you. Who couldn't possibly deserve you, but nonetheless wants to cherish you and your children for the rest of our lives with all the passion he possesses."

Before she could stop him, Teagan went down on one knee. "My dearest Valeria, will ye go adventuring with me? Will ye sleep with me in the shadows of the Pyramids, and walk barefoot with me on the sands of Cadiz? By the way, my employer—I'll explain that to you later—tells me there may be trouble brewing in Egypt, and wants to send me to investigate. We could make it our honeymoon trip."

"Egypt, is it?"

"Aye. Mayhap a bit of the Maghreb as well. Anything for my lady's pleasure. Ye like camels, do ye?"

A properly demure look on her face, Valeria rested her

chin on her fist, as if considering carefully. "Well, if you're prepared to offer all that, how can I refuse?"

And then that irredeemable rogue Teagan Fitzwilliams, in a delightful demonstration of some of the passion he possessed, showed Valeria right there on the public roadway just how thrilled he was at her acceptance.

*   *   *   *   *

Please turn the page
for a sneak peek
at Julia Justiss's next book,

MY LADY'S HONOUR,

coming soon!

Chapter One

Wales, 1812

"Your cousin Nigel—that is, the new Baron Southford, be awaitin' ye in the library," the maid informed her with a curtsy.

Gwennor Southford sighed and removed the apron with which she'd covered her mourning gown while she helped Jenny and the staff clear away the remains of the breakfast they'd served after her father's interment. "Thank you, Jenny. Tell him I will join him shortly."

While the maid departed, Gwen stopped to check her hair in the black-draped hall mirror, making sure no unruly strands had escaped her coiffeur to catch the eye of her punctilious cousin. A London dandy of the first stare, Nigel never failed to look at her without a slightly pained expression, as if she offended him by sporting soot on her nose or a spot on her gown. Which most of the time, she allowed, she probably did.

Or perhaps it was just that, not being able to peer down at her from a superior height, Cousin Nigel tried to intimidate her with his faintly contemptuous gazes. Though they did not succeed in leaving her in awe of him, she often felt like a large, ugly and not very interesting beetle being inspected under a glass.

Finding that her thick black hair, which had a tendency to curl wildly despite her efforts to subdue it, was still neatly braided, Gwen walked on to the library. She couldn't imagine what Cousin Nigel needed to say to her that could not have been expressed in front of a roomful of other guests.

Perhaps he merely wished to complain—again—about the meals or accommodations. Which, she had no doubt, he would soon be "improving" by the addition of a foreign chef to create dishes more suitable to his cultured palate, followed by an army of workmen to update the century-old rooms to a more fashionable mien.

She grimaced at the idea of her beloved home being transformed under his ruthless hand. Pray God she could convince him to send her to London for the upcoming Season, so she might find herself a husband, and her and Parry a new home.

Damping down a niggle of unease, she knocked on the library door, then entered.

She had to suppress a pang at seeing her cousin lounging in her father's favorite chair behind the massive desk. Wrenching her thoughts from reflections that could only bring on another wave of useless grief, she curtsyed and forced herself to focus on Nigel.

Once again he subjected her to a lengthy, critical inspection. "Well, Cousin Gwennor, I'm afraid the years have not much improved you, but at least you've the sense to keep that peasant's hair tightly braided, and your other features are not unpleasant. I suppose, with the addition of a small dowry, you will do well enough."

"Thank you, Cousin," Gwen said sweetly, with clenched teeth, "for your kind condolences on my father's death. And I am…gratified to meet with your approval."

"Your tendency to indulge in levity at inappropriate moments does not become you, Gwennor," he replied loftily. "I'm quite certain I offered you my sympathies upon my arrival yesterday. However, it does no good to linger in the past. Changes will be taking place at Southford now that I am baron, and you must adapt to them."

"Naturally, Cousin." She would not refer to him as "my lord," she thought mutinously, no matter that she was no longer the daughter of the house but merely a female relation dependent on his charity. "Does your reference to my dowry mean that you intend to send me to London for the Season, as I've requested? I shall be ready to leave as soon as my bags can be packed."

She cast her eyes down and clasped her hands in such a picture of maidenly humility that Nigel, no fool despite his affections, gave her a sharp look.

"I have given thought to your eventual settlement, yes. I think we both agree that it is not in either of our interests that you remain at Southford. After all, the quality of establishment you maintained for your papa, though adequate enough, I suppose, for a Welsh baron of rural tastes, will not do for me."

"No, Cousin, my sort of household—" which, she added silently, would be notable for simplicity, kindness and courtesy to all "—would definitely not suit you."

"I'm glad we agree on that score. And since with the alterations necessary to bring the manor and outbuildings up to the standards worthy of my stewardship, the estate is likely to suffer some heavy financial demands, I see no reason to throw away money on a London Season. You're well past the age of presentation, no great beauty, and your dowry is merely adequate. I do not wish to be unkind, but a dispassionate assessment must conclude that your chances of attracting the eye of a gentleman wealthy and influential enough to make a connection with his family worth the heavy expense of sending you to London are, I regret to say, remote. In this, you must trust my far greater knowledge of the sensibilities of ton gentlemen.''

So used to his disparagement that his strictures scarcely made her wince, Gwen's active mind considered instead the implications. Not London. Would he send her to Bath, perhaps? Or to the large assemblies in Gloucester?

"It was to announce my solution to this delicate dilemma that I summoned you. Of course, I am fully sensible that as a Southford and my cousin, you must wed a man of good reputation and standing, if not one as discriminating in his requirements as I am myself. I have chosen such a husband for you, Cousin. You may congratulate yourself on soon becoming the bride of Lord Edgerton.''

Shock riveted her to the spot. "Edgar Edgerton? B-Baron Edgerton?'' she stuttered, hoping there might be some misunderstanding.

"Indeed,'' the new Lord Southford replied, smiling benevolently. "I can see how overwhelmed you are by my choice. Lord Edgerton may be a trifle older than you, but he is still a fine figure of a man, and his six motherless sons, poor lads, will give you ample opportunity to practice your preferences for frugality and a rustic outdoor life.''

Gwen swallowed hard.

1004/04

MILLS & BOON®
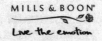
Live the emotion

Historical
romance™

MY LADY ANGEL by Joanna Maitland

Is Cousin Frederick as notorious as her family have led her to believe?
Lady Angelina Rosevale is about to find out. If only Frederick could
be more like the mysterious masked Max, with whom she's come
into contact in the most scandalous of circumstances. Being in Max's
company is pure pleasure – though Angel can't deny there's
something disturbingly familiar about him...

Regency

BEAUCHAMP BESIEGED by Elaine Knighton

England and the Welsh Marches, 1196

Sir Raymond de Beauchamp sparks fear through the Marches,
yet Ceridwen ap Morgan aches for his touch. Raymond sees no
advantage in wedding this Welsh beauty. Her presence raises
unwelcome ghosts of memory, and marriage will interfere with
the dark vows he's made. Yet his blood, once hot for revenge,
now burns only for her...

THE DARING DUCHESS by Paula Marshall

Sir Neville Fortescue comes from a long line of hellraisers – but he's
determined to live a decent life. He certainly doesn't associate with
women like the notorious Diana, Duchess of Medbourne. But
when he and Diana are plunged into a shady world of brothels,
plots and murder, Neville realises he has underestimated this
beautiful young widow – and his own love of adventure...

Regency

On sale 5th November 2004

Available at most branches of WHSmith, Tesco, ASDA, Martins,
Borders, Eason, Sainsbury's and all good paperback bookshops.

1004/153

MILLS & BOON

Live the emotion

GREAT READ, GREAT VALUE
for only £3.99 in November

SUPER HISTORICAL ROMANCE BRINGS YOU

An Honourable Man
by Rosemary Rogers

**Drama and passion in this sweeping,
sensual tale of love divided…and conquered.**

When her father dies mysteriously just before the onset
of the Civil War, beautiful, headstrong Cameron Campbell
must save the slaves on their Mississippi plantation from her
brother's cruel intentions. Her only supporter is the man who
once broke her heart, Captain Jackson Logan – a man who
is not what he appears.

Against the dramatic backdrop of the besieged South,
Cameron must learn to trust this most unlikely ally and
discover if he truly is an honourable man.

"The queen of historical romance."
—*New York Times Book Review*

**So don't miss out
An Honourable Man
will be available from Friday 5th November 2004**

*Available at most branches of WHSmith, Tesco, ASDA, Martins,
Borders, Eason, Sainsbury's and all good paperback bookshops.*

A Regency Invitation

to the House Party of the Season

Nicola Cornick, Joanna Maitland,
Elizabeth Rolls

On sale 3rd December 2004

Available at most branches of WHSmith, Tesco, ASDA, Martins,
Borders, Eason, Sainsbury's and all good paperback bookshops.

MILLS & BOON®

Live the emotion

Regency
Brides

A wonderful six-book Regency collection

Two sparkling Regency romances in each volume

Volume 5 on sale from 5th November 2004

*Available at most branches of WHSmith, Tesco, Martins, Borders,
Eason, Sainsbury's, and all good paperback bookshops.*

REG-BRIDES/RTL/5

When she was good,
she was very, very good.
And when she was bad, she was...

NAUGHTY MARIETTA

NAN RYAN

Published 17th September 2004

MIRA®

2 FREE

BOOKS AND A SURPRISE GIFT!

We would like to take this opportunity to thank you for reading this Mills & Boon® book by offering you the chance to take TWO more specially selected titles from the Historical Romance™ series absolutely FREE! We're also making this offer to introduce you to the benefits of the Reader Service™—

- ★ **FREE home delivery**
- ★ **FREE gifts and competitions**
- ★ **FREE monthly Newsletter**
- ★ **Exclusive Reader Service offers**
- ★ **Books available before they're in the shops**

Accepting these FREE books and gift places you under no obligation to buy, you may cancel at any time, even after receiving your free shipment. Simply complete your details below and return the entire page to the address below. You don't even need a stamp!

YES! Please send me 2 free Historical Romance books and a surprise gift. I understand that unless you hear from me, I will receive 4 superb new titles every month for just £3.59 each, postage and packing free. I am under no obligation to purchase any books and may cancel my subscription at any time. The free books and gift will be mine to keep in any case.

H4ZED

Ms/Mrs/Miss/Mr ....Initials ....

BLOCK CAPITALS PLEASE

Surname ....

Address ....

....

....Postcode.................................

Send this whole page to:
UK: FREEPOST CN81, Croydon, CR9 3WZ

Offer valid in UK only and is not available to current Reader service subscribers to this series. Overseas and Eire please write for details. We reserve the right to refuse an application and applicants must be aged 18 years or over. Only one application per household. Terms and prices subject to change without notice. Offer expires 30th January 2005. As a result of this application, you may receive offers from Harlequin Mills & Boon and other carefully selected companies. If you would prefer not to share in this opportunity please write to The Data Manager, PO Box 676, Richmond, TW9 IWU.

Mills & Boon® is a registered trademark owned by Harlequin Mills & Boon Limited.
Historical Romance™ is being used as a trademark. The Reader Service™ is being used as a trademark.